W9-BYI-360

SILVER

NITRATE

SILVIA MORENO-GARCIA

SILVER NITRATE

DEL REY

New York

Published in the United States by Del Rey, an imprint of Random House, a division of Penguin Random House LLC, New York.

Del Rey and the Circle colophon are registered trademarks of Penguin Random House LLC.

Hardback ISBN 978-0-593-35536-7
International edition ISBN 978-0-593-72415-6
Ebook ISBN 978-0-593-35537-4

Printed in the United States of America on acid-free paper

randomhousebooks.com

2 4 6 8 9 7 5 3 1

First Edition

Book design by Fritz Metsch

For Orrin Grey,
monster maker

The paper was narrowly examined. As Harrington had said, the characters on it were more like runes than anything else, but not decipherable by either man, and both hesitated to copy them, for fear, as they confessed, of perpetuating whatever evil purpose they might conceal.

—M. R. JAMES, "Casting the Runes"

OPENING

TITLE

SEQUENCE

MCMXCIII

1

An engorged, yellow moon painted the sky a sickly amber hue, illuminating a solitary figure. A woman, standing between two sycamore trees. It had rained, and the earth was slippery as, breathing with difficulty, she ventured toward the cabin. The woods felt awake and dangerous, with the sounds of crickets and rolling thunder in the distance. There was a thin humming. Was that a bird? It was too high-pitched, that noise.

The woman pressed a hand against her lips and stared at the cabin, with its welcoming lights. But that oasis of warmth was distant. A twig snapped, and the woman looked behind her in terror. She began to run.

The noises of the night were now mixed with the patter of her feet. She flew forward, and her hands desperately pulled at the front door—there was a *thump*, so loud it sounded like a cannon—until she finally managed to burst into the cabin. She immediately shut the door, bolted it, and stepped back, waiting. Her eyes were wide.

The crash of an axe against the wood made the woman jump. Splinters flew. The woman screamed, pressing back farther into the room as a man hacked his way through the door. The scream was an annoying squeal that made the levels jump into the red. The man lingered at the threshold, clutching the axe. He began advancing; his breath was heavy, punctuated with an annoying pop.

"Demon possession again?" Montserrat asked. Her eyes were on the VU meter; on her knee she balanced a notepad.

"Ghosts," Paco said.

She scribbled in the notepad. "I thought you were into ninjas."

"We're still doing the ninjas. Just not now."

"A ninja moratorium."

The woman screamed again. Montserrat pressed a button. The image froze on the screen. She spun her chair around.

The padded room smelled faintly of the pine-scented air freshener that the other sound editors liked to spray around to cover up the fact that they were smoking inside. The whole place was a bit of a mess. The editors regularly left pizza boxes and empty bottles of Pepsi around the mixing room, along with the scent of cigarettes. "No food or smoking in the editing room" said a sign half hidden behind the random stickers the editors had pasted on it over the years. In theory, this admonition made sense, especially when you were dealing with film. You didn't want to smear a workprint with grease. In practice, though, all editors were supposed to eat in front of the monitors. You were constantly working your ass off in post-production, trying to make up for missed deadlines. Montserrat had never been in a facility that was perfectly neat and organized. Editing rooms all looked like war zones unless a client was poking their head around.

Still, she might have tidied up if Paco hadn't ambushed her. Unfortunately for him, this particular mixing room was small and, unlike the bigger rooms, didn't have a client area with a couch. Paco was sitting uncomfortably on a chair, by the door, next to a pile of tapes and vinyl records, and from the look of his position he was probably getting a cramp.

"So, what do you think?" Paco asked.

"I think this is the kind of shit you shouldn't have to be fixing in post-production. Did you shoot these scenes inside a washing machine? The sound is terrible. Those levels are way too hot."

"I know, I know. But what can you expect with these budgets?"

"It's going to take me a couple of weeks."

"I need it to be done in five days."

Montserrat shot him a skeptical look. "Not likely. Mario will tell you as much."

"Come on, I'm not asking Mario, I'm asking you."

"I don't want to be stuck here from the crack of dawn until midnight because you forgot to hire a person who can hold a boom mike in the right position."

"Don't do this to me. I've got hundreds of units due at Videocentro and can't run the duplicates if the master is a mess. Don't you get overtime for this stuff? Must be a hefty check."

"I wish," she said.

Though there was the yearly discretionary bonus. The full-timers got the aguinaldo mandated by the law, but freelancers like Montserrat couldn't count on that. They had to rely on the gratitude of their employers. At Antares, Mario gave his editors a turkey, a bottle of cheap whiskey, and a Christmas bonus. It was never a generous bonus—it shrank or expanded at whim—this despite the fact she was by far the best sound editor at Antares. She was also the only woman on the Antares team, aside from the receptionist, which was probably why she never became a full-timer, never had the right to an aguinaldo, and instead had to rely on Mario's mercurial temper: the editing business was a boys' club. There were a few women working at studios writing the scripts that were used for subtitling and dubbing. There were also female translators, though those were often freelancers who were contracted for single projects. But full-time female sound editors? Those were as rare as unicorns.

"Look, I have to meet someone for lunch," Montserrat said, grabbing her leather jacket from the hook by the door and slipping it on. "Why don't you talk to Mario and we'll see what he says? I'd love to help, but he was raging about an unpaid dubbing—"

"Come on, guys, I always pay even if I'm a few days late. As soon as I offload those videos I'll be golden, I swear."

Montserrat didn't know how true that was. Paco had scored a modest hit with an *Exorcist* rip-off a few years before. Mexican horror movies were scarce these days. Paco had reaped the benefits of a nascent home video market a few years back. But he wasn't doing well anymore. Four years before, René Cardona III had tried the same concept: shooting a low-budget horror copy of a hot American film with *Vacaciones de Terror*. Although *Vacaciones* was a blatant attempt at mixing *Child's Play* with *Amityville*, the film had one semi-famous star in the form of Pedro Fernández, whose singing career had assured at least a few butts in seats. *Vacaciones de Terror* and its obligatory sequel had performed decently, but the market for local horror productions wasn't substantial enough to support two filmmakers intent on churning out scary flicks, and Paco didn't have a singer to put on the marquee.

Not that there was a market to produce anything with a semi-decent budget at this point. The best that most people could hope for were exploitation flicks like *Lola La Trailera*. Paco was, if anything, a little better off than most Mexican filmmakers, since he'd managed to rope a few Spanish financiers into his moviemaking schemes and so the bulk of his output was meant for the European market. He'd dump a bunch of copies at Videocentro, then sell the rest to Italy, Germany, or whoever had any dough to spare. Paco's work was slightly more nutritious fare than what most of the other exploitation hounds offered, but nothing to get excited about.

"Montserrat, come on, darling, you know I'm solid. How about we do this: *I* pay you the overtime. I'll throw in . . . oh, how much would you want?" he asked, reaching into his pocket and producing a wallet.

"God, Paco, you don't have to bribe me."

"Then you'll do it?"

Montserrat had been working at Antares for the past seven years. She'd never made it into the two big film studios, but you had to be the son of someone to edit at a place like that. Positions were passed down through the STPC and STIC like knighthoods. Now that Estudios América was being dismantled, the movie business was even more of a mess than before, and competition for positions was cutthroat. Antares had been, when you added all the pluses and minuses, not that bad.

Not that bad, that is, until the previous year, when the company had hired a new sound editor. Everyone loved young people and despised old ones. Help wanted ads always specified "35 and under," sometimes even "30 and under." Samuel, the newest member of the team, was definitely under thirty. Mario had funneled a bunch of assignments to Samuel, in part because his youth meant he was one of their lowest paid employees. Antares saved money with Samuel. And, as a result, Montserrat had been pulled from several projects. She'd gone from working five, sometimes six days a week, to three, and she was sure Mario was going to cut her down to two by December. Maybe they'd end up assigning *this* job to Samuel.

Crap, she needed to make more money. Her sister didn't ask her for anything, but Montserrat knew she was hurting a little. She had been working only part-time for half a year now; the cancer treatments were too exhausting for her to manage her usual workload at the accounting firm. Montserrat tried to chip in when she could.

"Follow me," she muttered, looking at her watch. She'd be late if she didn't step out now.

Paco and Montserrat walked down a long hallway decorated with wall-to-ceiling mirrors and back toward the reception area. The mirrors were supposed to be "wall art" and lend an air of class to the joint, but the results were more tacky than elegant. The reception area was the only part of the studio that looked semi-decent. Instead of shabby, patched-up furniture, the room boasted two black leather couches. Behind a big desk a big sign with silver letters said "ANTARES" all in caps.

Candy was behind the desk. She had bright yellow neon nails that week—she changed them often—and smiled at Montserrat happily. Candida, who liked to go by Candy, handled reception and all manner of assorted tasks. She was the person who kept track of who was using which editing bay at any given hour of the day. She wasn't supposed to schedule anything until Mario said so, but Montserrat sometimes skipped the queue.

"Candy, is Mario back from that business lunch yet?" she asked, hoping the answer was yes but the receptionist shook her head.

"Nope."

"Crap," Montserrat said. "Okay, this is what we'll do: Candy, can you slot me in for some night work tomorrow? Put me for the whole week, beginning at seven in my usual room. I need to work on Paco's latest picture."

"Oh, what's it called?" Candy asked, looking at Paco with interest.

"*Murder Weekend*," Paco said proudly.

"Sounds cool. But, Montserrat, I need to know the pricing, the green form—"

"Put it down before someone grabs the time slot," she said. "I'll show it to Mario later and fill in the green form."

Before Candy could ask another question, Montserrat waved them a curt goodbye and stepped outside.

She shook her head, thinking about the long nights that awaited her. Too many people thought they could skimp on the audio portion of a shoot. Then they ended up with ambient noise, cutoff tracks, or low sound quality. They often expected miracles, too, from their sound editors, and Montserrat had to deliver those miracles for a measly amount of cash. She wasn't even on staff, for God's sake. Mario didn't believe in hiring people full-time because it was cheaper and easier to keep them coming in by the hour. That way, when he didn't need some-one, as he had with Montserrat lately, he could cut them off without sweating it.

The problem was that Montserrat *liked* editing at Antares. A full-time job for a TV show would be steady money, but it also meant she'd have to work with a lot more people. Two audio editors in the same room, and then maybe the lead editor and the director giving notes while they worked. She knew someone who had made the switch to working as a sound recordist because it at least meant less insane schedules, but she despised sets, with all their technicians and actors. Small productions, low-budget flicks, these appealed to her because she often worked alone, no need for a gigantic team of ADR experts, foley artists, and music su-pervisors to suffocate her. People. She didn't wish to deal with people, although sometimes she feared she'd end up with a vitamin deficiency from spending all daylight hours inside, and she'd start talking back to the characters on screen, like an editor she knew did.

Montserrat wondered if she shouldn't poke her head around the set of *Enigma*. Cornelia could introduce her to her contacts, or there might even be an opening with Cornelia's TV show. She hated the idea of a desk job, but maybe there was freelancing she could do on the side to augment her paycheck. Research. Administrative work. Something other than audio editing, because audio was uncertain: canceled gigs, clients changing their minds, or the composer scoring a film being late, which meant *hurry, hurry, hurry*.

No one cared about the audio, anyway. People noticed only when you fucked it up, not when you got it right. It was a thankless job that had her sometimes catching three hours of sleep on one of the couches around Antares so she could keep working through the night.

Montserrat made it into the restaurant on time and took a booth, or-dered a coffee and a slice of pie. Tristán arrived twenty-five minutes later. His coat was a lush plum color with big buttons and a wide belt.

His hair looked a little ruffled, and he was wearing his sunglasses, which he took off with practiced theatrical panache as he sat down at the table. "Well! They were out of Benson and Hedges at my usual newspaper stand, so I had to walk around."

"I thought you were a snob who only bought imported cigarettes."

"I'm trying to save money this month. Dunhills are out of the question for a few weeks," he said, taking out his lighter and a cigarette. "You've been waiting long?"

"Yes," she said. "You shouldn't smoke."

"Keeps me thin, and I have to have at least one vice."

"Maybe, but we're sitting in the non-smoking section," she said, pointing to the sign behind him.

Tristán looked around and sighed. "Now why'd you seat us here?"

"Because it's full in the smoking area and they said there's no way we're getting in there."

"Maybe I can ask for us to be moved," he said and raised his hand, trying to attract the attention of a waitress.

"Please don't," she said, poking at the slice of pie she had almost finished eating. She'd assumed he'd be late and had been wise enough to order quickly.

"Miss?" he said.

A waitress turned around. He threw her his careless, sixty-watt smile that was all teeth. The smile had a success rate of 70 percent. The waitress approached him, notepad in hand.

"Are you ready to order?"

"I'd like a Diet Coke. Could you move us to the smoking section?"

"It's full."

"If there was a table that opened up, could we move there? What's your name? Mari. That's nice. Mari, would you be able to keep an eye out for a table for us?" he asked. "As a special favor for me, please."

He spoke with that deep, velvet-smooth voice he always used when he wanted to get something. The voice had a success rate of 90 percent. The waitress smiled at him. Montserrat could tell by her expression that she was wondering if she didn't know Tristán from somewhere. She had that curious look people got around him. Maybe she'd remember him later.

"Well, all right," the waitress said, blushing.

"Thank you, Mari," he said.

Tristán Abascal, born Tristán Said Abaid, was Montserrat's age. Thirty-eight. They'd grown up in the same building, and they both loved movies. But their similarities ended there. Tristán was tall and handsome. Even the years of drug use and the car accident hadn't completely marred his looks. He wasn't the same crazy-beautiful boy he'd been, but he still cut a striking figure. And although it had been about ten years since he'd acted in a soap opera, some people still recognized him.

Montserrat, on the other hand, was small and plain. When they were kids, the others mocked her limp. After three surgeries, her foot had improved quite a bit, though it pained her when it got cold. Now that there were bits of silver in her hair, her plain face was only growing plainer.

"So, the good news is I found a place. It's in Polanco and it's the right size," he said spinning his sunglasses with one hand and smirking. The doctors had done a good job with his left eye; there was but a faint scar under it, and the eye was still smaller than the right one, a little lopsided, that pupil permanently dilated just a tad more than the other. It gave his face a faintly mismatched air where once before it had possessed an elegant, near-perfect symmetry. Nothing terrible, but he was self-conscious about it, even after many years. He wore the sunglasses all year long, everywhere he went. In the first few months after the accident, he even wore them indoors.

"How much is it?"

He gave her a figure, and when she raised her eyebrow at him the smirk grew into a big smile. "It's a bit pricey, I know. That's why I'm laying off the Dunhills. I'll need all the voice work I can get. Work has slowed to a trickle."

"You too? We should buy a lottery ticket."

"Cash flow problems?"

"Not dire, yet. But I'd like to help Araceli with her expenses."

"How's she doing?"

"Good. I mean, as good as she can get. We're hoping it'll go into remission, but despite all the treatments and the limpias, nothing's changed."

"I should stop by and say hi to her sometime."

"She'd love that."

The waitress came back with his Diet Coke and a glass filled with ice. Tristán smiled at her as she poured the soda. He ordered a Monte Cristo sandwich and fries. She knew he'd poke at his food and eat little.

"I need to be out by the thirtieth, and I have the movers booked and everything, but I'll have the keys sooner than that. I was thinking we could look at it before the move. How about Friday?"

"I'm probably going to be stuck doing a rush job all week."

"In that case could I borrow your car? I wanted to take a few small things on my own."

Montserrat had three loves. One was horror movies. The other was her car. The third was Tristán.

She'd always loved him, first when he'd been simply "El Norteñito," that slightly confused boy from Matamoros with the funny accent. She grew up in Tristán's kitchen and had even learned to cook meatballs the way his Lebanese mother did. Montserrat's parents were divorced, her mother was seldom home, and her sister Araceli was a terrible cook, so she much preferred eating with him.

Theirs was the bountiful affection of children who sat close to the TV set, mouth open, and watched monsters carrying maidens away. After his braces were removed, Tristán morphed into a cute teenager, the one all the girls had a crush on; she too had a crush on him. Around that time, Tristán started taking acting and singing lessons. He was no good with the singing, but he did get work modeling for fotonovelas and as an extra in several forgettable flicks before landing a steady gig at Televisa.

By 1977, when the twenty-two-year-old made his debut in a soap opera, he had the chiseled good looks of a star, and Montserrat's love became a roaring passion that was eventually dampened by his utter indifference. She loved him still, but it was not with the desperate romantic yearning of her younger years. She'd eventually admitted that Tristán was a bit of a shit at times and more than a little fucked up. He could be a horrible, selfish prick, and his numerous personal problems took their toll on their friendship.

Yet she loved him.

However, despite this deep affection, she would not give him her car. She immediately tensed and put her cup down.

"Is that all you wanted? To borrow my car?"

"Come on, no. It's been a while since I last saw you. I wanted to say hello."

"And conveniently borrow my car."

"It would only be a tiny trip."

"No. You're not going to lug around your mattress on top of my car to save yourself money with the movers."

He laughed. "I'm not tying the mattress to the roof of your car. Come on, Momo."

"No. That's it, no. Take a cab. Or have Yolanda drive you there."

Tristán's lips were pressed tight together, and he was staring at her. But she wasn't going to let him have the car. She'd wanted a car the Saint drove on the TV when they were kids, a Volvo P1800. Since she couldn't get one, she'd settled on a Volkswagen that ran like a dream. It was white, immaculate, and kept safe and sound in a reliable garage spot she rented a block from her home. It was not the car of a TV hero, but it was her precious four wheels, and she didn't need Tristán stinking it up with his cigarettes, imported or not.

The waitress came by and told them she could move them to the smoking section. Montserrat took her cup of coffee, and he grabbed his soft drink. When they sat down again Tristán again toyed with his box of cigarettes. Montserrat extended a hand and placed it over his. "I'd like it if you stopped smoking."

"I've told you, it keeps me thin."

"If not for your health, think about your teeth."

"That's why I have veneers."

"Tristán."

"We switched sections so I could smoke."

"We switched because you're a stubborn fucker," she said, almost hissing at him.

"Mmm," he replied as he lit his cigarette and took a drag. "Yolanda and I broke up, so she's not driving me anywhere."

This startled her. Usually, Tristán called Montserrat at the end of his relationships. He used her as a confessional booth.

"What? When?"

"Two weeks ago."

"You didn't say anything over the phone."

"I was trying to figure out if I could patch it over. I mean, seriously patch it over, not just flowers and a box of chocolates. Therapy, maybe. Couples counseling."

"That's a bit—"

"Mature of me?" he asked.

"Unusual," Montserrat said. "I thought you two were going to work on that movie."

"We're not on speaking terms. It's impossible to get funding, anyway. You have to beg for grants and kneel in front of Conaculta," he said.

"What did you do?"

"Why do you always assume *I* did something?"

"You didn't cheat on her, did you? She was nice."

"You didn't even like Yolanda," he muttered, irritated.

"Well, she was nice for *you*," Montserrat said. "She was a bit of a snob, but you enjoy that."

"Are you still seeing that vet with the bad hair?" Tristán asked. He sounded a little spiteful, but she didn't take the bait.

"That was a year and a half ago. And 'seeing' is a big word. If you go out with someone twice you are not seeing them," she said calmly. "Anyway, we're talking about you and Yolanda, not me."

"I didn't cheat on her," Tristán said, tapping his cigarette against the small, amber-colored ashtray. "If you must know, she wanted to get married and have a baby."

"Kiss of death, that," Montserrat muttered.

"Maybe I should get serious about someone, do the whole wedding and baby thing."

"Do you want to have a baby?"

"No! But I would like to be happy, and sometimes I think I'm too fucked up to make it work with anyone. I'm going to die alone, wrinkled and ugly, devoured by my cat."

"Don't be stupid. You don't even have a cat. Besides, you're lovely."

"My God, I like it when you lie to me like that," he said, grinning with unmitigated pleasure. He really was too vain.

"I guess now I understand why you said you needed a new apartment. And I thought it was because your old apartment had a roach problem."

"Roaches and silverfish. I'm hoping the good thing about this new place is I'll at least avoid an insect infestation."

"Silverfish love eating starches, you know?" Montserrat said. "They'll eat books and photos. They're ravenous little monsters."

"That's why I never had you over. It wasn't a nice apartment. It was cheap, though," Tristán said with a sigh.

She knew he had never had her over because he had been fully immersed in Yolanda, and he didn't need Montserrat when he was captivated by the fresh bloom of a new relationship. When he was single, though, he stuck to her like glue. It irritated her when she recalled Tristán's inconsiderate behavior, his patterns. In six months, he would meet someone new and forget Montserrat's phone number until a malady befell him or he started getting bored.

"I need to run," Montserrat said and checked her watch. She folded her napkin and placed it by the empty cup of coffee.

"Where are you going?"

"I told you I had less than an hour for lunch and you were late."

"You can't leave me eating by myself."

"I am," she said. She grabbed her jacket and put it on.

"What about marriage? Should I crawl back to Yolanda?"

She took out a couple of bills and placed them on the table. "Because you're afraid of growing old and being alone?" she asked, her voice coarse, even though she didn't want to sound angry.

"Yes. What? Don't stare at me, it's a good enough reason. Isn't it?"

"It's not," Montserrat said as she zipped up the jacket. He was irritating her with his little lost boy look, that wounded, wide-eyed expression. "Maybe you'll meet someone interesting in your new building."

"Sit down and eat with me. I'm not done chatting with you."

"Maybe you'll learn to be punctual," she said, which earned her a glare and a huff from him.

She slid her hands into her pockets and walked out of the restaurant. When she got back to Antares the reception area was empty and there was a sign that said "Ring the bell," which meant Candy had gone to fetch herself lunch. Montserrat meant to head to Mario's office to see if he was back, but he ambushed her in the tiny closet-like space that passed as their staff room, with a sad, half-dried fern in a corner and a toaster that had a broken lever so you had to keep pressing on it. There was a working coffeepot, which was the reason Montserrat had headed there. She placed her jacket on the back of a chair and poured herself a cup.

Before she had a chance to take a sip, Mario walked in. He had splashed soup on his cheap tie during lunch. "Who exactly do you think you are, booking time for Paco without my permission?" he asked.

"I told Candy we'd fill out the green form when you came back."

"You are not supposed to do that. If I'm not around, you're supposed to talk to Samuel and let him figure out the schedule."

"I didn't see Samuel."

"He was right in the office. If you'd checked with him, you might have seen Paco has an overdue bill—"

"Fine. I'll fill out the green form."

"You have to start paying attention. I can't run a business if you're goofing around. You're a decent sound editor, but you have a terrible attitude," Mario said, moving past her and almost making her spill her cup of coffee as he elbowed her on the way to the coffeepot.

"What? How do I have a terrible attitude?"

"You do. Everyone complains about it."

"Who?"

"Samuel, for one. He organized that team-building exercise last month, and you were the only one who didn't show up."

"You're kidding me, right? The 'team-building exercise' was drinking beer in very big glasses and pinching waitresses' behinds. I don't need to play sexist caveman games with the boys to do my job."

"Sexist," Mario said, crossing his arms. "I suppose now you're going to say that you're getting picked on because we're all being sexist here."

"I *am* getting picked on. You're giving Samuel the best jobs, you're pushing me to the sidelines," Montserrat said, knowing she shouldn't be getting this worked up or speaking this honestly about the situation, but it infuriated her when people tried to belittle her. "Come on, Mario, we both know you're fucking with me."

"See? That's what I'm talking about. No one can talk to you because you simply explode," Mario said, rolling his eyes. "It's as if you get your period twenty out of thirty days of the month."

"I'm not the asshole pitching a hissy fit over a green form."

"That's it. Out you go. You're not scheduled this week," Mario said, majestically pointing a finger at the door.

"What? No! I'm doing that job for Paco."

"You're not. You call next week to see if you have shifts. You're getting seven days off unless you apologize for being disrespectful."

"I haven't done anything!"

When Mario was in a bad mood, he became a petty tyrant. She knew from experience that the answer was to bow her head and blurt out a half-assed apology. That's what Samuel or the boys did when Mario was grumbling and stomping through the building. But if there was anything she hated, it was having to stomach a bully. Every single fiber of her body resisted the impulse to grovel, even when she could see by the look in Mario's eye that he expected her to. Maybe it had been the comment on sexism that had gotten him riled up. Whatever it was, Montserrat would be damned if she was going to take a reaming from this guy.

"Well? Are you going to apologize?"

Montserrat slammed her cup down on the rickety plastic table where they were supposed to have their meals. "I'll take the seven days off. Maybe when I come back you won't be such an ass," she said, gathering her jacket under her arm and storming out of the room.

As soon as she opened the front door, she knew she'd messed up. She shouldn't have gone off on him. Mario had been baiting her. He was probably itching for excuses to let her go, and she was giving them to him on a platter. Well, there was nothing to be done about it that day. Mario would probably change his mind in a few hours. He usually did. If he didn't call her in the morning . . . well, fuck.

Montserrat put on her jacket with a quick, fierce motion and hurried to her car. She desperately needed to find alternative sources of income, because this job wasn't cutting it anymore.

2

Tristán had been without a phone for ten days now. On the one hand, he wasn't surprised because Telmex wasn't exactly prompt, but with the rent he was paying at his new apartment he had assumed things would proceed more smoothly. The apartment manager had certainly assured him he'd get all the trimmings at his new home.

Now, to be perfectly honest, the apartment wasn't the height of luxury. Sure, it was located right next to Polanco, but it was actually in Granada. Tristán told himself it was like Polanco, except it wasn't, not with the warehouses and ratty buildings nearby. Walk a few blocks and you'd be in a land of new sports cars and chic restaurants, but that was still a few blocks from him.

Tristán's building was five stories tall, painted green, and had been refurbished to serve a higher class of clientele in the past few years; he didn't doubt in a decade or two developers would bulldoze the whole colonia and build it anew, making it as shiny and elegant as Polanco. But for now the prosperity that the building owner had expected had not manifested.

Yet Tristán could not do any better. Already the new apartment was making his wallet bleed. He needed to line up more gigs.

That was why he wanted to get his phone up and running again. He was trying to land an ad campaign. He kept staring at his pager forlornly and running to a pay phone a block away to make calls.

The one good thing about this state of affairs was that the journalists might have a harder time getting hold of him. The anniversary of Karina's death was coming up. Ten years since she'd died. A guy who worked over at a miserable rag had called him a few weeks before looking for an interview. At least this way Tristán wouldn't be tempted to talk.

Ten days was ridiculous, though. Tristán reached the pay phone and dialed the number for the apartment manager's office. Because this was supposed to be a nicer building, there wasn't the usual portera in a check-ered apron, her hair in curlers, that people could harangue about a prob-lem. You had to phone a number.

The girl at the management office said she was aware of his phone issues, and no, there was no update on when that would be fixed and it was really Telmex's fault anyway so maybe he should be harassing them instead. When he pointed out that the apartment had been offered to him with three months of free phone service the girl replied that she didn't have his contract in front of her but it was still Telmex who had to fix his phone line. He hung up, muttered to himself, and began walking back to his apartment. Tristán was trying to cut down on his smoking, but frus-tration made him stop in front of a newsstand, where he bought a pack of cigarettes, some Chiclets, and an issue of *Eres*. He knew he shouldn't grab the magazine. It only upset him when he saw the well-groomed faces of younger actors who had obtained roles he'd been up for. And there was the danger that they would be running a story on Karina. But he felt masochistic that afternoon.

Karina. He managed to forget her for three quarters of the year, but eventually succumbed, took out her pictures—he carried one in his wal-let, but he had many others, tucked away in a shoe box—and spent too many hours staring at them. When he'd been younger, he'd believed he would be able to put the accident behind him. Now he could admit that might never happen, that in fact the ache was getting worse. Each year made the pain sharper. Most people couldn't understand that. Whether they said it outright or not, they considered him weak, foolish, a failure.

Tristán stopped in front of the mailboxes, fetched several letters, and stuffed them in his back pocket, then lit his cigarette and headed to the third floor. After he walked into his apartment and tossed his jacket on the couch, he finally looked at the envelopes and realized one of the let-ters was a welcome message from the management company and the other two were not addressed to him. Those letters were for Abel Urueta, apartment 4A.

That was a name you didn't hear these days. Montserrat and Tristán had spent more than one truant afternoon at the Palacio Chino and the Cine Noble eating mueganos and watching horror movies, including Uru-eta's old flicks. Nowadays the Cine Noble showed pornos, and the Palacio

Chino was falling to pieces, all its golden décor slowly tarnished by grime and neglect. Few folks made movies in Mexico anymore, almost everything went straight to video, and it was a stream of cine de ficheras and cheap comedies with men who pawed at a woman's tits. *La Risa en Vacaciones*, with its hidden cameras and cheap jokes, was what passed for entertainment. And now Abel Urueta, who had directed three magnificent films in the 1950s, was a mere footnote in the history of entertainment.

Tristán felt something close to childhood glee as he looked at the letter. He quickly walked the steps up to the fourth floor and knocked on the door of 4A.

A distinguished-looking gentleman, his gray hair parted in the middle and a handkerchief knotted around his neck, opened the door and regarded Tristán curiously. He'd never seen a photo of Abel Urueta, but he thought this was the right guy. He had Stanley Kubrick eyebrows—arched a little, the eyes intense—coupled with a half smile fit for Luis Buñuel.

"Mr. Urueta? I'm sorry, I seemed to have received your mail by accident," he said, extending the letters.

"That damn postman," the older man said, shaking his head. "One year I don't give him cash on Postman's Day and he acts like I spit on his face. Well, forgive me if I didn't have change that morning. It's practically armed robbery dealing with people these days. Accident! That fellow keeps slipping my correspondence in whatever mail slot he pleases."

"Sorry about that. I can drop by other letters if they end up in my mailbox."

"That's nice of you. You must be the new guy in 3C. The woman who used to live there had a yappy dog that pissed in the lobby. She coughed all the time, too."

"I hope I'm an improvement, then."

"Definitely. Well, I'm Abel Urueta, as you probably guessed by the envelopes," the old man said, extending his hand.

"Tristán Abascal."

They shook hands. Abel smiled. A flash of recognition crossed his eyes.

"I know that name. And that face. You're an actor."

"More like a voice-over actor these days."

"My boy, what a waste to do voice work! You have the face of a young Arturo de Córdova."

Tristán, who in his haste had dispensed with his trusty sunglasses, felt both oddly shy and proud. He was used to being admired—at least back in the day; there was less admiration and more dissection these days—but this compliment, from someone who had worked with the real Arturo de Córdova, touched him. Even at the height of his popularity Tristán hadn't starred in movies. He'd been a soap opera actor, an extra on several forgettable flicks, and he'd even done a toothpaste ad. Films were another realm, and for him film stars of the Golden Age were gods preserved in celluloid.

"Thanks. It means a lot. I have to say your movies were amazing, sir. *Whispers in the Mansion of Glass* was perfect," he said, hoping he didn't sound like an absolute dork.

"You saw that?"

"My friend Montserrat and I, oh . . . we love your Gothic cycle of—"

A loud whistling noise made Abel groan in irritation, but he motioned to Tristán. "That's the water for my coffee. Come in, come in."

Before giving Tristán the chance to reply, Abel left the door wide open and rushed into the kitchen. Tristán walked inside, hands in his pockets, and looked around the apartment. He recognized the layout from the agent who had shown him building plans. This was what was called a "deluxe," with the front door leading directly into the living room, the dining room and kitchen extending toward the right, while on the left there was a hallway that should lead to the bedroom, a space designated for an office, a hall closet, and a bathroom. Tristán lived in the "standard," which was a one-bedroom, more affordable option. He had been tempted to look for a bigger apartment—the place he'd shared with Yolanda had been wonderfully spacious—but reason had prevailed in the end. A small place, with a more modest rent, would suit him fine.

Yolanda had kept several pieces of furniture, which meant Tristán's apartment was sparsely furnished. Abel, on the other hand, had packed all his life between these walls. Tristán admired the sturdy bookcases brimming with reading material and the potted plants by a large window. A Remington typewriter was set atop a table, next to a Tiffany-style lamp. There was a bar cart with a decanter and glasses, a phonograph, and a vase of a magnificent shade of green with art nouveau flower decorations. Abel collected antiques, by the look of it. Lots of them. He also had a whole shelf filled with quartz crystals and stones. Geodes were split open, showcasing their sparkling interiors. A mineral enthusiast. No, a magpie.

He pictured the director walking around the city with a beret on his head. Classy man, this one. Tristán had not been born to wealth and worldliness; instead he'd borrowed his manners from films and soap operas. He could recognize the genuine article, the true sophisticate, and gawked, pleased by his surroundings.

"Do you want a cup of coffee, Mr. Abascal?"

"Tristán, please," he said, moving toward the dining room. Abel was still in the kitchen. He heard the clattering of cutlery and cups. "Sure, I'll have a cup."

"It's coffee from Veracruz. I put a pinch of salt in it, to make it less bitter, like our mother used to do. Do you like bitter coffee?"

"I prefer it strong. My mother is Lebanese. We added cardamom. I think most coffee at restaurants tastes like watered-down dirt, to be honest."

Abel laughed. He walked into the dining room carrying a tray with two cups of coffee and placed one before Tristán. On the tray there was also a plate with cookies.

"Is the name Tristán Abascal real or was it an invention by an executive at Televisa? Arturo de Córdova was born Arturo García, but they thought it was too common. Tristán is quite the unique name."

"The Tristán part is real enough; my mother named me after an opera. The last name is a fabrication. I was born Tristán Said Abaid," he said as he took a sip of the coffee.

"It happens. Show business is about remaking people. But you were saying you've seen *Whispers in the Mansion of Glass*?"

"*The Opal Heart in a Bottle* and *The Curse of the Hanged Man*, too. Montserrat even bought a poster of that. She wanted to get a poster of *Beyond the Yellow Door* for years, but they don't seem to exist even if someone once said they had one."

"*Beyond the Yellow Door*," Abel said, pausing and looking at him in surprise. "You'd have to be very interested in old movies to care about that. It wasn't even completed."

"I know. Montserrat is a huge horror movie buff. She told me about it."

"Who is Montserrat?"

"Sorry. Montserrat Curiel. She's a sound editor. My friend."

"A sound editor. For movies?"

"For everything, I guess. The coffee is pretty decent," he said, tapping the rim of the cup with his index finger. It wasn't, but he was trying to make a good impression. He was particular about the drinks and cigarettes he consumed. Pompous, was what Montserrat always said. Picky, he replied.

Abel offered him the plate with cookies. He took one cookie and another sip of coffee. He found himself lazily discussing film stars of old with Abel. The director knew everyone. Tristán always relished this kind of talk. The anecdotes and tales of decades past filled him with excitement. He loved chatting with Germán Robles, who had starred in proper films back in the day and had switched to voice-over work; now Robles grabbed every gig from the talking car on *Knight Rider* to dubbing flicks. Or he liked bumping into Joaquín Cordero, who'd also been the lead in a bunch of movies during the Golden Age and who lately played fathers and uncles on soaps.

The older actors were kinder. They didn't mind having a word here and there with Tristán. Tristán's peers, especially in the early years after the accident, looked at him like he was a leper. He supposed the has-beens and the seniors didn't see him as a threat. He was a bit like them. The young ones, though, had their reputations to worry about. Who wanted to be photographed with a murderer?

Of course, Tristán hadn't actually murdered anyone. He'd been in a car accident and had to have his eye reconstructed after that mess, and then got hooked on painkillers. But the newspapers were not much for nuance. If he'd played nice with the press before, maybe they wouldn't have jumped for the jugular. But he hadn't always played nice, and his image of youthful excess, which had once garnered free publicity, had sunk him, eliciting awful headlines: "Party Monster's Bacchanal Ends in Tragedy" had been one of the best ones. Plus, Karina's father, Evaristo Junco, was a vindictive asshole who had blamed Tristán for the crash. And unfortunately, Evaristo was friends with many important people.

When you've been excommunicated from TV by Evaristo Junco you don't get fruit baskets for Christmas anymore.

Tristán was munching his fourth cookie when his pager went off. He unclipped the device and glanced down at it. For a moment he thought to ask Abel if he could use his phone, but that might be a bit much, because the message was from Yolanda. Yolanda had insisted he'd taken a CD of hers, and although Tristán didn't have it, she wasn't letting it go.

Yolanda kept adding imaginary charges to Tristán's tab. Suddenly he owed her for this and that thing. And okay, fine, Tristán understood the impetus behind that, because they had been planning on going on vacation together. Now that they had split, that meant the vacation was down the toilet.

All he wished for was a bit of peace and quiet, and he suspected Yolanda would be in a foul mood. The breakup had been more tempestuous than amicable. Yet, as much as he didn't want to speak to Yolanda, he felt tempted. It might keep his mind off Karina. He was going to take out her picture that night and look at it. He simply must.

God. Maybe he shouldn't have a phone. He definitely shouldn't have a romantic relationship for the next three decades. He fucked them up with an expertise that was astonishing.

"I need to take off, sorry," Tristán said, clipping the pager back in place.

"No problem. Perhaps you'd like to come to supper and bring your editor friend?" Abel asked.

"You mean it?"

"Of course. I seldom have a chance to talk to interesting young people these days. How about Saturday? Around four."

"Sure," Tristán said, whip-quick. He felt like a child who has gorged on sweets, dizzy with joy.

They shook hands. Tristán hurried down the stairs.

Two days later he decided to stop by Montserrat's workplace rather than phone her, because the telephone was not connected yet, and because when Montserrat was in one of her double-down-and-work phases she simply yanked the telephone cord out of the wall and pretended the world did not exist.

He lounged in the reception area of Antares, flipping through a magazine, until Montserrat deigned to step out. She gave him a narrow-eyed look, pulling at the cuffs of her jacket like she did when she suspected trouble was afoot.

"I'm not here to borrow money," Tristán said, raising his hands dramatically in the air. "I have good news. Let's go for a coffee."

"No. It'll take you two damn hours to eat a salad."

"So? When's the last time you ate?"

Montserrat didn't reply, but he knew she was surviving on a salt cracker and two peanuts. She'd always pushed herself. When they were kids, she could outrun all the other children in the neighborhood despite her bad foot. He supposed she was still trying to outrun everyone. Tristán was aware sound editing was a boys' game. Montserrat was tough. She had to be. Nevertheless, he worried when he saw her straining that hard, driving herself to exhaustion.

"I saw your car parked out front. Let's go to the Tortas Locas."

"You're not getting inside my car with that fucking cigarette."

Tristán sighed. He'd been about to light it. He carefully stuffed the cigarette back in its pack. "Momo, I can open the window if it bothers you. Or do you want to go around the corner to that fonda? Forget that: let's hit a proper restaurant. Crepes at the Wings. That's better. Crepes suzette. It's too late for tortas."

"Tristán—"

"Bet you fifty thousand pesos that you don't even have milk at your apartment."

"What?"

He was attuned to Montserrat's phases, like memorizing an almanac and knowing if it was a gibbous or waxing moon without having to glance at the sky. He could tell it had been a long week for her, and personal matters tended to elude Montserrat during the long weeks. With her headphones on, she could notice any pop or crackle, but she wouldn't know if it was Tuesday or Friday. Because it didn't matter: what mattered was the sound.

"Let's drive to the supermarket."

"For God's sake," Montserrat muttered, but Tristán knew he was entirely correct about the state of her refrigerator. Even though Montserrat complained that he was immature, he didn't walk around wearing the same shirt three days in a row. Sure, her t-shirt looked clean enough this time around, but the jeans she was wearing were not fashionably ripped.

It looked more like Montserrat had stepped into the first thing she'd found that morning, and that included jeans with holes.

At least her car was immaculate. Montserrat might forget to purchase necessities, but she did not forget to pay the viene-viene who watched and washed the cars in front of her job. That car was guarded as if it was kept at Fort Knox.

They headed to the nearest supermarket. Tristán thought he might as well shop for himself, too, and Montserrat kept sighing as he checked the label of each item that went into the cart. He needed to know what he put in his body, attuned as he was to the dangers of extra calories and perilous sugars. There was also a paranoid voice in his head that said actors shouldn't be caught at the checkout counter with four bags of Sabritas as their dinner.

"What's the good news, then?" she asked while he was considering a box of crackers.

"I aced an audition, although it's still too early to say anything definitive about a paycheck. It might be people being polite rather than liking my performance. But forget that, the thing I wanted to talk to you about was Abel Urueta."

"What about him?"

"He lives in my building."

Montserrat stopped pushing the shopping cart and turned to him in surprise. "Urueta? The director Urueta?"

"Sure," Tristán said. He reached into the cart and looked at the label of a pack of instant noodles that Montserrat had dumped there. "How do you eat this?"

"With a fork," she said dryly.

"No, I mean how the fuck do you eat this? Shit, Montserrat, stop at the deli, get a slice of ham and a bit of cheese and make yourself a real lunch. No wonder your gums bleed. You probably have the nutritional deficiencies of a seventeenth-century sailor. Urueta invited you and me for dinner. We should get a bottle of wine for that."

She shook her head and stared up at him. Even with her combat boots, Montserrat barely grazed Tristán's shoulder. She mostly looked like a tiny, ferocious elf. A very shocked one at this moment, with her mouth open, awe and confusion overwhelming her.

"You're serious?"

"Of course I am. You don't eat right. I've told you a million times before, and then you complain that the dentist—"

"I mean about Urueta. You met him and he wants to have dinner?"

"Saturday."

"When did you meet him? How?"

"A couple of days ago."

She opened her mouth, closed it, opened again.

"I can't go Saturday."

"Why not? Don't tell me you'll be working. It's insane how busy you've been lately. All of July and half of August you were cooped up in front of the monitors."

"That was then. Besides, how would you know? You were too busy during the summer to see *Hellraiser 3* with me, and they only had that one special screening at Palacio Chino."

His love life had been imploding in July and August, but it wouldn't help if he mentioned that. Montserrat would probably think it was juvenile. Her solution to romance problems was to stop returning phone calls.

"Come on, you want to hang out Saturday. I know you do."

"I need the work," she said, with that stubborn grimace he knew well. "Mario has been treating me like shit, and I can't turn down anything right now or he'll use it to claim I'm unreliable. I got into a fight with him and he won't let me forget it. I'm trying to patch things up and be nice until December or I'm not getting a bonus."

"You're always fighting with him. I bet he doesn't even remember he got mad at you."

"He remembers."

"You can take one afternoon off."

"I told Araceli I'd drive her to the hospital. And afterward she'll probably want to buy candles at the Mercado de Sonora."

"That stuff doesn't work."

"Well, nothing does," Montserrat muttered, giving the shopping cart a hard push.

Tristán stuffed his hands quietly in his jeans pockets and walked next to Montserrat. "Sorry," he said.

"It's not your fault."

"I know you're busy, but it would be good to take a break. You'll burn out if you keep up this way."

"I don't burn out."

She turned to the left, almost colliding with another woman's shopping cart. The woman swore at them. Montserrat walked faster. She slowed down next to a large pyramid constructed with boxes of Zucaritas. Tristán reached for one of the boxes, flipping it between his hands. God, this was basically sugar in a box.

"Maybe I could skip the candles and take Araceli to the hospital," she said, giving him a hesitant look.

"Good. And you know what, we don't have to stay for dinner with the guy if he's boring. We can drop off the bottle of wine and then go to my apartment and order from Benedetti's."

"You said I eat shitty food and you want to order pizza."

"You do eat shitty food. But it's okay to eat shitty food when we're together."

They grabbed more groceries. Tristán refrained from commenting on Montserrat's purchases. At the checkout, he stared at a magazine on a rack and once again wondered if someone would be running a story about Karina. He didn't want to, but he was counting down the days to the anniversary of her death.

They dumped the groceries in the trunk of the car. Once they were seated, he took off his sunglasses and glanced in the rearview mirror, his eyes fixing on the scar under his eye. His left pupil was always a little more dilated than the right one because of the accident. He knew it wasn't very noticeable, but it would never cease bothering him.

Yes, he realized he was lucky to be alive. But no, he couldn't forget what had happened.

At least the dinner would provide a welcome distraction for both of them. Montserrat certainly looked like she needed a night of merriment, and he had to admit, seeing himself in that rearview mirror, that he too was stressed. Talk of actors in rubber suits playing monsters should cheer them up. Besides, he'd meant it when he'd said they could leave if it was a bore. He'd bought a second bottle of wine for that purpose. Just in case.

3

Montserrat despised hospitals. The sight of a doctor or a nurse cata-pulted her back to her childhood. Three. That had been the number of surgeries on her foot. The long, ugly scar running up her ankle and the eternally skinny, atrophied muscles of the left leg were her legacy. But the foot no longer turned at such an odd angle, and she didn't noticeably limp—not most days—even if cold weather made the limb ache. She had to watch how she walked. But after so many decades she knew how to lean her weight, and there was seldom an awkward shuffle as she moved. Except when she felt tired, and then there might be that old, unusual stride—the living dead mambo, that's what she called it—but toned down, like noise in the background of a recording that has been successfully muffled by the audio console.

No, she couldn't stand hospitals even if the days of treatments and pain were long gone. But her sister needed her, so Montserrat put on a smile and waited until Araceli came out and jumped back in the car. Araceli switched on the radio, settling on a station that played ballads. Montserrat glanced at her sister's delicate wrist and tightened her grasp on the wheel. It seemed to her Araceli was thinner each time they saw each other.

"I'm thinking of going by the Mercado de Sonora for those candles I told you about," Araceli said.

Probably for a limpia, too. Not that those worked, like Tristán had pointed out. Araceli believed in healing crystals and auras. Montserrat's faith in such remedies was lukewarm. She'd placed a statue of San Antonio upside down to get a sweetheart and tied ribbons around an aloe vera plant, but it was out of habit more than pure belief. She wished she could believe, though. Montserrat and her sister needed a miracle.

"I remember. I thought we could go later, but we can head there right away," Montserrat said.

"Oh, we can't drive there, you know that. I'm mentioning it in case you need something. I can drop it off at your place."

"Maybe we should do it the other way around."

"I can take a bus."

"The bus is crowded. And they always pass you by. Especially now, you shouldn't be wasting your energy standing around, waiting for one to roll by."

Araceli gave her a pointed look. "I can still ride a bus."

"I didn't say you couldn't," Montserrat said, but of course she'd implied as much. She didn't know how the hell to deal with Araceli's illness. She supposed Araceli simply wasn't used to having their roles reversed. It had been Montserrat who had needed care when they were young.

Araceli sighed. There was a pause. "You have plans. Didn't you say you're having dinner with Tristán?"

"I can have dinner with Tristán any day of the week."

"Have you seen his new apartment yet?"

Montserrat shook her head. "I've been busy," she said.

Not as busy as she would want, although she didn't dare tell her sister that. All she'd ever wanted to do was spend her life next to cartridge recorders, turntables, and mixing consoles. Library effects, loops, and multitracks, that's what she understood. Now with work drying up— Mario had not forgiven her, he simply needed her right this minute—what would she do? She wanted to look at cue sheets and figure out the layback, not have to fight with her boss for a couple of crummy shifts.

"Don't waste your Saturday with me. Go have fun. Have dinner with a handsome man."

"It's only Tristán."

"So? You might as well look at something pretty while you cut your steak. Better than staring at one of those gruesome posters of yours."

"He's not wall décor."

"You know what I mean. Drop me off at home and have a good time."

"Araceli, I should stay with you. We can rent a movie."

"No, you shouldn't. We can never agree on what to watch."

That much was true. Few people shared her taste. She'd scared a date off once by renting *Evil Dead*, another with *Videodrome*.

Montserrat took Araceli back to her apartment and then made her way home. She dropped the car at the garage, then walked the one block to her building. It was a shabby six-floor structure from the 1940s. Although it was not much to look at, it had weathered the earthquake of '85 without any issues, and its age meant her two-bedroom apartment was spacious, with high ceilings. And as a bonus, she having been such a long-term tenant, the rent was very reasonable.

Montserrat appreciated the height of the walls, which allowed her to showcase her posters. Although her sister thought the artwork macabre, Montserrat delighted in her collection. Her living room featured a beautiful poster of *Suspiria* and another of *Hasta el Viento Tiene Miedo*. She had framed lobby cards of other flicks. In her room, above the bed, Boris Karloff stared at her with his sad eyes. The second room, which was haphazardly used as an office, was stuffed with records, CDs, and movies. She had her computer there, a comfy chair, more posters, a desk, and a corkboard that was mostly used for pinning random photos, postcards, and tickets from concerts she'd attended. A poster of *The Curse of the Hanged Man*, Urueta's last horror film, was framed and placed above a file cabinet she used to store documents. The hanged man in question was a tiny figure in the background, dangling from a tree, and in the foreground there was a woman in a white nightgown, kneeling by what appeared to be a door that looked suspiciously coffin-shaped.

This was Urueta's best film. *The Opal Heart in a Bottle* had a beautiful sequence with a boat gliding through a swamp, but its framing story of a woman who remembers her past lives when pressed into a hypnotic trance felt tacked on, at best. *Whispers in the Mansion of Glass* redeemed itself with a delirious chase in a labyrinthian catacomb. *The Curse of the Hanged Man* had a tighter script, and one could feel Urueta was beginning to come into full bloom. It made her curious about what he might have done if he'd kept directing horror movies, but Urueta's filmography became entirely forgettable once the sixties were in full swing.

Montserrat riffled in her closet for clothes. She had been too busy to bother dragging her clothes to the laundromat, and therefore her wardrobe choices were limited. She owned a couple of blazers and skirts, which she never wore, and three good-quality dresses she had not dry-cleaned in ages.

She settled for a pair of black jeans and a Black Sabbath t-shirt that was only a little frayed at the neck. For a note of color she painted her lips a dark red. Her frizzy hair was always trouble, and most days she simply tied it back in a ponytail. Somewhere, under the sink, there was a hair dryer and a hair iron she seldom took out. She considered washing her hair and straightening it, but was immediately daunted by the idea. She stuffed her feet into a pair of old sneakers and congratulated herself on having found clean, matching socks.

She headed to Tristán's apartment at the appropriate time, although she knew he wouldn't be ready. Tristán complained she was too punctual, that this was un-Mexican. Montserrat simply shrugged. You had to adhere to schedules when you worked in dubbing. Studios were not revolving doors, open all day long. You clocked in and out; you were there when the client needed you. But there was no use explaining this to Tristán. He arrived on the dot for work, but in social situations his internal clock malfunctioned.

Montserrat parked her car a couple of blocks from Tristán's apartment, at a parking lot that she deemed trustworthy, then walked up to his building. The white façade and glistening numbers at the front made the structure easily identifiable. Across the street, there was a mechanic's garage and a tlapalería. It was as if the street had been vivisected. One side had a beautiful, new building. Meanwhile, stray cats sunned themselves on the opposite sidewalk, resting next to the cars parked by the mechanic's shop.

Montserrat pressed the intercom button. Tristán buzzed her in. When she stepped onto his floor, Tristán poked his head out the door, brushing his teeth with a towel around his waist. He motioned her in with one hand, mumbled something, and disappeared into the bathroom. Such a casual, careless greeting was normal between them. A half-naked Tristán did not even register among the list of unusual sights she'd seen in his apartment.

Montserrat sat on his couch with a frown. It was an uncomfortable couch. Gorgeous, but the leather squeaked if you moved a fraction of an inch. His apartment was sparsely furnished, and there were still boxes piled in a corner.

"Can you fasten my cuff links?" Tristán asked, walking out of the bath-room, now wearing a shirt, his hair still damp. He held out his wrists toward her.

"You're wanting to impress the old man. Now I feel underdressed."

"I always overdress, and you know it. You didn't have clean clothes, did you?"

Tristán smiled at her wickedly, knowing very well she had skipped the laundromat. She did not answer, instead simply adjusted the cuff links and brushed his hands away.

"If you're going to criticize my outfit, then you shouldn't ask me to come to this stupid dinner."

"It's not a stupid dinner. You're going to like Urueta. It wouldn't kill you to socialize a little, you know?"

"I socialize enough."

"Aha. Now don't give me that mean look or I won't give you this."

"This what?"

Tristán reached into his right pocket and handed her a key ring. "My apartment keys."

Montserrat shook her head vehemently. "No. I'll have to water your plants and feed your fish when you go on vacation."

"She kept the plants. As for the fish, it died a little while back."

"What if you adopt a dog or some shit?"

"I'm not adopting a dog. Come on, you always have a set of keys."

He meant she had a set of keys when he was between relationships, when he wanted her available to drop everything and come by on the evenings when he became melancholic and lonely. When he needed her to house sit. When his life was a bit of a mess and she was the one restocking his refrigerator. That's how things worked between them. Montserrat didn't know if it was simply that age was getting to her, but she didn't feel like grabbing the key and subjecting herself to the merry-go-round that was Tristán.

Habit, however, was a powerful force. She opened her palm, and he placed the key ring on it. She could always return it.

"I should put on my shoes," Tristán said brightly.

"You want me to tie your shoelaces?" she asked, her tone mordant. But he laughed her away and disappeared into the bedroom.

"I might have a great gig lined up. The audition? Turns out I was right: they like me a lot," he yelled from inside the bedroom.

Montserrat stood up at one end of the hallway and looked in the direction of his room. "What gig?"

"For that ad campaign I told you about."

Montserrat was honestly surprised. Tristán leaned against the doorway and smiled charmingly, brushing a piece of lint off his shirt. "I'd play a detective."

"A detective? Holmes or Marlowe?"

"Marlowe, I guess. I get to stand in a suit, light filtering through the blinds, glass in hand. It's for a brand of whiskey. Print and TV commercials. My face would be on billboards. It's not a soap, but the money is good."

"Forget soaps. Tristán, that's amazing!"

Tristán smiled again. This time it wasn't his crisp, canned smile, but a genuine one. He looked boyish and a little bashful when he smiled like that, the years melting off him.

When they were young they had played by the train tracks in Pantaco, wielding wooden planks as swords, reciting dialogue they scribbled on napkins.

Near the tracks were vast storage facilities filled with grain, a veritable ocean of corn, wheat, and rice, just a few paces from rickety fences with plenty of holes that were no deterrent for eager children.

The kids in the neighborhood would dare one another to jump into the gigantic piles of grain. They traded gruesome descriptions of rodents hiding in the corn, waiting to gnaw children's toes off. They whispered stories of people who had choked to death, suffocated by the grain. Stories to scare each other, and yet, there was real danger in this adventure. One had to climb up to the rafters, walking along a wooden beam like a trapeze artist. The dive into the grain was a good seven- or ten-meter jump.

Tristán wouldn't jump alone. Montserrat remembered plummeting into the grain, Tristán's hand firmly grasping her own. She remembered the way her stomach lurched for a second, the sweaty palms, the gasp escaping their lips. For a fraction of a second it felt as if they were weightless.

Then came the cushion of grain beneath their bodies and Tristán's wide, crooked smile as he turned to look at her, buried to his waist in kernels of corn. That smile before the dentist fixed his teeth, before the TV studio showed him how to grin for the flustered fans, before the world wore him down.

Montserrat slid her hands into her pockets and smiled back at him.

Tristán turned away and finished readying himself. They marched up to Urueta's apartment with a good bottle of wine as an offering. When Abel opened the door, Montserrat remembered a photo of the director she'd seen in a book about the history of Mexican cinema. He still sported a little mustache and his hair was slicked back in the same style as it had been in the 1950s. He had a firm, pleasant voice that paired well with his tweed jacket and the gray knit vest with big buttons. He watched Montserrat and Tristán with the eye of a connoisseur, of a casting director.

"I'm so glad you are joining us. Tristán said you are a fan of old horror movies."

"We both are," Montserrat said as they sat down in the dining room. Behind Abel there was an old cabinet filled with dusty china and knickknacks. Cameras from different eras, photos in silver frames, a stack of greeting cards. The table was set with some of that same ancient china, the glasses dusted off and filled with wine.

"Who is your favorite director?"

"I like Tod Browning," Montserrat said. "I like all the RKO horror movies, too. Jacques Tourneur's *Cat People* is a classic. Val Lewton produced wonderful work on a tiny budget."

"My father knew Browning. Back in the day, they shot films in different languages using different cast and crews but the same sets. My father was part of the crew on the Spanish-language *Dracula*. Browning shot in the daytime, the Spanish language crew shot at night. Have you heard of that?"

"Yes. With the Dunning method they could use a previously shot backdrop behind the actors, and therefore save money that way. No need to shoot a crowd scene twice. They'd substitute the silver in a black-and-white print with yellow dye and by lighting the set the right way, with yellow-orange lights against a blue background, you could create a rudimentary rear projection method."

She'd told Tristán this dinner was stupid, but she was actually nervous about making an appearance. She didn't want to seem too eager or too guarded, and she feared giving the wrong impression. Tristán was charming; she knew herself barely tolerable. Not that she wished to strike a sour note, but her favorite topics—forgotten films, horror, sound—were seldom the things others talked about. People's eyes glazed over when she spoke, if she deigned to speak. Sometimes, at parties or reunions, she preferred to simply stand in a corner and pretend she'd lost the ability to string words together.

She was rude, that's what people said, but she didn't want to be rude to Abel Urueta. She wanted him to like her.

"What a delight. Your girlfriend does know her old films," Abel said, beguiled rather than indifferent to her. She was used to indifference and smiled.

"Oh, Montserrat is not my girlfriend," Tristán said with a careless chuckle. How annoying, his nonchalance, and how annoying, too, the little jab of pain that accompanied it.

It shouldn't have bothered her, because he had spoken a true fact, and yet for a second there was that uncomfortable snagging of her heart before she shook her head and brushed the feeling away.

"We've been friends forever. She kept me from getting my ass kicked when I was a kid."

"She's a tiny thing, Tristán."

"Back then I was short, too. I didn't stretch up until I was fifteen. When my family moved to Mexico City the kids around our building made fun of my accent. I was from up north, my accent was thick, and the neighborhood was full of bullies who'd beat me up for the fun of it. But Montserrat knocked them down with her cane."

It was true about the accent. You couldn't tell where Tristán had originated anymore, he'd smoothed all his edges, but once upon a time he'd had the thickest of accents. It had been the same story with Pedro Infante. They had dubbed him in his first film because his accent was too thick and producers doubted he'd make it big. He was raw. That's what they had said about Infante in the beginning. Infante proved them wrong, though. And Tristán had possessed a similar rawness that he'd polished to a fine sheen.

"A cane?" Abel asked.

"I limped," Montserrat said, cutting into the chicken breast on her plate and shrugging. "I had to have surgeries to fix my foot. The kids called me Frankenstein because of my scar. Or they'd call me Peg Leg. I'd swing my cane around and beat the little pricks. When they laughed at Tristán, I beat them, too."

"And when you grew up you both went into the entertainment business. Did you attend university together?"

"God, no," Tristán said. "I dropped out of high school to act."

"What did your family say about that?"

"They had their reservations."

That was such a euphemism that Montserrat couldn't muffle a snort. Tristán's father had wanted his youngest boy to become a lawyer or a dentist, and they'd had a legendary row when Tristán quit school. The only reason why his old man had relented was because Tristán brought in good money back then, and they could use his paycheck—Tristán's dad was having a rough patch.

Montserrat's mother had criticized Tristán's decision loudly, too, warning that if her daughter ever dared to pull a stunt like that, she'd beat her bloody. Montserrat graduated from high school, studied accounting like her mom wanted—her sister was already working in that field, and her mother thought it was a sensible job for her younger daughter, too—and worked part-time at a business that rented audio equipment for musicians and for parties. She graduated with mediocre grades, spent most of her time trying to learn everything she could about audio, and quit her part-time job to get another part-time job at a post-production place with awful hours and awful pay.

Her mother still thought that was the worst decision of her entire life. Maybe the woman hadn't been so wrong after all.

"Who do you work for, Montserrat?"

The last thing she wanted to discuss was her job. This was a sore subject with her mother, and she insulated her sister from her workplace issues, but the way Abel asked the question was with real interest, without any judgment. She found herself answering with a smile.

"Antares. I work on a bunch of projects. I did a bit of anime in the summer."

"What is that?"

"Japanese cartoons. Tristán does voice work for a series from there. He plays Lancelot in *Legend of the Round Table*."

Japanese was the hardest language to dub. English was also problematic. People used fewer words when speaking in English; the language was full of contractions. When you had to speak the same lines in Spanish, the dialogue could balloon. Tristán, however, dubbed Japanese cartoons with ease. It wasn't so much that he synchronized his words to the lips of the characters, it was that he simply *became* the drawings on screen.

Lancelot, for example, was the most handsome and the bravest of the knights, and when Tristán spoke like Lancelot he sounded like an eager, twenty-something hero, brimming with bravado and courtly virtues. Other voice actors could master the art of the labial synch, but their performance felt wooden. Tristán seemed almost careless when he bumped into a studio, smiling, script in hand, but he was a pro nevertheless.

"Do you ever do any audio editing for films?"

"Yeah. Some post-production stuff, sometimes dubs for films they broadcast on TV, I've even done 'foley art.'"

"What is 'foley art'?"

"Sound effects: chopping a head of lettuce to make it sound like a person is being decapitated," she said, making a motion as if she were swinging an axe. "It varies."

"God. It's been so long since I worked, I probably wouldn't be able to recognize an editing bay," Abel said, shaking his head. "In the old days we didn't call it that."

"It was efectos de sala, yes. Or, to pull a 'Gavira,'" she said.

"Gavira! A genius, that one. Have you met him?"

"Oh, yes," she said. Gonzalo Gavira had been a legendary Golden Age sound man. He'd worked for Buñuel and invented the distinctive sound effects of *The Exorcist*. She doubted he'd worked with Abel, but the man might have a juicy tale about him after all. She suspected Abel Urueta had many juicy tales.

"A Gavira! You should have said that first," Abel said. His tone was that of playful admonishment, like a grandfather teaching a child a lesson.

When had Urueta shot his last movie? 1966, perhaps? And afterward he mustn't have had much contact with filmmakers. It was a little sad, when you thought about it, how a great director could be forgotten and detached from his previous world.

"Sorry, we use a lot more Americanisms now," she said. "When they shot *Tarzan* in Mexico they didn't shoot it with sound, and they had to send it to Los Angeles for all the sound effects. But we do that now."

"They shot that at Estudios Churubusco back when . . . oh, it would have been '69?" Abel said, rubbing his chin.

"From '66 until '68," she said breezily. Montserrat had a good memory. You needed it with editing. "It wasn't the first Tarzan production in Mexico: Weissmuller shot *The Mermaids* in Acapulco in '48."

"Weissmuller used to like eating at this little place near Caleta back then. Such a long time ago! I would have been twenty years old when RKO was rolling their cameras in Acapulco." Abel smiled wistfully and refilled her wineglass. "John Wayne owned the Hotel Flamingo in Caleta, did you know that?"

"And Errol Flynn anchored nearby and lounged around the Sirocco. But I can't remember if that was before or after his trial for statutory rape. A big creep, that one."

"Hardly the worst or most interesting of the lot," Abel said. "I'll tell you a fun story after dinner, since you like old movies and their stars."

The evening was flowing better than she'd expected. She thought she'd either clam up or talk too much, but Abel was a pleasant host; he knew what questions to ask and listened to the answers with real interest.

After the plates were cleared, they moved into the living room. This, like the dining room, was crammed with objects and furniture from previous eras, with shelves extending as high as they could, overflowing with dusty treasures. Two overstuffed velour couches were set in the middle of the living room, and that is where they sat. Tristán quickly took out a cigarette, and Abel handed him an amber-colored ashtray.

"Would you care for a brandy?" Abel asked, as he stood next to a bar cart and began filling a glass.

"I'll have one," Tristán said.

"I'm fine," Montserrat said.

"Nothing better than a brandy and a cigarette in the evening. It helps with the digestion," Abel said, filling a second glass for Tristán. The old man then sat on the couch in front of them.

With his handkerchief around his neck and his horn-rimmed glasses you could discern what Abel Urueta must have been like in his youth. A cool, snappy dresser. A rich boy. He spoke with a luxurious voice that plainly telegraphed the distance between their upbringings. Montserrat had grown up in a tough neighborhood and weathered a rough childhood. Urueta had not. And his history was imprinted in his voice. It was very difficult to erase such things. They lingered, like the scent of faded flowers. Of course, there were certain people who were able to shed their old skins and their primordial speech patterns. Tristán, for example, had the gift of mimicry. But these were rare creatures, and Tristán had never wanted to be himself in all the time since she'd first met him. When they watched horror movies, it was the sight of the monster, the Other, that terrified Tristán and the idea of becoming the hero that seduced him. Montserrat saw herself in the faces of monsters and did not wince.

"Tristán said you've been looking for a poster of *Beyond the Yellow Door*. That was a very curious movie and the last of the horror films I ever shot. Now, let me ask you something: what would you say is the most infamous horror film ever shot?"

"Infamous how? *Freaks* caused a scandal," Montserrat said, thinking back to Browning's pre-Code masterpiece. It was an oddly affectionate horror film, and in her mind far superior to *Dracula*. "And a few years ago Carlos Enrique Taboada was editing *Jirón de Niebla* when Salinas confiscated the film. I heard it from a trusty source."

That was a bit of a half-truth; she'd heard it from Paco Orol, and he wasn't a good source at all. Montserrat wasn't sure that something else hadn't happened to halt the editing of Taboada's fifth horror flick. The story went that one of the producers of the movie had been backing Salinas's political rival. When Salinas seized the presidency, he retaliated by either sending soldiers to steal the reels or accused the man of piracy and *then* had the reels seized. Of course, people also said that Salinas had murdered a maid when he'd been playing cowboys and Indians as a child and it had been covered up. All sorts of stories swirled around at parties, and when you were drunk the stories tended to become bloated. Nevertheless, as long as they were talking infamous films, surely *Jirón de Niebla* had to count.

"Those are good examples. What about cursed films?"

"Wasn't *The Exorcist* supposed to be cursed?" she ventured. "The set burned down. They hired a priest to perform a blessing."

"Mmm," Tristán said, taking a quick sip of his brandy. He turned to her. "We rented *Three Men and a Baby* to see if a ghost had been caught on film. Remember that?"

She did. They had frozen the frame and moved close to the TV set, but all Montserrat could distinguish was a shadow. It was something silly to do on a Friday night when the pizza from Benedetti's was running late.

"A ghost is a ghost. But a curse is entirely different."

"Is *Beyond the Yellow Door* cursed or infamous?" she asked.

It was neither, as far as she knew, but it was clear he wanted this question asked. She'd heard stories about the movie through the years; there had even been that guy who swore he'd seen a poster for it. But nothing ever materialized. It was too small a film and Abel Urueta was too obscure a director for it to garner more than a sentence in publications about Mexican cinema, if that. From what she understood it would have been another horror film, slightly different from Urueta's previous historical entries because this one would have been a contemporary story. No-name actors in the cast, or marginal ones, which was par for the course. The plot? A cult, evil shenanigans. One theory was that Urueta never meant to release the flick, that it was commissioned by a consortium of Americans laundering money and the negatives destroyed. A second rumor was of embezzlement by one of the investors, who fled with much of the film's budget to Brazil, as the reason for its implosion. Another one was that it didn't get beyond the pre-production stage, and if it did Urueta only shot a third of it. But it wasn't Jodorowsky's *Dune*, or Welles's *The Other Side of the Wind*. People were not muttering excitedly about it and hoping for a belated release. The only reason Montserrat had ever heard about the flick was because she had a soft spot for Abel Urueta, which in itself was a rare endeavor.

Abel sat back, laced his hands together, and smiled at them. "Yes and no. It's too obscure for anyone to remember it. But it should be remembered if only for Wilhelm Friedrich Ewers. It's not every day you run into a German occultist who is writing movies in Mexico City."

The name was alien to her, and she thought she would have remembered such a name.

"It sounds like you're about to recite a tall tale," Montserrat said, raising a skeptical eyebrow at the old man. "German occultists?"

"There's a healthy history of German occultism. In fact, there was a fellow called Arnoldo Krumm-Heller who moved in Parisian circles before making his way to Mexico City, where he served as a physician for none other than President Madero. In 1927, he founded the Fraternitas Rosicruciana Antiqua in Mexico City."

"Maybe that's true, but I happen to know the scriptwriter for *Beyond the Yellow Door* was Romeo Donderis, if that's where you're headed," Montserrat said and she plucked Tristán's glass from his hand and took a sip of it. She hadn't felt like drinking, but the mood was changing. Whatever defensive measures she'd erected were swiftly brushed aside, and she felt festive, even giddy, since she knew she'd caught Abel fibbing. "He was also the scriptwriter on a Western that I quite appreciated."

"But I didn't say Ewers was the sole scriptwriter. Ewers worked on the treatment, so to speak. He also modified bits of dialogue and polished certain scenes."

Montserrat considered that.

Tristán took the glass back. He looked very relaxed as he stretched out his legs and inclined his head. "An occultist *and* a writer. I can't even remember my appointments for Monday," he said with a cheeky grin. "But I do admit people can get into bizarre hobbies when they're in show business. Is that why the film ought to be infamous? Because that German boy said abracadabra and presto?"

"Oh, no. It's more than that. It's the whole of it. The Nazi connections, the secretive little stories."

"Nazis! We're not in Argentina," Tristán said with a hearty laugh.

"I take it you've never heard of Hilde Krüger, or Hilda, as she called herself in Mexico. She was a Nazi, an actress, and a spy, who cozied up to many Mexican government functionaries in the 1940s. Gabriel Soria auditioned her for a role or two, which is how I learned about her. There were Nazis floating around Mexico around that time."

Tristán's smile faded a little. Montserrat leaned forward, looking carefully at Abel. "You're serious? You worked with a Nazi writer?" she asked.

This no longer sounded like a fib, or an elaborate joke. They were at the edge of something special.

"That's the thing. Ewers told different versions of the same story. In one version, he's a young man who stumbles into the circle of Nazi occultists, in another there're no Nazis at all but he's studying with Erik Jan Hanussen, who teaches him hypnotism, before he must flee Germany when Hanussen is assassinated. Even Ewers's age was in question. In 1961, when *Beyond the Yellow Door* was filming, he looked to have been in his thirties, and at the time of Hanussen's death in 1933 he would have been barely fourteen, which contradicts some of his stories.

"But it didn't matter what version you heard, what wild tangle of events Ewers spun for you; after you met him you believed that he did possess secret knowledge. It was how he spoke, how he carried himself. It made folks nervous on the set, especially since we were shooting a horror film. Then, suddenly, Ewers died. He was mugged one night. We lost our funding, we couldn't complete the film, and misfortune seemed to follow the crew."

"What kind of misfortune?" Montserrat asked.

"Anything and everything. If you ask theater performers, they'll tell you *Macbeth* is cursed, but they probably can't pinpoint the exact source of the trouble, and it was the same with *Beyond the Yellow Door*. People who worked on it had accidents, or couldn't get new roles. Vague stories, half rumors about things that happened on set. I had a friend who joked that the film had been cursed. 'Remember Abel's cursed movie?' Some people had heard about Ewers and his magic talk, and they also knew it had been a horror film. Altogether it made a spooky story. I had to admit it was fun to bring it up at parties. If you have a failed production, you might as well have one that is cursed."

Abel poured himself another glass of brandy. "Of course, that only lasted for so long. Eventually, people forgot all about the curse. Poof, gone, even that. Say *Beyond the Yellow Door* nowadays, and no one can remember I worked on that."

"What happened to the reels you were able to shoot before your backers pulled out?" Montserrat asked.

"The reels were destroyed when the backer left. And my work? It doesn't amount to anything. All I can do is tell you stories of dead people, and of Ewers, the sorcerer who swore one day I'd be one of the greats."

She thought he might add something else, that he was about to elaborate on what he meant, but his face turned sour and distant.

A painful silence, and then Abel chuckled. "Well, I thought I was going to tell you a fun and interesting horror story, and it seems I've simply told you a sad one. I'm sorry."

Abel's eyes looked glassy as he clasped his hands together. He reminded her of Boris Karloff in *The Black Cat*. His visage was both elegant and worn down, and his hands looked frail. Before, she'd been able to envision the younger Abel Urueta with a colorful handkerchief around his neck, but now that image had faded. She was left only with the impression of age and melancholy.

The grandfather clock in a corner struck the hour. Montserrat turned her head, looking at the time. She groaned.

"I should get going. I have a shift," she said, springing up from her seat.

"Oh, boy, Momo, tonight?" Tristán asked.

"Yeah. Gotta catch the work when you can."

They all stood up. Abel walked them to the door. He smiled at them, with a sad, tired smile. "It was nice talking to you both. You'll come back for a visit?" he asked.

"Sure," she said and shook the director's hand. She meant it, too. This was seldom the case. Tristán wasn't wrong about her social life. She preferred the solitude of the sound cabin and the headphones to having to clink glasses with people. But Urueta's mournfulness made him more, not less, appealing to her.

Tristán accompanied her down the stairs. He jangled the apartment keys in his jacket pocket as they walked through the lobby. "Interesting fellow, isn't he? He told me a story about Irma Dorantes that I'd never heard before. A raunchy one."

"Were there any occultists in that one?"

"No."

"*Beyond the Yellow Door* is the kind of stuff they might cover on *Enigma*," Montserrat mused. "Cornelia's still working there."

"That's a terrible show. I don't understand how it's on the air."

"Because people watch that stuff. Nino Canún has guests talking about UFOs every damn month on his show. He and Jaime Maussan, that's all they talk about."

"What's going through that devious little brain of yours?"

"Nothing," she said, sliding her arms into her jacket and adjusting the collar.

"Liar."

But he was right. There was something going through her mind, and that was the simple fact that *Enigma* had money and needed content. American money, to be exact. The backers for that show were folks from Miami who were trying to slide into the Latin American market. Telemundo was now aiming to make their own soap operas, and the folks backing *Enigma* were looking for the same thing: original programming.

Montserrat didn't know how to pitch stories to TV suits, but Cornelia did. You could get a two-hour special out of a German occultist if Nino Canún could get eleven hours and ten minutes on the air showing grainy video footage of lights that were supposed to be spaceships.

Amphibian babies, little gray men who abducted women in the middle of the night, pyramids designed by people from Atlantis. That's what people wanted, and there was money to be made in that stupid line of work. She knew it because she'd seen Cornelia's condo and her fancy furniture. Meanwhile, editing audio at Antares wasn't leading her anywhere, and her sister was in a tight financial spot.

She checked her wristwatch. "I've gotta run."

"Wish me luck," Tristán said as he held open the front door for her.

"What luck?"

"For the ad campaign."

"No such thing as luck, but I'll tell Araceli to buy you a rabbit's foot next time she goes to the Mercado de Sonora."

"Very funny. Have lunch with me next week. You can help me run a few lines."

"I need to finish the project I'm working on."

"Phone me!"

She smiled, taking three steps from his doorway, hands in her pockets. "Go get that gig, handsome!" she yelled before she trotted off to find her car.

4

Tristán's coping tactic was erasure. He was avoiding newsstands, he had vanished the calendar from his home, he had placed the box with Karina's photos at the back of his closet where he couldn't get to it easily. The little picture he carried in his wallet remained there because he never took that one out, but otherwise he was determined to pretend this was an ordinary month.

He had plenty of other things to worry about, anyway. The ad campaign for the whiskey was going to another guy, and Yolanda had phoned—the line was finally working—still talking about the missing CD, but really suggesting they should meet for dinner. Well . . . for fucking. Tristán felt everything was a bit too raw to think about having sex so soon after their breakup, and he suspected Yolanda might want to get back together with him, because that had happened once before. That would be unfair to her since he was as lukewarm about their relationship as he had been for the past few months. They had patched things up after their first, brief separation, only for Tristán to regret it within days. He suspected the same thing would happen again if he started seeing her: breakup, together again, breakup. It was not a pattern he relished. But he was also wildly, desperately, in need of distraction.

The days felt endless, and he couldn't depend on Montserrat to keep him distracted, even if he longed to simply sit in a corner of the editing bay while she worked her magic with the controls. But Montserrat was busy. She had shifts at her job right now, and he was in one of those downward periods when the opportunities were scarce and the tedium kept mounting. The new apartment had cable, and he kept browsing through the channels or else sat on the couch, listless. No new gigs were going to manifest like this, and yet he felt less and less inclined to even try. In his early audio days, he'd gone to the big dubbing studios at nine a.m. and lounged around, fishing for work, waiting to see if a voice actor who was scheduled that morning had missed roll call so he could take his place. It was miserable, unproductive, hard work, and he was reluctant to head down that route again. It was better to stay put, to wait for the telephone to ring, than to be reduced to those awful, mendicant sessions.

On a rather gray and dreary Thursday he managed to gather the energy to clean his living room and make his bed. He even went for a walk, and while watching pigeons bobbing for crumbs on a stretch of greenery that passed as a park, he resolved to tell Yolanda that he didn't think it was wise that they meet for dinner, rather than offering bland replies that could be mistaken for "maybes."

When he returned to the apartment he was in decent spirits. Tristán, despite his multiple failings, was an optimist. He told himself each new day could bring a fresh beginning. He'd learned this from his mother, who always hummed a tune as she cooked; who always smiled despite his father's meager paycheck and their modest apartment. His mom adored opera, she loved the great dramas and the beautiful arias, and she could reliably conjure good cheer despite her interest in the sorrows of the great heroines created by Verdi.

He'd have to give mom and dad a call that Saturday. He'd also take Montserrat and Araceli for ice cream or another treat. Yes, he told himself, it was going to be a fine day and an even better weekend. Optimism! That was the trick.

The phone was ringing when he walked in. He was surprised when the person on the other end of the line said she was a writer for *De Telenovela*. No one cared to interview him anymore except when it was to ask tawdry, exploitative questions, but the writer quickly said she was writing a story on actors who were doing dubbing for TV shows and his name had come up as someone she should talk to.

"Would you have a few minutes?"

"Oh, sure," Tristán said, feeling delighted someone was paying attention to his voice work. "What would you like to know?"

The writer asked about his role as Lancelot on the Japanese show Tristán had been working on, then they discussed how he'd transitioned to voice work—to be frank, he owed a lot of it to Montserrat, who had been the first one to suggest it—and the basics of the job.

"Do you mind if we talk about your soap opera roles? It'll help contextualize the shift to audio," the reporter said.

Tristán, who had been more used to puff pieces than serious interviews in his youth, immediately agreed. He wondered how many pages this interview might yield. It could all end up being nothing more than a paragraph, but he was praying for something meatier.

"Your last soap, it was *Juventud*. You were the romantic lead and worked with Karina Junco."

His voice was cool as he spoke, mostly because he'd learned to sound cool when he talked about his girlfriend. "That was a long time ago," he said, hoping to parry the question, hoping they'd move to talking about another co-star or another soap.

"What was she like?"

Wild, he thought. He'd been attracted to her from the moment he walked on set. She was TV royalty. Her father was a producer, her mother a former movie star. She'd grown up two paces from the limelight, which had made her spoiled, but she was also charming enough that you could ignore her flaws. Tristán hadn't been an innocent by the time he worked on that soap; he'd climbed his way to the summit and learned the ropes, and he could recognize a self-destructive personality when he saw one, but he also savored that type and so was mesmerized.

He twisted the cord between his hands. He tried to say her name and couldn't. "She . . . she was sweet. Energetic," he said, choosing politeness and euphemisms instead of blunt honesty.

"You had a long-term relationship."

"We were together for over a year," he said. Fifteen months and twenty-two days. He had not forgotten that number. They'd broken up three times during those fifteen months and each breakup hadn't lasted more than a handful of days. Patterns. Tristán did love his patterns.

"There was talk, back then, that Karina was doing drugs. That you were doing drugs, too. That you were, in fact, doing drugs the night of the accident. There was a lot of talk about you. About your special parties."

Yes, he knew that tale. Tristán, the pill pusher who had stuffed Karina Junco full of chemical substances. This was a great exaggeration. For one, back in those days, Tristán didn't do any hard drugs. It was only after the accident that he'd gotten hooked on painkillers. Karina was the one who liked to put whatever illegal substance she could find inside her system. In the early eighties, he was still worried about showing up to work looking a mess. Tristán had never attended an orgy either, nor given Karina herpes, as one bullshit story had claimed. He slept around as much as might be expected of a good-looking young man who graced the covers of magazines, but he was careful about STDs.

He was also bisexual, and he'd been sternly advised by the top brass at Televisa to be discreet about it. A few of the directors and casting agents and other actors frowned, aware they were working with a fellow who went both ways, but Tristán had been devastatingly, almost impossibly handsome, sexy enough to send chills down a viewer's spine, and extremely sellable. So they ignored that aspect of his life, just as they'd turned their blind eye to other stars from decades past who dabbled in decidedly un-Catholic activities.

Then, when the accident happened, the salacious rumors about his sex life began to circulate, and he was labeled a pervert. But not openly, no. No one ever admitted stars like Enrique Álvarez Félix were gay and nobody ever would. Nobody printed the names of Tristán's ex-boyfriends in magazines. It was all innuendo and coded phrases, but it did the same damage.

It had been Karina's father who—despite retiring from producing, he still maintained his connections—had spearheaded that smear campaign; it was Karina's father who had loaded the ammo and taken a shot at the young actor. Tristán couldn't prove it, but he knew it, just as he knew his career was over. God forbid a leading man make the mistake of looking the least bit queer.

The rumors ballooned, and Tristán's father yelled at him, saying he had shamed his whole family. Eventually, people lost interest in him. The bruises from the accident faded, but so too did Tristán's name from gossip columns. Nevertheless, Tristán had to wade with caution when it came to his family. His father was still going on about how he had been corrupted by deviant producers and directors, even though he hadn't minded those "deviants" when the dough started rolling in and Tristán shared his wealth with his family. The less said to his brothers about his romantic life, the better. His mother simply worried people would be mean to him if they learned he dated both men and women.

There was a lot of talk about you, back in the day. About your special parties, yeah. Such a snide little remark with such huge implications.

"I did not organize a party the night of the accident," Tristán said tersely.

"I thought—"

"I did not. Check stories from that day, you'll see it wasn't my party."

"People said you were cheating on Karina," the reporter said, quickly pivoting, perhaps unwilling to admit a mistake.

"Who have you been talking to?" he asked, his cool slipping, the nonchalant, smooth tone he cultivated turning coarse. This was bullshit. But so much had been whispered about him. "Forget about it, I'm hanging up."

"Were you driving the night of the accident?" the reporter asked. "Did you in fact kill Karina Junco?"

Tristán set the receiver back in its cradle and went into his bedroom. He found his wallet and took out the snapshot he'd been ignoring for the past few weeks and stared into Karina's face. He imagined the photo *De Telenovela* would run of Karina. She might even get the cover, looking sweet, with ribbons in her hair, as she had looked in the promotional images for *Juventud*.

The tragic end of a would-be star.

Tristán would be a vulgar footnote in her two-page spread.

By one a.m. he was plastered and had to call a taxi.

He pressed the wrong button when he stumbled against the intercom outside Montserrat's building and had to dial again, but he climbed the stairs with the ease of an Olympic champion. He knew, without looking at her as she opened the door and he walked into her apartment, that she was furious. The door slammed behind him. He tossed himself on her couch.

"It's late," she said.

"I didn't get the part."

"You could have told me tomorrow."

He looked at her with half-lidded eyes. She was wearing an oversize t-shirt that reached her thighs and thick socks that were pulled almost to her knees. Her big toe poked out from one of the socks.

"You sleep in that?"

"Are you coming to consult on my wardrobe?"

"I came to tell you I lost the campaign. They're going with someone younger. They want to reach the twenty-something demo. Something like that. They're going with a blond dude. A clone of Luismi who cut a record two seconds ago. Maybe he modeled instead of singing, who the fuck knows. I'll tell you, I—"

Montserrat hit him in the face with a cushion. She wasn't gentle about it, either. She swung it with all the force she could muster. "You're a thoughtless, drunk prick! I'm exhausted!"

"It's not that late!" he yelled, tossing the cushion back at her. She swatted it away.

"No? Maybe you're confused; this is not a nightclub. Were you partying and forgot your address?"

Tristán stared at Montserrat, rubbing a hand against his face, his eyes now wide open.

"Did Yolanda dump you a second time?" she continued. "Or were you unable to score at the bar? What's the motherfucking stupid reason why you're here at this hour?"

"Karina's ten-year anniversary is next week," he said, his voice low and rough.

Montserrat's angry snarl turned into a shocked open mouth. She grabbed hold of the hem of her t-shirt and twisted it with one hand. "I'm sorry, I forgot," she said. Her voice sounded uncharacteristically soft. It reminded him of when they'd been kids. She'd been sweeter, then. Not with everyone, but with him. She'd made sure to cover his eyes when there was a monster that was too scary on the screen and told him when he could look again. When he broke his arm, she wrote in their secret alphabet on his cast. She composed the eulogy for his pet turtle's funeral.

"So did I. For a second. I agreed to an interview, and I didn't think it would be about that."

She stood next to the couch, looking at him, and he in turn looked at the ceiling, clasping his hands together and resting them against his chest. They'd played at pirates, but Montserrat played at vampires. Sometimes she made him pretend he was the vampire in a coffin made of cardboard, his hands pressed against his heart like that.

But vampires didn't grow old, and when he'd looked in the mirror a few hours earlier, he was definitely riddled with gray hairs.

"Ten years," she said.

Tristán clasped his hands tighter. Karina would have been thirty-six. He could hardly believe it. Time had slipped through his fingers.

"I forgot about it, yeah: a whole decade next week. The reporter started asking questions, and I thought she wanted a story about me. But it was about her."

"I forgot, too."

Tristán shook his head. "Yes, but I wouldn't expect you to remember. She didn't die in your car, after all."

"What did the reporter say?"

"You know what she said. And if she didn't say it, she implied it. They all do. Fuckers."

He hadn't been driving, but nobody seemed to care or remember that. What they remembered was that Tristán Abascal was a party animal who demanded that innocent, pure-hearted Karina Junco drive him home after feeding her a vast number of drugs during an orgy in Cuernavaca. Every single quote and commentary had been about how Tristán had guided her to perdition.

It was the way Karina's father sought to cleanse his child's image. It was a lot better to say her perverted boyfriend had practically murdered Karina than to admit she'd been an alcoholic and a junkie.

The shame of it . . . the fucking shame he felt, in the hospital, his body aching, and then the shame as his mother cried on the phone, as his eldest brother read him a headline . . . Shame, pain, guilt. It didn't end.

"They always talk shit."

"I should have called someone," Tristán muttered.

She sat down, resting on the couch's arm. "Tristán, don't start. It wasn't your fault."

"I should have gotten help."

"Your face was smashed with glass. You couldn't run to a pay phone."

"She needed help, that night—" he muttered and stopped, catching his breath.

He remembered he'd been wearing a burgundy jacket, and they'd both overdone their drinking. He remembered the tears in her eyes as she clutched the wheel and kept begging him to look at her, and then he pretended to fall asleep.

Tristán unlaced his hands and now dug his fingers into the couch, as if he could rip the upholstery apart and puncture his hands with wooden splinters and metal springs.

"I should have gotten her help before that. I knew she was overdoing it with the drugs and the drinking, but I never complained."

Karina and Tristán looked good together, and they were going to have another major hit, and if the press found out about her addiction maybe they'd cancel the project. He wanted that role. It was a great part.

What a selfish thing to think! Even these days, when he thought about Karina, he didn't consider how horrible her death must have been, crushed under that car. He thought about his face. He thought about the surgery and how his eye would never look the same, or about the scars on his chest. And right now he was angry because he thought Karina was probably going to get the cover of a magazine next week, but *he* would never have another magazine cover again.

Selfish, selfish prick, and Montserrat didn't know anything about it, she didn't understand. He wanted to tell her everything and could not.

Tristán sat up and let out a pained laugh. Montserrat was looking at him from the other end of the rickety couch.

"I'm exhausted, Momo. Sometimes I think it would be easier to drive off a cliff and re-enact that crash. Give the public the ending they want."

She stretched out a hand. He shook his head and brushed her hand away. Montserrat stood up and went to her bedroom. When she returned she had a blanket and a pillow. She handed both items to him, wordless. Tristán placed the pillow under his head and wrapped himself in the blanket.

He heard the click of the light switch and her sock-clad feet against the wooden floor. The numbers on the VCR next to the TV glowed a bright red, and he stared at them, burning the minutes into his retinas until at last he fell asleep.

He woke up to the scent of fresh coffee. In the kitchen, Montserrat was frying eggs. He stretched his arms and turned his head as she walked into the room with two plates in her hands and placed them on the round dining table.

Tristán sat in front of her and took a sip of coffee. The eggs were burned. Montserrat was a terrible cook, but he ate them all the same. His stomach was gurgling. The previous day he'd limited himself to a liquid, alcohol-based diet.

"I have a shift. I can give you a ride home before I head into the studio," Montserrat said.

"It's fine. I don't want you to be late."

"I wouldn't be late."

"I guess that would be nice, then."

Montserrat nodded. Tristán focused on his plate. She cleared the table. He followed her into the kitchen and watched her as she placed the cups and plates in the sink.

"I'm sorry I woke you up last night."

"It's not the first time."

"I'm still sorry."

She scraped the fork against a plate, brushing crumbs into the drain. Her hair was pulled back with a scrunchie, and he was surprised to see Montserrat, like himself, also looked older than he remembered. Her face seemed to have acquired a couple of wrinkles on the forehead during the night.

But no, it was the simple passage of time, which he did not ordinarily recognize.

"Back when the accident happened, and afterward, when things were bad with you . . . the night with the painkillers when you . . . well, when I called the ambulance . . . that was the most scared I've ever been in my life," she said. "I'm not sure what I'd do without you. I'd probably go mad."

Montserrat's face was calm as she spoke. She set down the dish she'd been holding and turned to him with cool eyes, but her words had burned him as bright as a match under his fingertips.

"Momo, I wouldn't. Not again. Not really," he assured her.

"But I know you might. One day. Maybe."

"Don't be silly, no. I was drunk last night, that's all," he replied, sounding a little breathless. "I'm fine."

They both knew he was lying. He'd tried to kill himself once only five years before and thought about attempting it half a dozen times since then. Even if he didn't contemplate suicide anymore, he might slide into another period of drug use and destruction that would sink him into the gutter for good.

He forced a smile on his face and gave her a playful jab on the shoulder. "I'll run a comb through my hair and try to look half-decent before we get into your car, okay? We don't want to have the neighbors thinking now you're sleeping with hobos. Though you did bang that German backpacker that one time, and he looked like he slept on a park bench."

"Twelve years ago," she said, rolling her eyes. "The one time I pick up a guy at a bar and you'll never let me forget it."

"You have terrible taste in men."

Montserrat smirked and gave him the finger. Tristán turned around and headed into her bathroom, where the mirror confirmed his suspicions. He did look like shit and needed to desperately scrub his face clean and attempt to freshen up his breath.

He shook his head and decided he should purchase an answering machine. That way he could screen his calls and burn the tape if that reporter ever phoned again. This, at least, might provide him with a better coping mechanism. For now, though, he tried to think happier thoughts.

"Urueta wanted to go antique hunting on the weekend," he yelled from the bathroom, as he grabbed the bottle of mouthwash sitting next to the sink. "You're invited."

"Where?"

He opened the bottle and took a swig of the mouthwash, gargling and spitting. Montserrat stood at the bathroom door and looked at him in the mirror as he washed his face and patted it dry.

"I don't know. La Lagunilla, I think. That's how he makes a living these days. He buys antiques and resells them for a profit. He hasn't shot a film in decades. But if you're busy, it's fine."

"This shift, it's my last one for a couple of weeks."

"You have something lined up after that?"

"Nothing solid," Montserrat said. "They keep giving work to others rather than me."

"But you're the best!"

"You know how it is. I don't drink with the boys, and the boys don't like me much."

"I thought that didn't matter to Gabino."

"Gabino retired, remember? It's Mario assigning the work now, and I got into that fight with him, so he's assigning work with a medicine dropper or moving my shifts around."

"Fucker."

Montserrat shrugged. "It gives me a chance to keep an eye on you."

"Forget about last night. I'm fine. I'll only be a minute here and then you can get ready for work."

He grabbed a comb and parted his hair. She gave him a cautious nod and moved away, heading toward her bedroom. Tristán tried smiling at the mirror, flashing his very white smile. Then he made a mental note to keep avoiding the newsstands in case anyone did decide to run a picture of Karina on the front page.

5

She stopped at Woolworth to buy sewing patterns for her sister. They were decorating a section of the store with plastic pumpkins for Halloween. NAFTA was supposed to have brought prosperity to Mexico. She wasn't sure how much prosperity was rolling down her street, but they were getting a lot more American products, including American movies. Now with the passing of the Ley Cinematográfica, movie theaters wouldn't have to show as many national films. COTSA had already been butchered, and there were hardly any screens left to show local flicks. Not that COTSA had kept to the rule of exhibiting 50 percent Mexican films before it was dismantled; they skirted the law, preferring to play what sold, and what sold was *Rambo*. On top of that, the movie palaces were being replaced by American-style multiplexes.

Film was a shambling zombie of an industry; she'd worked on the periphery of it and only succeeded in having half a life. *Enigma* could be her ticket to financial stability. God knew her current job wasn't a fountain of riches.

She looked at one of the pumpkins and decided she still preferred sugar skulls. She bought a bag of peanuts at a newsstand and headed to the restaurant. Cornelia arrived wrapped in a great, fluffy coat and dumped her leather purse on the table with a sigh. Her eyeglasses were round, and behind them her eyes looked perpetually surprised.

"Well! I couldn't find a parking spot. I had to circle the block forever. And the rates they have now! It's armed robbery."

A waiter made the mistake of heading toward their table. Cornelia immediately turned to the poor kid and began talking at a brisk speed. "I'd like tuna on lettuce. No, no mayo, no mustard, no tomato, just tuna on lettuce. Okay, maybe tomato. Yes, one little tomato. I'll have a Diet

Coke with a twist of lemon and a cup of coffee. Forget the coffee, I drink too much coffee. Mineral water and a twist of lemon. Can you bring everything out at the same time? You know what, make it a chicken breast with a salad on the side."

Montserrat had already ordered, so she simply raised her glass of water at the waiter in solidarity. He turned around in silence, with the professionalism of a man who had seen his share of eccentric customers and was not fazed by anything anymore. Cornelia was, as Tristán liked to put it, an acquired taste.

"I'm trying this nicotine patch, and all it does is piss me off," Cornelia said as she leaned forward and set her elbows on the table. "What about you? I was going to phone you last month but then I got stuck with an assignment and how have you been?"

Montserrat informed Cornelia that she was doing fine, and Cornelia replied by beginning a long story about a mole on her back that she was having checked. Conversations with Cornelia were never linear. They diverged, her thoughts doubling back then steamrolling forward, but she was a decent friend and a good production assistant.

Finally, Montserrat was able to guide Cornelia toward the topic of *Enigma* and their current episode lineup.

"My hours at Antares are getting cut all the time."

"I told you if you trained that kid, soon they'd have him doing your job in no time. Never teach anyone anything! How long have you been there? For years and years! It's because you're not in the union. Leeches. That's what these people are."

"If the owner even heard the word 'union' he'd fire us on the spot. Which brings me to *Enigma:* I have an idea for an episode."

"Finally! I told you to get out of the sound business. It pays peanuts. What's the idea, then?"

"I met this director, Abel Urueta. He used to make horror movies back in the day and turns out he worked on a film that was written by an occultist: Wilhelm Ewers."

"They don't ring a bell," Cornelia said, scratching the spot on her arm where she wore her nicotine patch.

Montserrat talked about Urueta's filmography and explained she could get an interview with him. By the time their food arrived, and Cornelia began picking at her chicken, Montserrat suspected she was fighting a losing battle.

"I thought you said you might have something for me if I came up with ideas for the show," Montserrat said. "Get into production, you said."

"Yes, but I was thinking something more like finding the Mexican Amityville. Haunted houses. Lloronas and chaneques. Jaime Maussan has people talking about energy lines, and the cover of *Conozca Más* is about the fate of Atlantis. You have an unknown director and a dead German writer."

"And *Año Cero* says we can discover the secrets of ancient civilizations by mediating with a crystal pyramid. My story doesn't sound any crazier than that."

"That's the problem. It doesn't sound as meaty, at least not the way you're selling it. You're making it all sound very proper and elegant."

"It's a retrospective about a lost film."

"Yeah, and the Nazi occultist is the interesting part. So, what else do you know about him?"

"Not much," Montserrat admitted, although she'd spent plenty of hours daydreaming about *Beyond the Yellow Door*.

"There's your problem," Cornelia said, waving her fork at Montserrat. "You need to get more info on the guy."

"Could you give me an advance on this? That is, if I began the research," she said, feeling that tickle of excitement she hadn't felt in a long while with a project. At Antares they kept her on a leash.

"If you want to work for the show, you need to give me more than that. Can you sit Urueta down for a pre-interview? I can tape the formal interview in the studio, but a pre-interview would help me figure out what we have here. And show notes, research. Otherwise, it's too difficult to gauge the material."

"You want him on camera?"

"Yes. Nothing fancy. If it looks meaty, our going rate for freelancers is good, but without some proof of concept I can't do anything. It's the way the system works."

"I know. Leeches," Montserrat said, balling her napkin tight.

"Oh, come on. Don't make that face! I don't make the rules, if I could,

I'd pay you ten advances. You think about it, all right? Otherwise, we
could wait and see if anything opens up in the sound department."

Fat chance. Montserrat knew she could be waiting for years for that.
On Friday, Montserrat checked Riera's *Historia Documental del Cine Mexi-
cano* and searched for information on Urueta's movies. There wasn't anything in the eight-volume compendium about *Beyond the Yellow Door*, not
that she expected there to be, but there was no harm in double-checking.
She phoned the Cineteca and asked if she could drop by the archives and
look at their fact sheets and press clippings for Urueta's other films. She
typed up a page of notes with whatever she remembered about Urueta
and what she'd heard about *Beyond the Yellow Door*. She had no idea who
had worked on the production aside from Urueta and the screenwriter,
Romeo Donderis. She'd check his filmography at the Cineteca, too.

On Sunday, she met Urueta and Tristán at an agreed-upon intersection, and they walked to the market.

Montserrat didn't haggle and she was afraid of pickpockets; therefore
the market had little appeal for her. Tristán, on the other hand, seemed
eager to explore the stalls. He was wearing his trademark sunglasses and
a loose plaid jacket. He looked bohemian, which was fine. There were all
kinds of people at the Lagunilla, from the homeless to a ritzier clientele
hungrily searching for a bargain. Some of the goods sold were illegal, and
when the police felt like it, they raided the place. But not that day.

The three of them looked at nineteenth-century chairs and plastic
Barbie dolls with their hair in disarray. There was fayuca and genuine
porcelain. Paintings of idealized adelitas sat next to posters of José José.
Urueta was concentrating on watches. When he found an item that interested him, he took his glasses from his front shirt pocket and examined
the item, then stuffed the glasses back in their place. He repeated this
motion a half dozen times, sometimes nodding to himself and muttering
under his breath.

"I sell them in the Zona Rosa," he explained. "There's always a clientele for watches, and I know a guy who is good at fixing them."

They walked past a stall full of Nazi memorabilia. It had jackets em-
blazoned with red armbands and swastikas, Nazi war medals, old pistols,
helmets, even flags and an Adolf Hitler doll. Montserrat stopped and
stared at the display. She supposed it hadn't been that hard for Hitler's fol-

lowers to make it to America, not with greedy people willing to harbor them. Some of those mass murderers must have been flush with Jewish loot, with the belongings of the poor Romani they tried to exterminate, and the coins stolen from the corpses of disabled people. And so they'd come to the Americas, to be greeted with open arms by Perón and others like him.

"You told us Ewers might have been a Nazi," Montserrat said as Urueta stood next to her, a blue plastic market bag dangling from his wrist. He was carrying a couple of watches he'd bought in it. "Was he an agent in Mexico, like the actress you mentioned?"

"I still find it hard to believe there were actual Nazi spies in Mexico," Tristán said, brushing a lock of hair away from his face. Montserrat saw Urueta and herself reflected in the dark lenses.

"They had their sympathizers. Ever heard of the Gold Shirts? They were around in the thirties, and even later. Rubén Moreno Padrés organized two anti-Semitic meetings right here in La Lagunilla back in 1940. They handed out a lot of leaflets that year, accusing the president of allowing Jewish immigrants into the country and leading it to its ruin. But I can tell you Ewers didn't join flashy demonstrations of that sort, and he wasn't with any particular group. It was more . . . well, it stretches farther back. Ewers was into runes and magic and film. All of it, combined."

"Runes?"

They strolled next to a vendor displaying rugs and others selling heavy rotary telephones from the fifties.

"There were many magic systems in Europe in the early part of the century. Krumm-Heller, the physician I told you about before, he studied runes and also developed a therapeutic system based on scents."

"A belief in nice-smelling candles sounds innocent enough to me," Tristán said. He was taking off his glasses now, biting at their arm.

"Krumm-Heller also believed that certain races were inferior to others."

"That is definitely not innocent," Tristán added, shaking his head. He put the sunglasses on again. "Was every occultist a racist?"

"Helena Petrovna Blavatsky, who founded the Theosophical Society, also talked about higher and inferior races and the evolution of humans.

Guido von List conceived of a magical runic alphabet and thought humanity had entered a cycle of decadence and was firmly in favor of eugenics. Then we have Jörg Lanz von Liebenfels, who was also an occultist and believed the Aryan people were threatened by lower races."

"But was he a Nazi, then?" Montserrat asked. "You haven't answered that question."

"Maybe he was a soldier," Tristán ventured. "Wehrmacht."

"No, he wasn't a soldier. He was an occultist. But plenty of occultists had bizarre racial theories, and Ewers wasn't above listening to what pro-Nazi groups had to say. He mentioned the Vril Society and the Germanenorden. He claimed he stole knowledge from them." Urueta took out a handkerchief and wiped his forehead with it. "He was opportunistic, would befriend anyone who might assist him. Let's finish looking at this aisle and then we can head back to my apartment. I'll tell you more there."

They spent another half hour at La Lagunilla even though Urueta did not acquire anything else.

When they reached the apartment the old man offered to pour all of them a brandy, and they sat down in the living room.

Tristán relieved himself of his sunglasses and accepted a brandy. Urueta leaned back in his chair and removed his shoes with a groan, then he donned a pair of slippers. The plastic bag with the two watches had gone into one of the many drawers of a cabinet. On a coffee table Montserrat spied a thick stack of old issues of *Cahiers du Cinema*.

"The Lagunilla bleeds me dry. It takes a lot of energy to look at the merchandise and figure out what's what."

"You were speaking of Ewers," Montserrat said, quickly, wishing to jump back on the subject.

"Mmm? Yes. It's funny, I haven't spoken about him in a long time. I have a friend, José López, who would tell you that you should never speak of the dead. But then again, you are interested in him, and I seldom have interested guests."

"You said Ewers stole knowledge. How?"

Urueta rubbed his hands together before taking a sip of brandy. "Ewers was not that different from many men who came before him. His occultist ideas were a mishmash of other ideas. Inspired by people like

Krumm-Heller, Ewers thought Aryans were a superior race and therefore endowed with the capacity for spellcasting, but he also thought the Aztec and Inca were capable of such feats. And Mexicans, due to this ancestry, could also achieve a certain level of magic mastery."

"But Mexicans are not Aztecs any more than all Italians are descendants of Roman generals," Montserrat said.

"I'm definitely not Aztec," Tristán said with a shrug. "Both of my grandparents were from Beirut."

"Ewers's concepts were, shall we say, a little fantastic. He saw parallels between European runes and Aztec and Maya ideograms and glyphs. His true innovations, the element that made him popular in Mexico in the late fifties, were his mishmashes of ideas about film and magic. Tell me, have either of you heard of Anton LaVey? He was the founder of the Church of Satan."

"I don't think LaVey was his real name," Montserrat said. Since she was friends with Cornelia, she got to hear a bit about the topics that they covered on her show, and LaVey had come up at one point.

"Of course not. Everyone reinvents themselves. Rudolf 'von' Sebottendorf was no 'von,' either. LaVey was a showman, and so was Ewers. But if you asked him, he'd tell you his affinity for orbiting around movie stars and directors wasn't so he could get a taste of showbiz: Ewers believed films were magical."

"Where did he come up with that idea?" Tristán asked. "I know we talk about movie magic, but that's a stretch."

"Aleister Crowley, probably one of the most famous occultists that ever lived, organized the *Rite of Saturn*, a play performed in 1910. Crowley then went on to oversee several other theatrical performances. His idea was to embed ceremonial magic within the play. Certain gestures, certain costumes and symbols, were authentic and used by occultists. Ewers believed that Crowley was on the right track, that magic rites needed to be performed in front of a large audience, whose energies would power the spells being cast. But he didn't think theater was the right medium for this."

"Film," Montserrat said. "A lot more people will see a movie than your average play. I guess they're more immersive, too."

Urueta snapped his fingers and nodded enthusiastically. "Exactly!

Crowley wanted to induce a state of ecstasy in his audience; Ewers thought they would be better used as a battery. He also thought film had particular properties which intensified magic."

"Such as?"

"The film was shot with silver nitrate stock because silver is a powerful conduit for spells."

"In 1961?" Montserrat replied, incredulous. "It was phased out long before that."

"They were still using nitrocellulose film base in Europe. Franco's people bought nitrate stock that Kodak was trying to dispose of on the cheap, and Madrid Film used that to shoot flicks. We got ours from the USSR. It was unusual, but then the whole production was unusual. And you should see nitrate film stock when it is screened! The whites look like bleached linen, the blacks are so rich you feel you could bury your hands in that velvet darkness," Urueta said, his eyes wide with childlike glee. "God, the film looked beautiful."

Beautiful and liable to burst into flames, Montserrat thought. That's exactly what had happened at the Cineteca some ten years before. Hundreds of Mexican films had been lost in a fire that had probably been caused when a loose wire made the nitrate film stock in the vaults explode. She'd heard of Moviolas blowing up when the sun's rays focused on a lens. Nonsense, probably, but scary enough to make you careful around nitrate film.

"It must have been expensive to shoot with an outdated film stock," Tristán said.

"Not as much as you'd think, and anyway Ewers had a wealthy patron," Urueta said. For the first time since he had begun talking about the occultist, the old man looked uncomfortable. He shifted in his seat. "But yes, there were expensive choices, and the production schedule was not ideal. The complicated sound mixing meant we would have to spend more time in post-production."

"How?" Montserrat asked. "Was the film scoring going to be laborious?"

"It wasn't the music that was the problem, it was the dialogue. Ewers wanted the film dubbed. It would be post-synchronized."

"Like in Italy? Fellini sometimes didn't write dialogue until a scene had been shot," Montserrat said. "Was it an artistic statement? Or was he hoping to sell this to a foreign market and dub into another language?"

"No, it was driven by Ewers's ideas about magic systems, some bits from Crowley, some bits from God knows where. He thought when the image and sound are shot separately and then brought together, it's like closing a circuit."

"Then when you say he stole knowledge . . . he stole Crowley's ideas and spliced them with his own?"

"Yes, Crowley. I believe Antonin Artaud's Theatre of Cruelty inspired Ewers, too," Urueta said, looking thoughtful. "Artaud thought theater was the only medium that could create a 'communion' with the audience that was akin to a 'magic exorcism.' Artaud went to Mexico, by the way. He lived with the Tarahumara, consumed peyote, and participated in a shamanic ritual. Ewers obviously found Artaud's ideas delicious, but he loved film, not theater."

"And those two things you mentioned . . . the Vril . . ."

"The Vril Society," Abel said. "An occultist society based on the ideas of a British writer called Edward Bulwer-Lytton. They thought there was a life force called *vril*, which, when controlled, could grant someone immense power. Of course, they also thought it was ancient Aryans who harnessed these powers. Ewers said he fraternized with them. There seemed to be a very active occultist scene in Munich when he lived there."

It sounded like something out of *The Devil Rides Out* or another Hammer film, but rather than feeling put off Montserrat was intrigued. The post-synchronization, the silver nitrate film stock, they both contributed to make this more charming than macabre, although she appreciated the disturbing vein of darkness to the whole tale. Abel seemed to relish telling the story, too: he was a kid narrating ghost stories late at night. Tristán seemed less impressed. Ghouls and monsters were not his favorite dish. He watched them for Montserrat's sake, stood in line for Freddy Krueger and Pinhead because she wanted to attend the late show.

"He sounds like a weirdo. A maybe-I-was-a-Nazi-weirdo, to boot," Tristán said, his voice languid as he nursed his glass and threw his head back. "It's hard to imagine anyone taking him seriously."

"There once was a lovely lady called Marjorie Cameron. She became popular among certain socialites and the avant-garde set in 1950s California. She even obtained a couple of bit parts in movies. What is less known is that Marjorie was the wife of Jack Parsons, an occultist and rocket engineer."

"That's a résumé," Tristán said.

"Well, yes, and Marjorie's résumé was equally interesting. Marjorie was the founder of a group called The Children, which practiced sex magic rituals hoping to create a third race of 'Moonchildren.'"

"It's starting to sound like eugenics," Tristán said, cringing.

"Of a more benign nature, I suppose. Marjorie believed it was the mixing of different races that would create these special children."

"It still sounds awful. So, what you're saying is there were a lot of nutjobs hanging around thirty years ago," Tristán concluded as he lit his cigarette.

Montserrat gave him an irritated look. She didn't want Abel to stop talking about this, and Tristán had that mildly hostile tone he bandied around when he was growing bored.

"I know it sounds silly *now*, but people like Marjorie or Ewers could easily find their place among a certain social set."

"So could Charles Manson," Tristán said dryly.

Urueta opened his mouth to protest, but Montserrat spoke before he could. "Who was Ewers's patron?" she asked.

Urueta again looked uncomfortable. The glass he had been idly toying with was placed aside. He looked at her as if trying to figure out what her line of thought was.

"It was Alma Montero. You wouldn't know her, but she used to be—"

"A silent film star," Montserrat said immediately.

"I should have guessed you would know after all," Urueta said.

Montero had made the jump to Hollywood, along with Gilbert Roland and Ramón Novarro, but couldn't cut it in talkies. Neither could Norma Talmadge or John Gilbert. For every Joan Crawford there was a Vilma Banky, whose career was snuffed out with the advent of microphones. Accents, squeaky voices, stiff performances spelled doom for dozens of performers.

"Alma Montero was bankrolling a German occultist," Montserrat said.

She couldn't suppress a snort. It was like hearing that María Félix regularly attended Ouija board séances with Zabludovsky. Oh, it was better than the plot of any Hammer film she knew.

"I've told enough stories for a day and have errands to run," Urueta said, standing up quickly. There must have been something about Montero that bothered the old man. He'd been chatty as hell so far.

"You're kicking us out so soon?" Tristán asked. "What are we supposed to do with our evening now?"

"Would you mind if I came back with a tape recorder and asked you a bit more about Ewers? I'm thinking of doing a piece on *Beyond the Yellow Door*," she said quickly, perhaps too eagerly. Abel, who had been about to reply to Tristán, likely with a joke, froze and looked at her with suspicion.

"A piece?" Urueta asked. "What kind of piece?"

"Montserrat has contacts at *Enigma*. They do a weekly show. It has a lot of viewers. It could be good for you," Tristán said, dropping his cigarette in an ashtray. "It would be very classy."

It wasn't the way Montserrat had hoped to introduce the topic, and she wanted to slap Tristán on the back of the head.

Urueta shook his head firmly. "I know what show you mean, and there's nothing classy about it."

"If we could talk it over a little," Montserrat said. "If we could work out an angle."

"Not now," Urueta said.

Quickly, stiffly, Urueta bid them goodbye, and Montserrat and Tristán ended up standing in the hallway, looking at each other.

"Why did you have to mention *Enigma*?" she asked, stomping toward the stairs.

Tristán shrugged and raised his hands helplessly in the air. "How was I supposed to know he'd take it so badly? He was willing to tell us Ewers's life story until that."

"And until he mentioned Montero."

"Meaning?"

"Meaning there's more to that there. We'll have to find what. I need to pay a visit to the Cineteca."

"Does this mean Cornelia got you a job at *Enigma* or what?"

"Nothing solid. Freelance assignment, if that. But Ewers is what I pitched her, so that's what I should be working on. I have to do more research."

Tristán patted his clothes looking for his keys. "Do you need to do research? I thought these were the kind of folks that broadcast stories about how Pedro Infante is alive and living in Mazatlán because he was horribly disfigured à la Phantom of the Opera after his plane crashed."

"You must fill the screen with something for forty-five minutes between commercial breaks. It might as well be a semi-coherent story."

Tristán found the key and opened the door. "You know who advertises on that show? Those people with astrology hotlines. They must make a bundle by the minute."

"Also singles hotlines," she said, remembering the numbers that scrolled across the screen on certain shows late at night.

"Want to have a bite before you head home?" Tristán asked. He went straight to the kitchen and opened the refrigerator. It was a large kitchen. The refrigerator looked like it had recently been rolled into the apartment and so did the stove. A bright yellow phone was attached to a wall.

"You're cooking?"

Unlike Montserrat, whose mother had been uninterested in teaching her child how to cook, Tristán's mother had shown him the secrets of the kitchen. He had been her baby, the little one clinging to her skirts. Montserrat's mother was made of sterner stuff. She barked orders when she was around the house, but she usually got in late anyway, sometimes because of work and sometimes because she'd brought a date home. Montserrat learned to either ignore the men her mother called her "co-workers" instead of her lovers, or to step out and into Tristán's apartment on the evenings when her mother had company. The Abaids had liked her, anyway, and Tristán's mother piled her plate high with food.

"I would cook if I had anything decent in the cupboard. But you know how it is. You get used to cooking for two and then it's too depressing to go back to one. I ate all the beef yesterday. Maybe there's chicken somewhere."

Tristán unbuttoned his plaid jacket and tossed it on a counter. Even a simple gesture like that could evoke beauty and grace when Tristán performed it. Now that Montserrat thought about it, today he had looked a bit old Hollywood, his outfit vaguely matching the antique setting. His face had been made for a different decade. Silent films, maybe.

She thought about Montero. She couldn't remember when the woman had been born. Could she still be alive? If she was still around, it might be a good idea to interview her.

"No chicken. Sushi Ito opened up a few blocks from here," Tristán said as he rummaged inside the refrigerator and pushed containers aside.

"Sushi Ito is no good. There are real sushi places in the city, you know?"

"Well, I don't want to go all the way to a decent place. I don't have any proteins. Fuck. This milk expired."

Tristán took out a carton of Leche Lala and dumped its contents into the sink. Montserrat peered into his refrigerator. If she was guilty of not having enough food in her apartment, Tristán was guilty of having too much and always eating out anyway. Everything went bad in his refrigerator. He maintained a carefully curated collection of moldy tomatoes and overripe fruits. Montserrat didn't know why he even bothered venturing into the supermarket if he was going to scarf down enchiladas at the Sanborns anyway. Nevertheless, when the fancy struck him, which, granted, was less and less these days, Tristán could cook a veritable feast. Montserrat knew how to make five dishes, and four of them she'd learned from Tristán's mom. The lush red of pomegranates and saturated green of pistachios. The scent of rose water and warm bread. That was Tristán's kitchen, and he hummed an old song as he chopped vegetables. It was usually one of the same melodies his mother used to sing to them.

Montserrat checked the expiration date on a yogurt container.

"Have you ever used those phone lines?" he asked.

She handed him the yogurt, which had also expired, and he began scooping out its contents into the sink. "Have I asked an astrologer to draw my natal chart over the phone?"

"No, the singles hotlines."

"They're scams. I'd rather be alone than pretend someone cares about me when they don't give a damn."

Tristán seemed to consider that, thoughtful, as he stood by the sink. The light from the refrigerator traced shadows and lines across his face, emphasizing the faint scar under the eye that worried him so much and

that he thought marred his looks. A few hairs at his temples glinted silver. He could not have been photographed better if von Sternberg had
brought reflectors and lamps into the apartment.

She thought about what Urueta had said, that Ewers believed magic
could be performed using film stock, and for a second she believed he
wasn't so off the mark. Maybe certain people could cast spells with one
look and a line of dialogue.

Tristán opened the tap, let the water flow, then closed it again and
closed the refrigerator door, tearing away the wispy enchantment of light
and shadow he'd conjured.

On the refrigerator he had a magnet with the number of a pizza parlor. "Now here's a truly important question: triple cheese or quadruple
cheese?"

She smiled and picked up the receiver. "Quadruple."

FEATURE

FILM

6

Montserrat still missed the old Cineteca. She fondly recalled watching many films in the Salón Rojo before an inferno that raged for fourteen hours gutted it. They said the person responsible for that mess had been Durán Chávez, that he had fired the people who checked the air-conditioned vaults and made sure the temperatures did not rise above ten degrees Celsius. He'd been trying to save a few pesos, and instead the whole building exploded when the silver nitrate became unstable. But there were also tales of faulty wiring and even arson. There had been a fire at the UNAM Film Archive five years before the one at the Cineteca, and Manuel González Casanova, who designed the storage vaults there, had privately whispered that someone had stolen the reels inside and then torched the place to conceal the crime. If that was the case, perhaps the fire at the Cineteca was also deliberate.

Whatever the reason for the fire, the new facilities were soulless. The original Cineteca had been built atop two of the sound stages of Estudios Churubusco. One could say it had old films in its bone marrow.

The real problem with the new Cineteca was not aesthetic, but practical. Thousands of books, magazines, scripts, and films had been turned into ashes. Montserrat was looking at reduced holdings. Perhaps at some point there might have been more information, but now she was faced with the reality of finding only meager film stubs and capsules. The dregs of cinema, rather than the crown jewels.

In an attempt to be thorough, Montserrat combed through whatever material she could uncover on Urueta and Montero even if the pickings were slim: a few press clippings, publicity pictures of Montero from her heyday as a star, a filmography that didn't even include all of Urueta's flicks.

She found nothing about Ewers.

Beyond the Yellow Door. Urueta's movie . . . She thought of film turning brittle, growing yellow with age, opaque, full of scratches and blemishes. But sometimes you could immerse film in hot water and restore it to its raw materials; recast it, bring it back to life. A coat of fresh emulsion . . . but the film Abel Urueta had shot was long gone. She wished she might have been able to see it. There was no trace of it. It had vanished. Just like Ewers, if he'd ever existed. Maybe Abel had told them a tall tale and there was no German occultist with a mysterious past. She'd never heard his name whispered by any of the film junkies she hung out with.

Tuesday, she dropped by Antares to collect a check and hopefully se-cure more work in the upcoming weeks, but Mario was still being evasive about future projects. At night she thought of the time a construction crew accidentally found more than a hundred nitrate negatives hidden under an ice rink in Dawson City. Strange discoveries happened at times, stories you wouldn't believe if someone told them to you. Abel could be speaking the truth; Ewers might have been real. She kept going back and forth about him. Wednesday, she ventured to her sister's place and they watched TV together. She hardly paid attention to the images on screen, thinking again of *Beyond the Yellow Door*. How much film had Abel shot before production shut down? What were the "half-stories" that happened on set that Abel had alluded to? All she'd ever heard was that Urueta had abandoned horror after *Beyond the Yellow Door* and picked other genres, something that was confirmed by his filmography. He hadn't done too well and his career had quickly fizzled out.

Afterward, Montserrat went browsing around a shop that carried vintage magazines, looking at issues of *Mexico Cinema* and *Cinelandia*, with their yellowed pages and pictures of ancient actors. How things had changed since those golden years, not only at the box office, but also when it came to post-production. There was something kinesthetic about editing sound that would soon be lost as computers took hold of the business. Her thoughts whirled around negatives and lavender stock care-fully wrapped in tissue paper, hand-winders, Moviolas, tables and joiners and cleaning machines. She'd met a negative cutter who told her you should never put nitrate in a tight container. It should have enough space to breathe. Breathe, like a fine wine! It had a special scent, too, once it had begun to deteriorate, but she couldn't remember what it was.

She grabbed one of the magazines and went to the counter. Behind it sat an old woman who was doing a crossword. She smiled at Montserrat.

"Hey, Trini, you know every actor and director that set a toe in films in the fifties, don't you? Ever heard of a guy called Wilhelm Ewers?" she asked, placing a copy of *Cinelandia* on the counter. Sonia Furió was on the cover and it had an interview with Urueta, from when he'd shot *The Opal Heart in a Bottle*. "He would have been a hanger-on in the late fifties, beginning of the sixties. Used to date Alma Montero and did a movie with Abel Urueta, but it never got released. *Beyond the Yellow Door*. I don't know if he appeared in anything else, but I'm trying to find out."

"He doesn't ring a bell."

"Ever heard anything about *Beyond the Yellow Door*?"

"No, but he had a spate of films that fell through in the sixties. Not that he was the only one; cinema took a dive around that time," the woman said, shaking her head. "Urueta didn't help himself by being difficult. I heard he spent more time at the racetrack than reading a script back in the day. I heard he got involved with gangsters and almost had his legs broken. Didn't he die last year?" the woman wondered.

"He's still around," Montserrat said, handing her a bill.

"What are you looking for?"

"I'm not even sure," she said, and it was the truth.

There was a guy she knew, Fernando Melgar, who sold movie memorabilia and who once told her he had a script from *The Curse of the Hanged Man*, Abel Urueta's last horror flick, annotated by Romeo Donderis. Nando's prices were steep, which is why she didn't bid on that, but he had mentioned that he could get Donderis himself to authenticate the script. At the time, she had thought it was a ploy to try to impress her—Nando was a horny creep—but maybe she ought to call him and ask if he knew anything about *Beyond the Yellow Door*. She was even tempted to drop by his apartment uninvited, see if he'd chat with her. Then she thought better of it. Nando would see it as a come-on, and she'd be stuck fending him off. Besides, was a random idiot who sold autographed pictures of Lilia Prado in tight leopard-print dresses really going to know anything about Wilhelm Ewers? Nando might have heard a story or two about *Beyond the Yellow Door*, but it would be the same rumors about financing gone sour she'd heard, or the stories that Abel had a gambling problem.

When Montserrat returned home she phoned Tristán and complained about her futile attempt to build a story. Wilhelm Ewers remained faceless, only a smudge in her mind, like the discolored bottom of a film can.

"All the stuff at the Cineteca is useless. If I was doing a piece about Abel's career it might fly, but I'm looking for this one movie and this one fucked-up German who wrote it and I'm not having any luck."

"Don't panic yet. Urueta is going to give you the interview you need sooner or later."

"He doesn't like us."

"He got a little tense, but Urueta loves talking. He wouldn't shut up about Liz Taylor and Richard Burton and how he had cocktails with them several times when Burton was shooting *The Night of the Iguana*. He's an old soldier sharing war stories. He wants to be heard."

"Not by me anymore. Not if *Enigma* is involved. This is bullshit."

Editing was changing. The Moviola and the Steenbeck machines were yielding space to video monitors, tapes, and computers. *Beyond the Yellow Door* was an item from another era; it enchanted her with its antiquated film stock and post-synchronized sound: it was like meeting a gentleman in a tweed suit and a monocle these days. She wanted the story about its troubled production. She wanted to discover its secrets, and there was nothing to be known. In her mind, the picture she had assembled of the film was vanishing, like decomposing celluloid.

"What isn't! Listen, hang in there. I'll soften the old man. Be ready to come over on Saturday."

"Yeah, yeah," she muttered without enthusiasm.

Friday instead of going to the Cineteca she headed to the archives at Lecumberri. She found more of the same: stubs, film capsules, a few reviews. An old issue of *Cinema Reporter* dated 1960 provided her with the only significant piece of material she was able to dig up: a black-and-white photo showing Ewers.

The picture in fact showed four people. Two of them she identified easily. Abel Urueta had his trademark scarf, and Alma Montero, although older, was recognizable from the publicity photos from her silent era years. A pretty, young woman in a strapless dress was new to Montserrat. She had the air and smile of a socialite if not an actress. The fourth person was a man in a dark suit. They sat with Alma at the forefront, the lens more interested in her, then Abel, the girl, and finally the man at the farthest end of the table almost an afterthought. The occasion must have been a birthday celebration or a big event, for there was confetti in Alma's hair.

The caption read: "Film star Alma Montero, director Abel Urueta and his fiancée Miss Clarimonde Bauer, and Mr. Wilhelm Ewers enjoy an evening at El Retiro." The story that accompanied the picture was a stub and useless filler, like everything else she'd found, but at least the image made a ghost tangible. Because until that moment she had begun to believe there was no Ewers. He had evaded her, but at least she was able to contemplate the reality of the man.

Yet stubbornly, as if he had known he was being sought, the man in the picture appeared almost out of frame, his head inclined, so that you couldn't get a good glimpse of his face no matter how much Montserrat squinted and tried to make out more details. She could see the balloons decorating the background, but not Ewers.

"Slippery motherfucker," she whispered, but at least she now could pinpoint a man going by that name who had made it into the local film publications on at least one occasion. If she kept looking, perhaps she would find more mentions of him somewhere.

That same afternoon Tristán called and said Urueta wanted to have them over the next day. Montserrat, with her usual punctuality, arrived notepad and pen in hand at the arranged time. Tristán told her to stuff the notebook in her purse. It might scare Urueta off.

"Let me do the talking," Tristán added.

"Last time you did the talking and you screwed it up."

"And I'm fixing it."

"What's wrong with me doing the talking?"

"You have the subtlety of a steamroller."

"I do not!"

"You do! Let him drink, let him relax, then ask questions."

Although reluctantly, Montserrat agreed to zip it, and they marched up the stairs to the old man's apartment. Abel Urueta received them with a whiskey in his hand and a yellow scarf knotted around his neck, and asked them what they wanted to have. He then launched into a story about Ava Gardner who, according to Urueta, favored gin as her drink of choice.

Soon enough, Montserrat was nursing a soda, Tristán was imitating their host by also having a whiskey, and Urueta was looking placid. Montserrat bit her lip and didn't make a peep.

"Montserrat thought you had excommunicated her," Tristán said, stirring the ice cubes in his glass and leaning back in the couch they were sharing. "She was ready to pray twelve rosaries as penance."

Across from them Urueta laughed. "I overreacted. You must understand, I don't want details of my personal life and my friends shared with a show like *Enigma*."

"It's not as bad as that. Besides, it would mean a lot to Montserrat. She's trying to land a few gigs with them. All she wants is to hear a bit more about an old movie. What's the harm in chatting about it? There are no cameras rolling here."

Urueta glanced at them hesitantly. He wanted to talk, she could tell that much. Tristán was right. With Urueta, chatting about his glorious cinematic past was as much a compulsion as the gin and tonics, whiskeys, and other drinks he regularly imbibed. He was never in a room without a glass in hand for long, and he wasn't without a story for long, either. In an odd way he reminded her of Tristán. Or maybe he looked like what Tristán might become in a few years if he kept walking the same path.

"I saw a picture of you and Ewers this week," Montserrat said.

Tristán gave her an annoyed stare. So much for letting him talk. But rather than looking upset, Urueta seemed intrigued.

"Where?"

"It was an old magazine story. Alma Montero was in it, too, along with a young woman. Clarimonde Bauer was her name."

"Clarimonde was my fiancée," Urueta said. He set his glass down, stood up, and pulled a book from a shelf, turning the pages. "She wanted to be an actress. Here she is in 1960. She was twenty-two and I was twenty-eight. A couple of young fools. See?"

She had been wrong. Urueta had grabbed a photo album, not a book. She took it from his hands and peered down at the open page. There were several snapshots showing two young people holding hands. The girl with auburn hair was indeed beautiful, and the young man had a cheery smile on his face.

Montserrat did a little math in her head and realized Urueta was now sixty-one. It surprised her. He looked older, worn down. The booze had carved his face with a rough hand.

Tristán peered down at the pictures. "You were awfully young to be directing movies at that age," he said. Montserrat could recognize the note of rehearsed admiration in her friend's voice, but Urueta was immediately taken by the compliment.

"They called me 'The Kid.' I had three movies under my belt by then. It runs in the family. My mother was a script girl, my father was a cinematographer. I grew up playing around the prop department. I knew anyone there was to know in the movie business."

"Including Alma Montero?"

"She was a friend of the family."

"Was Ewers a friend of the family, too?"

Montserrat turned the page of the album. There were more pictures of Urueta, some alone, others with people she did not recognize. Her fingers drifted across the edges of the photographs.

"No. I met Ewers through Alma. In 1960, I had shot three films. Yes, low-budget horror films, but I knew I'd get bigger projects soon enough. Unfortunately, I had developed what you'd call a little bit of a credit problem. I owed money, and it kept me awake at night. Alma heard about this and told me she was going to be financing a film and wanted to shoot the following year. She would pay me a decent salary, and when the movie was done she'd get me in touch with her old Hollywood friends so I could try my luck there. Turn three more pages and you'll see him," Urueta said, pointing at the album.

Montserrat did as he said. She turned those three pages and there he was. The picture startled her, not because there was anything unusual about Ewers's appearance, but because his face had been half hidden in the other picture she'd seen, as if he feared the camera. But there was nothing shy about Ewers in this photograph. In fact, the photo dripped with self-possession.

Ewers was seated with his hands resting on his thighs, and he was leaning forward. His legs were spread wide. His face might have been bland if it hadn't been for his firm mouth and the piercing blue eyes that stared at the viewer. Something in the tightness of the jaw, in the sharp slope of the eyebrows, demanded attention. There was a trace of rancor in those features. This was a hungry man.

"He looks like a dude who would stab you in an alley and go through your pockets for spare change," Tristán said, peering down at the picture. "He looks pissed."

"I don't think I ever thought that exactly, but he made a vivid impression on everyone who met him, although in the beginning I admit I assumed he was a garden-variety gigolo."

"How come?"

"Ewers changed his biography and age depending on the listener, but the birth year that seemed to stick was 1923. Alma was born in 1906. With such an age gap, I assumed Alma was simply infatuated with Ewers and wanted to please him by shooting that silly film of his."

Montserrat held the album closer to her face. Ewers wore a double-breasted trench coat of a light, sandy color. Around his neck hung a large circular silver pendant carved with spidery lines.

"What's that pendant he's wearing?" she asked.

"A vegvísir. That Which Shows the Way. It's supposed to be an ancient Norse talisman to help travelers return home safely."

"Let me see," Tristán muttered, taking the album and frowning. "You can probably buy that at El Chopo for a peso from one of the darketos."

"I doubt it. The runes carved on it were designed by Ewers. But I thought exactly the same thing you are thinking now: that Ewers was a phony."

"Why did you change your mind?" Montserrat asked.

Urueta retrieved his glass and took a sip. He was smiling as he looked down at the floor. "The script Ewers had worked on was not terribly special. A young woman reveals the secrets of a magical cabal and is punished by the members of that secret society. Her boyfriend saved her six minutes before the movie ended and killed the bad guy. An ordinary movie.

"I had heard Alma was dating an eccentric German guy. He talked about runes and said he could predict the future by gazing into a bowl of water. But then, so what? I'd met plenty of astrology consultants for the rich and famous. Sydney Omarr studied in Mexico City before making his way to Hollywood. Psychics like Jeane Dixon appeared in *Parade*. I had lunch with Alma and Ewers and he was polite, charming. He didn't seem odd. We didn't even talk magic that first time. Then, I attended one of Ewers's séances."

There was a pause as Urueta contemplated his glass and downed its contents swiftly. "There was food, drink, music. It was like any regular party except he said we would summon a spirit. Around one a.m., Ewers had us recite several phrases. He had us chanting, in fact. In one hand he had a little bell, which he rang at certain intervals.

"I was drunk, and I was not very interested in all of this, but as the chanting kept getting louder and the bell rang, Ewers began to make motions with one hand, as if asking someone to come closer. He kept doing this with one hand and ringing the bell, and at one point I felt there was someone standing directly behind me and then that someone brushed past me and stepped forward. It felt like a breeze, almost, but the windows were closed and there wasn't anyone behind me, we were all in a circle with Ewers at the center of it. It was the first time I believed Ewers was in fact a sorcerer as he claimed."

Tristán was about to say something, but Urueta held up his open palm and shook his head.

"No, you don't have to tell me about the power of suggestion. He had a gift. When he wanted to, he'd flip a switch and shine, and you'd fly to him, a moth attracted by the light. He made magical charms for me and for my girlfriend, invited us to other séances. We began talking about magic.

"Ewers believed in willpower. It was the engine of magic. This was not particularly novel. He got many of his ideas from Golden Dawn, and I'm sure others said the same thing. But willpower alone is not enough for magic; you also need rituals. Ewers was fascinated with movies. He thought the merging of sound and visuals could produce powerful magic. It was the perfect ritual."

"And post-synchronization was the way to cast spells? But how exactly?" Montserrat asked, remembering their previous conversation.

"We would shoot a regular horror film. But we would also have three short scenes with a small amount of dialogue throughout the movie. Those were the key magical components. The dialogue was the spell, and the three people on screen were the magicians. There were runes, which he designed, and those would be projected during the credits, before and after the movie. The act of post-synchronization was what brought all these components together."

"If he only needed three scenes, why shoot a regular movie at all? Why not borrow a camera and record all three on a weekend?" she asked.

"Weaving the three into the film was what helped give the spell its shape. It granted it a certain cohesion. Otherwise, it would be too . . . hmm, I think he said it would be too crude," Abel said, frowning. "I can't remember what word exactly he used."

"Maybe it was like tape splicing," Montserrat said. "If you cut and join tape at a ninety-degree angle, it gets the job done, but you end up with a 'click.' It's better to slice at an angle. More elegant, I suppose."

Abel snapped his fingers and nodded excitedly. "Yes! That was the word! It was more elegant. Besides, Ewers thought magic built up, a bit like a pressure cooker. Day one of shooting the magic was weak, but by four weeks it was getting much warmer in the pot."

"I guess a Polaroid needs to be exposed to the light for a while for the film to develop," Montserrat mused. "Do you know what spell Ewers was trying to cast?"

"A good luck spell. Alma had been out of work for a long time. She dreamed of making a comeback. The spell would rejuvenate her, return some of her old beauty and therefore ensure she would get new parts."

A magical face-lift, Montserrat thought, but she was careful not to say that. Next to her, Tristán seemed amused, and she wondered if he was thinking something similar.

"Who were the magicians that agreed to perform on screen?" Montserrat asked. "I imagine Ewers was one of them, but what about the other two?"

Abel stood up and reached for the bottle of whiskey, refilling his glass. He topped up Tristán's drink and then stood in front of them, glass in hand pressed against his chest, before letting out a sigh. "I was one of them. Ewers thought you needed three spell casters. The father, the all-powerful male force, was the role he played. Then there was the son, the innocent. That was me. The 'Kid Urueta.'"

"Who was the third?" Montserrat asked.

"Originally, it was Alma. She represented the mother, the feminine principle of magic. But then Ewers confided in me and said he wasn't going to cast a spell for Alma after all. He was ill, you see. He needed a spell to save his life. We would cast a different spell instead. But he couldn't let Alma know because she wouldn't agree to it. So, he recast the part."

"You went behind Alma's back and got another woman to read the lines he needed?" Montserrat said.

"I didn't want Ewers to die, and I loved Clarimonde."

"Your girlfriend was the third magician?"

Urueta clutched the glass and spun around, his back to them. "Ewers believed she was more powerful than Alma, and it solved the problem of the modified spell. Alma wasn't supposed to know about it. But then José went and babbled to her, and also told her that Ewers was sleeping with Clarimonde."

Tristán opened his mouth in surprise and let out a snicker. "Wait. Your girlfriend was banging the crazy German? Did you know about that?"

Urueta turned around and looked at the younger man angrily. So much for Tristán's tact and for letting him speak. Then again, the men had been pounding back the whiskeys as if they were water. Montserrat was certain they were both a little drunk or Urueta wouldn't be talking so freely.

"After we met Ewers, Clarimonde became interested in magic, in occultism, like I did. Call me stupid, but no, I didn't think she had an interest in him beyond that, and neither did Alma. José was another member of our circle, and he somehow learned about it and told Alma, then told me. We were in post-production, and I had to stop our work for a few days because Alma was furious. Then Ewers died and everything went to hell. Alma wouldn't let me finish the damn picture. She cut off the money and had the film confiscated. It was a bad memory for her, she said."

"He was mugged," Montserrat said, remembering that detail. "So it wasn't disease that killed him in the end."

"No, it wasn't. It was bad luck. Bad luck followed all of us after Alma shut down our production. My relationship with Clarimonde didn't survive. I heard she married a guy who made his money in real estate and she had children with him, but they all died in accidents. The scriptwriter? He fell down the stairs and broke his neck. The stuntman? He was thrown from a horse and never walked again. The musician who was supposed to compose the score? Died of a blood clot at the age of thirty-five. My career ended after *The Yellow Door*. I made smaller and smaller movies. I was done less than a decade later. I couldn't even shoot a shampoo commercial."

Suddenly Urueta leaped forward and let go of his glass. It shattered, making Montserrat jump in her seat. Urueta snatched the album she had been holding from her, feverishly turning the pages. "Look at this! A review from 1959 talking about my excellent sense of timing! Look at me here, on the set of *The Opal Heart in a Bottle*. A career doesn't vanish from one day to the next! We were all cursed!"

Urueta took a big breath then slowly walked back to the couch in front of them and sat down, closing the album and placing it on his lap. He smiled, the corners of his lips lifting only a tad.

"I guess you can see now why it's a bad idea to interview me. I'm a crazy old man."

"You're not crazy," Tristán said.

Montserrat was surprised by the sureness and honesty in his voice. So far, Tristán's attitude had been one of wry amusement. But he sounded sincere. He did like the old man.

"Maybe you had bad taste in friends back in the sixties, but you're not crazy," Tristán added with a shrug, showing a little of his trademark mordancy after all.

"Thank you for that."

They were quiet. Urueta's living room, which she'd found cozy on previous occasions, now seemed to her stuffy, and the man's antiques and knickknacks had an air of stale sadness. The broken glass shards lay scattered between them.

"I don't normally talk about this, this story . . . about Ewers because . . . when I said I talked about 'the curse' at parties, I did, but I was drunk when I brought it up. I learned not to, after a while. People stare, they think you're a nut. But I like you both. You're good people and I'm telling you the whole story, the whole truth," Urueta said, looking at Tristán, then at Montserrat. "I don't want to be interviewed about that movie, but I will agree to do it if you help me. I do need help."

"I can ask the TV show if they'd pay for the interview," Montserrat suggested.

Urueta shook his head. "I don't want money. I want your help in completing the film."

"I don't get it."

Urueta placed his hands on the album, gripping it tight. He looked like a starlet who is about to sign an important contract, all nerves and sudden shyness.

"I've thought long and hard about what happened with *Beyond the Yellow Door*. All that lousy luck. I abandoned any magic practices after that, but my friend José kept at it, and he had a theory that everything that happened was because we didn't complete the spell. Ewers died, Alma confiscated the reels, and we were never able to finish the dubbing. He said we caused a short circuit. And we didn't pull the breaker. I want to finalize that film."

"But you can't," Montserrat said. "You don't have the film anymore, and Ewers is dead. He can't provide the voice work. You said you needed three people."

"Two men, one woman: that's us," Urueta said excitedly.

"I've played many roles, Abel, but I'm no sorcerer and neither is Montserrat," Tristán said.

"I know that, but maybe it'll work anyway. We dubbed two of the three scenes. It was the third scene that we didn't get to work on. And I still have the pages Ewers gave us. I didn't throw them out."

"Even if we agreed to provide the voices, we don't have the film."

Urueta sat up straight. His nervousness was bleeding away. "I have that scene. It's the only can of film I was able to hide before Alma pounced on us."

"You have a can with a nitrate print in this apartment? That thing heats up, you're toast," Montserrat said in horror. "It can continue to burn even under water!"

The Kineopticon in London, Laurier Palace in Montreal, Esmeralda Theater in Chile, the Madrid Film laboratories, the Cinémathèque headquarters on the Rue de Courcelles. Nitrate fires through the decades. The ingredients of film—nitric acid, methyl alcohol, cotton liners—were the same as those for explosives. Burnt offerings for an invisible god, that's what nitrate was.

"It's not in the oven. It's in the freezer!" Abel protested.

Montserrat had a vision of TV dinners and cuts of meat stacked against a metal canister. She hoped he didn't mean *that* freezer.

"It's perfectly safe, all right? I shot a whole movie with that film stock, I'm not going to be lighting a match anywhere near it."

"You do have it?" Tristán asked.

"Of course I do!" Urueta said vehemently. "Do you think we could dub it?"

Montserrat didn't reply. Instead, she pried Tristán's whiskey from his hand and took a swig.

7

The end of October was their season, when sugar skulls adorned the windows of bakeries for the Day of the Dead and the video stores tried to push their horror catalogue onto customers. On Channel 5, there might be a late-night movie marathon. The Cineteca and the art clubs went for higher brow fare, Cronenberg's *Dead Ringers*, or Bergman's *The Seventh Seal*. It was the time to read out loud the mordant rhymes about death printed in the morning edition and smile at the cartoons done in the style of Posada, but also the perfect week to pop a copy of *A Nightmare on Elm Street* into the videocassette player, followed by the remake of *The Blob*.

Yet Montserrat was quiet that year. She wasn't deriving much joy from the last week of the month. The latest issue of *Fangoria* in Spanish lay discarded on the table between them, even though Tristán had bought it expressly for her: he could live without pictures of latex monsters. Montserrat looked her usual self, complete with a t-shirt that said "The Howling" in distinctive red letters, but it didn't feel like her.

Tristán raised his cup of bad coffee to his lips and watched her. How Montserrat could fuck up something as simple as coffee, he didn't know, but she managed it. He had to admit she could cook meatballs the way his mother did, though. It was the one dish she had been able to master.

"Are we going to help Abel or what, then?" he asked, because they had been circling around the topic for the past twenty minutes, and he was getting tired of her scowls and the way she sat, arms crossed, frustrated and anxious at the same time. Abel had begged him to beg Montserrat in turn, and Tristán had tried his best to bring up the topic organically and failed. It was time for a direct offensive.

"I don't know."

"If you don't want to do it, tell him. You don't have to look at an old bit of film he stuck in a freezer."

Montserrat stared at him, her voice firm. "I love the idea of getting a glimpse of a few minutes of *Beyond the Yellow Door*. It's all I can think about lately."

"Then what the hell is going on?"

She stood up and went into the kitchen. He heard her opening the refrigerator, and the sound of an ice tray slapped against the sink.

"I don't want to get Abel's hopes up," she said.

"What?"

Montserrat walked back into the room, a glass filled with Fanta in one hand and a mug in the other. She set both of them down on the round table and sat down across from him.

"He thinks this is a spell, Tristán. Not any spell, but a spell that is going to break whatever curse was placed on him. He expects something to happen after we finish. What will he do when no one's phoning to give him an Ariel next month?"

"Come on, you know he's not expecting that."

"He isn't? Are you sure? He seemed convinced his old German buddy was a sorcerer."

"So, what if he expects a little something? Your sister shops at the Mercado de Sonora all the time. How many ribbons does she have tied around an aloe vera plant right now?"

"Don't compare my sister to Abel Urueta. Going for a limpia is not the same as joining a cult led by a delirious would-be sorcerer, then thinking that decades later you can cast a spell he taught you."

"I'm not saying it's identical. But people want to believe a rabbit foot is lucky and that you can attract good vibrations with quartz crystals. Hell, that's what *Enigma* is all about. Wanting to believe a silly alien conspiracy for five seconds, but it doesn't mean anyone is thinking a UFO will land on the roof of their apartment tomorrow and the Martians will dance the cha-cha for them."

"I don't know," Montserrat muttered, and she shoved the mug toward him. "Smoke if you want."

"I thought I couldn't smoke in your apartment or your car."

"I can't stand your stupid face. You look like you are about to pass out from nicotine deficiency."

Tristán gave Montserrat a sharp look. He wanted to prove to her that he could spend the afternoon without a cigarette, but he was savoring the taste of it already. He popped the cigarette into his mouth and lit it with dexterous fingers.

"Can you do it?" he asked.

"I'd have to look at the film," Montserrat said. "The problem with silver nitrate film is it can deteriorate dramatically if it's not well handled. It can self-destruct and gives off acidic byproducts. It can even damage other films and prints."

Montserrat's face became more animated as she spoke. She loved spewing nerdy details; it was as addictive and delicious to her as a cigarette was to Tristán. Or as telling stories was to Urueta.

"You have six stages of degradation. After stage three, you're toast. You can't duplicate that film. Urueta's film could be white powder residue and nothing more."

"Like Dracula, when the sun hits him. Ashes in a coffin. Or a tin can in this case. But you don't know that yet."

"No. I don't. Which makes it even more annoying."

"Point is, the film could be fine," Tristán said, tapping his cigarette against the rim of the cup. "You could have a guaranteed interview with Abel Urueta, a glimpse at a rare horror film, and all it takes is studio time."

"The rarest of horror films," she muttered. "But it's the same problem. What if he really thinks it'll work?"

"Why *shouldn't* he hope it does?" he replied, his voice off key. "If I could go back and stop Karina from getting into that car, I would. And on bad days, if you told me what I had to do to time travel was rub chicken's blood on my face and dance around the living room, I might. It's stupid, but it's also a bit of hope, and hope is hard to come by."

Hell, if someone told Tristán he had to kill the chicken by gnawing at its neck to improve his lot in life, he'd do it.

That week he'd seen the latest issue of *De Telenovela* at a newsstand. It featured a picture of him and Karina on the cover. He'd bought a copy, then tossed it next to his bed without reading it. Why? He knew what it would say. He didn't wish to rehash the past, and yet he hadn't been able to stop himself from getting the stupid magazine.

"It's a fantasy," Montserrat said.

"We lived off fantasies when we were kids. All those matinees, those were our tickets to dreamland," he said a little roughly, because whenever he thought about Karina something ached inside him. It was the cumulative scars of the accident, of his addictions and mistakes, his lost career and hopes.

"He's over sixty years old and we're thirty-eight."

"I looked in the mirror this morning, but we all indulge in games, even at this age."

"You're saying we should indulge the old man."

"It can't hurt. Besides, you said you liked the guy."

"It's because I like him that I don't want to hurt his feelings."

Tristán drank a little Fanta, and Montserrat went back into the kitchen and brought out a plate with peanuts. They cracked the peanuts open and popped them into their mouths.

"Maybe it's not Ewers on camera in that film. Maybe the negative is blank."

"Or powder, like you said," he replied.

"Or Ewers wasn't a sorcerer. He was some guy Abel knew and he made up the story about them casting spells together."

"That too. Magic films! It's insane. But we do this little thing, and you might have a real story. I bet you Abel even lets you borrow that photo album of his. Boom! We have your story for *Enigma*. You profit, we make an old guy happy, and we get to see a few minutes of a rare film."

The sun was setting. The smog outside made the sun look like a great red ball of fire, like they were in an apocalyptic film. The shadows on the floor were elongated and deformed by this reddish twilight. Montserrat's plants by the window wove elaborate organic patterns of darkness. On the walls of the living room, the monsters in the posters stared down at them both, and the clock behind him, shaped like Felix the Cat, marked the hour as it shifted its eyes.

"I'm not sure Abel will let me get him on camera and talk about the movie, even if we dub the film. And I'm even less sure that *Enigma* will want a story out of this," Montserrat said, slowly scratching a peanut with

her nail. "What if we're taking advantage of a delusional old man? Maybe
he needs, I don't know, a therapist instead of us hanging around him."

"He doesn't want a therapist, he wants to relive his glory days for a
few minutes."

"We shouldn't be doing this on a weekend," she said, of all things, and
he knew she was out of excuses.

Tristán exhaled. The smoke rose from his lips with an elegant, practiced abandon. "Do you have anything more exciting planned?" he asked.
"Cutting your toenails, maybe? Adopting a stray cat?"

Montserrat was looking at him, her fingers drumming against the
glass of soda. "Fuck you," she said, but the words had no barbs. She was
agreeing with him. Like when they sneaked behind the rickety fence, into
the storage facilities, and walked along the long wooden beam before
plummeting into the grain. *I dare you*, she said and he repeated it, he said
it back, and then they jumped together.

Montserrat opened the door of the studio to Abel and Tristán at exactly
midnight. They couldn't do the work in the daytime because her boss
would have thrown a fit, but at night the employees sometimes sneaked
their personal projects into the editing bays. It was fine as long as no one
was charging anyone outside the studio for their time, and even though
Montserrat's shifts that November were rather limited, her seniority at
Antares still provided her with a certain freedom of mobility. In other
words, they could work on the dubbing when the others had left the facility. If need be, Montserrat might work into the morning. The early hours
were slow. Or she'd fit it in during her supposed lunch time. For now, the
important part was to record their voices.

Tristán and Abel followed Montserrat down the long hallway with
mirrors. Her t-shirt that day had *The Hunger* written on it and her hair was
tied up in a messy bun. She looked as plain as usual, but it was a plainness
Tristán liked, even if he teased her about it. He wouldn't have known
what to do if Montserrat had suddenly decided to color her hair or slip
into tight dresses. Part of their unspoken agreement, he thought, was that
Montserrat must always remain the same. She must be a constant in his
life, his true north.

There was a monstrous selfishness to this attitude. He understood this the same way he realized he was sometimes annoyingly childish in his demands and affection. But it was the only way he truly knew how to love someone.

"I made a duplicate of the film so we could work with that to produce a final mix, but I wanted you to at least see the original nitrate print one time," Montserrat said, as they approached a door. "I was afraid the film might have shrunk, or that I wouldn't have the right projector and equipment to work with it, but I can play this film fine. I'm not sure I'd want to be projecting an entire film with no assistant—you want two people switching reels and you want to be in a safety booth—but it's a few minutes of film."

"Then the film is in good shape," Abel said nervously.

"You'll see," she said, holding a door open for them.

Tristán and Abel entered a small screening room with only three rows of seats. Tristán had been there on previous occasions. Antares had been top of the line, once. A 35-millimeter projection room, an editing room with a sturdy Moviola, a KEM and two computers that could run Avid, multiple editing bays with MIDI synchronizers: it was nothing to sniff at. But from what Tristán had heard, courtesy of Montserrat, Antares wasn't doing so hot anymore. The equipment was aging, and there were new players in the market. Audiomaster 3000, which had already swallowed several other companies, dominated the dubbing market in no small part because of their ties to Televisa. Things were getting worse now that Audiomaster was the only dubbing studio capable of recording in stereo rather than the monoaural system once prevalent in Mexico.

Magic, if it does exist, would sure be helpful right about now, Tristán thought. Antares could use it, and so could Montserrat with the way her career was going. Then again, so could he.

Tristán and Abel picked their seats while Montserrat fiddled with the projector. Abel clutched the typewritten pages of the old movie script he had kept. He coughed and muttered to himself. Tristán, on the other hand, tossed a mint into his mouth. Montserrat had warned him there would be absolutely no smoking inside the studio, and he had to have a palliative.

The reel began with no fanfare, interrupting the darkness of the room, and he gazed at the screen.

Tristán had seen many films and never paid much attention to the stock they were shot on. That kind of trivia was best left for people like Montserrat or Abel to discuss. To him, it didn't matter, and it must not have mattered to many others because Montserrat had mentioned that the majority of silver nitrate films had been recycled to extract the silver and celluloid.

But as he looked at the screen, he finally understood what those granules of silver could do for a film in the hands of a skilled director. There was a clarity to the images that belied their age, a depth to the shadows that made them almost touchable, and a luminosity that entranced the eye.

The first shot was of an empty altar with black draperies. Then two people walked into the frame, dressed in dark clothes. On the left was a beautiful woman, her hair pulled back with a ribbon across her forehead. Her hairstyle made her look like a Greek priestess, but her eyes were vacant or glancing in the wrong direction, away from her co-star, as though she were searching for a cue card. Clarimonde Bauer might have been a wannabe starlet, but she did not know what to do in front of the camera.

The man on the right was Abel Urueta, as young as they'd seen him in the album, a pale scarf tied around his neck. Clean-shaven, with the light hitting his face, he looked younger still. His mouth, twisted into a boyish smirk, added to that sense of greenness. Abel had wished his smirk to appear knowing, but instead it made him look panicked. He had been made to stand behind a camera, not in front of it.

Tristán had memorized the lines they would speak into the microphones that night. Even though Abel clutched the pages, and even though it was too dark to peek at them right that instant, he knew the words that were being mutely spoken on screen, and his lips traced each syllable.

"I greet you upon this most sacred of hours," Abel was saying.

"I greet you as the moon bares her face to the sky," the woman replied.

Two more lines, spoken in the silence of the projection room, and then a curtain was lifted in the background, and a hooded figure stepped forward. He walked without haste, his face shielded from the camera. Although Tristán could not be sure, this being black-and-white, he had a feeling the cape he wore would have been yellow, same as the gloves that encased his hands. It was a hunch.

The figure stopped suddenly and removed his cape, letting it fall upon the ground and finally showing his face. Although Tristán had not understood Ewers's magnetism from gazing at a still photograph, he was now able to appreciate the man's talent for showmanship.

Ewers had a fluidity that was ripe for the camera. Fittingly, he reminded Tristán of silent film actors, and he wondered if Alma Montero had tutored her lover in the art of theatrical gestures and movements, showing him how they shot movies in her day.

Ewers's silver pendant glittered against his chest. He laced his hands together and moved them up, almost covering his face with them, then pulling them down as his lips parted.

"I greet you as the light that cleanses the dark," his lips said.

The black-and-white backdrop rose, revealing a multitude of elaborate silver candelabra arranged behind the trio, the curtain of darkness substituted with a curtain of light as the candles gleamed like tiny diamonds.

"Give me your hands, dearest brother and sister, for now we call upon the Lords of Air, the Princes in Yellow, to witness our rites."

There were more lines like this, sentences that Tristán could not comprehend—the mumbo jumbo dreamed up by screenwriters. In the background came attendants bearing implements that they laid upon the altar. A knife, a walking stick, two porcelain bowls.

The next scene would see the heroine tied upon that altar and then quickly rescued by her boyfriend. But for now, the screen remained exclusively occupied by the three performers, and although Ewers's words were pompous and Clarimonde Bauer looked vacantly at the camera and Abel was much too nervous, the sum of all these elements was a vivid, enticing sequence rather than an amateurish disaster.

"Witness my might, for I am Sorcerer of Sorcerers, and I anoint myself the lord and master. The king is I," Ewers said. Or he would have said, if the sound had been recorded on film. Again he laced his hands together, as if holding up an invisible crown while his two acolytes fell to their knees.

Slowly the man placed that invisible crown upon his head and stared at the screen. The light hit his eyes, making them shimmer as he lowered his hands. Then came nothing but blackness, and the reel ended and the lights went up.

Tristán sat in his chair, suddenly remembering his days of drug-dazed abandonment. There had been a feeling he had chased back then, which had been close to what the film had captured. Something sweet and dark and beautiful.

"The whole of the film, it wasn't like that," Abel said, as if guessing his thoughts. "But this and the other two sequences, they were like a dream, weren't they?"

Or a nightmare, Tristán thought. Although maybe the difference didn't matter to people like Montserrat and Abel, children who had wanted to hold the hands of monsters and ride fabulous celluloid beasts.

"I thought it was a bit like Cocteau when I shot it. But I had forgotten it. I had forgotten how beautiful it would look on screen," Abel continued and smiled. "There's magic there, isn't there? Real magic."

It was in that moment that Tristán finally understood Montserrat's reticence, because the way the old man looked right at that instant, with all the hope in the world brimming from behind his tired eyes, made his heart ache a little.

The film was gorgeous. But so was that old vampire movie *Nosferatu* that Montserrat had taken him to see at an arts club that also doubled as a bar in the Condesa. The glow of Ewers's pale hair was almost a blinding fire, but so was Harlow's mane, and he had seen a dozen sequences draped in beautiful shadows, like the ones in this film, on a dozen screens. When they watched *The Old Dark House*, *The Mummy*, when Lugosi grinned at them across the ages.

This was no different from that: it was the alchemy of moviemaking, not of sorcerers.

Tristán's silence must have betrayed him. Abel turned his head quickly, looked at him with anxious eyes.

"The missing ingredient is the sound, of course. Once we hear it with sound, you'll get the full effect."

Abel Urueta's face was wasted and brittle. It almost hurt to look at him after seeing him walk across the screen in his youth, full of promise, with his smile betraying his nerves like now, decades later, his lips curved into another agitated grin.

And for a few seconds Tristán wished with all his might that there really were spells and curses could be lifted.

"Yes, there's magic," Tristán said gently. Although he was egotistical by nature, he also had moments of great generosity and tenderness, and he esteemed the old man. He was a weirdo, but so were he and Montserrat.

The door behind them opened, and Montserrat walked into the room, hands in her pockets. She smiled at them shyly, as if tiptoeing into a church, and he could tell by the way her eyes shone that she was as excited about this bit of film as Abel.

"Are you gentlemen ready to record a few lines?" she asked.

Tristán turned to Abel, who was still holding the pages with a death grip. The director nodded.

8

Montserrat arrived with the fury of a sudden autumn rain, stomping into his apartment, dry-cleaned clothes in hand. Her frizzy hair was like a dark cloud above her head. He did not understand her sour face at first, but the source of the problem became quickly apparent: it was Abel Urueta, again, like a musical motif that gets repeated when the monster is about to pounce on an actor.

"I warned you we were getting his hopes up," she said. "Last night he phoned, and he spent thirty minutes telling me about Ewers."

"Hmm," Tristán said distractedly. He was trying to pick a tie and regarded the choices he'd laid on the bed with skepticism. "What about the little sorcerer boy?"

"Ewers had to leave Germany in 1941, after Hitler passed a law kicking out practitioners of 'secret doctrines.' "

"What exactly is a secret doctrine?" he asked, his interest stoked for a second.

"Anything to do with magnetic healers, astrologists, faith healers, all that stuff. But occultism was fine for military applications, so some people were able to escape punishment by working for the Nazis. And even though Ewers sometimes said he had left Germany before the end of the war, he also said he practiced radiesthesia to save his neck."

"You've lost me," Tristán admitted.

"Swinging pendulums around to locate Allied ships and sink them."

"That could be useful background for your story."

"Maybe it would be, if I could believe it and confirm it. Urueta has several different background stories for Ewers: he left in 1941; no, he stayed; no, he wasn't working for the Navy and maybe he'd been conscripted by them." Montserrat shook her head. "Besides, that's not the point. Abel's talking magic and counting the days until the spell begins to work," she said, pointing up at the ceiling, presumably at Abel's apartment.

"You enjoy chatting with him!"

"Seven days since we dubbed the film and seven days of calls. He's even calling me at my job. He phones more than once. Yesterday he called three times. This is serious."

Tristán sighed and tried to maneuver her out of the bedroom, but Montserrat stood her ground. She practically hissed at him. So she was going to be in *that* kind of mood today.

"What are you going to do about this?"

"We didn't promise him results."

"No, but that's what he wants. He's asked twice if I did the dubbing correctly. He even wants me to screen the nitrate print again, and he keeps calling me. You told me you'd phone him."

"I've been busy."

"He's drinking too much. Double whiskey hour is turning into double whiskey evening."

"Oh, Abel downs a drink or two, but it's no big deal."

"I guess you're not one to judge."

Tristán frowned, prickled by the implication. "What's that supposed to mean?"

Montserrat met his eyes. "Talk with Abel."

"I'll have a chat with him."

"When?"

"I don't know, tonight or tomorrow. Sometime next week," he said, his irritation mounting. He hated it when people pressured him, most of all Montserrat, because she was aware that he hated it. He also hated reminders, he hated veiled threats, and he hated the way she was pursing her lips at him.

"He called at eleven p.m. last night."

"I need to finish getting ready. Can I have my suits?"

"The bill wasn't paid, and I had to cover it myself. Let me find the receipt," she muttered, as she tried to fish inside her purse with one hand while holding the hangers with the other.

"Oh, give me that!" he said angrily, tugging at the hangers. "I should tell the cleaning lady to pick it up next time. Then I wouldn't have neurotic fights over my clothes."

Montserrat opened her mouth in surprise. Two seconds later she tossed the garment bags in his face.

"Yeah, you *should* pay the cleaning lady to pick up your clothes," she said. "You should pay a cab driver to take you places, too. In fact, why don't you start doing that right now?"

"For fuck's sake, Momo, I have an appointment with Dora! I thought you were giving me a lift!"

"I'm not your chauffeur."

She left, slamming the door shut so hard he thought it would fall off its hinges. Tristán hurried to his bedroom and changed. As he buttoned his shirt and stood in front of the mirror, he noticed that the tap was dripping again. It was unbelievable that his brand-new apartment could have plumbing issues, but it was the second time that week that he'd closed the tap only to find a trickle of water flowing when he walked into the bathroom later in the day. He did not want to call a plumber.

"Dorotea, good to see you," he told the mirror, smiling with the same zest that had first gotten him his break in fotonovelas. "Dora, you look great."

Tristán had never been good at being alone. That was one quality he admired about Montserrat. She did not seem to have that compulsion to seek others. Tristán, on the other hand, jumped into more than one doomed relationship simply for the sake of hearing someone's voice in the other room.

Yet despite his need for others, he was consistently terrible at maintaining any relationships. He seldom asked anyone out for lunch or cultivated the usual social niceties, instead expecting people to materialize before his door. In his youth, this had been an easy achievement. At twenty-three, Tristán had not lacked invitations and attention. He had a crowd of adulators practically hounding him. As the years went by and his perfect beauty dimmed a little and his fortunes dipped, that constant court of friends and fans had thinned.

That was why he'd been surprised to hear from Dorotea. She was a big fish now, working as a creative director and churning out teen soap operas. *Alcanzar una Estrella* had hit it big three years before, and they were trying to find other products that appealed to that same youthful demographic.

He was nervous about the meeting and needed a pep talk, not Montserrat's agitated recriminations.

"Fuck you, Momo," he muttered as he closed the tap. He'd picked a brown suede jacket and a dark green shirt, plus his trademark sunglasses, for the lunch meeting. He smiled again, wider this time, and telephoned the cab company.

The Angus in the Zona Rosa wasn't his kind of joint. Men went to the Angus for the hostesses, who were supposedly from the northern states and supposedly naturally taller, paler, and therefore prettier—there were a staggering number of pale Mexicans and blondes in ads and commercials. Tristán had always felt uncomfortable with all those women and their plastic smiles. It reminded him, in a way, that he himself was all plastic and had been sold as easily as the steak the women brought to the table.

He suspected Dorotea didn't like the Angus, either, that she simply had acquired the habit of eating there after noticing leering men she wanted to do business with were easily soothed with cuts of meat and beautiful waitresses. Dorotea hadn't climbed the ranks by being an herbivore; she ate other people up.

Tristán could have told her she shouldn't have bothered to conjure beautiful girls for someone as lowly as him, but at the same time, being so lowly, he knew suggesting a change of venue was out of the question, and he was too curious to see what Dorotea wanted with him to invent an excuse.

"Dora, good to see you," he said, smiling, as he approached her table.

"Hello, darling," she said, standing up and depositing a quick kiss on his right cheek, then the left one in the Spanish fashion. Dorotea was some twelve years older than him and hailed originally from Sevilla. She'd been living in Mexico City since the mid-seventies after marrying her second husband, who had imported both a new wife and several cases of good wine into the country.

"Sit and take off those sunglasses. I want to take a good look at you. How are those little crow's feet doing?"

Tristán's smile trembled, threatening to become a grimace, but he removed the sunglasses. "Fine, I think. I hardly look like a Shar-Pei."

"Are you using right now?"

"Not for a while."

Tristán kept smiling, not because he was accustomed to Dorotea's bluntness, but because a waitress was approaching them, and he donned a placid mask in public. He ordered a soda rather than an alcoholic beverage, even though he was tempted to start pounding whiskeys. Montserrat had rattled him. She said Abel sounded depressed, and she was worried about him, and then she kept bugging Tristán about it like he was supposed to do something. What could he do about the old man? Tell him he was sounding nuts? That he was getting stalkerish with all the phone calls? Recommend a therapist? Should he pour the fellow's booze down the drain?

"No relapses? You've had your share of them."

"It's cigarettes and booze these days, and I'm cutting down on both of them," Tristán said once the waitress had stepped away.

It was more a half-hearted attempt at reducing his alcohol and cigarette consumption—and now he felt a twinge, thinking maybe he was a lot like poor old Abel Urueta with his double whiskeys—than a real effort to wean himself off them. But Dorotea did not need to know that.

He could already imagine what Dorotea was going to propose: a bit part in an anthology show. Maybe *Mujer, Casos de la Vida Real*. He could play a wife beater or a kidnapper—Pinal's show was a tearjerker that squeezed female misery like a lemon—for half an hour and get a quarter of what he should be paid. Dorotea had dangled parts like those in years past, but even that tripe had not materialized.

He didn't even know why she bothered with such things anymore. Maybe it was a misplaced sense of guilt. After all, Dorotea had cast him on the last soap he'd ever done, the one where he met Karina. *Juventud*. The corniest variation of Romeo and Juliet to hit the airwaves, complete with its own cheesy theme song.

"We're casting a role, and the director thinks you'd be perfect for the part. But due to the nature of the role, I had to ask."

"What, I get a five-minute guest spot somewhere? I can do five minutes drunk and high, no problem. But don't worry. There's no funny business in my life right now."

"It's a lead role."

Tristán's smile finally shattered, giving way to frank surprise.

"Yes, a lead in a soap. I'll be Fernando Mondego, Count de Morcerf, the villain in a new take on *The Count of Monte Cristo*," he said, holding his glass up with two hands. Otherwise, he'd spill Abel's bourbon over the carpet.

"I knew it! I knew it would work!" Abel declared, raising his own glass. "I got a call this morning: the Cineteca wants to do a retrospective of my work."

"That's fantastic! But we should have toasted to that instead of me!"

"Oh, there will be plenty of toasts to go around from now on. It's like I said: the spell worked, our luck is changing. We need music!"

Abel quickly walked toward the audio console and began looking at the pile of records next to it. Tristán sat down next to Montserrat, who was toying with an olive she had speared with a toothpick.

"I'm going to have to go on a diet," Tristán said, looking at Montserrat in wonder. "God, I have to lose at least five kilos."

"You're mad," she said.

"Definitely not. I've let myself go lately."

"Nonsense, my boy. It's all in the face," Abel declared as he dropped the needle and Chet Baker's "So Che Ti Perderò" started playing. "James Dean wouldn't diet."

"Mmm, but James is dead," Tristán declared as he leaned forward and popped the olive Montserrat had been holding into his mouth. He laughed, and she gave him a frown. Yeah, she was still ticked off even if she had agreed to attend Urueta's get-together. He'd thought it would be a serious conversation where they'd both tell Abel that he needed to cool it off with the phone calls and obsession about spells, but it was turning into a celebration.

"Don't worry, my dear, your luck will change, too. Give it a little time," Abel said as he walked back to where they were sitting.

"I'm glad you're feeling more relaxed," Montserrat said, which was a diplomatic answer considering she had been ready to strangle the old man only twenty-four hours before. "By the way, I have your duplicate here."

She reached into her purse and held out a small can of film. "I have the original at Antares's vault. You need to find a safe place for it, maybe at the Cineteca."

"Not my freezer, then," Abel said with a smile.

"I'm not letting you have it back unless you promise it's never going to sit next to your ice cube tray again."

"I promise. And I have something for you, my dear, to thank you for the sound editing you did." Abel handed Montserrat a book. "It belonged to Ewers. It's one of the souvenirs I keep."

"*The House of Infinite Wisdom* by Wilhelm Ewers," Montserrat said, opening the book and reading out the words printed with a simple type-face on the first page, for the book was hardbound and lacked a dust jacket. "It looks like a manual."

"It's part of the literature he distributed to his followers. I thought you could use it for your TV segment."

She looked up at Abel in surprise. "You'll do the interview?"

"Why not? Maybe after my retrospective is solidified, but it's as you said: free publicity. Now, do we need to get more olives onto this table?" Abel asked, picking up the bowl that Tristán and Montserrat had ran-sacked.

It was late by the time they stumbled down to his apartment. Well, Tristán stumbled. Montserrat drank little and tended to keep her head straight even when intoxicated. He, on the other hand, did not struggle with in-ebriation. He let it wash over him.

Urueta's music was still ringing in his ears, and he hummed that tune sung by Billie Holiday that played as they had said their good nights. "For Heaven's Sake." He couldn't remember the third line, so he kept repeat-ing the first two as Montserrat guided him to the bedroom.

"Is it that late?" he asked, the digits of the digital clock jumping at him in the semi-darkness of the room. He bumped a leg against the bed.

"Yeah."

"Wow. We kept at it for a while, didn't we?"

"Sure did."

He peeled off the sweater he'd been wearing as he sat at the edge of the bed and yawned. "Does that mean you're not angry at me anymore?"

"The problem seems to have resolved itself. Lucky you."

"Luck," he said, grinning as he took off one shoe, then another. He rubbed one foot against his ankle and yawned. "I'm horny."

"You're drunk."

"Well, I get horny when I'm drunk," he replied, flopping back on the bed and staring at the ceiling. "You should slip under the covers and whatever happens, happens."

"That would be a lousy idea."

"That's the whole point of being drunk," he said, closing his eyes. "It's doing every stupid thing that comes into your head and then worrying about regrets in the morning. By the way . . . I feel bad about yelling at you. I know you're not my maid, or my chauffeur. I was angry. And dumb. Very dumb. Sorry."

"Good night, Tristán," she said, and he felt her fingertips against his forehead for a second, brushing a strand of hair away from his face.

"Yolanda said we had a codependent relationship. I think she got that from one of those self-help books she loves to read. But I like to think we have a partnership.

"I feel so alone sometimes, you have no idea. And the loneliness seems to seep into my bones and I get scared because I feel numb. Not depressed or upset: I'm a blank tape. Like someone dragged a magnet against the tape inside my brain and erased all the information. There's nothing left to feel. I felt it all and I'll never feel anything new again and I'll always be alone.

"But when we are together, it's like when you explained about control tracks. Every videotape has this track that allows it to calibrate properly and ensures it plays back at the right speed. Only sometimes you need to adjust the dial to align it. That's you and me. You're this dial, that when it's turned properly it makes the picture clearer, better. Everything is suddenly in perfect unison and I'm not empty. Do you understand?"

There was silence. She had left. Not that he had expected her to stay, or his speech to be anything but a monologue meant for himself.

"Momo," he muttered.

When he woke up it was still dark. He rubbed his eyes and made his way to the bathroom. He stubbed his toe against a table in the hallway before stumbling forward and into the bathroom, where he slapped his palm against the wall until he landed on the light switch.

The bathroom lights turned on, making him blink in discomfort. The tap was dripping again. He'd have to call the plumber.

He peed, then sleepily thrust his hands under the faucet and closed it with a sigh. He left the lights on and the bathroom door open to help guide himself to his bed and avoid crashing into another piece of furniture.

As he walked back toward his room, he saw a figure standing in the hallway. The apartment was in semi-darkness, and he was still half asleep, but even in that twilight space he could tell it was a woman. He couldn't see her clearly, though, because of the angle at which she was standing; her back was to him, and her clothes were dark. She looked like a black smudge against gray paper.

"Momo. You stayed?"

He took a couple of steps toward her. The woman's shoulders were slouched, and she was pressing her hands against her face, as if sobbing or hiding from him. The woman shivered.

There was something about her posture that didn't correspond to Montserrat.

There was something wrong, very wrong, about her.

In the bathroom, the tap was dripping again. Tristán had sobered up, and he swallowed.

"Momo," he whispered, even if he already knew it was not Montserrat. The sound came unbidden. It was a plea for help rather than an attempt at recognition.

The woman turned around and slowly lifted her head. The light emanating from the bathroom was not enough to allow him to glimpse her in her entirety, but he saw her eyes and he recognized her: Karina.

As she shuffled forward, he got a better look at her. Karina Junco. With her same makeup, her same hair, the locket with the gold "K" she liked to wear around her neck.

Only Karina was dead. She'd been dead for ten years, and the last time he'd seen her she'd been crumpled against the wheel of the car, with glass slicing her skin.

Now she stood in his apartment, her movements slow and somewhat delicate, somewhat monstrous.

Tristán pressed himself against the wall to keep himself upright and stared at her, his mouth open, and then Karina opened her mouth, too. Her tongue darted out of her mouth, as if she were attempting to wet her lips and failed. Or perhaps she meant to speak.

If I blink she'll be gone, he thought, but he couldn't stop staring at her. His eyes were pinned open. His breath was shallow, and he felt nauseated.

She didn't speak; instead she made a gurgling noise, and when she opened her mouth again blood poured from it. It spilled as freely as water; it dripped down her clothes onto the floor. Her fingertips were now stained with blood, and she was leaving a tracery of dark footprints behind her.

She shivered and little bits of glass dislodged from her skin and rained upon the floor, sparkling in the darkness, crunching beneath her feet.

He slid down, his back against the wall, raising a shaky hand to try to cover his eyes.

9

M ontserrat didn't mind the early mornings when she had to drive to Araceli's place and take her to an appointment, but she minded the ride back after her sister had her chemo. Araceli looked so worn it was like sitting next to a ghost. But at least that morning it was a checkup, and as Montserrat listened to the radio and drummed her hands against the wheel, waiting in the parking lot, she was able to keep her thoughts away from the cancer that was gnawing at her sister's body.

Her thoughts bounced back to Tristán, whom she'd tucked in late the previous night, remembering his offer of sex and wondering if he was awake yet. Jerk. She knew him too well to interpret his clumsy overture as anything more than stupid babble, designed to irritate her. If she'd been younger, maybe it might have made her heart stutter a little. But now she knew it had nothing to do with her, that it was only his neediness and loneliness that drove him into the arms of others.

He was constantly reaching out, while Montserrat slipped more and more inward.

She eyed her purse and the book stuck inside. She grabbed it. *The House of Infinite Wisdom* came with an illustration on the second page: a crude, black-and-white drawing that resembled the pendant Ewers wore in the photograph she'd seen of him. Eight interconnected lines set within a circle.

The vegvísir and the words "follow me into the night" were printed beneath the symbol along with the author's name.

The door opened, and Araceli jumped into the passenger's seat. Her eyes were wet with tears. Montserrat dropped the book on her lap and stared at her sister.

"What happened?" she asked.

Araceli would not reply. Montserrat extended a hand and touched Araceli's wrist.

"It's good," Araceli said, nodding and cracking a smile. "The tumor's almost vanished. The doctor couldn't believe it. Montserrat, I'm going to be fine!"

It was Montserrat's turn to stare at her sister before they broke into laughter.

Montserrat returned to her apartment late that night, carrying with her a Tupperware with two tortitas de papa that her sister had cooked for her and another plastic container with starters for making yogurt. Montserrat didn't want to be responsible for any living organism, even if it was bacteria and even if according to Araceli the little organisms would multiply and produce yogurt automatically. Araceli was into natural foods, and Montserrat had been lucky that her sister didn't try to also convince her to give up tortillas in favor of slices of nopal. After their meal, Arcaceli had phoned their mom, and they had taken turns on the phone. Montserrat and her mother had little in common, but the joy of knowing Araceli was doing much better loosened Montserrat's tongue, and her mother spoke with warmth in her voice.

The day had been long, and Montserrat thought to simply turn on the TV and watch one of the movies she'd rented. She was already late returning the tapes. But when she looked at the plastic box showing two bleeding eyes and the words *Terror at the Opera* beneath it, she suddenly didn't feel too eager to start an Argento film. There were other matters nagging her.

Montserrat munched on a cold potato patty, then washed her hands and sat in the living room and opened Ewers's book.

There are four cardinal points, but a congregation is led by three, for the fourth point is the haven of the Lords of the Air who serve as a conduit for our will. Thus, let there be three. The son, who will rule the West. The mother, who is both whore and divine, Lady of the South. And upon the Eastern King, the Mighty Father. Thus three become four and four are one, united by the might of man.

Montserrat turned the page and saw a drawing of a circle, sectioned into quarters, which seemed to depict the "four" points Ewers had mentioned, and in the middle a smaller, black circle and a white dot inside the black space.

She thumbed through more pages, landing at an entry with a heading that said, "The Permutation of Water," followed by "The Whispers of the Earth." She stopped at the page titled "The Cipher of Fire."

Fire, as the alchemists of old knew, is the most challenging of elements. We fear fire, yet without the sun's fire we would perish in an endless winter. Fire cleanses as much as it destroys, removing all vapors and impurities. Water nourishes the Earth, but fire perfects it, and it is fire that brings day into night. As Valentinus said, at the end of the world, the world shall be judged by fire. After the conflagration, there shall be formed a new heaven and a new earth, and the new man will be more noble in his glorified state.

This all sounded to Montserrat like the kind of literature that would definitely appear in *Enigma,* with mentions of this and that alchemist, or an occultist she'd never heard of. She'd tried to understand the book but was having a hard time of it. Maybe she was going into this from the wrong direction. Maybe she needed to talk to a historian. But the one historian she knew was Regina, and Montserrat tried to stay away from her exes, even if the breakup had been relatively clean.

In this case, Montserrat's crime had been the fact that she didn't like hanging out with Regina's friends, the lot of whom were professors and grad students from the UNAM. Montserrat found herself gritting her teeth at parties as someone yelled about Foucault. She couldn't help but look at all those strangers gathered in her girlfriend's living room and wonder at the fact that they were supposed to be members of the same species.

This wasn't an especially novel sensation, as she'd felt the same thing when previous boyfriends or girlfriends had attempted to induct her into their social circles. On each occasion she cycled through bewilderment, then irritation, finally ending in boredom. Not that she'd dated that much. Dating was but an impulse that flared every three or four years, but she

could identify a pattern. A few weeks of affection, then months of growing cold animosity, until Montserrat simply stopped returning calls.

At least she'd never made the mistake of moving in with someone,
unlike Tristán. And at least her three significant relationships had not
ended in spectacular drama—no yelling, no recriminations: a muffled
conclusion.

Regina had not taken the breakup badly, partially because Montserrat suspected she had never been all that interested in her, which made
Montserrat in turn feel better. Besides, Regina and Montserrat had lasted
together a little longer than usual, certainly longer than Ismael, whom
she'd ditched after a marathon of nine weeks. Her more leisurely half
year with Regina had, perhaps, smoothed their finale.

One of Regina's historian buddies would know if the stuff Abel Urueta
had told her about radiesthesia and Nazis had any truth to it, or if he had
made it up, but Montserrat didn't feel quite ready to pick up the phone
yet.

Montserrat went to the kitchen and put water on to boil. The battered
kettle stretched her face across its surface, deforming her reflection as she
crossed her arms and waited for the steam to rise. The instant coffee was
insipid, but she wasn't fussy, and she carried her cup back to the living
room to continue her reading.

The opener of the way, the book said, and there was an illustration of
a man seen from behind with his arms raised toward the sky, while a gigantic eye stared at him from the heavens. Urueta had called the vegvísir
"That Which Shows the Way." And here was the "opener of the way."
There was a symmetry to the book, and not only in the text, but in the
illustrations. The circle with the four sections aligned perfectly with the
drawing of the vegvísir, and when you paid close attention you realized
that the black circle was in fact an eye with a pupil in the center.

She stopped, her finger resting upon the page, feeling odd at the realization that there was a logic to Ewers's manuscript and perhaps she was
beginning to get the hang of it. In fact, it was quite the elegant, artistic
little book. A bit garrulous. Ewers favored long paragraphs and never-
ending sentences, although there was an undeniable allure to the way he
structured his thoughts. In person, had this delivery been amplified, had
the words been even more insidiously charming when spoken?

"'Fear gives a sorcerer power over a person,'" she read out loud. "'Never let fear control you: rage will be your shield. Forge an armor out of anger and bile.'"

She flipped to the last few pages of the book to the black-and-white headshot of Ewers with a tiny biography beneath it—nothing useful, merely two sentences declaring Ewers an occultist and expert in all matters magical. A water stain marred the back of the book, as if someone had left it near an open window when it rained or spilled a cup of tea, and the headshot in turn was deformed, and the details of the face were smudged by the ravages of time and the elements. And yet, once again, there was something vivid, bewitching, about Ewers's gaze, staring at her across the decades.

The next day, she dropped by Araceli's place. They were both still giddy with her diagnosis and besides, her sister had wanted to take a bunch of clothes to the laundromat and run errands. When they were done with that, Araceli suggested they have supper together, and therefore it wasn't until eight p.m. that Montserrat walked into her apartment and saw the answering machine with the number four blinking on it.

She groaned, figuring that the guy from the video store was going to scold her.

She pressed the button to rewind the messages.

"Montserrat, give me a call," Tristán said. "Something's wrong."

Then another message. "Montserrat, you're not in yet? Why don't you have a pager? Call me."

Were all the messages from Tristán? Had he gotten himself in trouble? Before she could listen to another message the phone rang and she picked up.

"Finally!" Tristán said. "Where the hell have you been? I'm tired of talking to your machine."

"Out. What are you, my mom?"

"I saw some fucking shit and today it's even more fucked up."

"What?"

"You better get over here."

"Sure, boss. Do you want me to swing by with Cheetos or anything else you might want? A pizza, maybe?"

"I'm not kidding. It's important."

Montserrat scoffed as he hung up, then she grabbed the keys she had dumped next to the phone and went to get her car. When she arrived at Tristán's building, he was waiting for her outside, arms crossed. She had been ready to yell at him, but he looked tense and truly worried.

"What happened?" she asked as they went into the building.

"After that celebration at Abel's apartment the other night I saw Karina," Tristán said, walking briskly toward the elevator.

"Were they showing a rerun?"

"No, she was in my apartment."

"You were looking at pictures of her?"

"She was *standing* in my apartment."

Montserrat stared at Tristán as he jabbed the elevator button. Before she could ask another question he spoke again. "I freaked out. I got dressed and checked in to a hotel, and I spent a whole day there."

"You went to a hotel because you had a nightmare?"

"I saw her. And don't look at me like that. I'm not doing any drugs, and alcohol doesn't scramble your brain."

You're having a nervous breakdown, she thought. They'd been through one already. And whatever he said, he might be lying about the drugs.

"Well, the pressure of the new soap opera, the excitement—"

"I don't see my dead girlfriend when I'm excited, trust me!" Tristán yelled as he jabbed the elevator button one more time.

The doors opened, and he stepped in with a huff. Montserrat followed him and watched as he pressed the button for his floor. She was trying to watch her words and gently suggest he needed to talk to a doctor, but then Tristán muttered a low "fuck," and she figured she needed to ease him into that conversation.

"Look, I told myself that I had a nightmare, too. Just like you did. And I was willing to believe it because frankly even if I wasn't doing drugs that night, maybe all the stuff I snorted and injected through the years dislodged a few components inside my head. I was willing, until two hours ago, to toss myself on a couch and tell a psychiatrist how the other kids bullied me when I was little and that I wasn't potty-trained until I was three."

"But?"

"Oh, I'll show you 'but,'" he muttered, slipping his hand into his pocket and taking out the apartment keys.

He unlocked the door with an angry curse word, then stomped toward the dining room table, where he extended an arm and pointed at a yellow manila envelope.

"Look at it," he said.

The manila envelope had been ripped open, but she handled it carefully, sliding its contents onto the table: it was full of feathers, as if someone had plucked a chicken. There were also seven long nails, old with rust, and a long piece of thread, knotted seven times. She contemplated this strange assortment of objects with a raised eyebrow, then looked again at the envelope, searching for a sender. There wasn't one, but the recipient's address and name scribbled with a black marker did not belong to Tristán. She raised her head quickly.

"You stole Abel's mail?"

"I didn't steal Abel's mail. The postman keeps leaving it in my mailbox, and I was distracted today so I opened it before I paid attention to the name. And look what I found! I saw my dead girlfriend and now he's getting a fucking witch's kit in the mail."

"We don't know what that is."

"You go to the Mercado de Sonora and shop around blindfolded or what? That looks like witchcraft!"

Montserrat had not, in fact, paid too much attention to the wares sold at the market, but what she had seen were candles, powders, sprays, soaps, and incense, all packaged with silly labels that promised money, love, or fortune. She had not come across an assortment of feathers and nails like this; it didn't look like any of the amarres Araceli might buy.

"Why don't we talk to Abel?" Montserrat asked, as she began stuffing the contents back inside the envelope.

"And ask him what, if he's signed up for the hex-a-lot club of the month?"

"Don't be a dick. We need to hand him his mail anyway."

"Great. We can hire an exorcist after that."

"Yeah, I'm sure there're a few in the Yellow Pages."

"You think I was drunk and made this all up, don't you?"

Tristán stared at her, and Montserrat stared back until finally she let out a sigh and shook her head. "I don't know what you saw, and maybe this funny envelope is a coincidence. But in the unlikely event that it's not, I'm guessing you can't afford to move to a hotel permanently, so we need to figure out what's going on."

"Promise you don't think I made it up."

"I don't think you did."

"And swear you think I'm clean."

Montserrat wished she could reply with an enthusiastic yes, but all she was able to do was press her lips together and slowly nod. Tristán had been a very active addict, to put it mildly, and his behavior during the lowest days of that addiction had been erratic; there had been moments when he said he could feel bugs under his skin, and one time when he saw flashing lights. He'd kicked the habit, but there had been one relapse a few years ago.

"Okay, look, come with me," Tristán said, grabbing Montserrat by the arm and pulling her with him.

They stood next to the bathroom's doorway and looked inside. Folded towels were stacked on a shelf, and there was a wicker hamper for the dirty laundry and a fluffy bathroom mat by the sliding shower door.

"What?" Montserrat asked, unable to discern an oddity. If anything, Tristán could be accused of being a little too neat.

"When I left my house the taps were closed. But look now."

Montserrat starred at the thin trickle of water going down the sink's drain.

"You probably left the tap open when you left."

"I did not. Someone was in this apartment."

Montserrat stepped into the bathroom, taking one more look around, then reached for the tap and closed it. She glanced at the mirror and saw Tristán's troubled face reflected there.

"I'm not lying, Momo," he said.

"I know," she said, turning around and clutching his hand between hers.

10

H ave a drink," Urueta told them, his hands flying toward the bottle and the glass. But Tristán shook his head.

"You need to tell us what this is about," he said, brandishing the envelope, which the director had simply tossed aside on one of the couches and Tristán had snatched up immediately.

"It's nothing bad. A protective spell."

"You order them from a catalogue or what?"

Urueta laughed. One of the feathers from the envelope had adhered to his shirt, and he carefully removed it. "I became uninterested in magic practices after Ewers's death, but others continued their studies. My friend José López was one of them. I mentioned we cast a spell, and he sent this as a gift. It's no different than buying a bracelet against the evil eye."

"Why would you want a bracelet against the evil eye? You didn't say that would be necessary," he said and extended his hand, holding out the envelope.

Urueta took it, peering into its interior. He set it down on the bar cart and continued mixing his drink, his brow furrowed.

"It's not. What's wrong?" Urueta asked.

"Tristán saw something," Montserrat said.

"Can you be more specific?"

Tristán was a bit of a coward, always had been, and he was not ashamed to admit it. That was why, when they were kids, he'd depended on Montserrat. Even with her limp and her small stature she'd had no qualms about standing up to the other kids or engaging in mischief. She was the one who invited him to run past the train tracks and break into the grain storage facilities. Therefore, it was hardly surprising that he merely stared at Abel, not wishing to say it out loud.

"Tell him," Montserrat whispered.

Tristán licked his lips. "I saw my girlfriend standing in my apartment. She passed away ten years ago. And now that thing came in an envelope for you. Abel, what's happening?"

"Your girlfriend?"

"Yeah. She was in my apartment."

Rather than laughing at them or calling Tristán crazy, Abel put his bottle and glass down. "The permutation of water and the water bearer," the old man muttered.

"That's something from *The House of Infinite Wisdom*," Montserrat said. "What does it mean?"

"It's the levels of magic Ewers talked about."

"Could you explain it to us?" Montserrat asked.

"Well, yes, but I'm sorry, it's nothing to worry about, to be a necromancer you'd need years of—"

"Please explain," Montserrat said, cutting him off, her voice cold and sharp.

Abel looked like he was going to protest, but it was Tristán's turn to glare at him. The director sat down on the couch across from them and clasped his hands together.

"I don't know where to start. Ewers left Germany and originally went to South America looking for extinct magic. He believed, like others did, including Himmler, that there had been an ancient Aryan civilization that preceded all other civilizations. While men evolved from monkeys, the Aryan people were part of this superhuman race.

"Ewers knew an author and amateur archeologist named Edmund Kiss who made a trip to the Andes, where he claimed to have found a sculpture with Aryan features. He also claimed the ruins at Tiwanaku were of Aryan origin. Ewers ran with this idea. He thought the Aryan superhumans had founded great cities, but needing workers, they had created the perfect vassals themselves. This explained the Aztec, the Inca, the Maya empires, even the legend of Atlantis. All these people were made by the Aryans, but then they revolted and overthrew their masters. Eventually they forgot most of the magical practices of their ancestors, although they retained snatches of rudimentary knowledge. Ewers went to South America and made his way up to Mexico because he was trying to gather those fragments of knowledge."

Tristán had heard similar bullshit in shows like *Enigma*. It was always aliens who had built the pyramids. Nobody could conceive of any Indigenous group erecting anything more complex than a hut.

"When Ewers began organizing his magic circle, he said people like him, people of Aryan descent, were naturally suited for magic practices, seeing as it was they who had essentially come up with this technology millennia before. Then there were Indigenous people who had preserved their culture and bloodline, the Mayas for example. And then you had everyone who had basically evolved from monkeys. Therefore hierophants needed to have some of that pure Aryan or Indigenous strain to wield the higher forms of magic. Other people could cleanse themselves of the harmful Christian ideology that had stamped out Aryan magic practices and handle the lower forms of magic. They could be adepts, but not hierophants."

"All right, you're saying that what, Montserrat and I are monkeys?" Tristán asked, gripping his hands tighter together.

"No, that's what Ewers would have said. I thought . . . well, look it doesn't matter, the point is he created a magic system, and he designated a level of high magic that could be wielded by the hierophants, the leaders of the congregation. This high level of magic included the ability to know the past by speaking to the dead, to know the secrets of the present, and to glimpse the future. He associated this with certain elements. Water was for necromancers. But you couldn't be one. When Ewers picked us to be his hierophants he looked at our birth dates, our family histories, our—"

"Maybe he was bullshitting you," Montserrat said. She had an expression like she had caught sight of a loose thread and was about to pull it.

"I'm not—"

"He said you were special, didn't he," she continued. "He couldn't have said you were a Maya prince by looking at you. He must have said you were the descendant of a great Aryan lord. Yeah, you couldn't be a monkey, not with those light eyes."

Tristán had grown up knowing that there were skin color scales. The whiter you were, the better. Even his "exotic" looks were only allowed on television because he had the correct mix of facial features, height, and skin tone. Yet he still stared at Montserrat in surprise and then at Urueta.

The director rubbed his cheek, glancing down. He appeared clearly uncomfortable. "It was something of the sort, though not so coarse as that."

"His upper tier of followers must have been pale as fuck," Montserrat mused.

"It was complicated! I didn't understand everything, and I didn't necessarily believe everything he said, either. Atlantis, Hyperborea, ancient magic . . . he mixed and matched, okay? All I know is that hierophants were hard to find, and neither you nor he should be seeing any dead people. That is a higher ability. One spell would not give you this power."

"What should one spell give us?" Tristán asked.

"Nothing except good luck! We were simply completing an old circuit. And it worked. I have my retrospective; you have that new role. I'm sure there's a positive development in Montserrat's future."

"My sister is doing better. The treatment worked," Montserrat said, frowning.

"You see? This is a cure for all of us. For all our souls," Urueta said. He looked so excited Tristán thought he would clap.

But Tristán was not going to join his little celebration, no whiskey and soda and listening to the old man's stories tonight. He reached for his pocket and took out his lighter and a cigarette to keep himself cool, although he still tapped his foot nervously.

"I'm no sorcerer, and maybe I'm even an ape with good manners, but having spent a long time in the hospital after a crash, I do know that there is such a thing as side effects. And that you shouldn't mix certain chemicals. So let me be blunt here: could there be side effects after this spell we performed?"

Urueta looked at Tristán, then looked away, then stared back at him again. "I don't know," Urueta finally said.

"What do you mean you don't know? You've been talking magic this and magic that to us," Tristán said. His hand was shaking a little, and he was dangerously close to yelling. He had been afraid to talk at the beginning, yes, but Urueta's vacillation both pissed him off and emboldened him.

"I don't know! I was not the best magic practitioner. Clarimonde was superior to me. José knows more."

"Well, at least *we* now know that your superhuman Aryan powers can't accomplish everything," Tristán muttered.

Urueta looked surprised, as if he'd been slapped. Then he merely seemed contrite.

"You're right, I did want to be special," he said. "Who doesn't? When people believe they lived previous lives, they never imagine themselves as peasants covered in shit. Yes, Ewers told me I was special. He told all of us that. We descended from lost Atlanteans, we could have power, we could guide the congregation. He promised us high magic. I'm sure you wanted to be special, Tristán. No one becomes an actor because they want to be commonplace."

"Oh, what do you know," Tristán said, taking a drag from his cigarette and shaking his head. "I started doing modeling work because my parents could use the cash, and I took acting classes because I couldn't take boxing lessons. That's what you were supposed to do if you were a boy, learn to throw punches and play pool, and I sucked at those and wasn't any better with school."

"But that wasn't all, was it?"

It wasn't. There had also been the allure of the silver screen, the comfort of those flickering images Montserrat and Tristán watched on the weekends. Outside the movie theater the world was littered with sharp edges, but inside there was the softness of the weathered movie theater seats. There was the possibility that he might one day be up there, his face in full color for all the world to see, for all to admire. Those boys who had bullied and mocked him would die of envy when they saw his name on the marquee.

"No, it couldn't have been all," Urueta said, his voice gentle. "Dear boy, you were not there. When Ewers talked, everything he said sounded reasonable and it made perfect sense. He tapped into something in me. Call it a lack of confidence, or a weakness, but I followed him."

Tristán's impression of Urueta was that he was a polished man. But that was now. He thought of him as he'd looked in the film, a young man in his twenties. A privileged man, perhaps, because you couldn't start directing at that age unless you had sufficient contacts. But one who was still a little awkward, a little green, and maybe even a little scared. Someone who would have been lulled by Ewers's chatter, who wouldn't have asked questions. Ewers would have known how to pick them, he thought.

Tristán shook his head, almost snorting, and grabbing the amber glass ashtray by the couch.

"You said your friend still practices magic. Could he help us understand what Tristán saw?" Montserrat asked.

"José turned his attention in other directions. He disagreed with Ewers's philosophy, so his studies have taken a different shape."

"He sent you that talisman with the feathers," Montserrat said, pointing at the manila envelope.

"It's a generic talisman, so to speak. Besides, he wouldn't want to get involved. José is a recluse, and he doesn't like talking about Ewers. It wouldn't do any good."

Tristán pictured himself now seriously going through the Yellow Pages and looking for an exorcist. Maybe he would get a ticket to Catemaco and see if that town really was teeming with warlocks, even if that kind of junk was ridiculous and no better than when his mother told him never to open an umbrella inside a house. Or how the phases of the moon were propitious for certain tasks. He remembered her cutting his hair only on certain nights so it would grow slower or faster as she hummed a song and they sat in the middle of the kitchen. There had also been the statue of San Charbel, tied with ribbons inscribed with prayers. All these relics of his childhood now seemed to acquire more weight.

Midnight sorceries, curses, and phantoms. What had they gotten themselves into?

"Nevertheless, maybe we should talk to him," Montserrat insisted.

"You've only seen your girlfriend once, haven't you?" Urueta asked.

"Once was enough," Tristán replied, dumping his cigarette in the ashtray and remembering the blood dripping to the floor.

The vision hadn't lasted long. When he'd opened his eyes, Karina was gone, and he had turned on the lights in his room and dressed himself with trembling hands. But he was still scared. He wanted to get the Ghostbusters in there, along with José López and a whole team of parapsychologists.

"Light white candles around the apartment. The dead appreciate the light. It appeases them," Urueta said. "Get flowers, too. Ghosts absorb the scent. Incense will also work. A ghost can't harm you."

"How long should I do that?"

"It's hard to say. You've only seen her once, correct?"

"Yes. But the water was running in my apartment today, and I did not open a tap."

"She might be gone already."

"Which doesn't explain why I would have seen her in the first place."

"Necromancy was not among my skill set, so I can't say I understand it."

"What was your skill set?"

Urueta stood up and stared at the shelf displaying his crystals. His back was to them as he leaned forward and caressed a large piece of quartz. "Clairvoyance. Not that I could ever bet on the ponies nowadays. Whatever skill I had has atrophied. It was not much to talk about in the first place. Ewers said I'd come into my true power one day, but then he died, and whenever I've tried it on my own it didn't work."

"And Ewers's skill set was radiesthesia," Montserrat said.

"He told us that. He *knew* things. If you misplaced your keys, he'd be able to tell you where they were."

"Your girlfriend, you said she was more skilled than you? Was she also clairvoyant?"

"Necromancer."

"Then why don't we talk to her?" Tristán said, snapping his fingers.

"I wouldn't know where to find Clarimonde. She married and remarried and then she moved away. It was ages ago," Urueta said, waving his hand vaguely. He set the quartz down, and then he turned around and looked at them. "If José and Clarimonde had been available I would have completed the spell long ago. But José would never agree to such a thing and Clarimonde left me."

"If you'd told me I might end up seeing dead people I might not have agreed to it either," Tristán said.

"Ewers never harmed me, Tristán. When he was around, the world was exciting! He always seemed to get his way, and he bristled with power, and he shared some of that power with us. I'd go to the track and pick five winners in a row. He made people who had dismissed me into my admirers, rid me of enemies . . . I thought this spell would be good for us."

"And I thought we were doing you a big favor."

"No, you thought I was crazy, that I'd made the whole story up," Abel said angrily. "You thought you were humoring a silly, tired geezer."

Well, of course Tristán had thought it was a silly story! Montserrat, too. They'd both agreed to help Abel precisely because it sounded like a ridiculous game. Tristán couldn't help himself. "You *are* a tired geezer!" he yelled. "A drunk one, too. And I thought *I* had problems!"

Montserrat turned to Tristán and clutched his arm. "Stop it," she whispered.

Abel stared at him with hurt pride and outrage. "Light the candles, buy the flowers. I'll pay José a visit, see if he has any advice to offer," Urueta said. He sounded tired. Tristán was tired, too. Yeah, he'd do that. He'd also get a bucket filled with holy water, probably.

They left after that and stood in the hallway. Tristán slid his hands into his pockets and looked at the ground.

"Can you stick around?" he asked Montserrat. "Maybe even sleep on the couch? Or you can take my bed and I'll take the couch."

"I'm not going to sleep on your couch."

"Why not?"

"I can't move in with you to keep you safe from ghosts."

"I'd make a fabulous roommate."

"I have things to do. I want to get hold of Regina tomorrow," she said, taking his arm as they began walking down the stairs.

"What for?" Tristán asked, trying not to sound alarmed. Unlike him, Montserrat didn't get back together with her exes, but maybe she felt like trying something new. Not that he would chide her about it, it was . . . well, he liked it when there wasn't anyone else butting into their conversations and tagging along on movie outings.

"I need to talk to someone who knows about all those occultists in mid-century Germany. Ewers didn't exist in a vacuum. He took his ideas from somewhere. Maybe if I understand the where, I can understand his magic system."

They stopped in front of his apartment door. He sighed, relieved. "Then you do believe me after all."

Montserrat shrugged. "I'm not sure what happened to you, but something happened."

"My apartment is haunted, Momo. That's what happened," he said, turning the key and opening the door. He poked his head inside. Everything looked fine. He took a tentative step inside, then another. Montserrat didn't follow him; she was still standing by the doorway. "You're not hanging out for a bit?"

"I won't sleep over."

She sat on the arm of his couch and watched as he went around the living room, looking for the candle he knew he had somewhere. Finally, he retrieved it, along with a candlestick, and placed them both on the coffee table. The match's flame burned quickly, and he shook it out.

"Araceli is going to be okay then?"

"Seems like it," Montserrat said, but her shoulders were hunched, and she was biting her lip.

"I thought you'd be happy."

"I am. It's this talk of spells and magicians that is bothering me," she said and opened her purse. She took out the yellowed book Urueta had given her and stared at the cover, holding it with both hands.

"You're not scared, though. I can tell. I guess it's not surprising. Nothing ever scares you."

She looked up at him and shook her head wearily. "Plenty of things scare me. Maybe I'm not as nervous as you because nothing bad has happened to me."

"Do you think he was telling the truth? Will the candles help?" Tristán wondered.

"I hope so."

He would stop by a florist the next day and order two dozen roses; he'd get more candles. He'd get veladoras with pictures of the Virgin of Guadalupe or the Sacred Heart painted on them. Incense, too. But who knew if it would be any good, and he could tell she was thinking the same, that even if she was not afraid, she was concerned about him. He thought about asking her a third time to stay with him but refrained.

He found himself thinking about the day he'd met Montserrat. Three boys had cornered him behind the stairwell and were teasing him, their taunts a crescendo that would soon no doubt end in a beating. She'd had her cane back then, and he remembered how she'd come into the apartment building, carrying a sturdy bag of groceries in one hand.

He hadn't seen her at first. He'd heard the *tap-tap* of her cane, heard the distinct patter of her shoes, and then her voice, loud and clear. "What are you up to?"

The boys had turned in surprise and then, seeing the girl with the pigtails, they laughed and swore at her. Go away, they said. But she was insistent. She stood there, gripping her cane and her grocery bag, and glared at the boys.

"You go away," she replied.

Two of them scuttled toward the front door, but the biggest boy stared Montserrat down. She stared up at him, though, and before he could open his mouth, she hit him with that cane. The way she landed the blow, Tristán could tell she had done this before, and the big boy yelped and stumbled, but he did not raise his hand against her.

"Come on," the other boys said. "You know she's nuts!"

They ran off. Tristán stood with his back pressed against the wall, warily looking at the little girl as she adjusted her stance and gripped the cane properly again.

"I'm Montserrat. But you can call me Momo. Wanna play?"

Just like that, with a boldness that made him immediately agree that yes, he wanted to play after he helped her carry the groceries up to her apartment. Which proved his point that she'd never been scared, while he on the other hand had possessed a long résumé in the art of being a coward. This haunting couldn't have happened to a worse person.

He was going to buy five dozen roses the next day.

Tristán adjusted the candle on the table, scraping off a drop of warm candle wax with a nail, and looked at Montserrat as she turned a page. The sight of her fingers upon those yellowed pages made him grimace.

"Should you be reading that?"

She glanced up at him. "Why not?"

"Urueta gave you a racist magic manual circa 1960. Very vintage, and also probably the equivalent to a fucking *Necronomicon* in Spanish."

"There was a kid from the UNAM who told me he photocopied the real *Necronomicon* one time. He wanted to barter my copy of Fulci's *Zombie* for it."

"The laserdisc of Fulci?"

"That one. He also wanted a blow job for it. There's always someone wanting to sell you a lie around El Chopo."

Tristán wondered who had been the kid who had the gall to ask Montserrat for a blow job, not because she was unappealing—she had, as he liked to say, her angles—but because she looked like the kind of person that would knife you in the bathroom stall if you asked for that. She was a Tlaltecuhtli, not a Venus.

"Of course, but that's a real magic book in your hands," Tristán said.

"Why? Because Ewers might have been a real sorcerer?"

"I'm sure he was. His spell worked, and I saw Karina standing right here in this apartment," Tristán said, pointing in the direction of the hallway where he'd seen the dead woman.

"It doesn't mean the book is correct."

"What, he wrote all that down and lied?"

"There's something about this book," Montserrat said, tapping a nail against the page. "It's like Urueta said, it's a mishmash of ingredients. And there are pages missing."

"Where?"

"From the back," she said, carefully sliding her hand along the spine. "Page seventy-one jumps to seventy-three. There's no table of contents, so it could be a misprint, but I don't think so. I think someone gave this book a new binding. Printed 1961, Talleres de Ediciones BE, Doncellas eighty-seven, Mexico City."

"It's creepy. Everything about this is creepy."

"That was the point, wasn't it? That it might make a good story for *Enigma*?"

"Only now I wish you'd worked on a piece on UFOs. By the way, you're not going to turn this whole thing into a video segment, are you? I can't sit on camera and say what I saw. I'd look crazy."

"No, I won't make you do that."

She shook her head, closed the book, and he was certain she'd depart any minute now.

"Let me get you a soda," he said. "Or a coffee."

He made a much better coffee than the abomination Montserrat had served him at her place. He had real beans, for one, and his mother had made sure, like any good Lebanese boy, he could make a decent cup. Anytime someone came to visit you had to serve proper coffee. Tristán still kept the rakweh his mother had gifted him before his father changed jobs and his family moved back up north. They'd wanted him to go with them, too, worried that his acting career was turning from a side gig into a full-blown profession—his father didn't quite approve of showbiz as a vocation—but by then it was too late. Tristán was determined to be a performer, and all talk of going to university and studying for a career fell on deaf ears. Even nowadays, when Tristán phoned his mother, she sometimes mentioned that one of his uncles might employ him at his furniture shop.

"I don't want coffee."

He was already halfway to the kitchen but paused to turn and look at her. He didn't know what Montserrat saw in his eyes, but her expression softened. She nodded.

"One cup."

Tristán, who had been kneading his hands together, now smiled brightly. He tried not to glance at the clock on the wall, for it would show the hour and the inevitable fact that sooner or later she'd go home, and it would be night outside, and he'd be utterly alone and helpless, with only a candle to keep him safe.

11

W hat I'm interested in is occult doctrines and occult sciences in 1930s and 1940s Germany," Montserrat said, quickly glancing at the notes she'd jotted down and adjusting the telephone against her ear. "It's for a possible gig with a TV show."

"I'm surprised to hear that. I thought you were married to audio," Regina said.

"It's not paying that well these days. Besides, it's merely a possible gig. Nothing final. Anyway, would you know any books that would be useful? I don't mean half-researched junk but some stuff with teeth."

"It's not exactly a common subject. Can I call you back in a bit?"

"A bit like an hour or a bit like a few weeks? Because I'd rather have it be an hour."

"Are you in a rush?"

"Tick tock," Montserrat said.

"Okay, fine. An hour. Call me back."

Montserrat called at an hour and ten minutes, and Regina answered at the third ring.

"I got two books to recommend to you. Do you have pen and paper?"

"Sure."

"The first one . . . oh, honey, no, I'm on the phone."

Montserrat heard an exchange of muffled words, as if Regina had pressed a hand against the receiver. In the background was the sound of a record player. Regina was living with someone new. It neither surprised Montserrat—it had been two years, after all—nor filled her with jealousy. She felt only that vague curiosity she sometimes had about other people. She had never lived with anyone. She couldn't stand the thought of having to surrender her movie posters to the tastes of a lover, or having to engage in the domestic compromises such relationships entailed.

Idly she ran a hand down the spiral of her notebook until Regina finally spoke again and indicated the titles of two books. Before she hung up, they made a brief exchange of goodbyes and promises to meet for coffee that Montserrat did not intend to keep. She'd have to make a trek to the used bookstores at Donceles and see if anyone carried them. Otherwise, she could try Gandhi, but that might be more expensive. She grabbed the Yellow Pages, made a few phone calls, and found a store that said they had the two history books she was looking for. She asked the woman on the phone to put them aside for her.

The trip downtown was quick, and she sprinted up the stairs to the second floor of the bookshop. It was a stuffy, small business that was packed with books from top to bottom. Books in piles, books on shelves, books occupying chairs. The cash register looked ancient, but the girl behind the counter was in her twenties, with a Walkman clipped to her jeans and her hair painted a glossy black. Her eyes were lined with kohl.

"I called about a few books, Golden Dawn and all that stuff," Montserrat said.

"Yes, right. Let's see: Aleister Crowley. Wow, that dude was nuts."

"You know much about these magician types?"

"A little, I guess. I read this one," the girl said, looking at the back of one of the books and looking for a sticker. "It was creepy. Do you like scary stories?"

"Depends. You have more stuff like that?"

"More Crowley? We have a special section at the back for antique books. We had a copy of *The Diary of a Drug Fiend* a while back, it was pretty old."

"I'm not looking for collector's items. You wouldn't have a . . . I don't know, anything else on magic?"

"We have an esoteric and spiritual section. We got a book about how to talk to guardian angels. It's down there," the girl said.

Montserrat found the bookcase labeled "Esoteric and Spiritual," and discovered that nearly half of it was dedicated to astrology. She ended up picking a couple of other books at that store, then went next door, to another bookstore that smelled musty and looked like an exact replica of the previous one except that this one had an old dude behind the counter. She repeated this process two more times before heading home.

Back at her apartment, she cleared her desk, took out a notebook, pens, Post-its, and began reading. She learned about Aleister Crowley, Jack Parsons, and Thelemea, and even found out more about Marjorie Cameron Parsons. It turned out she had lived in Mexico and had performed blood rituals, hoping to communicate with her dead husband by slashing her arm.

Over the next few days, she alternated between the books she'd bought and Ewers's book. Crowley's main idea seemed to be that theoretically anyone could take old systems of magic and strip them to their symbolic core, using them in a modern age. Ewers seemed to replicate this idea with his emphasis on cinema as a technology that might permit an optimal kind of spell casting.

She thought back to her idea of nitrate film as a burnt offering, ritual sacrifice upon a tabernacle of silver.

At work, she kept quiet; she read during breaks and scribbled in a notebook. She was jotting a question she wanted to ask Urueta the next time they met when Samuel walked into the lunchroom.

"Are you studying for something?" Samuel asked, pushing aside her book.

Montserrat clapped *The House of Infinite Wisdom* shut and stuffed it back in her purse. She glared at Samuel. "Are you spying on me?"

"No. I saw you hunched over, looking like you're cramming for a final."

"It's none of your business."

"Wow, you're tense. Here, Mario prepped next week's schedule."

Montserrat snatched the piece of paper from Samuel's hands and gave it a quick look. "I'm not on for anything. He's got you in six days in a row."

"I know, but—"

"Oh, shut up, you boot-licking pig," she said, shoving away the sandwich she'd been eating and pushing Samuel aside as she went toward the door.

"Hey! You can't call me that!"

"Go tell Mario about it," she replied, relishing his anguished face.

Samuel, predictably, did tell Mario, and Montserrat had a second yelling match with her boss. She called Tristán after work, intent on complaining about her job, about the lousy shift system and her co-workers, but Tristán quickly told her he was heading out.

"I have a meeting," Tristán said.

She twisted the corner of an index card that she'd used to jot notes. "I thought you were locked at home, terrified of ghosts."

"I bought three vases, which are currently crammed with flowers. I'm burning candles at every hour of the day. I haven't seen or heard anything strange since we spoke to Abel last week," he informed her.

"Nothing, then? Not a single thing?"

"No. Thank God."

"Hmm," she said, tapping a nail against the card.

"You sound disappointed."

"No . . . well, I was hoping to talk to you for a bit, but you're going out."

"I can call you later."

"Not in the middle of the night, please."

"I'll call you at a decent time. How about eight a.m.?"

"That would be nice."

When he hung up, she looked at the index card and the words she'd copied from Ewers's book. *Seize the world, squeeze it for every drop of power, smite your enemies.*

"Some days I could do a little smiting," she muttered, thinking of her job, and she reclined in her chair, contemplating the pile of notes and scribbles she was assembling.

Tristán didn't call. Not later that night, not in the morning. Although it irritated her, it also meant he had not seen Karina again. She was sure he would have phoned if he'd been frightened. Maybe November was not a month for ghosts, after all. Maybe Ewers was a phony and had never cast spells.

She had the nagging feeling, despite this, that she had missed something when she'd gone through Ewers's book the first time, that there really was a secret to be pried from those pages. So she started back at the beginning, opening it to the first chapter, then thumbing to the second. Which is when she noticed the word penciled in at the top of the page.

Find, it said in small, flowing letters. She had not paid attention to this marginalia the first time she'd read it, but now she stared at that single word, which seemed to her like the discovery of a fingerprint at a crime scene.

She went through every page and found words in pencil at the top of three other chapters. *My words* showed up in chapter three. *Beneath* made its appearance along chapter seven, while *the skin* was the last annotation.

She wrote all of them down.

" 'Find my words beneath the skin,' " she said, reading the sentence out loud.

The phrase was elusive. It told her nothing, just as she felt all those chapters on magic practices had revealed little. There were two chapters dedicated to runes and sigils, and another one about how performances could be used for spell casting, but it was all couched in cryptic language and florid imagery that made it difficult to discern Ewers's meaning. The thing she had understood most clearly, having now sampled much of Ewers's magic system as well as books about other occultists, was that the man was a dedicated collage artist who could mention Icelandic runes one second, then talk about Peruvian shamans in his next breath. It was cheap romantic exotification, but she could also glimpse what Abel Urueta had seen: Ewers had a sense of grandeur, and he knew saying something plainly would not be as effective as going full-on rococo.

Montserrat turned the volume between her hands, when suddenly she remembered what she'd told Tristán the other day: that she thought this book had been rebound.

"You crafty bastard," she whispered.

Montserrat went to the kitchen and opened a drawer, shoving forks and spoons aside until she found a sharp knife.

She sat back in the office and opened the book flat, plunging the knife along the interior fold of the cover. It was a harder task than she had anticipated, but she managed to take off the cover and remove the pages, revealing two pieces of paper, as thin and delicate as the skin of an onion, which had been neatly hidden in the binding.

She unfolded the pages and saw that they were written with ink, and in the same tight, small letters she'd seen penciled along the margins. Smaller, still. Had he written this with a magnifying glass? She turned on the green desk lamp and adjusted the angle.

The following is a brief but accurate account of my life, written this April 4 of 1961, at the age of 38. I was a sickly infant. A bout of rheumatic fever left me with a weak heart and I spent the bulk of my childhood cloistered at home, for my delicate constitution could not abide the outside world. My parents heaped praise upon my older brother and left me to spend lonely afternoons in my room, anticipating my early demise. But I did not die then and proved to be a precocious and brilliant child.

It was my intellectual father's personality which bestowed upon me the gift of culture and wit. From my mother I inherited a certain melancholy and inquisitiveness, as well as an ease for languages. I found solace and companionship in books, paying special interest to the works of Guido von List and other thinkers of that ilk.

When I was eight years of age my older brother drowned in a terrible accident. My mother, distraught, asked my father to consult with mediums and magic practitioners in a quest to contact her dead child. Years before his marriage, my father had been engaged in such explorations, and now he returned to them.

Thus, I became accustomed to perusing the same books my parents read and listened to the conversations they maintained with learned practitioners of the magic arts.

My father was acquainted with members of the Thule Society, the Ordo Templi Orientis, and other similar organizations. I was introduced to the many spiritualists, dowsers, astrologers, chirologists, and clairvoyants who assembled in Munich, which, in those days, numbered quite a few, and who visited my father, whose vast library contained valuable tomes. We maintained a salon, and I enjoyed this motley group of guests.

My mother, at first keen to organize elaborate reunions and séances, drifted into a pit of melancholy after a few years. The one reason why those activities interested her had been the possibility of regaining her dead son, and once this goal proved unachievable, she plunged into a mixture of drug addiction and depression, neglecting me and my father.

My mother killed herself on the fourth anniversary of my brother's death. After my mother's suicide our salons seemed to take place more often, although I noticed my father, rather than conducting the serious studies he had followed before, now seemed to organize any reunions as excuses for drinking and socialization. I began to correspond directly with several of

*our guests, amassing whatever knowledge I could. I was especially
interested in the idea of rune magic and was inspired by Kummer, Wiligut,
and others of their ilk to develop my own runic system.*

*My father's connections were at first a boon for me and then a liability,
for the month of June of 1941 saw the arrest of numerous astrologers and
occultists, including people like Krafft, who had been widely considered a
favorite of Goebbels. We'd thought him and ourselves untouchable. We were
wrong.*

*My father was not among those arrested. He had learned that a team of
pendulum users was being put together by the Navy High Command to help
them sink British boats, and he convinced a man in charge of these
experiments to let us join the dozens of men and women who spent hours
with their arms stretched out across the nautical charts, attempting to
discern the smallest motion of their pendulums. Therefore, although many
astrologers and occultists faced imprisonment, we were spared.*

The year 1941. Montserrat opened a book, then another. She plucked
a note from her desk. That was the year Reinhard Heydrich ordered the
Gestapo to take action against "fringe" sciences. The Krafft in the letter
must be Karl Ernst Krafft, who had been recruited by Goebbels into the
Propaganda Ministry so he could produce a new edition of Nostrada-
mus's prophecies; an edition that would pinpoint a German victory. Krafft
had eventually fallen out of favor. This part of Ewers's story had the ring
of truth.

*Our luck did not hold for long, and we found ourselves in a precarious
position by the end of 1942, when we were both thrown under house arrest.
My father's reaction was to drink whatever he could get his hands on, and I
understood, from his feeble mutterings and complaints, that he was
ultimately a weak-willed and pitiful man whose possibilities had been
exhausted. My poor health, ironically, kept me safe during this time as few
people thought an alcoholic and his wan, feeble son could cause problems.*

*It was in 1943 that Mussolini was kidnapped, and in desperation
Himmler decided to assemble a large group of occultists, ranging from
astrologers to pendulum users, to locate the man. My father and I were
among those invited to join this motley group at a villa on the Wannsee.*

Although the purpose of the congregation was to gather for work, the atmosphere was of that of a great bacchanal, with enormous quantities of food, drink, and tobacco available to energize us, plus the promise of one hundred thousand Reichsmark for anyone who could provide the required coordinates. My father promptly sunk into a stupor, and I watched the fools around me carousing and eating until I thought they might explode, all while I considered our situation and its inevitable conclusion.

For I must confess that my experiments with the pendulum had never yielded many results, and my studies of runes and astrology charts produced few effects. I knew, therefore, that just as we had been marched into those vast rooms filled with wine and food, we would be marched out to our doom once we were proven to be frauds and fools. There was not one amongst the lot of us that could claim access to a higher power.

After paying attention to the layout of our abode and studying the guards who kept watch over us, I determined that security was lax. No doubt this was because few people would wish to abandon such luxurious accommodations. At any rate, I arranged, through clever subterfuge, to make my way out of the premises. I carried with me what few belongings I had, including my pendulum. My father attempted to bar my way, but he was drunk. I managed to land a blow against his head, and he lost consciousness. I ran.

This was the first turning point in my life. I realized that my father would be punished for my escape, maybe even killed, but he was too much of a liability to me, old and weak as he was. I understood, at that moment, that the universe was inhabited by those who trample and those who are trampled, and I was determined to survive this war. No one would tread over me.

I lived in terror for days, not knowing where to go or how to get there, unable to chart a route. I was hungry and tired; one evening my luck took an even worse turn when I was suddenly beset by a man by the name of L, who was a thief. L pointed a gun at me and went through my belongings, pocketing what little he could find before he noticed my pendulum and a map. Curious, he asked what it was, and I explained to him the work I conducted, quickly adding that not only could this be used to locate British boats, but to locate anything at all.

L was greedy, that I immediately understood. I also understood if I did
not make myself useful to him, I'd end up on the side of the road with a
bullet in my gut, thus it's no surprise that I steered our conversation toward
the topic of finding hidden valuables. I managed to convince L of my special
abilities, and he agreed that we would journey to Berlin.

Soon I found myself in trouble once more, since L demanded a
demonstration of my powers before we reached the city. My abilities with
the pendulum were meager, but I had no choice, and I sat in a cold room
with my arm extended, as I'd done before, and assumed I would be killed by
a bullet to the head.

Yet in that moment when I should have resigned myself to death, I felt
the fiercest desire to live. It was that same flame that had burnt in my chest
the night I left my father behind and made my escape, and as I clasped the
chain from which the pendulum hung, I vowed I would not perish there.
There was an itching of my palms and a sharp spark of pain in my head.
Then, as if possessed, I uttered coordinates for a nearby building that was
abandoned and where L promptly uninterred a box filled with coins.

From then on, my gift did not fail me—though I developed a propensity
for migraines after calling upon it—and I did not need a pendulum to locate
objects, either, although I liked to use it for show whenever L was around.
Weapons, food, money, art objects. I retrieved them for my companion like a
dog sniffing for truffles.

L was rapacious and had no allegiances, two qualities I learned to
admire. He lacked my father's sophistication and intelligence, and I despised
his crudeness, but I admired his tenacity.

After the war ended, we found ourselves in trouble once more. L's past,
before he became a deserter and a thief, included certain crimes that would
earn him the noose, should the authorities catch wind of him. He knew a
forger who could provide him with papers that would allow him to change
his identity and secure passage to South America.

L's plan was to leave me behind and steal our share of the loot we had
amassed, which is how I arrived at the second crucial moment of my life. In
a fit of rage, I sliced his neck open. Panicked, I utilized the forged documents
L had secured and assumed a false identity, boarding a ship from Italy to
Argentina.

*At first, I thought myself quite clever. For a while, I focused on my runes
and filled pages with them, and found my quiet studies as rewarding as they
had been in my childhood, but soon a bitter melancholy overwhelmed me. I
hated South America and longed for home. I cursed my stupidity, because, I
must admit, my departure had been made thoughtlessly.*

*One afternoon, walking through the streets of Bueno Aires, I chanced
upon a beggar, sitting on the side of the street and performing a small type
of divination magic using pebbles. At first, I paid him little heed, but then I
felt a distinctive tug similar to the sensation I had when I used my
pendulum; not quite pain in this case, but almost like feeling the snapping
of a branch.*

*I stood in disbelief looking at the brown-skinned man and realized I was
feeling magic. This man was performing an actual spell.*

*My studies of von List, as well as knowledge acquired from my father
and other learned men, had taught me that magic was the divine right of
my kind. Here, however, was this leathery little man stirring pebbles and
telling fortunes.*

*This marked the third crucial point of change in my life. I began to prod
for answers, intent on understanding what I had witnessed. I thought back
to Ernst Schäfer and Hans F. K. Günther, both of whom had theorized that
Nordic tribes had at one point escaped into Asia after a great catastrophe.
Walther Wüst spoke of an empire of Aryans that had declined due to
miscegenation, giving birth to the high castes of ancient India and Persia.
Eventually, my thoughts solidified. Had Edmund Kiss not told my own
father that after the fall of Atlantis the ancient Aryans had fled to the
Andes? Had I not heard chatter about geomantic lines across continents? I
had derided those around me as untermenschen capable of only inspiring
pity, yet I began to rethink my ideas.*

*I had, in many ways, stumbled in the dark, ignoring the ultimate truth
of my abilities. For I had tapped into a web of power birthed by the ancient
magic of my Aryan ancestors. There was no doubt that these ancestors, who
had once ruled over mankind, had left their marks on the world and on
certain people. I therefore determined to meet with as many priests,
shamans, and sorcerers as I could throughout South America, attempting to
seize the remnants of knowledge they preserved from the ancient times.*

Montserrat checked another note that she'd pinned to her corkboard. Walther Wüst had been a high-ranking official in the Ahnenerbe, and Edmund Kiss believed the ruins of Tiwanaku were built by an ancient Nordic race who had migrated from the Lost City of Atlantis. Ewers had apparently been familiar with a large body of Nazi pseudo-scientific theories and racist rants. He'd held on tightly to them, so that by 1961 he was probably muttering many of the things he'd babbled in 1941.

My progress was at first slow, but my natural ease with languages and my determination allowed me mastery not only of Spanish, but an understanding of Quechua and Aymara. Thus, I met with and acquired the knowledge of many talented soothsayers and sorcerers.

Some of these people turned me away, but this did not deter me. Yet there was one encounter that affected me. I had sought audience with an old woman who practiced a certain type of magic I was interested in, but the woman refused to converse with me, saying that she did not trade in blood magic. When I asked for clarification, she said that I carried two deaths and again reiterated that, although powerful, blood magic was not something she would abide, nor would she abide me.

That meeting rattled me. I realized that the woman was referring to my father's death and L's death, indicating that these deaths had been used as an ingredient in my spell casting, all of which at first disturbed me. But then, it made sense. My powers with the pendulum had only manifested after I had left my father behind; presumably he had been killed due to my actions, or perhaps the blow I had given him had felled the old man. And it was after I disposed of L and went to South America that my powers seemed to increase even more. Of course, I had done plenty of learning in that time, but now I considered that perhaps it had been these deaths in combination with my rudimentary magic knowledge that had kindled my latent abilities.

The thought of blood magic, of sacrifices and perhaps greater powers, drew me to Central America, where I explored ancient Mayan ruins, felt the dim magic left in old stones, and spoke to elders who had safeguarded bits of knowledge from the Spanish conquistadores. In Mexico, I hoped to find traces of the mighty Aztec people, but Mexico City proved to be a disappointment. The inhabitants of the metropolis were mixed to a great extreme. While the purest form of magic is Aryan, and Indigenous magic is diluted and deformed, the mestizo possess no great reservoirs of knowledge. I had nothing to gain from these people. I was amongst untermenschen, once more.

Having exhausted most of my funds, I had to survive by writing horoscopes or performing parlor tricks. In my spare time, I tried to perfect my spells, drawing runes and scrying. By chance I met a few people in the film business and was invited to the screening of an old silent film, which I did reluctantly, hoping merely to drum business for myself at the party after the show.

I did not realize that this screening would mark the fourth and most important moment of my life. As I sat in the third row of a small theater, bored and brooding, I felt once again that electric tug that heralded magic. I gazed in wonder at Alma Montero, whose shimmering image upon the darkened screen oozed a power unlike my own and yet of a similar nature.

I became obsessed with meeting Alma, and although it was no easy feat, I managed to become well acquainted with her. Yet these meetings only led to disappointment, for in person Alma did not exude anything but a vague power. I had thought her a sorceress and found a woman.

I was baffled when, at another screening, I once again felt that same elusive power but in person could only discern an ordinary actress and retired performer. One evening, I was at Alma's house idly listening to a few people chatter, and one of them made a quip about celluloid goddesses and their acolytes. This random uttering was the key to the puzzle. I understood that Alma's power derived from the medium. It was the film itself that seemed to amplify whatever latent abilities she possessed. And it was not only the film, but the act of watching the film with an audience that granted it its might.

A movie is a spectacle, but so is a sacrifice atop a pyramid. It was the truth that Aleister Crowley glimpsed when he staged "The Rites of Eleusis," a knowledge which I have now perfected.

Through trial and error, I have come to understand the importance of silver nitrate and sound in the creation of a most powerful spell. My runes, by themselves, are child's play, and therefore I reach the fifth and most important point of my story: my death.

My heart, fragile as it has always been, is sure to fail me soon. I've grown weaker and weaker, and I foresee my end. But, as the serpent sheds its skin, I will merely shed one skin in exchange for another. I will rise anew.

My whole existence has been nothing but the prelude to this great event. I can now see how each of the turning points in my life embroidered the picture of my destiny. I have learned from every single sorcerer and shaman who ever crossed my path, and when they would not share their secrets, I have stolen them. I have lied, I have cheated, I have bled and made others bleed. I have amassed all the knowledge that could be had that was mine for the taking.

My will has been honed, and as my body has turned frail, my feeble heart now almost grinding to a halt, my mind has become stronger and will overcome the natural limits of the flesh.

Should everything proceed as we have planned, then upon my rebirth I will burn this letter and with it all traces of Wilhelm Ewers, becoming someone new.

But should an obstacle present itself, do not let this letter go astray.

For I write my story and my will upon these pages, and in doing so I affix myself to the world.

For I preserve my will upon my image and in doing so affix myself to the world.

My dear Clarimonde, I affix myself to your memory, let nothing come between us. Await me.

Wilhelm Friedrich Ewers.

Montserrat examined the thin sheets of paper with their tiny black scribbles, and she had the thought that she was grasping a piece of an ancient exoskeleton, as if indeed Wilhelm Ewers had left a part of himself upon these pages, as though the letter and the book itself were smudged with his fingerprints and his magic. She closed the book and placed it on her desk.

She walked back into the living room, her movements slow. There was something almost voyeuristic about this act of reading Ewers's letter, yet it had been extremely helpful.

Wilhelm Ewers, she could now confidently state, had grown up during

the time of burgeoning occult movements in Germany. When such esoteric groups were suppressed, he survived and moved to South America,
where he perfected a syncretic magic bible that liberally borrowed from
other magical systems. He took ideas from Crowley, yes, but also numerous unnamed local warlocks and healers. Ewers had learned from or
stolen from a vast number of people before making himself at home in
Mexico.

The picture of the dead man was acquiring colors and details in her
mind, to the point that she could almost picture what Ewers might have
said if she'd asked him a question. She supposed that was to be expected,
considering that she was interested in doing a story about him for *Enigma*,
but it also made her feel oddly close to him. She didn't want to admit
Ewers was an interesting fellow, but she supposed he'd had a certain flair,
and you could still taste that long after his death. Plus the spells, the idea
of magic as something that could be imprinted on film, the delicate systematization . . .

The phone rang. She was tired and stared at it as though it were a
strange plastic beast, as though she had never seen a phone in her life.
She thought it might be Tristán, suddenly remembering he'd promised to
phone and had not called her the previous day. It took four rings for her
to pick up the receiver and press it against her ear.

"At 2:29 I will be dead," Abel Urueta said.

didn't know who to speak to. Tristán is not home and I remembered your number and I have no idea what to do." Abel sounded agitated, out of breath. Had he been running?

"What happened? Where are you?"

"I was selling watches at a shop near the Angel."

"Are you still there?"

"I'm . . . yes . . . I'm at Liverpool and Amberes. Montserrat, I'll be killed!"

"Listen to me, there is a shopping mall nearby, head to the food court. At this time of the day there will be tons of people. You are not going to get killed in front of the frozen yogurt stand. Sit there and wait for me."

"Montserrat, I saw my death. At 2:29, and it's already 1:30."

Montserrat checked her wristwatch. "I'll be there as fast as I can. Wait for me at the food court."

"Yes, yes, I will."

He hung up. Montserrat fetched the book she had been reading and stuffed it in her purse. Without its cover, removed so she could peruse its binding, its weight felt different; it was a thing transformed, devoid of its skin. Traffic was heavy, and Montserrat gritted her teeth, afraid Abel might get tired and rush off without her. But she found him sitting in the food court, as she'd asked him to. Gone was the sophisticated, put-together gentleman she had met a few weeks ago. Instead, there sat a nervous old man who jumped up the moment he saw her.

"Abel, what the hell is going on?" she asked.

"Last night she called me and today I had a vision."

Montserrat sat down, placing the purse on her lap, and he reached over for her hand, clutching it tight.

"Who called you?"

"Alma Montero. I hadn't heard from her in years, but she phoned me and she said she knew I'd been dabbling with Ewers's spells and that I must set things right or I'd be sorry."

"What did she mean by set things right?"

"She wants the film and anything that I own that belonged to Ewers. I always disliked Alma," Abel said, shaking a finger in the air. "She was loaded, but she was a prickly one, even back then. She hardly let me speak this time and called me names. The filthy mouth on that one."

"How could she know you were dabbling in spells, or that you had the film?"

"It must have been José," he muttered as he relaxed his grip on her hand. "Tristán complained so much about seeing his girlfriend the other night that I had to consult José. I had not told him . . . he sent the talisman with the nails because I said I was casting a spell, but I didn't specify what kind, just that I might need a little something for protection. He took his time and sent what you saw. When I phoned him and specified we had dubbed the nitrate print, he became upset."

"Then you lied to us," Montserrat said. "You didn't say there was any danger—"

"I didn't realize there was any danger," Abel said earnestly. "I thought it through, I tried to remember the sort of things Wilhelm had taught us. It made perfect sense."

"Why would José tell Alma anything? I thought he was your friend. Does he have something against you?"

"I don't know. José had money problems a few years ago, and I think Alma helped him out. Maybe he thought he owed her something. It could be she found some other way, too."

"What other way?"

"Spells, magic." Abel was nervously palming his jacket. "Do you have a lighter?"

"I don't smoke. Now tell me what she said exactly."

Abel took out a cigarette case and placed it on the food court table. He finally produced a lighter and lit the cigarette with a huff. "She said I needed to return all the items that had belonged to Ewers, or I'd be sorry. She accused me of being a thief. I had a right to that bit of film, you know.

I directed the damn thing, and I'm no thief. She probably thinks she can hex me, the bitch."

"Well, did you steal the film from her?"

Abel emphatically shook his head and let the ashes of his cigarette fall on the glossy plastic food court table. "Never."

"But you did take that book from Clarimonde Bauer."

"What are you talking about?"

Montserrat produced the mangled copy of *The House of Infinite Wisdom* and placed it on the table. "This book was meant for Clarimonde. You intercepted it or stole it. He hid a letter for her inside the binding. It was never meant for you."

"What letter?" Abel said. "If you found something you better hand it over."

"Tell me how you got hold of that book and that print."

"I don't have time for your bullshit!"

He stood up, tugging at his jacket and giving her an irate look. Three teenagers who were munching on fries at a nearby table chuckled.

"The letter is at my apartment and the silver nitrate print is at the Antares vault, so you better watch your language and sit down."

Abel muttered a curse under his breath, but he sat down and took out a monogrammed handkerchief and dabbed at his forehead.

"The book and the nitrate print were in Wilhelm's apartment. I wasn't supposed to take them, but I did. Alma didn't confiscate the film reels, she destroyed them. This was what I could salvage. If I stole from anyone, I stole from him."

"So you could cast the spell."

"I wasn't thinking about spells back then. I was angry."

"Because the film collapsed?"

"The film was over, Clarimonde had been cheating on me, the whole of it."

Abel gave her a weak smile and scooted forward, leaning his elbows against the table. He took a drag.

"I should have known. She helped finance the printing of that book of his when Alma wouldn't. Clarimonde's family was in the book business. Alma was getting fed up with Ewers. The film cost so much money, and Ewers kept on with his talk of spells and alchemy, but there were no results. Endless spending, spending. Anyway, Clarimonde financed his stupid book, even printed it in record time. She insisted it was for us. Ewers was a powerful magician, and he was going to do so much for us, one day. I had no idea she was seeing him behind my back, not until José told me about it."

"What happened next?"

"The weekend Ewers was shot, Clarimonde was in Puebla, visiting friends. Hours after it happened, I heard Alma Montero was seizing film reels and shutting us down. I knew Ewers had a safe in his apartment. We were going to do our dubbing in a couple of weeks, so he was storing the print there. I went to the apartment, found the reel and the book and took them with me. Alma didn't know, and neither did Clarimonde."

"You said you did it because you were angry."

Abel rested a hand flat against the table, then closed it into a fist and smiled wryly. "I didn't think it was fair I was about to be left without anything. I took the reel because I wanted *something*. Mementos, right? Everyone wants a memento."

"Alma Montero certainly wants yours. Did she say she'd kill you and specify the time?"

"She said I needed to return the things that belonged to Ewers. She said she'd be stopping by."

"Then she didn't threaten to kill you."

"I saw it later," Abel said. "I was standing in front of a mirror and I saw it, and the time it would happen too. Someone is going to slice my throat at 2:29. I know you don't quite believe in magic, but once upon a time clairvoyance was my talent."

"But you could not bet on the ponies nowadays," Montserrat said, remembering his words. "You said your talent atrophied."

"When he died, yes. But maybe it's all come back. I must do something, I must go, I'll die—"

Before he could stand up she pointed behind him. "It's after two thirty."

"What?"

He turned his head and looked at the clock in the food court, then he glanced at his wristwatch. He put out his cigarette and sat back, pressing his hands against his face, then ran his fingers through his hair and let out a sob.

The teenagers who had been smirking at them now looked worried.

"I need to lie down. Montserrat, can you give me a ride back to my apartment?"

"Sure," she said immediately.

When he stood up and they began walking, he threw a couple of nails on the floor. "Throw nails behind you when you walk so you cannot be followed," he mumbled.

"A spell?"

"A counter-spell."

He stopped once in front of a store with faceless mannequins to fetch more nails from his pocket and sprinkle them on the ground, and to light another cigarette. The glass of the shop window reflected Montserrat's worried face. Behind her someone had stopped to stare at them, probably alarmed by the old man who was throwing nails on the ground as though he were tossing crumbs to pigeons. She couldn't see the stranger's face, only the outline of his silhouette, the shape of a trench coat.

She grabbed Abel by an arm and pulled him quickly through the doors of the mall and onto the street before someone called security on them.

Montserrat let Abel smoke inside the car because it seemed to calm him down, and by the time they reached his building, he was quiet and serene. Once inside his apartment, Montserrat set the kettle on a burner and prepared a cup of coffee. They sat at the table together.

"You think I'm mad, but I'm not," he said, his voice low, as she pushed the cup his way. He pressed his hands around it without drinking.

"I don't think you're mad. I'm simply trying to understand what is happening. Why would Alma care if you cast a spell?"

"I don't know and I can't ask her or José, assuming that it was José who informed her of my comings and goings. Magic was a game for me, a youthful impulse. But others took it seriously."

He sipped his coffee, then contemplated the many photographs and memorabilia in the glass cases behind Montserrat. "What did the letter you found say?"

"It narrated Ewers's life story. The real one, not whatever lies and fragments he shared with you. Abel, you said that what we were doing was completing a circuit and you didn't expect any negative consequences, but there are consequences now. Maybe we should undo it."

"You're not untying a knot, Montserrat. We could make it worse. We could turn our luck even blacker than before."

"You and Tristán are both having hallucinations."

"Visions," Abel said angrily. "I had a vision. I had them before, when Ewers was around. I was able to glimpse future events. I did bet on the ponies back in the day. I won several races. He died and it all went away. And Clarimonde, she left, too. All of it, gone."

He slammed a hand against the table, but his anger was burning down quicker than the cigarettes he'd consumed. Abel stared at Montserrat, his lips trembling.

"Can you get me the film and the letter, please?"

"Are you going to give them to Alma?"

"Very likely."

Montserrat hesitated. It was not that she particularly relished the thought of keeping Ewers's possessions, nor that this would surely destroy any chances at a TV segment about the occultist, but she felt a preservation instinct that told her they ought to hold on to this material. But ultimately all these were borrowed items. They did not belong to her.

"I'll swing by Antares on Monday. The vault is kept locked, and I have to ask for someone higher up to open it, I don't have keys for that. I can give you the letter at the same time unless you want me to bring it by tomorrow."

"Monday is fine, I suppose. Maybe I was mistaken about my vision. Maybe I shouldn't give these things to her. What do you think? Should I? And what if she wants the duplicate we made, too? I couldn't part with that."

"Where are you keeping it?"

"Oh, in the living room next to my crystals. It was such a lovely piece of work we did on that. I wanted to show it at my retrospective. She'll probably cut it into pieces, like she did with the rest of my movie. It's a pity. I was never as great a sorcerer as Clarimonde, or even José. If I was, I might attempt—but never mind."

Abel didn't say much after that, and she eventually bid him goodbye.

She knocked on Tristán's door before exiting the building, but he didn't answer. She left him a note under the door asking him to call her. Around eight p.m., she phoned Abel.

"How are you doing?" she asked.

"I'm fine. I'm watching a movie."

"Is it any good?"

"It's Ninón Sevilla, my dear. Good does not begin to describe her. I met her through Libertad Lamarque, who had been blacklisted after getting in a tiff with Eva Perón. She slapped the dear lady across the face, then ran off to Mexico."

She pictured Abel wrapped in a robe, the glow of the television on his face, ancient actors reflected in the lenses of his glasses.

"And you?"

"I'm watching *La Telaraña*. Taboada's show. I have the VCR programmed so I never miss it."

"Taboada doing TV . . . who would have thought! And I was so much better than him, back in the day. But I heard they don't like him at Televisa and he doesn't like them. Still, I suppose a paycheck is a paycheck. Not that TV can approximate film in any way."

She could hear drums playing in the background. Sevilla must be about to dance one of her musical numbers.

"You want me to stay on the line while you watch your movie?"

"No. I'm fine. I'm sorry I bothered you today, Montserrat."

"It's okay."

"I didn't think anything bad would happen when we dubbed that film. You need to believe me about that. It had been so long since I cast any spell, why . . . I was almost sure it wouldn't work! When Ewers died, I couldn't do anything. The spells he taught us were useless. I tried a dozen times, drew his runes . . . nothing. I think I stashed the nitrate print away for that reason."

"Because you didn't think it was magical?"

"Yeah. I was scared to do anything with it. If I kept it locked away, I figured maybe there might still be a little magic left. If I opened it, it would be like exposing a negative to the light. Montserrat, I wanted it to be good again, like it used to be. They put my name on posters when I was young."

"I know, Abel. I know."

"I should let you get back to your show."

"Call me in the morning, all right?"

"Sure."

After Montserrat hung up, she walked back into her office and stared at the corkboard. She'd promised Abel she'd hand him the nitrate print and the letter, and of course it was the right and the smart thing to do. Both Abel and Tristán had seen something odd; it could be if she clung to these items soon she'd be seeing weird things. Yet in a way she wanted to find out if there was some truth to Ewers's talk of spells or if it was nothing but odd coincidences: the vivid imagination of an old man, nightmares, perhaps even too much booze.

She looked at the last page of the book, with Ewers's badly distorted photograph, and pressed her palm against the paper.

She phoned Tristán again, and when she got no answer, she sent a message to his pager. Montserrat changed into her pajamas, which consisted of a t-shirt with the cover art from the *Killers* album by Iron Maiden. Her gray sweatpants hung loosely around her hips. She flipped through channels and dozed off in front of the TV.

The phone woke her up. She picked up, groggy from sleep, assuming it was Tristán. He always called at ungodly hours, never worried about everyone else's schedules. But it was Abel again, the words frenetic.

"Montserrat, please, you have to help—"

There was a loud thud, then a click.

"Abel?" she said, but he'd hung up.

Montserrat called him back immediately. The line was busy. She phoned Tristán. She got his machine. She thought to send him a message via his pager, but she didn't want to wait. Tristán could be anywhere.

Still half in the grip of sleep, she stuffed her feet into a pair of sneakers, plucked her keys from the hook by the door, and put on the leather jacket she had been wearing earlier that day.

The walk to the garage seemed to take an eternity even though it was only a block away. When she reached Abel's building, she used the spare keys Tristán had given her to open the front door. As she climbed the stairs she wondered if she was going to have to pick the lock on Abel's apartment, like she did when she and Tristán went into the grain storage buildings. But when she reached Abel's door, she saw that it was open a couple of inches.

Montserrat stepped into the apartment. It was dark in there, and the first thing she did was slide her palm against the wall, trying to find the light switch.

"Abel," she called out as the lights went on. "It's Montserrat."

She walked slowly, not wanting to frighten the old man. Everything seemed in order in the living room. His books were arranged on the shelves, the oval portraits with signed photos of long-dead movie stars sat right above Brownie cameras, and old issues of *Cahiers du Cinema* were stacked on the coffee table.

Montserrat poked her head down the hallway. "Abel, I'm here."

The apartment was quiet. A thin shaft of light escaped from underneath the door of one of the bedrooms. He must be in there.

"Abel, can you come out?"

She felt unnerved. Rather than proceeding, she stepped back and went into the kitchen. She grabbed a knife from a drawer and headed back into the hallway and stood in front of the door, taking a deep breath.

"Abel, I'm coming in, okay?" she said.

She waited a few seconds, hoping he would reply. But the only answer was a thick silence. It made her think that Abel was not home, although she had the definite sensation someone was waiting for her inside the bedroom. She turned the doorknob and walked in.

Abel's bedroom was large, but it was full of antique furniture that crowded her view. In front of the bed there was an armoire outfitted with two mirrors, one on each door. The bed was of cast iron and piled high with blankets. A dresser was covered with boxes, two bookshelves were stuffed with more antiques and knickknacks, and there was even a chest with another chest on top.

"Abel," Montserrat said, slowly rounding the bed.

There he lay, on the ground, belly up, one hand pressed against his stomach. His eyes were wide open. His neck had been cut from side to side and blood had seeped onto a thin, beige-and-blue Persian carpet, staining it red.

She pressed a hand against her mouth to keep herself from screaming.

From the corner of her eye Montserrat spied movement, and she turned around, knife in hand, staring at her reflection in the armoire's doors. The apartment was still silent, but there was a strange charge in the air.

She knew silence and she knew *silence*. When working with tracks, any audio engineer would record a couple of minutes of silence to establish room tone. Later, that silence could be used to seamlessly bridge gaps. Dead silence, however, was a different thing. Dead silence was the absence of all sound. No room, outside of a soundproofed studio, could be dead silent. There was always the sound of traffic outside, the tick of a clock, the buzzing of an alarm in the distance.

Yet silence thick as tar enveloped her, threatened to suffocate her.

She saw herself in the mirror, frozen in the armoire's panes of glass. She could not move. A terrible fear had gripped her heart. It was the terror of this unnatural silence, of the brightly illuminated room that nevertheless seemed to hide stark shadows, and even of the shape of the blood upon the carpet.

She thought the patterns on the rug, mixing with the spilled blood, traced strange glyphs.

And that silence . . . that silence was louder than a hundred decibels, louder than shouting, or a siren or firecrackers going off in the night. Yet that room, if measured with a sound level meter, could not have registered any more noise than the ticking of a watch.

In the mirror there was a spark. That silvery, shimmering second that unsettles the retina, the accidental transition as the light of a projector hits a clear frame.

A flash frame.

Fear, which had rooted her to her spot, now gave her the courage to move. Montserrat jumped toward the room's entrance, her fingers brushing against the door jamb. It was scorching hot. She let out a yelp, which broke the terrible blanket of silence, and dropped her knife, stumbling out of the room and running back into the living room where she found a phone and picked up the receiver. She yelled for an operator even though none could answer her desperate plea because the other phone was in the bedroom, off the hook, smeared with blood.

13

Outside the police station Montserrat paused to look at a newspaper stand with its collection of magazines, newspapers, and comic books on display. The new Gloria Trevi calendar had arrived in time for the holidays, and her nakedness would soon adorn all the mechanics' shops in the city. A tiny Christmas tree, decorated with tinsel, sat in a corner of the stand, promising cheer and good tidings. Montserrat kept perusing the headlines, looking at the papers hanging from clothespins, as if searching for the answer to a puzzle.

Tristán steered Montserrat away from the newspaper stand and toward a taxi.

"When will they have the results of the autopsy?" Montserrat asked after he'd given the driver his address.

It was the first sentence she had uttered since they'd walked out of the police station. She looked haggard, an actor rehearsing the part of a zombie, with dark circles under her eyes and the occasional grunt that served as answers to his questions.

The taxi driver eyed them through the rearview mirror, and Tristán stuffed his hands in his pockets. "We can't discuss that now," he muttered.

"Why not?"

"Because no," he said.

The driver knew Tristán. It was the same casual recognition he experienced on occasion, that raising of the eyebrows, the feeling that people had seen him somewhere before. He had forgotten his sunglasses, which might have ordinarily rendered his face anonymous. The driver might not figure out who he was in the end, it might remain at that nagging level of half-acknowledged recognition, or he might put two and two together and realize it was Tristán Abascal. After all, the anniversary of

Karina's death had been in the magazines recently. They had run Tristán's picture, too.

Or maybe the driver stared because Montserrat's hair looked like Elsa Lanchester's in *The Bride of Frankenstein*, an unruly mess of curls that stood up in every direction, and it was easy to see she wasn't wearing a bra under her thin t-shirt with her jacket unzipped. She looked like she had both rolled out of bed and spent forty hours awake.

"I want to discuss it," Montserrat insisted.

"We're not alone," Tristán practically hissed, leaning close to Montserrat's ear.

"I'll be getting off around the corner from here," Montserrat said.

"What? No. Montserrat, you can't get—"

But the driver had obediently turned the corner. Montserrat pushed the door open and jumped out of the car. She began walking away without as much as a goodbye. Tristán took out a bill and handed it to the driver, then rushed to catch up with Montserrat, who was walking at a quick pace despite her slight limp.

"Are you nuts or stupid? That driver was listening to every single word we said. I think he recognized me."

"I doubt it."

"I don't. I have a major part coming up. I can't have people tying me to anything scandalous."

"Don't worry, the one who was detained was me, not you."

"Yes, but I just picked you up."

"Where were you the night Abel died? I tried beeping you, I tried phoning, I tried knocking and you were not there," Montserrat said. Her tone of voice was flat, so he replied in an equally flat voice although he knew this would only incense her.

"I was with someone."

"*Fucking* someone," Montserrat said, almost biting into the words.

Tristán's masterful plan to meet Yolanda for drinks, so he could hand her the CD—to remain friends, to be adults about this breakup—had morphed into a patchy attempt at trying to give their relationship another chance. They had headed to Cuernavaca in her car for a mini-vacation, booking themselves into a cute little hotel. The first twenty-four hours

had been fine, then sometime around dinner the second day Tristán had
been distracted and morose. He had taken the trip, and he was trying to
mend this relationship, partially because he kept thinking about the terror of loneliness and Karina's death. Normalcy. That's what he needed.
A shot of normalcy.

Yolanda assumed his melancholic mood had something to do with her,
and when Tristán assured her that was not the case, she asked what was
bothering him so much. Afraid of confessing he was, perhaps, going insane, he'd been evasive and grown more and more irritated. Yolanda lost
her temper, they bickered, and in the end Tristán sat at the bus terminal,
chain-smoking and waiting to buy a ticket home.

It had been a disaster, the last nail in the coffin of his relationship with
Yolanda, and he did not need Montserrat giving him a sermon about it.

"Yeah, I was fucking someone, if you must know," he said, his tone
cool, but with a bite. "I'm allowed to fuck, unless they've established a
new morality police I haven't heard about. Screw you, Montserrat. If you
can't get any it doesn't mean I'll go without it."

He didn't mean to say all of that. The words came tumbling out because of the stress of the last couple of days when he'd been in the panicked position of discovering one of his friends was dead and the other
was being held for questioning. Not to mention his catastrophic fight with
Yolanda. It was like getting punched three times in the face.

"I don't care if you fuck a man, a woman, or sign up for a threesome
with a set of twins, what I care about is the fact I kept trying to get in
touch with you and you simply weren't there. I needed you to keep an eye
on Abel. You are an unreliable—"

"Do you know how much money it cost me to get you out of the slam
mer? How many favors I pulled?"

There was a chill to the air, and the businesses were starting to pull
down their rolling steel shutters. Montserrat stopped in front of a haberdashery and stared at him.

"Well, do you?"

Montserrat did not reply. She started walking again, and he followed
her, his voice rising with each step. "You're wearing an Iron Maiden t-shirt
with the word 'Killers' printed on it and you found Abel's corpse."

"So?"

"It's dumb, my eyes, my love. You might as well have held up a sign that said 'murder suspect right this way.' "

Montserrat hated it when Tristán slipped into using endearments during arguments. It had been common in his household growing up, but there was nothing that could fuel her rage more than his passive-aggressive dropping of a sweet word. Especially "my love."

She shoved him, and he collided with the shuttered front of a shop, his back making a loud thud when it hit the steel.

"Excuse me for panicking. Next time I stumble onto a dead man I'll wear a suit!"

Montserrat's hands were pressed against his chest, and she glared up at him before attempting to slide away, but he caught her wrist and held her in place.

"Don't you remember what happened with that Molinet kid a few months back? They found the maid dead in his house, and they said he'd done it because he was a Satanist. And the proof of his Satanism was that he had a Stephen King collection, a copy of Süskind's *Perfume,* and a few heavy metal records in his room.

"Cops always try to pin it on an easy target. I should know," he added, recalling the fuss after Karina passed away. "Orgy in Cuernavaca ends in deadly crash," that's what the newspapers said, and he had never been able to shake off that aura of crime and debauchery from himself.

Montserrat gave him the tiniest nod, looking away from his face. "I was scared, okay? That's why I'm pissed off. I needed you that night."

"I know," he muttered.

The tension between them was dissipating. He hated it when they quarreled. It left him a mess. He never knew how to properly apologize.

"Why were you in Abel's apartment?" he asked.

"Abel said he was going to die. He had a premonition. Everything seemed fine and then he called me in a panic."

"Did you tell the police this?"

"No. I may be dumb, but I'm not *that* stupid."

He sighed and let go of Montserrat's hand. The haberdashery closed its shutters with a loud clang at the same moment the lamps went on.

"Tell me what happened."

She did, starting with their meeting at the Zona Rosa, then ending by recounting her conversation with the cops and the questions they had peppered her with. Tristán reached into his pocket and took out a cigarette, toying with it before pressing the tip against the lighter's flame and giving her a weary look.

"There's something else, isn't there?"

"When I was in Abel's room there was a silence."

"You mean a noise?"

"No, a silence. Or rather, it was a presence that seemed to muffle the room. It was unnatural; I have never experienced anything like it. I don't think Abel lied when he said there are such a thing as curses and spells. We need to get back into Abel's apartment. I can pick the lock, it won't be a problem."

"It would be a big problem if someone saw us doing that."

That, plus the fact that they would be breaking into the place where someone had recently died. It felt to Tristán almost like desecrating a tomb.

"We'll go late tonight."

"His death is not our fault."

"No, but we need to know who was behind it. Can't you feel it? This is not over."

Insects began to fly around the lampposts, attracted by the lamps' glow. He opened his mouth, letting smoke curl up to the heavens, and narrowed his eyes.

"You don't know that," he said and started walking.

"Did Abel's death make the news today? I checked the headlines, but there was nothing. Did it get any play on the radio or TV?"

"No."

"Don't you think that's strange? It's the kind of story that should be in the tabloids."

"Maybe it'll make tomorrow's edition."

"I spent forty-eight hours being bullied by cops. They would have tipped off the reporters if there was anything juicy cooking. If they didn't, it's because someone didn't want his death to be a big deal. Reporters writing nota roja don't suddenly grow shy."

"You're getting into conspiracy theory territory. Maybe the stories Cornelia peddles at *Enigma* are rubbing off on you."

"Someone murdered Abel, and it was connected to the film he shot decades ago. That's no conspiracy theory."

The businesses on the street they were walking down had grown sparser, and now they were going past houses and the occasional apartment building. The windows of an apartment turned red when someone switched on a string of Christmas lights.

"If someone did, then we should leave it alone."

"I don't think we can."

"Why not?"

"Because of that silence I heard in the room. Because something has gone terribly wrong. I don't think the worst we're going to encounter are apparitions of dead girlfriends and invisible presences."

The stretch of sidewalk where they stood was bathed crimson by the Christmas lights. Tristán eyed Montserrat wearily.

"We don't know that. Let's get you back home. You can shower, change your clothes, and it'll be fine in the morning."

"I need to find out the truth more than I need a shower."

"God damn it," Tristán replied, slapping a hand against his thigh while he hurriedly took another puff of his cigarette.

"Alma Montero, Clarimonde Bauer, and José López," Montserrat said, holding three fingers up and counting them. "Those are the people Abel kept talking about, and those are the folks who can help us figure out what is going on and why Abel is dead. I'm going to find them."

He closed his eyes and tried to focus on the rich taste of the cigarette coating his tongue.

"Maybe I don't want to know why he died."

"He was our friend and someone sliced his throat open."

The bitter smoke escaped the corner of his mouth as he snapped his eyes open. Ahead of them another house had turned their Christmas lights on. They were green.

The first week of December. It was the season to devour empanadas, eat rosca de reyes, and listen to the fireworks exploding late at night. He was hoping to drink all the way through the posadas—he'd work off the calories in January. It was not the month to be chasing after murderers.

"Montserrat, the worst thing to do is to get involved in this mess."

"Well, I'm going to go to his apartment to see if I can find a Rolodex and track down his contacts."

"God, no! Breaking in—"

"You can stand guard or you can stay out of it, but I'm headed to your building and I'm picking that lock."

"With what?"

"I know how to pick locks with a pencil cap, in case you don't remember," she said and gave him a brazen look he recognized well from their days playing by the warehouses stuffed with grain. He was acquainted with this iron stubbornness. There was no point in attempting to dissuade her.

"Maybe I could ask my contacts around Televisa and get a phone number for Alma Montero," he ventured. "That way you don't have to commit a crime to get your way."

"I'm still going to have to look inside Abel's apartment. The dub we made should be in there, and I want it."

"The cops might have taken it."

"Why would they take a can of film?"

"I don't know what counts as evidence."

Montserrat edged close to the green lights and away from the red ones. Half of her face was bathed in emerald green as she zipped up her jacket and tipped her chin up at him. "Well, are you with me?" she asked.

"Always," he said, tossing his cigarette away and grabbing her by the arm with a cool aloofness that disguised his nerves. Then again, he was an actor and could play the part of the tough hero for a bit.

14

They hailed a cab and headed to Montserrat's building. As soon as Montserrat walked into her apartment, she noticed the red button blinking on the answering machine. She tossed her purse on the couch. The first message was from Samuel.

"Hey, Montserrat. I have no shifts for you for the second half of December, but I might have something for you in January. I need to talk to you about the Christmas party. We're doing a gift exchange. Phone me."

She did not intend to go to the party and waste her time having to pretend she liked whatever idiotic gift the guys had picked. She'd get her bonus and tell Mario and his buddies that she had plans that day. She deleted the message. The next message was from her sister asking her to call her back.

"You didn't tell her I was detained, did you?" Montserrat asked, turning to Tristán. But he shook his head no.

Montserrat dialed Araceli. Her sister sounded cheerful when she picked up. In the background she could hear the muffled sound of Christmas music. Great. She had started playing José Feliciano. Things would only get more insufferably cheery from there. Still, she was glad to hear Araceli's voice after her forty-eight-hour marathon session fielding questions from cops.

"Hey, mom's been calling you. She says you're not picking up the phone."

"She didn't leave a message."

"You know she hates machines."

"She called you to tell me that?"

"Yup. She wants to know if you're going to Morelia for Christmas. We could drive together."

Montserrat's relationship with her mother remained somewhat distant, but she made an effort to visit on her birthday and during Christmas. Araceli was closer to their mom; they talked often on the phone. Montserrat knew she was expected to make an appearance, but she couldn't promise that, not with the way things were.

"I've got work," she lied. "That's why I haven't been answering the phone. I'm in the middle of a research project."

"I thought you were having trouble getting hours at Antares. Are they changing their mind?"

"Something like that. You should go, though."

"You'll be alone for the holidays if I drive to Morelia."

"I'll be with Tristán."

"He doesn't have a new hot date yet?"

Montserrat glanced at Tristán, who had plopped himself on her couch and was glancing at her curiously. "Status unknown."

"Well, if you change your mind let me know. I'll head out on the seventeenth, to avoid all the traffic. Work is slow and I might as well go there early. If you want me to take a gift for mom I can wrap it for you."

"Sounds good."

"You need to buy red-and-gold underwear, Montserrat."

Red was for love, golden was money. Araceli followed her New Year's superstitions rigorously. What would she say if Montserrat told her magic was real, and sorcerers might walk the streets of their city?

"Are you listening? It works. But you have to make sure the panties are red and the bra is gold."

Araceli enumerated the cons of not wearing red underwear and Montserrat said her ahas and sures like a metronome. At last Araceli said goodbye and Montserrat hung up.

"Everything okay?" Tristán asked.

"My sister wanted me to go with her to Morelia. Are you spending Christmas with your parents?"

"So I can savor the recriminations?" Tristán replied. "No, thanks."

If Montserrat and her mom treaded carefully around each other, then Tristán's relationship with his parents was a tangled knot. It had been his mother, a dreamy woman who had an affinity for operas and named him after Wagner's *Tristan und Isolde*, who nurtured her youngest son's artistic pursuits. His father didn't think much of it, and his brothers had raised their eyebrows at his acting career, especially when it careened out of control and Tristán wrestled with his addictions. In the old days, when Tristán's escapades made the tabloids, his father had promptly picked up the phone, berating him. But the man had tired of calling, and now barely bothered asking Tristán about his personal life. Tristán's mother was in touch more often. Sometimes she even called Montserrat, asking how her son was, begging her to keep an eye on him.

But Montserrat had thought they were on good terms that year.

"Something happen?"

"Not really, just the coverage about Karina's death. The ten-year anniversary and everything. I can't imagine what my mother thought, stopping by the newspaper stand and seeing our photos. *De Telenovela* practically ran a special on us."

"She wouldn't read that garbage, Tristán."

"Wouldn't she?" he replied wryly and crossed his arms.

She waited for him to say something else, but he was sitting with his lips pressed tight and his head bowed. She knew when to make an exit, and she needed a shower anyway.

Afterward, she changed into a black turtleneck and a pair of jeans. They went out for dinner at a fancy French restaurant in Polanco, a few blocks from Tristán's home, after he said he'd pick up the tab. The waiter frowned when Montserrat ordered a beer, but she didn't much care what the man thought of her taste in drinks.

They took their time eating and then lounged inside Tristán's apartment before Montserrat rummaged among his things and found two paper clips she could use to pick the lock. Tristán didn't want to break in and kept wondering what would happen if anyone saw them, but at midnight the hallway was deserted, and they were inside Abel's apartment in less than a minute. She hadn't lost her touch.

Tristán closed the door and turned on the lights. Montserrat went toward the shelf with the crystals.

"The film's not here," she said, pushing aside geodes and quartzes, then standing on her tiptoes and trying to see if he had placed the film can on another shelf.

"Maybe the cops took it after all."

"Why would they?"

"I'll look in the dining room."

Montserrat moved from the living room into Abel's office, which was decorated with a couple of large posters from his movies—*The Opal Heart in a Bottle* and *Whispers in the Mansion of Glass*—and a myriad of photos of movie stars of yesteryear. There were bookcases stuffed with antique clocks and watches, objects he probably planned to resell. A rolltop desk was placed by a window. She opened a drawer and found an agenda with names and addresses and pocketed it. The photo album Abel had showed them lay open atop a reading chair. She closed it and tucked it under her arm.

Montserrat stood at the doorway to the bedroom, watching Tristán as he pulled drawers open.

"Anything?" she asked.

"Nothing like a can of film."

"Did you try the freezer?"

"He didn't stick it in the freezer."

"I wonder what he did with it. Or whether someone stole it when they killed him."

Tristán was looking down at the floor, frowning.

"What?" she asked.

"There's a bloodstain on the floor."

Montserrat swallowed. She'd been trying to keep her cool and succeeded, but the mention of blood brought back the memory of Abel's face. "We should go," she said.

Tristán walked Montserrat to her car, which was still safely parked around the corner where she'd left it the night Abel had phoned. On top of everything, she had feared someone might make off with her wheels.

"Call me when you reach home," Tristán said, leaning down next to the window.

"You're going to get Alma Montero's contact information, right?" she asked instead of answering his request.

"Sure. I'll try tomorrow. But call me when you arrive."

Montserrat didn't want to promise she would. It sounded like she was a kid answering to her parents, but she nodded.

Back in her apartment, she refused to go to bed and instead opened Abel's address book, turning the pages in search of contact information.

But Alma Montero, José López, and Clarimonde Bauer were not there. She grabbed the phone book, her hands sliding down the pages, but neither Bauer nor Montero were listed. She didn't want to phone half the city to find the right López.

She threw her head back on the couch and stared at the ceiling. Still restless, she ended up in the kitchen boiling water for a cup of tea. Back in the living room, cup in hand, she opened Abel's photo album, slowly flipping through the pages. Snapshots of Abel's youth showed him grinning at the camera. There were many photos of Clarimonde.

She found the snapshot of Ewers staring at the camera, leaning forward. She kicked off her shoes and sipped her tea.

There were other pictures of Ewers, all of them showcasing that practiced, piercing gaze. In a series of full-body shots he wore a loosely belted beige trench coat with the collar pulled up high. Something in the poses and the way the photos were shot reminded her of Tristán's photographs when he was looking for work as a model. Photos for a portfolio. She remembered a stray line she had read in Ewers's book and turned to that, finding the correct page.

> *Silver is, of course, an important element of spell casting, and it should be no surprise that mirrors are reputed to have occult uses, seeing as they are coated with silver. Silver nitrate film, therefore, naturally offers an acolyte a perfect medium for sealing spells. Magic rites, shot with silver nitrate film, and shown to an audience, will multiply their potency tenfold. A spell caster must be seen and heard to have a powerful effect. Magic in the dark, in the privacy of a room, does not suffice. Witchcraft cannot be hidden between walls.*

She slid Ewers's photograph out of the album and held it up.

"Of course you wanted to be seen and heard," she said. "I think you wanted to be an actor."

She realized how ridiculous she sounded, speaking to a picture of a dead man, especially when this was nothing but an idle conjecture, but the practiced tilt of Ewers's head indicated many hours spent in front of a mirror.

"How'd you do it?" she asked his photo. "How do you make magic real and not just words on paper?"

She set the photo down and retrieved Ewers's letter. The apartment was quiet, but it was not the quiet of the other night. It was merely the usual silence laced with the humming of the refrigerator in the kitchen and the barking of a dog on the floor below. Blocks away, a siren wailed. She took more sips of tea.

The warmth of the beverage and the lovely, comforting sight of all her possessions had a soothing effect, and she found herself yawning. She scribbled on a napkin—Ewers, Wilhelm, magic, spell—then crumpled the napkin, smudging the words.

The phone rang, and she picked it up.

"I told you to call me when you got home," Tristán said.

"I got here five minutes ago."

"You left my apartment over an hour ago."

"I lost track of time," she said, glancing at the clock on the wall and setting the cup on the coffee table. She rubbed the back of her neck with her free hand.

"What are you doing?"

"Looking for information," she said, flipping the pages of the book on her lap and turning to the chapter titled "The Cipher of Fire." It was conveniently illustrated with the image of a flame within a circle.

"Did you find anything interesting?"

"Nothing yet. I need to give his book another look, with more care. I skipped through a lot of bits the first time I looked at it. I should give his letter a lengthy reread, too. And the film in the vault . . . I need to retrieve that."

"Don't tell me you plan to put it in your freezer?"

"No. I want to see that scene we dubbed again. I have a copy of the pages we used for the dubbing. I should check that," she said, sliding the book aside so she could take another sip of tea.

"Why?"

"'Give me your hands, dearest brother and sister, for now we call upon the Lords of Air, the Princes in Yellow, to witness our rites,'" she recited carefully, setting the cup down. "I'm pretty sure those were the words."

The black-and-white clock of Felix the Cat moved its eyes and its tail to a steady, hypnotic rhythm.

"What did you say?"

"It's Ewers's line, in the scene we dubbed. Remember? And then he crowns himself king. 'Witness our rites.' Ewers's magic relies on being heard and seen. His spells don't exist without a spectator."

"If a tree falls in a forest and no one is around to hear it, does it make a sound?"

"Exactly. He needed a coven so they would observe him. It was part of the magic."

"It sounds nuts."

"No. Look, when Valentino died, what happened? Thousands of people lined the streets of Manhattan to see his coffin go by. Women were hysterical. Some of them even threatened to kill themselves when they heard he had passed away. A riot broke out because so many people wanted to view his corpse. We remember Valentino even if we've forgotten actors who were equally as famous as he was, perhaps even more famous."

"I don't get your point."

"Ewers's plan was to kill himself, remember? He was going to die and be resurrected by his coven. I bet it would have been a grand spectacle, a super performance. And then he expected to spring back to life. Only it didn't happen that way because he was mugged. I wonder what happened to the body? I doubt his lover paid for a nice funeral."

"So you're saying that, what, if Ewers had had a big funeral celebration he would have come back from the dead?"

"Well, no. The film was never completed, and Abel said that caused a short circuit. But he did expect to be reborn, after his film was done and he killed himself by his own hand. I think I'm missing a clue—"

"Momo—"

"When we dubbed the film, when we completed that part of the circuit, maybe it changed something. Like putting a new pair of batteries into a remote control."

"We're not sorcerers. We can't have started anything."

"What if it was a piece of code he had already written, and all you had to do was press a key? Or a VCR that you've set to record something?

All you need is someone to pop in the tape," she said. "I know this goes against Ewers's ideas of hierophants having to be special people with a precious lineage, but maybe he had no idea what he was talking about. Even if he knew, he might not have admitted it, because he was incredibly racist and obsessed with all that Aryan bullshit."

She was breathless. It was because she was nervous and excited by her line of thought, though, as Tristán liked to point out, she did tend to run on a bit. Before she could continue Tristán spoke up.

"This sounds fucking creepy, and I'm alone in an apartment surrounded by candles, so please stop."

She could picture his hand shaking as he lit a cigarette, the smoke rings coming out of his mouth.

"You were the one who wanted to prove to me you were not imagining Karina not so long ago."

"Yes, and exorcising her, if needed. You are going on about weird and frankly scary theories. I want to forget the whole thing," he said. His voice had an edge. His eyes would be very bright right now, his hands clenching like they did when he was truly upset.

"Tristán—"

"Momo, our friend is *dead*."

"I know. I found his corpse," she said, her voice growing harsher in response to his. "And the reason why I'm telling you all of this is because I want to know what happened to him, not because I'm trying to spook you. I'm trying to understand. Don't you want to understand?"

"I can't say that I do."

Montserrat let out a loud grunt and tugged at the phone cord. She lay back on the couch with the phone resting on her stomach.

"Momo? You there?"

"Yeah, I'm here," she said, pressing the phone against her ear.

Tristán sighed. "Look, I said I'd help you find Alma Montero and I will. But that doesn't mean I want to discuss spells after midnight. I'll never go to sleep like this."

"Would seven a.m. work better for you?"

"Haha. Very funny."

"Tristán, I don't think he was mugged."

"Huh?"

"Abel said what happened to Ewers was bad luck. He was killed before his project could be completed. But that sounds like a big coincidence to me. What if someone wanted him gone before the spell was cast? What if that same person killed Abel, fearing Ewers would come back from the dead?"

"That would be who, Alma?"

"Maybe."

"She would be in a wheelchair by now."

"You can cast spells in a wheelchair."

"I'm hanging up."

"Tristán—"

"I'm asleep," he said. His voice had lost its edge and was growing drowsily pleasant. He sounded quite lovely when he spoke like that; no wonder he had nabbed several dubbing gigs. No wonder, too, that soap opera viewers had once been thrilled when he uttered his hammy lines. Hooked, from the very first scene.

"Jerk."

"I do have to go to sleep."

"Go to bed. I'll be fine," she said, picking at a loose thread from her sweater.

The silence on the line was velvet soft, and she pictured him licking his lips, which he did much too often when he was nervous.

"I'm sorry you had to find Abel on your own. I should have been with you. Are you okay?"

She was tired and she was stressed, and when that happened her old leg acted up, but all things considered she figured she was doing fine. The eyes of vampires and monsters watched Montserrat from the posters on the walls. The garish artwork comforted her. She stretched a hand and set it beneath her head.

"Nothing an aspirin won't fix," she said.

"I won't leave you alone again. I'll keep the pager clipped on. I'll return any phone calls."

"You'll check on me before bedtime."

"I am checking on you. Keep me informed."

"I know. Thanks."

She hung up. The TV in the living room beckoned her to explore its late-night programming. There would be cheap thrillers on Cinemax or perhaps she might catch the last half hour of a colorized, bastardized classic on a channel showing classics. Cable offered many more delights than the TV set with the rabbit antenna had provided in their childhood. But the day had been long and she felt wrung out. She placed the album, the book, and the letter in her office and went to bed.

15

When Tristán desired something badly enough, he usually obtained it. The only problem was that he easily lost his impetus. Determination and steadiness were Montserrat's tools. He relied on charm. And charm he did during the next couple days, swiftly going through his address book and calling friends and associates and anyone he could think of until he managed to jot down Alma Montero's number.

He spoke to the old lady's niece, who was her caretaker these days, and told her that he and a friend were working on a documentary piece on Abel Urueta and wanted to discuss his unfinished film. Although the niece requested that any questions be submitted beforehand, Alma Montero was willing to talk to them without delay.

Alma lived in a six-story apartment building near Parque México. The earthquake of '85 hadn't leveled it, unlike many other ancient buildings that were condemned or razed, and it stood proud and elegant, the touches of Art Deco in its façade giving it the alluring air of a grand dame slowly going to seed.

The dim lobby of the building had two rows of brass mailboxes and an ancient elevator the size of a coffin that creaked when it began its slow ascent and outright rattled when the doors slid apart and they stepped out onto the hallway leading to Montero's penthouse apartment.

A maid opened the door and guided them to the living room. The furniture was mid-century modern, all teak and rosewood of a deep golden brown with curved, streamlined shapes. It bore no comparison to Abel's packrat surroundings. Abel's home had been a shrine to the past. Alma's apartment evidenced a fondness for a décor of decades gone by, but it was not a chaotic jumble of memorabilia. It was as if she had culled all the unnecessary frills and kept only the treasures of a long life. For example, the green tweed armchair on which a woman lounged, artfully balancing a glass against her knee.

When they walked in, she stood up and shook their hands.

"I'm Marisa Montero," she said. "Alma's niece."

She was a slim woman, fifty-something in age. Her makeup was heavy, her hair short, her nails red. Every detail of her seemed lacquered and deliberate.

"Tristán. And this is my colleague, Montserrat."

"Pleased to meet you. Won't you sit down? And what would you like to drink?"

"Water's fine," Tristán said, eyeing Marisa's cocktail but abstaining. He was trying to keep his nose clean and his apartment dry. This whole spell and curses business had him nervous, and when he got nervous, he went back to Olympic levels of drugs and booze. He didn't want to tumble off that cliff again.

Marisa repeated their request for water to the maid, who had been hovering behind the couch where they sat, and laced her hands together. She observed them with a practiced half smile.

"You said you are working on a documentary piece about Abel?"

"Yes. It's very nice of your aunt to let us talk to her about her time working with him," Tristán said and took out the mini cassette tape recorder Montserrat had procured for this occasion. "We need to tape both of you. I hope you don't mind," he said, pressing the red record button.

"I'm afraid my aunt doesn't give interviews anymore. She had a stroke years ago. It slows her speech and keeps her in bed. She's at our home in Acapulco for the winter. The city is too polluted this time of the year for her."

Alma Montero was eighty-seven years old. He had checked before the meeting. It was a ripe old age, but he had hoped she'd be lucid and mobile enough to speak to them.

"Don't worry, I relayed the questions you had for her and took note of her answers. Plus, I know her very well. I'm sure you'll have enough material."

Marisa reached for a leather pad and a pencil resting on a low table. Those must be her notes. Next to the pad there was a silver cigarette case and a matching lighter. The case was decorated with lapis lazuli and enamel, yielding a design of fans. Tristán placed his tape recorder by the cigarette case. The tape was spinning.

"You resemble her quite a bit. Except for the nose," Montserrat said.

"I'll take that as a compliment. She was a great star."

"*Beyond the Yellow Door* was the only film she ever financed?"

Marisa nodded. "It was a complete failure. She almost lost all her money in that venture. That's why production had to be shut down."

"Because of money issues?"

"That and a series of production difficulties."

The maid came back with a pitcher and two glasses. Marisa filled them with practiced elegance.

"Abel told us the film was cursed," Montserrat said, carefully taking a sip of water.

"What a silly thing to say."

"You don't believe it, then?"

"My aunt read the tarot, she had a horoscope made for herself. A curse is entirely more dramatic."

"But she dated Wilhelm Ewers, and he was a sorcerer."

Marisa's manicured finger tapped her glass languidly. She leaned forward, resting her left elbow on her knee, her chin against the back of her hand. The glass now dangled from the right hand.

"I think she dated a fellow named Ewers, but I'm not sure what you're talking about or why it matters. This was not on any of the questions you submitted."

"She financed a whole film for the guy and you don't know about him? Maybe you're not as well informed as you say you are about your aunt's life. We could, of course, drive to Acapulco and ask her about Ewers. But I think you know about him," Montserrat said. Tristán had to give it to her: she spoke with a steely aplomb that matched Marisa's polished, neutral face.

The women stared at each other, like duelists gazing across a field, pistols cocked.

"I see Abel still has a big mouth," Marisa said, breaking the bitter silence in the room.

"Abel is dead. He was murdered a few days ago."

"That's tragic. I'm sorry to hear it," Marisa said in a tone that was sufficiently polite but lacking emotion.

"Your aunt was in touch with him before his passing."

"They haven't spoken in years."

"Why would Abel lie? He said they spoke. She was angry at him."

"What are you suggesting?" Marisa asked, and now irritation had crept into her voice. Not that he could blame her. Montserrat barked like a hound.

"Montserrat is simply trying to tie up some loose ends. Abel's passing has left us with pages of notes and many questions that we can't answer without help. He talked about Ewers, and he said your aunt was aware he was in possession of a few items he used to own."

Marisa set her glass down and picked up the silver cigarette case, opening it and selecting a slender cigarette. Tristán reached forward, thumbing the matching lighter, and pressing its flame against the slim tip of the lady's cigarette. She seemed to appreciate the gesture and gave him an interested look. Good cop, bad cop. He'd played the role in a show, ages ago.

"What we want is more background material," Tristán continued, seeing he had captured her attention. "We need to know if we're headed in the right direction, or toward a dead end."

"Very well. I will talk to you about Ewers. But this needs to remain background material, you understand? You can't quote me."

"No, of course not."

"My aunt was, as I said, an avid fan of the tarot, astrology, the Ouija board. All those activities. She met Ewers at some party or another. He was an aspiring actor and part-time fortune teller. He'd read palms at the gatherings of socialites. She quickly took a shine to him."

"He wanted to act?" Montserrat asked.

"Very much so. She thought he had something, and tried to show him a few tricks. How to pose, how to speak. He was a performer back then, but not a very good one. Not yet," Marisa said, and she gestured to a heavy green glass ashtray. Tristán handed it to her with a polite tilt of the head.

"But he never got into movies. Except for *Beyond the Yellow Door* and his bit role there. Three scenes," Montserrat said.

"Did Abel tell you about the book?"

"*The House of Infinite Wisdom*. He let us read it."

"Then you know about Ewers's magic system," Marisa said. "An eclectic mix of occult learning, with digressions into the nature of the elements, and a theory about the importance of sound, film, and spectacle. I said he wanted to act, not that he wanted to be a movie star. The 'act' was the magic."

The smoke rose from Marisa's parted lips, shrouding her face for a second before she waved the thin veil away and smiled.

"My aunt paid for several . . . I suppose you'd call them 'screen tests,' except Ewers wasn't trying out for a part. He was attempting to find the right combination of film, light, sound, movements, voice, that would allow him to cast spells. He thought cultures of old strengthened their magic with pyramids, even embedding spells into the stones that served as foundations for these buildings. He thought you could do the same with film. It's all there, in that book, if you read it carefully. Of course, that's what my aunt said. I never saw a copy of it. She got rid of his possessions ages ago."

"She financed a whole film for him. One would have thought she would have wanted to keep a few of his things, seeing as she loved him that much. Why did she confiscate the film rolls and destroy them?" Montserrat asked.

"There was no point in finishing the film, not when he was dead."

"Even though it was practically finished?"

"It was not practically finished."

"Abel believed everyone connected to the movie suffered from bad luck because it was not concluded. When your aunt called him, she wanted a bit of film that he had kept. She told him he'd be sorry if he didn't comply with her request. I think she was worried about the magic Ewers embedded in the film, like those pyramids you mentioned."

Marisa raised her glass, holding it at eye level and looking at Montserrat above the rim, frowning.

"That's ridiculous."

"Not if you've read his book. Which I have. Why did your aunt destroy that film?"

Marisa's eyes narrowed sharply, she pursed her lips.

"He started a cult, recruited followers. She loved it, at first. He did his magic tricks, and they seemed to yield results. And she'd always had a hankering for that sort of game. She believed in magic, in a special power controlling the universe. Besides, he was handsome. Charming."

"What happened?"

"He wasn't quite as charming anymore."

"He had a new girlfriend, was that it?"

Marisa stubbed her cigarette in the ashtray. Her manicured hands now toyed with the glass, which was practically empty.

"He wanted power, that's what my aunt said. No, I don't know the specifics of what that means, but I do know his cult and his spells were making her nervous. Ewers was becoming reckless. It's one thing to cut off a rooster's head, and another to steal a corpse from a cemetery.

"He was always trying to perfect his magic. When he died, my aunt destroyed his things because some of the people in that cult were crazy. True fanatics who would have done God knows what with his possessions. She thought he'd died, and that magic nonsense should die with him. Abel passed away, right? Well, you should ask Clarimonde Bauer and José López about that, they were his most beloved disciples and they both are practicing magicians to this very day."

"You're kidding," Tristán said. "What, they're still following his teachings?"

"Clarimonde Bauer kept reprinting his works for years and years. She only stopped with the book because she fell into financial duress. José López still goes around with a flask of graveyard dirt under his shirt and a chicken foot to cast hexes. And if you look around the city, you'll see Ewers's runes pop up here and there, among the graffiti."

"His runes," Montserrat said. "You mean his cult is still active?"

"My aunt doesn't only spend time in Acapulco because of the weather. A few years ago, when she had that stroke, she felt it was related to Ewers. That someone or some people were casting spells using his magic system. She saw runes on an abandoned building, not far from here, and recognized them. Since then, she tries to stay away from Mexico City as much as she can. There is still magic in these streets, magic Ewers once wielded. His congregation may not be as numerous as it was when he was alive, and Clarimonde's money does not stretch as far as it once did. But there are always true believers who recall the good old days."

Tristán felt a shiver go down his spine. He remembered an empty lot near his apartment, surrounded by a tall wooden fence that was plastered with posters for concerts, boxing matches, and even pornographic movies. Sometimes, the posters were covered with graffiti before another wave of posters camouflaged the scribblings. He wondered if, underneath layers of cheap paper and colorful ink, there were symbols of old magic, like corpses bricked into walls.

"Would your aunt have contact information for Clarimonde and José?" Montserrat asked.

"No, she wouldn't. Clarimonde married and I think remarried, but that must have been a long time ago."

"And she became a publisher?"

"Sure, I suppose. She was certainly not going to make it as an actress," Marisa said scornfully. "Not that she tried to stick to it after Ewers died. José kept writing, but I'm certain he hasn't had any credits in ages."

"He was a writer? What did he work on?"

Marisa seemed surprised. "Why . . . on *Beyond the Yellow Door*, of course. He co-wrote it. Abel and he were friends, they'd worked together."

"José López is Romeo Donderis?" Montserrat asked. Now it was her turn to sound surprised.

"You didn't know?"

Abel never specified what José López did for a living, only that he worked on the film. Montserrat looked thoughtful. "Abel said your aunt gave him money one time when he needed it. She might have his contact information, after all."

"No, she would not. She does not wish to talk about those days. Spells? Cults? You understand why I asked that this all be background? And why you can't tell anyone that I was the one who mentioned these things?" Marisa said. Her words were calm, but her eyes flitted quickly from Montserrat to Tristán. "Anyway, I'm busy, and I do have another appointment."

"We understand. But could we ask you one more question? And, if necessary, could you relay this question to your aunt? We can leave you a number to call back."

"It would be awfully kind," Tristán added, the implication in his tone being that he would write down *his* phone number.

"Very well."

"What do you know about Ewers's death?"

"Nothing. They said he was mugged."

"That's not nothing."

"That's not anything, either," Marisa said. She looked at her wrist and tapped at her watch with her perfectly manicured nail, as if indicating, not so subtly, that this conversation was at an end. "You'll forgive me, I have to go."

"No problem. We'll throw nails behind our steps when we leave," Montserrat said.

He didn't know what she meant by that, but Marisa clenched her hands together. She smiled as she stood, but the smile looked a little crooked, like she was trying too hard.

They shook hands. Tristán did indeed scribble his pager number on a piece of paper and then pocketed his tape recorder. He gave Marisa a big grin, for the hell of it, and she responded with an interested motion of the head. Tristán still had it. He suspected that, had he been alone conducting the interview, she might have revealed more. When it came to good cop, bad cop, Montserrat steered toward the "beat the suspect until they confess" end of the spectrum. He mentioned this as they waited for the elevator, observing the needle on the brass indicator.

"You mean to say you would have fucked the answers out of her," Montserrat replied.

"No, but older ladies adore me."

"You would have gotten distracted without me, and you would have chickened out. You would have fumbled it."

"That's a great opinion you have of me."

The elevator doors opened, and they stepped in. Tristán jabbed the lobby button, and the elevator began its slow descent.

"When we went to the corner store to steal candy, it was me who did the actual stealing," she said. "You never could."

She could run faster if they stole, too. The limp didn't matter. Montserrat was always two steps ahead of Tristán.

"Stealing and talking are two different things. I'm fine with talking. Hey, what was that about nails, by the way?"

"A spell. I don't have nails. I wanted to see how she'd react."

"And?"

"She's nervous."

"So am I. What do you want to do now?"

"Keep digging. There was something wrong with Marisa."

"Wrong how?"

"I don't know. Something . . . crooked," Montserrat said.

They stepped out of the elevator and exited the building. Montserrat walked with her hands in her pockets and a determined, stiff strut. The conversation with Marisa had left him wishing for both a cigarette and a drink. He could have neither, not with Montserrat by his side. She'd give him another sermon on throat cancer. He ought to quit the tobacco, he knew that, but a fresh pack of Dunhills seemed awfully enticing.

"That lady said Ewers's old friends are still up to their magic tricks. They could have murdered Abel," he said, slipping a hand into his jacket pocket and putting on his sunglasses.

"Maybe. But she also clammed up right when I asked about Ewers's death. And why would Ewers's followers kill him?"

"Why would his girlfriend kill him?"

"He was cheating on Alma."

"Could be he was screwing around on Clarimonde, too."

"Could be. We better ask her, and ask José, too."

"How do you plan to find them?"

The leafy oasis of Parque México, with its stone benches and its beautiful fountains, was tantalizingly near, and he thought it might be more pleasing to stroll through its paths than to walk through streets that could be dangerously tinged with spells. Who knew, after all, if Ewers's runes would indeed be painted along the walls of an underpass? But Montserrat steered him in the opposite direction. They were headed toward the Patriotismo station.

"Abel said Clarimonde published Ewers's book, and she kept it in print for a long time. Could be the publisher that printed it is still in business. As for José López, I'm thinking I could pay Nando Melgar a visit."

"You told me Nando was a creep."

"He is. But he tried to sell me a script of one of Abel's films a few years ago. He said it had notes by Romeo Donderis in the margins, and he offered to have it authenticated by the man himself. I'll talk to Nando tomorrow."

"Listen, tomorrow I'm booked all day. I have this publicity thing for the new role. But if you postpone it, I'll tag along."

"I won't be in any mortal danger."

"So, I need *you* to ask questions properly, but you don't need *me*?" he asked without bothering to conceal his irritation.

"I don't need you, no."

He frowned. She was his co-conspirator, his best and truest friend, but sometimes she annoyed the hell out of him.

Montserrat let out a laugh. She placed a hand on his arm, as if trying to soothe his feelings. "I can handle Nando. He tries to pinch my ass, I punch him in the nuts. He knows how it goes with me."

"What if he's a masochist who enjoys having his nuts squeezed?"

"You worry too much."

"I do, not all about Nando, either," Tristán said, warily eyeing the crosswalk signal. "This talk of runes has me scared."

"You should never be afraid of magic. That's what Ewers said in his book. Fear gives others power over you and clouds your mind. It makes the magic go sour. Which makes sense, if you think you've been hexed, you live looking for signs of danger."

"I would think that is logical."

"Not the way he saw it. You had to be fearless."

"Why are you following this guy's advice?" he asked, irked by the way she spoke. She sounded almost pleased.

"I'm trying to understand the logic he employed, the underlying mechanism. Like Abel said, Ewers wasn't coming up with these ideas out of nowhere. He was mixing and matching. He wasn't that original."

"What is original? Every soap I was ever on was another soap with different names."

"Precisely. So even if Ewers thought a little much about himself, he might have stumbled onto a few good tips."

Tristán paused at a corner and looked down at Montserrat, taking off his sunglasses and staring into her eyes. "Be careful. I mean it, Momo," he said, dropping his voice. "This shit is dangerous."

She didn't blink, tilting up her determined chin, and spoke with a polished brashness. "I was caught off guard at Abel's apartment, but I won't be caught again."

"You're a terror," he muttered, and he meant it.

16

I t was colder that morning, and Montserrat's leg ached. She could do nothing about it except rub the limb and plug in the electric blanket. She dallied in bed, comforted by its warmth, and went through the notes she had gathered.

Her meeting with Nando wasn't until two p.m., so she had time to craft a defensive charm. Ewers's book was at first glance disorganized. But this was a mirage intended to either ward off dilettantes or enhance the book's mystique. Anyway, Montserrat had grasped the method he used to explain his magic knowledge. He divided magic into a system of levels and elements, with corresponding runes. According to him, adepts could only grasp the barest glimpses of this magic, while hierophants were able to wield it.

Water was associated with death—Ewers made his case by citing both Lethe and the Styx—and therefore with the past. Necromancy, automatic writing, retrocognition were detailed in the chapter he called "The Permutation of Water."

"The Whispers of the Earth" focused on the earth element, and therefore was associated with precious metals and with minerals. He also connected earth with plants and fungi, and thus, it was not difficult to discern why Ewers associated this element with potions and medicine—but also with hexes, as the same elements that could heal someone could also kill them. Ewers tied earth to visions of the future and clairvoyant powers, reasoning that all mirrors and crystals, which can be used for scrying, ultimately came from the depths of the earth. He even mentioned John Dee's obsidian mirror, made from volcanic glass mined in Mexico, which he used to foretell events.

"The Cipher of Fire" included long paragraphs on radiesthesia. This was not surprising, considering it was Ewers's specialty. Ewers associated fire with passion, transformation, and willpower—the phoenix, reborn from its ashes, appeared as a common motif, but the fire salamander also received lovingly detailed paragraphs. He placed telepathy, illusions, and defensive magic in this chapter.

There was no hierophant who could control air by itself. This element was a wild card, something that altered the other elements and was not found alone. Only a master magician, such as Ewers himself, could hope to control fire, earth, and water, and gain access to the ever-elusive aether or "air."

Movies were interesting to Ewers because they seemed to bring together all the four elements he relied on with his magic system. The silver nitrate used in films came from the earth; the spooling film was to him like a river of images; and the carbon arc lamps used to project movies were close to torches in his estimation, and thus connected to fire. These elements were unified and perfect with the inclusion of sound, which he identified as the air element. Air was an amplifier, like old audio systems, like Vitaphone, had amplified sound.

Films were also spectacles, and Ewers seemed to be fascinated by the idea of many people coming together to increase the power of a spell. Movies were a perfect amalgam of all the magical elements Ewers sought to harness, but Montserrat wasn't sure whether he had become interested in them before he met Alma Montero or after. According to his letter, his realization of the value of film came upon a screening of one of her movies, but Alma had made it clear Ewers was a wannabe performer by the time she met him.

Montserrat turned to the "Cipher of Fire" chapter and looked for the section on defensive magic. There were two pages on warding charms, which included the advice to "burn candles" to dispel noxious spirits—she supposed Abel had gotten the idea for the white candles from there—and a small spell that necessitated the pricking of a finger. You'd then smear the blood on a white handkerchief and draw a rune, tying it in three knots, and top it all off by burning a stick of incense in front of this bundle.

Montserrat's sister liked burning incense and had left a package of sticks at her apartment. She didn't have a proper incense burner, so she simply dangled the stick atop a cup. As for the handkerchief, Montserrat pricked her finger but did not draw Ewers's rune, instead tracing the word "shield" on a cloth napkin. She did this because she didn't fancy Ewers's complicated runes, but also because magic, from what Ewers seemed to be saying, was an exercise in belief and the self.

She didn't think it mattered as much whether you drew a rune or a word. It was the process of concentrating on the ritual that might yield results. Runes were important, personal, to Ewers. They meant nothing to her, and so she went with a word that did have the significance she sought.

Now, whether this would work was another question. And it could be that Tristán and she were simply going crazy in unison, but in the event that there were indeed murderous sorcerers lurking around the city, Montserrat decided to be prepared. Her meeting with Alma had, despite her indifferent façade in front of Tristán, jolted her a little.

After she was done knotting the handkerchief, she pushed her chair back and contemplated the corkboard that was now pinned with photos of Ewers along with notes and drawings. Her office was becoming a laboratory for understanding *The House of Infinite Wisdom*.

She zeroed in on one photo of Ewers surrounded by pale socialites and grinning men in their fine suits, all of them with wineglasses in hand. Where would she and Tristán have fit in with a crowd like that? Nowhere. In the late 1930s, in Chihuahua, where Tristán's father had lived before moving to Tamaulipas, merchants accused Middle Easterners of carrying diseases, of unfair business practices. They called them Turks, no matter where they came from, they said aboneros should be expelled from the country, like the Chinese had been kicked out. By the late 1950s, when Ewers presided over his crowd of admirers, Mexico City was warming up to certain Lebanese businesspeople who wielded their wealth as an entry card into society, but it didn't mean a poor boy like Tristán would have been welcomed with open arms. It also meant Montserrat, with her swarthy complexion and large nose, would not have made a good impression on those snobs.

Nevertheless, Ewers struck her as an opportunistic, slippery creature. A man who would not see a problem in draining as much money or knowledge from those he considered unsuitable companions before discarding them. They might have been allowed to attend one party, two, before being tossed away. Ewers had been a vampire, with his little book under his arm and his honeyed tongue serving as mesmeric tools.

Was studying him dangerous, as Tristán said? She supposed she could pretend nothing was amiss, erase the man from her mind, but that would only leave them more defenseless. Ignorance was not protection.

Montserrat copied the instructions for the spell on a piece of paper. She could give them to Tristán the next morning, if he was available. Or else she might call him that night.

Handkerchief in pocket, Montserrat took the subway to San Cosme. The trick in Mexico City was to know your method of transportation. Some neighborhoods should be approached only by subway, and others were fine for driving. Montserrat preferred not to take her car when it came to Santa María la Ribera, although the subway came with its own set of problems.

The car she boarded was crowded, which she'd expected, but the guy who practically slammed her against a pole and almost made her trip painfully reminded her of the benefits of her vehicle. Two teens laughed as they watched her wobble and hang on to a seat. She glared at them, thinking of Ewers's hexes. Paint a rune on the back of a spider and then crush it in your left hand: *so those who have wronged you shall be crushed in turn.*

She turned her head, glancing at the window of the subway car. Everyone's reflections were smudged in the glass; she was nothing but a blurry shape surrounded by other shapes. There was a guy a head taller than her standing behind her, looking down. She could see the muddled reflection of his head in the glass. Sometimes pervs tried to cop a feel or look down a lady's shirt, and she stood with her elbow at the ready in case he got close. She'd jab him in the ribs. Her leg still ached, and she closed her eyes and snapped them open when the train reached her station.

Nando used to exhibit his wares at El Chopo, selling videotapes to darketos, punks, and other alternative types until internal strife with the civil association that controlled the vendors forced him to look for another place to hawk his wares. He decided he didn't want to rent a storefront and settled on selling items from his apartment.

Nando sold cassette tapes and records that his cousin from Tijuana purchased in the USA and mailed to him, but when Betamax and later VHS hit the market, he settled on movies as his item of choice. Later, he concentrated on memorabilia, which fetched a higher price.

Nando lived on Fresno, three blocks from the Moorish Kiosk, in an ugly building that had been once painted "Mexican pink" and now looked like it was caked in dirt. The colonia had once aimed for a French look, with its Art Nouveau museum of glass and iron standing as a witness to great expectations that had long been dashed as the area grew grayer and more impoverished. Nando's apartment building did not have that old European flair some buildings sported, with mansard roofs and iron work. Instead, it looked like a box of tissues with squares carved to form windows.

She stood in front of his building and yelled out his name until Nando opened a window on the third floor and lowered a basket with the key. There was no intercom, and inside there was no elevator. You either yelled for someone to open or pounded the door until the super deigned to let you in, if she was around. Montserrat climbed the staircase cursing the cold weather and her aching leg.

Nando received her with a kiss on the cheek and a big smile. He made a show of walking her to the living room, which was clear of junk. The rest of his apartment was filled with carefully labeled boxes containing his merchandise and rolled-up movie posters, or else remained the domain of his mother.

"You want a beer?" he asked, offering an open bottle of Sol that was on the coffee table.

The room was wallpapered with a pattern of flowers, in the style of Nando's mother, who was the one who paid the rent. The old lady didn't allow any redecoration. She did permit Nando to cram a huge TV and a stereo into the living room, although, at this time of the year, the TV was half blocked by a plastic Christmas tree with blinking lights and an excessive amount of tinsel.

"It's a bit early for me."

"I wouldn't know. I was at a tocada in Santa Fe until four a.m. I just woke up."

Nando was only two years younger than Montserrat, but acted like he was fifteen and looked fifty.

"Where's your mom?"

"Off to the market. It's the two of us in the apartment," Nando said with a wink.

A painting of the Santo Niño de Atocha surveyed her from above the couch, where Nando had plopped himself, patting the space next to him. Montserrat pulled up a chair instead.

"How's the job?" he asked.

"Same old story. It's a bit slow this month. I want to pick up my bonus tomorrow, and I'll enjoy the quiet weeks until it picks up again."

What she wanted was for Mario to open the vault and let her grab the film she'd stored there, but the bonus would be as good an excuse as any. She might also be able to guilt Mario into throwing her a bunch of shifts in January. This whole magic business was leaving her life in disarray.

"I heard Mario was cutting hours at Antares, and he chopped a bunch of yours."

"Who told you about the hours at Antares?"

"Lalo Podesta was here a few days ago. We were playing cards. He says Samuel is bringing in a friend to replace you."

"How does he know what Samuel is doing?"

"Lalo loves to gossip."

If Lalo was flapping his mouth there might be some truth to it, but she didn't want to think about that right now, so she shook her head and glared at Nando. "Lalo should mind his own business and so should you. Anyway, I'm not here to discuss my job."

"Why are you here? You're looking nice, Montserrat. I love the thing you did with your hair."

The only thing Montserrat had done with her hair was tie it into a ponytail, but Nando was a horny dog trying to butter her up like a succulent lobster. She'd dodged enough creeps to know how to deal with this one.

"A while back you had a script for sale. It was by Romeo Donderis, and you said it could be authenticated by the writer himself because it was pricey."

"Sure, but that was a while back. It's long gone."

"I'm not interested in the script. I want to know about Donderis. Do you have his phone number or home address?"

"You're going to go see him? Are you trying to cut out the middleman in these transactions? I won't have that. How am I supposed to make a living?" Nando asked, spilling a little of his beer as he set the bottle down.

"What? No. I'm doing research on something."

"Oh? What are you working on?"

Nothing. The plan for a documentary piece was over. Maybe Tristán was correct, maybe they ought to cease their inquiries and pretend they had never heard of Ewers or his movie. But she couldn't look away and must find out who had killed Abel. That she knew, like she knew when a musical cue was about to play on screen. She didn't want to attribute any supernatural qualities to this feeling, but perhaps there was something of that to it. Abel had said once a spell is in motion, it must conclude.

It could also be a run-of-the-mill obsession, simple boredom. The tiresome echoes of her humdrum life that now pushed her to find that frisson of excitement. She felt alert and eager, like she hadn't in a long time.

"It's none of your business," she told Nando.

"When you ask for someone's help you should at least *pretend* to be polite. I thought you were going to buy something, but you're wasting my time," Nando said, scratching at the skin right above the elastic waist of his sweatpants.

Montserrat took a couple of bills from her wallet and slammed them on the table, next to the beer bottle. She didn't have money to be throwing around, but she also didn't want to spend an hour chatting up Nando. "There. Now give me his contact information."

Nando took both bills and stuffed them in his sweatpants' pocket and shrugged. "Beats me."

"You don't know."

"I have no idea," Nando said, shaking his head and taking another swig of beer.

"You fucker. How were you going to get the script authenticated, then?"

"I met the guy when I was selling at El Chopo. He stopped by my stall, I gave him my info. I've bought a few things from him. Lobby cards, other scripts, that kind of stuff. But he's the one who contacts me."

"Give me back my money, you bastard," she said, stretching out a hand and glaring at him.

"You're cute when you're pissed off. If you want to play detective, maybe you should seduce me to get your answer."

"You touch me, I'll kick you in the balls," she said matter-of-factly.

He rolled his eyes. "Fine. If you need him, you could try the coffee shop where I normally meet him. It's always the same place. The Maupassant. They sell crepes, about two blocks from Metro Chilpancingo. I think he's friends with the owners. What's your research about? Golden Age writers?"

"Something of the sort. Does he still write?"

"No. I think he's a copy editor. He has memorabilia from back in the day and sells it from time to time, to pay for a vacation or whatnot. Nice fellow."

"What does he look like?"

"Tall, gray hair, has a beard. Wears a hat. Do you want to look at a new shipment—"

"Thanks," Montserrat said. She quickly stood up, shook Nando's hand, and before he could attempt to give her a kiss on the cheek, hurried outside the apartment. Creep.

"Crush a spider in your left hand," she muttered to herself, wishing she could crush this guy.

The Maupassant was on Minería. It advertised authentic Parisian crepes as well as enchiladas on its windows. Neither offering seemed to be drawing in the crowds. When Montserrat walked in, the place was deserted. The small, white tables had vases with plastic flowers, and the walls were decorated with cheap posters showing the Eiffel Tower and the Arc de Triomphe. A white board announced the weekly special: empanadas de atun a la vizcaína and Nutella crepes for dessert. The woman behind the cash register was watching a small black-and-white TV set. She'd set a glass with a sign that said "tips and donations" on the counter. It only held a couple of coins.

"Sorry to bother you. I'm trying to find a gentleman by the name of Romeo Donderis. He also goes by José López. I was told he knows the owners here."

"The owner's not here today."

"Could I leave my number? He could call me back."

"You can leave it, but I don't know when he'll be coming in," the woman said with a shrug.

Montserrat wrote her number on a napkin and handed it over. "Hey, can I look through your Yellow Pages?"

"I suppose. Come behind the counter."

Montserrat did. The Yellow Pages were next to a battered Garfield phone with the cat's pupils rubbed out. Montserrat opened the second volume, looked under "Publishers" for Ediciones B. But it wasn't listed. Marisa had said Clarimonde Bauer had run into financial issues, so maybe the company had gone out of business. Still, she remembered the address printed in the book. It was downtown.

"Do you have change for a bill?"

"What do you think this is, a bank?"

Montserrat took out a bill and stuffed it in the glass for tips. She handed another bill to the woman, who frowned but gave her the coins she needed.

Montserrat thanked the woman. The creperie employee waved her away and went back to watching television.

At the corner there was a public telephone, its plastic shell defaced with crude graffiti. She tossed in a coin and dialed the number for Tristán's pager. After all, he did say he would keep it clipped on and wanted to be informed of what she was up to. She left a message with the address she was going to and indicated she'd stop by his apartment that night.

Montserrat took the subway to Bellas Artes and bought a map from a newspaper kiosk a few paces from the station's exit, and after consulting it walked around the Alameda, avoiding the vendors who occupied it this time of year, offering to take pictures of the kids with Santa Claus or the Three Kings for a modest sum of money. She dodged pedestrians and peddlers of plastic trinkets, ignored decorations of giant artificial poinsettias hanging from buildings and signs advertising romeritos con mole, and followed her map down a small net of streets filled with ancient gray buildings.

The building that corresponded to Ediciones B was a turn-of-the-century construction with very tall, narrow windows that had been boarded up. A frieze with flower shapes ran above the windows, and the cornice was also decorated with floral motifs. Two wooden double doors were locked with a large chain and a padlock. The wall by the door was plastered with a sign that had been painted over with so much graffiti you could not read what it said, though it was obvious it had once spelled the word "condemned." Now only the letter "c" was clearly visible.

The building in front of Ediciones B was a toy store or kids' clothing store. It had a sign that said "Pingos" in colorful letters, but its steel shutters were rolled down. The street was quiet, with no street vendors or nosy neighbors to watch her. Montserrat decided to take a chance and reached into her purse, pulling out the two paper clips she had used to open Abel's apartment, and went to work on the padlock.

It was exceedingly simple to figure out its mechanism, and after looking both ways and making sure no one was watching her, she removed the chain and pushed one of the doors open, slipping inside.

The lobby of the building was impressively vast, and then came a flowing wrought-iron staircase and behind it a long hallway. The interior was half in shadows. She walked past the staircase, following the hallway, and reached what must have been a ballroom at one point. It was now an expanse of dust and darkness, a chandelier glinting and catching a stray ray of light as she poked her head inside. It was empty.

Montserrat changed directions and went back to the staircase, ascending it with a hand firmly on the banister. Darkness gave way to light as she reached the second floor; they had not bothered boarding up the windows at that level, and although it was getting late, light still streamed in, making it easy to find her way. She walked into offices that had a desk or two, or a chair that lay upturned, like cargo that had spilled from a shipwreck and been left abandoned on a lonesome beach.

A couple of windowpanes on this floor were broken. Rain had filtered in through the years, licking the floorboards and staining the walls. Pigeons had also drifted inside, nesting in filing cabinets. There were droppings on tables. A few of the birds, startled as she walked into a room, flew away. But others remained, eyeing her from above empty bookcases.

She stumbled onto a series of bluelines, tucked in dusty drawers, and opened boxes that had been piled in a corner. She pulled out a copy of *The House of Infinite Wisdom* and gazed at its familiar first page with the vegvísir.

Alma was right. Clarimonde Bauer had kept reprinting her lover's book.

On the third and top floor she paused in front of a bathroom without a door—it had been pulled off; only the hinges marked its passing—to rub her leg. A tap could be heard dripping, the sound of the water echoing against the white tiles.

She kept looking, opened more doors or poked her head into abandoned offices. In one room there was a calendar that said "1985" and a metal filing cabinet. She pulled at a drawer and found dusty invoices from years past. That office had an interconnecting door with another room, and when she opened it, she found herself in what must have been Clarimonde Bauer's office. At least, it was her photograph hanging on the wall, behind a desk.

Montserrat approached it, looking up at the face of the young girl she had seen in pictures, now sliding into middle age. She opened a drawer and found business cards bearing the address of Ediciones B. She chanced upon an old invitation for a party organized by Clarimonde, printed on ivory cardstock with an address in Las Lomas. She pocketed the invitation and looked in other drawers, but they only yielded stationery and envelopes. Montserrat exited the room and went back to the hallway.

When she passed by the bathroom it was quiet.

Montserrat froze in her tracks. The sound of water dripping, which had been so evident minutes before, had vanished. It was as if someone had closed the tap, or something was muffling the noise.

She took a step back and stood in the doorway of the bathroom. Light streamed through a frosted glass window, and the mirrors above the sinks reflected tiles, peeling walls, the bathroom stalls. The ordinary sights one would expect.

But on the mirror closest to the window, she saw a shadow that had the curious shape of a man. Just a shadow that gave the impression of someone in a trench coat, standing in profile. It could have been a trick of the light, an object reflected across the bathroom. Except then the shadow shifted, a silver spark rippling across the glass, reminiscent of a flash frame.

The silence strained her senses, making her wince.

It was a silence she recognized, that she'd met back in Abel's apartment, and which had threatened to burst her eardrums and now seemed to encase her in a velvet softness.

Montserrat reached into her purse and clutched the napkin that she'd smeared with her blood. Her throat was dry, and her heart was pounding. She was afraid of moving, of walking down the hallway, because if she turned she'd see *something* behind her, but in front of her there was the bathroom with its mirrors that held within them impossible reflections.

You should never be afraid of magic. That's what she had told Tristán. Fear gives others power over you. But her hands were trembling.

"Leave me," she told the silence, mouthing the words, although she could hardly hear them, and made herself turn around and hurry down the hallway.

She reached the stairs and began her descent, moving carefully, rapidly, yet without running. She had the impression that something was following her, something that moved with a quiet, liquid ease, and left no echoes as they descended the stairs. Something that she could not see, but only feel, although, as she reached the second landing, there in the corner of her eye—the edge of something. A coat. The flap of a loose belt, perhaps, trailing on the floor.

But there was nothing, no one.

"Leave me," she repeated, the handkerchief clutched in her left hand. She gripped it so tightly she was afraid she'd cut off the circulation to her fingers.

Montserrat could see the doorway now, and the feeling that someone was coming behind her only intensified as she reached the last few steps. But ahead of her, the lobby was onyx dark. A vault.

She hesitated, her fingers feeling the cool ironwork of the banister, and contemplated that darkness that seemed to silently breathe and heave before her. Awaiting her. A trap of silk and gloom.

Nevertheless, that was the only way out. To ascend the steps again would only mean to retreat into the soundless heights of the building, and toward that presence that chased her like a disembodied shadow.

Montserrat swallowed and closed her eyes, forcing herself to take a step.

She thought, as her foot reached down, that the someone behind her was about to lean down and whisper against her ear, breath brushing the back of her neck.

Montserrat.

But no. Those were her frazzled nerves. It was still quiet in the building. Even her steps were soundless. She breathed in dust and dampness, felt sweat trickle down her forehead, heard nothing.

The silence was like silk, toying with her, wrapping tight around her body after allowing one quiet, muffled noise to reach her ears: the tinkle of a circular pendant, nestled against folds of clothing. Vegvísir. That Which Shows the Way.

Someone slipped closer, creeped up behind her and gripped her hand. Taut fingers encased her own.

She stumbled and almost lost her footing as she reached the ground floor, but she was holding on to the banister and gritted her teeth before opening her eyes and shouting.

"Leave me!"

The echo of her voice across the lobby was a slap, reverberating within the building. Somewhere, pigeons batted their wings and flew up and away. The silence drifted up, too, like smoke escaping a chimney. It was gone.

Montserrat whirled around. Behind her, on the staircase, there was no one, and the lonesome hallway on the ground level was also empty. The lobby was dark, but it was the usual darkness of old buildings and enclosed spaces.

She yanked the front door open and stepped out into the street, colliding with a wild-eyed Tristán. The collar of his shirt was smeared with blood.

17

Tristán had hoped he'd be able to duck out of Dorotea's apartment and meet up with Montserrat downtown, at the address she'd pinpointed as the offices of Ediciones B. But he now doubted that would happen anytime soon. He'd already asked Dorotea twice how long this might go on and had received no real answers. Instead, Dorotea had palmed his cheek and offered him a diet soda.

He supposed he should have been grateful to Dorotea for organizing a full-fledged photo shoot, with makeup artists, a hairdresser, wardrobe, and all manner of assistants coming and going, rather than handing out an old file photo. But he was feeling rather tired. All this attention, coming after years of indifference and neglect, was like gorging on sweets. He was overwhelmed and nervous as a boy who had never stood before a camera lens.

It didn't help matters that he hated the clothes Dorotea had picked for him. He had thought to have his photo taken in a suit or a tasteful turtleneck, but Dorotea had brought costumes in the style of the soap he was going to star in. It was a riff on *The Count of Monte Cristo*, a historical melodrama where the ladies would wear anachronistic dresses that showed too much boob and Tristán would be stuffed into slim, dark suits with cravats at the throat. Tristán's role demanded a long, Fabio-like mane of hair. Tristán's hair was cropped short, which meant they'd brought wigs.

The photographer regarded him with a critically raised eyebrow and declared he wanted an "Eduardo Palomo as Juan del Diablo" look, not whatever the fuck was going on with that rat's nest on his head. Off came the wig they had given him and on came a different one.

Tristán had never acted in a period piece. His soaps were contemporary Cinderella tales, stories of country girls who moved to the big city and caught the eye of millionaires. Or else sickly sweet ensemble teenage dramas. He played fresh-faced playboys and heirs to enormous fortunes. Karina had served as his perfect foil. She had that upbeat look and sassy smile that made for good posters.

He wasn't even sure he could pull period garb off. Some people had faces that were too modern. You couldn't imagine Bibi Gaytán as a French courtesan.

"I thought you said this was a sure thing," Tristán muttered.

"Soda, darling?" Dorotea replied.

"I'd like to smoke a cigarette."

"The photographer doesn't smoke, darling."

"And? I do."

"You should stop. It'll stain your teeth."

"So will Coca-Cola," he said, pushing away the can of soda Dorotea's assistant was trying to wave in his face. He moved to the side, pulling Dorotea with him by the arm. "This feels like a casting call."

Dorotea daintily drank her diet soda with a short straw. "You know very well a casting wouldn't be taking place at my apartment."

"Then?"

"I told you. The director wants to be sure. We must show him you're still looking presentable. Anyway, once you do a reading and with these photos, it will be a done deal. I've been told we can even use the pictures for the announcement in *De Telenovela*, once it goes through. When was the last time you had a double spread?"

"Not in ages, but I don't have the role yet, and I've never had to pull any of these stunts to land a part."

"Last time you landed parts you weren't close to forty with a bit of gray in your hair," Dorotea said with a chilling finality. "Smoking also fucks with your skin, Tristán. You could use a little less nicotine and a bit more humility."

The wig they'd put on his head itched. Tristán excused himself and headed to the bathroom. He simply stood there, arms folded, contemplating Dorotea's black shower curtain with its gold starbursts and the black tiles on the walls.

Tristán removed the wig and looked at himself in the mirror, which was fancifully surrounded by light bulbs like something an actress would

employ when applying her makeup. He paid close attention to his left
eye. The stark, unrelenting lights around the mirror did not flatter him.

He ran a nail underneath the scar, pulling at the skin, smoothing away
the small wrinkles. He smiled at his reflection, showing his teeth. At least
constant dental treatments had kept those in good shape. There were no
stains, no matter what Dorotea said.

Tristán smoothed his cravat with a sigh, thinking about his first roles,
the days when he made the lists of Top Teen Idols. He thought about the
time Karina had posed with him for the cover of *De Telenovela*. He even
remembered the headline: "Karina Junco and Tristán Abascal reveal who
was their first kiss." Karina's first kiss was her neighbor, the son of an
industrialist who graced the society pages. Tristán invented a high school
girlfriend, even though he had not dated anyone seriously. He'd been too
focused on his modeling work and the acting classes. His first kiss had
been during a gig for a fotonovela. He'd turned bright red. It had been
embarrassing. So he'd made up a story of a girl and a romantic date.

His whole biography, as narrated by the magazines, was a lie anyway.
It never mentioned the Abaids, nor the neighborhood where he grew
up. It erased those cheesy photo shoots and replaced them with talks of
a miraculous discovery at a discotheque where Tristán had been spotted
by a talent scout.

Karina's biography had also been a sham. She was sold as a "good
girl," the kind who might go dancing on the weekend, but was waiting for
Mr. Right; a girl who longed for marriage and motherhood. But Karina
threw epic tantrums, outdrank men twice her size, and had more drugs
in her purse than a pharmacy. He'd dug that about her; her wildness and
unpredictability were what had attracted him in the first place. Her sense
of humor, sexiness, and wiles completed the picture. None of that made
it into the specials about her death. She was treated like a vestal virgin.

He supposed the inventors of plastic stars would craft an equally false
narrative for him for his triumphant comeback.

*Tristán Abascal, who has spent the last few years focused on traveling
the world, has decided to take up the mantle of actor once more. "I went
into an early retirement because I felt overwhelmed by the impositions of*

fame and I needed to find myself. But acting is in my blood," he said. The handsome actor hasn't been entirely removed from show business, and has dipped his toes into the world of TV dubbing.

Yeah, he could recite the whole puff piece already, even though it had yet to be written. They'd have to mention Karina, but that would be in the fifth paragraph, and there would be a heartfelt quote about her talent and sad death, without any gory details of the car crash. His substance abuse issues would be airbrushed away.

Tristán splashed water on his face and watched it go down the drain. He closed the tap and lifted his head, turning toward the towel rack. A sound came from the shower: the light tinkling of a curtain rod.

Tristán stood still and breathed in. He wanted to leave, he did. The sound, ordinary and commonplace, made him shiver. Yet he remained rooted to the spot, his eyes glued to the black plastic curtain with golden starbursts. It reminded him of a body bag. Yes, you could picture the outline of a body wrapped in black plastic.

The curtain rippled. It pulsated. Like a vein, or a living thing, like it was breathing. He had the sensation that he was moving forward, even as dread held him in place, even as the curtain was yanked aside by a hand, making the curtain rings rattle against the rod.

The shower curtain fell to the ground: an insect molting.

Karina stood in the shower, her clothes askew. He might have recognized her by the gold locket with the "K" around her neck, or her hair, or even by the simple fact Karina had been the only ghost he'd ever seen in his life. But instead, it was the low sob she let out that made him whisper her name.

She stood there, her head tipped down. Her lips moved without uttering words; she was a fish gasping for air, and then came that horrible gurgling noise that was seared into his mind as blood began to pour down her mouth, staining her chin.

The lights in the bathroom were as bright as they had been seconds before, yet the quality of the light seemed different to him. He would not have been surprised if the bathroom had suddenly been drenched in ghastly reds and blues.

He was trembling wildly. Tristán reached for the sink, attempting to steady himself. He thought he might faint.

Then Karina lifted her head and looked at him. Her eyes were terribly dark. Not the dark brown he remembered, but the black of a starless night. Black like a raven's wing. The eyes did not see him. They were fixed on something else, something far away.

He feared to make any movement, thinking it would attract her attention. He also felt oddly tired and out of breath. His stomach churned. Yet even though he remained frozen in place, she stepped forward, moving toward him. Her hands, which had been closed by her side into tight fists, now opened and dropped glass fragments onto the floor. They crunched as she stepped on them, slicing her feet, making them bleed.

Tristán found the strength to turn around and run.

In his terror he smashed his face against the locked door. Pain blinded him, and he let out a hoarse cry. He felt the blood sliding down his nose, staining his lips, and his eyes were tearing up from the pain. He closed them and managed to find the door handle by touch alone, yanking it open and stumbling out into the hallway. His hands brushed against picture frames hanging from the wall as he tried to steady himself.

"Tristán!" Dorotea said.

He opened his eyes and realized she was standing a few paces from him, together with the photographer. They both stared at Tristán.

"A no-nosebleed," he stammered. "I have a nosebleed."

"Let's head back into the bathroom."

"No! Not the bathroom."

"Tristán! Where else—"

"I should go," he said. "I feel shitty."

"Okay, look, fine, get out of that costume before you stain it with blood," Dorotea said, reaching into the bathroom and handing him a towel, which he pressed against his face. She pushed him toward her bedroom, where he'd left his regular clothes.

Tristán changed as quickly as he could. His hands were still shaking, and he had a hard time with the buttons of his dress shirt; in his haste he smeared the collar with blood. He was putting on his jacket when Dorotea knocked and opened the door, looking at him with a severe face.

"You said you were clean, Tristán."

"I'm not on anything," he replied, running a hand through his hair. The nosebleed had finally stopped. The terror remained, his stomach an uncomfortable knot, and he knew despite his protestations Dorotea must be thinking he was now into even worse stuff than before. "I should go. We can finish the shoot another day."

Dorotea did not reply. Or if she did, he did not hear her over the roaring in his ears. He had the beginning of a headache, and his nose still ached brutally. He put on his sunglasses, hailed a cab, and went in search of Montserrat.

18

The shock of seeing Tristán's face gave way to relief. Tristán steadied Montserrat and wrapped his arms around her. "Dear God, Momo," he said. "I didn't think I'd find you."

Montserrat clutched him tight and let out a sigh. Her mouth felt dry. "What are you doing here?" she asked.

"You left a message."

Did she? Montserrat could hardly remember what she'd done earlier that day. The building had left her with trembling hands and a quickly beating heart. She took a deep breath, glanced at the doorway behind her as if making sure nothing or no one had stepped outside. Then she took his hand and pulled him down the street. "Come on, let's go. I saw something weird in there."

"You too? Well, I guess trauma comes better in pairs."

"What do you mean?"

"I saw Karina again."

Montserrat turned a corner, unsure where they were headed. She walked quickly despite the pain in her leg. "What, at your apartment?"

"No. I was at a shoot. A ruined shoot now. I messed up."

"What was she doing?"

"I don't know . . . she was standing there. Dead and standing there."

She gave him a side glance. "The blood—"

"Mine. I banged my nose. And the damn shoot! Fuck! Everyone is going to say I'm doing LSD, crack, and cocaine all at once. Just you wait. I won't blame them if they do, either."

"They won't fire you, Tristán."

He snickered. "They haven't even hired me. Enough is enough, let's hail a cab, head to the Mercado de Sonora, pay for a limpia—"

"You think that's going to work?"

Tristán paused, pushing his expensive sunglasses up the bridge of his nose. "No. You're right. We burn all of Ewers's things, we get a limpia, and then we pretend we never heard of the man."

She stopped and stared at him. Burn them! The thought outraged her, but before she could say a word, Tristán was speaking again and raising a hand, trying to attract the attention of a taxi that was headed their way. "It's the only way to handle this, Momo. We forget about all this shit and burn it, and then burn the ashes, too."

She pulled his arm down and pulled him with her, across the street. "Are you kidding? I'm not letting you touch Ewers's book."

"Why the hell not? We throw gasoline on it and burn it in an alley."

"It's not going to solve anything!"

"How do you know?"

"Because I've been reading. Look, I made a protective charm," she said, taking out the napkin and showing it to him.

Tristán grabbed the napkin from her hands and inspected it. "You know, that's the problem. You're getting too involved in this abracadabra crap."

"Someone has to try and figure it out."

"You don't know the first thing about witchcraft."

She didn't like the tone he was using. It reminded her of her co-workers and her boss at Antares who were constantly underestimating her.

"Yes, I do," she said. "Ewers wrote it in his book, and I can tell you that you don't stop a hex by pretending it didn't happen."

"So we are cursed?"

"Ewers talks a lot about cycles, circuits, things that are interconnected to each other. That's why he loved movies. They were an endless loop. Magic, trapped forever and forever spinning through a projector. Magic fixed in time and space with silver."

"It's a simple question. Are we cursed?"

"Not quite. I don't think so."

"See! You don't know anything!" Tristán said and he raised and dropped his arms dramatically in the air.

"For fuck's sake, I'm trying to be honest with you. I don't know exactly what's going on, but Clarimonde Bauer and José López might, and we are going to find them. I have no idea where he is, but I have her address."

"Sure, Montserrat. Let's walk into the house of a witch and ask her about the ex-leader of her cult. You know what, you go alone. I'll head to the market," Tristán said, and he took two steps back from her.

Montserrat couldn't help herself. She did not try to contain her words—they came out fast and furious. "You fucking coward! I knew I couldn't count on you. You always leave me alone!"

"What are you talking about? I'm here, no? Even after I saw my dead girlfriend in the shower."

Montserrat crossed her arms and shook her head with a scoff. Tristán took off his sunglasses and pointed at her with them. "What?" he asked, exasperated.

"You always leave, you do. You find a new fling and off you go, merrily forgetting I exist, and then you come back six months later once that's done and you need attention. You're never there when *I* need *you*."

"Oh, okay. We're going to quarrel about my love life again?"

"You lousy bastard, you stupid   "

"I'm the smart one. You're the one who wants to investigate all this paranormal crap! Did you sleep through all the horror movies we rented?"

"We're part of Ewers's spell now. You don't undo a spell by pretending it was never cast. Fear is not going to help us."

"Fear is a natural reaction to seeing ghosts."

"It doesn't matter if it's natural. Fear gives a magician power over their rivals. It's reflected back at you, like looking into a mirror."

Tristán shoved the napkin back into her hands. "You have no idea what I've been through. I saw Karina, with blood dripping down her body. I'm not going to star in this episode of *Bewitched* for you."

Montserrat stuffed the napkin in her pocket. "You didn't ask what I saw in the building."

"What?"

"Back there, you didn't ask what I saw. You don't care. It's the Tristán show, twenty-four hours a day, seven days a week."

"What did you see? Your German boyfriend?"

"You're an asshole."

"I'm asking because you're awfully fond of his writing and ideas. Oh, look here and look there, Ewers this and Ewers that," he said in singsong. "Maybe you have a schoolgirl crush. God knows you have a tendency for those."

Montserrat opened her mouth in shock. Tristán meant her crush on *him*. Of all the low blows to throw, that was the lowest one. Sure, when they were young she knew the other kids made fun of her for it. Montserrat, trailing like a dog behind Tristán. But Tristán had never said anything about it. Until now.

"Fuck you, Tristán," she said, giving him the finger.

"Very mature, Montserrat."

She lifted her other hand, now holding up two fingers, before turning around and walking away from him. Tristán did not follow her. She heard him huff and his steps moving in the opposite direction.

Montserrat made it back to her apartment without any delay. Ewers's book and letter and her notes on his work were on the desk where she'd left them. Angrily, she pried the book open. It landed on the chapter called "The Opener of the Way," with its drawing of the great eye in the heavens.

"I'm not reading you," she told the book and headed into her bedroom, but it was too early to slip into bed. She stepped back into her office and riffled through the vinyl records and CD cases. She pulled out videotapes from the shelf where they were lined up—*The Keep, Lifeforce, Little Shop of Horrors*—then returned them to their place. Irritated, she stomped back to the desk.

"For fuck's sake," she muttered and leaned over the book, her hand sliding down the page.

Magic is the alchemy of soul and desire, the rarest of fusions. You can dig into the earth and find hundreds of pebbles, but diamonds are scarce. Equally rare is the Opener of the Way, the sorcerer that may rise above all other sorcerers, his willpower so mighty that he may control all aspects of magic. Recall the words Nietzsche spoke: "You must be ready to burn yourself in your own flame; how could you rise anew if you have not first become ashes." The truest form of sorcery requires the sacrifice of the self. Transmutation: it is the key to the highest echelons of existence.

When Montserrat had first looked at *The House of Infinite Wisdom* she had not understood what Ewers meant, but now she thought he was talking about his suicide, which would have resulted in a rebirth.

"Didn't quite work out, did it, buddy?" she muttered. "But you must have had a backup procedure. I would."

She turned the pages, looking at the section where Ewers discussed hexes. She considered Abel's idea that the reason behind his bad luck had been the fact that the movie had not been completed. That the dubbing had not taken place in that third scene. That might have been the case. Perhaps Ewers had embedded a curse into that film, something that demanded completion or else a web of bad luck was activated. In theory, then, their dubbing should have completed the circuit, negated any curse. But what if the cycle was not concluded with the dubbing? What if there was yet another step?

Ewers's book did not provide more information about what had to be done. Clarimonde Bauer might know. Or else José López. They had been privy to Ewers's preparations for resurrection, and they might have understood the shape his curse would take, should anyone interfere with his plans, and how to truly finalize this spell.

Was there no other way to avoid Ewers's curse? Must completion be the only answer? They were now part of Ewers's magic workings, unintentionally perhaps, but this was a fact. What to do, then? She had theories and no solid answers.

The next morning, she went to Antares. Candy smiled at her tiredly when she asked if the checks for their bonus were ready to be picked up.

"You'll have to talk to Samuel," she said.

Montserrat frowned, but the receptionist picked up the phone and called Samuel, who promptly came to greet her. The sterile reception with all its mirrors multiplied his reflection.

"Montserrat, how's it going?"

"It's going fine, but I was looking for Mario. I figured our bonus would be ready, and I wanted to pick up a film I left in the vault."

"Mario is not in the city. He left two days ago. His mom is sick."

"You didn't think to tell me?"

"I phoned to say you didn't have shifts this month but said you were still invited to the party and that we'd talk about the bonus. You never phoned back."

Montserrat huffed and stared at Samuel. "Okay, do you have the keys to vault two?"

"No. You know he keeps those with him. I don't have the checks, either, before you start asking."

"That sneaky bastard! I bet he's trying to get out of paying us on time! Or did he cut them? Are we all out of bonuses?"

"I don't think so."

"Then why didn't he leave the checks behind?"

Samuel shrugged. What did he care? Mario was treating him as his right-hand man now, so he probably had been paid without a hitch. Montserrat would have questioned him about Mario's exact coordinates, except she already knew it was a futile endeavor. She should have guessed Mario would pull a stunt like this. He'd hole himself up at an all-inclusive resort and reappear in January, phoning Montserrat when he needed her and delivering her money four weeks late. It probably helped him balance the books.

"Come to the Christmas party," Samuel said. "It'll be fun."

"I don't know when that is."

"The seventeenth. Look, I did phone you to tell you about the party."

"Well, I didn't get the fucking message," she snapped at him. "And I'm not interested in your gift exchange, I want shifts. I have seniority here. Why am I being placed at the bottom of the list for jobs? And why are you bringing in a friend to take my shifts?"

That seemed to catch Samuel by surprise, and it was his startled eyes that made her realize the rumors were true and she was not on the way out of Antares: she had basically been shoved out the door already. "Montserrat, let's get a coffee. I do want to get you shifts for Jan—"

"You're a snake."

Samuel frowned. "Have a merry Christmas," he said and walked back the way he came. Montserrat gritted her teeth, wishing she hadn't gone off and knowing she had ruined any chance of nabbing a check before the new year. She'd ruined the next year, too.

The receptionist gave Montserrat a shake of the head. "I can't blame you. Mario didn't even order turkeys for everyone this year. What a loser, right?"

"Yeah, right," Montserrat said. She didn't care about the turkey, but she did mourn the lack of extra money; 1994 was going to begin on a downward spiral.

As she walked, clutching her leather jacket closed with one hand, she wondered what Ewers would have done in such a situation. The spell with the spider wouldn't have been enough, that was a tiny hex, a minuscule jolt of power. He would have conjured something bigger, something more complicated. At the very least she found his ambition admirable. Big: he thought big, aimed high.

He would have told her to burn it all, trace runes of fire.

"Fuck Antares," she whispered. "Fuck them all."

Montserrat drove back to her neighborhood, left the car at the garage, and walked the one block to her building. Sitting outside her front door, twirling his sunglasses, was Tristán. When she stopped in front of him, he stood up. He had two plastic bags with him. His smile was sheepish.

"I went to the market," he said.

Montserrat frowned, but held the front door open for him, and they walked up the stairs to her apartment. Once inside, he placed the bags on the table and began taking his purchases out.

Montserrat looked at the candles and packages curiously, reading the cheesy, garish labels with exotic names out loud. "Jinx Removing Powder, Black Chicken Soap for Spiritual Cleansing, Authentic Hunchback Oil."

"I didn't know what to buy, so I figured more is better, right?"

"Venus Soap for Attractiveness," she said, showing him the crude rectangle of soap wrapped in pink paper. The label had the picture of a naked woman.

"They threw that one in for free. It's for me."

She laughed. "Of course. Not that you would need it."

"Well, Dorotea did say I'm getting a bit old."

"Nonsense. You're beautiful and talented," she said, taking out two red envelopes with crosses printed on them and adding them to the pile of objects.

"You should be my new publicist," he said, winking at her.

She scoffed, but the sound carried no real exasperation. He was being a clown, but she could deal with that.

"I didn't mean to upset you yesterday. It's . . . this stuff is dangerous," he said, pointing at Ewers's book, which lay on the table. She'd been reading it at breakfast. "And you can get a bit obsessed with things."

"I'm not—"

"It's not a bad thing. That's why you're such a good sound engineer. Because you are methodical and careful, because when you have a problem, you don't throw your hands up and give up. I've seen you work way into the night trying to get a sound mix right. It's great. But I see some of those same dynamics at play here."

"Don't lecture me about compulsions," she said, pulling out a chair and grabbing one of the red envelopes and shaking it, making its contents rattle. "I mean, you of all people."

"Me, yes. Who else?" he replied, pulling out a chair in turn and sitting next to her. "Because I care, okay?"

Montserrat nodded. She dropped the envelope and folded her hands in her lap, looking down, not glancing at him.

"I'm scared, Momo. Real scared."

"I know. Doesn't mean you should be such a dick."

"Doesn't mean you should be a dick to me either, yet here we are."

Tristán bumped his shoe with hers. Like they did when they were kids, telegraphing their thoughts, grinning as they planned mischief in his mother's kitchen. He smiled. It was such a warm and friendly smile; the first time she'd seen it she'd been infatuated with him. A second was all it took.

"What time are we going to see Clarimonde Bauer?" he asked.

"I didn't mean . . . you don't have to go with me, Tristán."

"What else do I have to do? It's not like my phone is ringing off the hook with calls from producers."

"You were right. It could be dangerous."

"Oh? Did you find something else in that book?"

"Well, no. Not really."

"Then we'll go—oh, shit," Tristán said. His beeper had gone off. He unclipped it from his belt and checked the message. "Can I use your phone?"

"Sure."

He promptly picked up the receiver and dialed. Montserrat ventured into the kitchen to fetch a glass of water and give him a little privacy. When she came back, he was standing looking thoughtful in the middle of the living room.

"Was that about the photo shoot?"

"No. It was Marisa Montero. She said she wants to meet with me this evening. She's worried about her aunt. I said I'd see her at a restaurant near her home. Somewhere public sounded like the best idea. I don't trust her. Could be she slices me with a machete like she's Jason Voorhees's mom if no one's looking. Sluts like me always get killed midway through the picture."

"How would you know? You closed your eyes all through *Friday the 13th*, you coward."

"I kept them open when people were getting naked."

"Liar."

"What, were you watching me?"

"Only when you flinched."

"That would be ninety percent of the movie," he said, but he did it with a laugh, and she shook her head, smiling back at him.

"You'll require a charm. I'll show you how to make one."

"A charm?" he asked blankly.

"We need a handkerchief."

"What about all the stuff I bought? Won't any of that help?"

She looked at the candles, powders, and soaps Tristán had brought with him. "No. You can't buy magic for twenty pesos and expect it to work."

"Does Ewers say that?"

He did, and he said plenty more. She'd found a certain comfort in the pages from his book. She liked the idea of systematization; an orderly world appealed to her nature. She could understand his methodic outlook—and there was a method to it, it was only that at first she'd been unable to grasp it. Tristán blossomed in chaos, but Montserrat liked control. Zeroing in on the details, looking at life through a macro lens. Ewers shared this tendency.

"Something like that. Magic is willpower made tangible," she explained. "You must immerse yourself in it, so to speak. The warding charm I made is easy enough. Prick your finger and draw a rune. Or well, a word, I guess."

"What is it, a rune or a word?" he asked, frowning.

"Ewers used runes, but I used words. I think you could use a stick figure and it might work."

"Isn't that like changing ingredients in recipes? Why would it work?"

"Why not? Don't you personalize recipes? Give them your own touch?"

"Sure, but *you* don't cook. When you do, it's ghastly. Except for the meatballs," he said, spinning one of the soaps he had bought between his hands.

"Be serious, Tristán."

"I am serious."

"The runes meant something personal to Ewers. But they don't mean anything to us. They were his secret code."

"Like what, like when we invented our own language in the fourth grade?" Tristán asked, tipping his chair back.

Montserrat stared at him. "What?"

"Don't tell me you forgot. We invented our own language so we could pass messages back and forth. It was fine until Miss Mireles caught us sending each other notes and gave us detention. We spent one month sitting outside the principal's office, writing down 'I will pay attention in class' in our notebooks."

Of course. They'd always played like this. At one point, they'd gotten hold of a pair of walkie-talkies and tried to talk to each other at night.

"Do you remember any of the alphabet we invented?"

"Sure, some, I guess," Tristán said, scratching his head. "Why would that be useful?"

"Because that was our language, yours and mine alone. Same as the runes were Ewers's. Here," she said, tearing out a piece of paper from the notebook she'd been using and handing him a pen. "Write something."

"All right. Um . . . there."

Montserrat looked at the letters he'd scribbled in blue ink. It was a crude, silly alphabet. A half-moon represented the "t" and a square with an X in the middle was the letter "m." They hadn't used it for ages. But she could still read it.

"Tristán and Montserrat," he said, tapping the page. "And we abbreviate it . . . here. You and me, like that."

Their initials. They'd carved that into their chairs at school and doodled it on random bits of paper, signing off their messages this way. The half-moon, filled in, and the square with the X. A line beneath each symbol served as a rudimentary flourish. It was the first signature they ever drew. The code for me and you.

"Okay, write the word 'shield,'" she said.

19

The restaurant Marisa Montero selected was a Spanish venue close to her home. Montserrat parked across the street and stayed behind the wheel, as if she were the driver of a getaway vehicle. Tristán felt more Cantinflas than James Bond, despite his sharp outfit. The vision of Karina remained fresh in his mind. He couldn't shake it off and had smoked two cigarettes before they parked and he stepped out. The charm he'd made, following Montserrat's instructions, lay heavy in his pocket.

Montserrat had been correct. He was not the right person to conduct interrogations. But they'd both decided maybe this time his charisma might be more effective than Montserrat's bluntness. Besides, Marisa had called him and made no mention of having Montserrat at their meeting.

Tristán straightened his jacket and stepped into the joint. It was the kind of place that sold overpriced cabrito al horno and imported wines. Marisa had a table at the back. The lighting in the restaurant, or perhaps the makeup she wore that evening, did her no favors. He'd thought her fiftyish when they'd first met, but now he calculated she was edging close to sixty. The blouse she wore was a pale blue, the shoulder pads on her navy suit jacket were quite large, like something Joan Crawford would have worn in her heyday. Or else it was the power suit women used to favor a few years before when the look had come back in vogue.

She had a martini already and was smoking a cigarette.

"I'm not late, am I?" he asked. His voice was perfectly poised, despite his nerves.

"Not at all. Just on time. I like a man who's prompt."

Marisa raised her hand, summoning the waiter with a casual motion of the wrist. Tristán asked for mineral water. He was still trying to steer clear of alcohol.

"You do smoke, don't you?" she asked, opening her silver cigarette case and offering him a slim cigarette.

"I'm trying to quit my vices."

"But I like a man with some vices."

"Prompt, but with vices, then? What a combo."

She smiled. Tristán mimicked the gesture. This part was easy. He could flirt with his eyes bandaged and both hands tied behind his back. It had been helpful, back when he'd started. He caught the eye of men and women alike. Maybe it wasn't fair, but he had secured his first few gigs like that. Flirting and sleeping his way through the auditions. It felt a bit cheap, now, and Karina had never had to do that. She was quality goods, she came from the top. A father who was a producer, a mother who was a former movie star. He, on the other hand, was a nobody who got lucky. Until the luck ran out.

"I'm glad you came alone," Marisa said. "Your friend is a little rough around the edges."

"Montserrat is very dedicated to her work," he replied, toying with the menu. The special of the month was bacalao, a necessary element for the December festivities. He felt hungry but at the same time did not want to order any food, not with someone he didn't know. He'd suddenly become superstitious, afraid of people slipping poison into his food or cursing it. It was the reason why he wouldn't take one of her cigarettes, either. Who knew what could be rolled inside it.

"Documentaries must be awfully complicated projects. How long have you been working on this one?"

"We only knew Abel a short while."

"It's a pity, his passing," Marisa said, but her tone was flat. Polite, but with no warmth. Announcers spoke like that when they read the news. "Well, I wanted to thank you for meeting with me on such short notice. I talked to my aunt earlier today. She wants to know if you have any of Ewers's things. Your friend, she mentioned that she'd read *The House of Infinite Wisdom*."

"Abel let Montserrat read a copy of that."

"Does she still have it?"

Tristán was a decent actor, and now he was sliding into the part, so he gave Marisa a shrug that looked perfectly innocent. "I don't think so."

"Perhaps you have something else that belongs to Ewers. Items you might be utilizing for your research. If that's the case, I'd like to buy them off you."

According to Montserrat, Alma Montero had ordered Abel to give her Ewers's film and other possessions before he was murdered. But Marisa had denied the two of them had been in touch recently.

"Why do you want them?"

"It's my aunt who wants them. She wants to destroy any artifacts connected to that movie they worked on."

"Is that so?"

Marisa rested an elbow on the table and leaned forward. "Yesterday I saw one of Ewers's runes near my home. My aunt believes his cult is more active than ever, and more dangerous."

He might have grimaced, but the waiter arrived at that moment and set a glass of mineral water in front of Tristán. He glanced down, glad for the brief interruption, and looked back at Marisa.

"I don't understand."

"My aunt suspects Abel did something. He cast a spell. And it's made Ewers's old acolytes restless."

"But why does she want to destroy Ewers's things?"

"The same reason why she burned his film all those years ago: Ewers was a dangerous man. Perhaps he still is."

The present tense Marisa utilized did not sit well with him. He thought of Montserrat back in the car, all alone, with sorcerers lurking around dark corners. He debated getting up and leaving immediately, but he stayed still. Montserrat would want him to find out as much as he could.

"How did Ewers die?" he asked.

It was not a question Marisa had been expecting. She raised an eyebrow at him as she took a drag of her cigarette. The silver case lay on the table, next to her martini glass. There was something subtly wrong about this woman, a sour note he could not pinpoint. It unsettled him.

"Stabbed. He was robbed," she said, picking up her drink and nibbling at an olive.

"An important sorcerer and he didn't have any bodyguards? Any charms to keep him safe?" In his pocket there was the handkerchief he'd smeared with his blood. He slid a hand into that pocket as he spoke.

"He grew cocky. Perhaps he was also distracted. He was ill, you know?"

"Yes, I heard. That's why he wanted to cast a spell in the first place. Although, to get his financing, he told your aunt the spell would be for her."

"You know a lot about Ewers, but you're playing innocent. I think you're only pretending not to have items that belonged to him. There was a film," Marisa said, and then she was quiet, as if expecting him to fill the gap.

"Oh?"

"Yes, there was." She was not amused by his evasiveness. She was not charmed. Not anymore. "Abel had been casting spells again, he'd been using Ewers's old things."

"How do you know that?"

"My aunt found out."

"Then she spoke with him before he died. You said they were not in touch."

"There are ways to find out about things without picking up a phone, young man. Especially when you remember a few spells."

"Your aunt is a practitioner still? She follows Ewers's teachings?"

Marisa shook her head and looked him straight in the eye, a quiet fury in her steady gaze. "Are you joking? She despised Ewers."

"You didn't say so before."

"I thought it was implicit. Listen, Mr. Abascal, I don't know why you're interested in Ewers or his film, but I can tell you the only thing you'll get if you hold on to anything that belonged to that man is grief. The rune I saw, it's a warning."

"Why would that cult be after you?"

"After my aunt, not me. Perhaps they mean to frighten her, to let her know she must not interfere in their business. My aunt thinks they are incredibly dangerous and the only way to be safe is to destroy those artifacts. I want you to consider selling them to me. I'll pay a good price."

"Wait a second, I didn't say I had anything," Tristán replied, but he knew she didn't believe that.

They sat in a silence that was not quite hostile but was not friendly either. The tide had turned. She wouldn't give Tristán anything else; still he tried one last question.

"You said Ewers is a dangerous man. What did you mean by that? He's been dead for decades."

Marisa smiled then. "Spells can last for a very long time. Ewers's power remains. And perhaps, a part of him remains, too. He was trying to cheat death, after all. Who says he didn't manage it somehow? Give me that film, Mr. Abascal. I think you know the one I mean. If you don't, you and your friend might be in a very risky position."

Tristán stood up and bid the woman goodbye. She waved him away. He felt flushed by the time he reached Montserrat's car and opened the door, anxiously looking at her. Montserrat was fine, listening to heavy metal of all things, and he breathed a sigh of relief. Marisa had royally spooked him.

"What did she say?" Montserrat asked, lowering the volume of the song by Luzbel that was playing. He didn't like that type of music, but being around Montserrat he had absorbed the names and songs of a few bands she preferred.

Tristán tugged at his tie and sat next to her, staring ahead. "She says Ewers's cult is having a good time. She recommends we get rid of anything he owned, especially the film."

"She knows about the dub."

"The dub, or maybe the silver nitrate print. Maybe both."

"Hmm."

"Hmm, what?"

Montserrat turned the key, and the car began moving down the street. Tristán rolled down the window a little.

"She says Ewers himself may not be dead. That a part of him remains."

"I think I saw him, at that building downtown."

Tristán stared at Montserrat. "Why didn't you say so before?"

"You were mocking me, remember? Asking about my German boyfriend and latest crush?"

Tristán felt like smacking himself. Yeah, of all the things to say, all the things to needle her with, he'd picked that. It was a low blow. He was aware, although he didn't like to acknowledge it, that Montserrat had liked him quite a bit back in the day. One afternoon she had even attempted to verbalize this attraction, at which point he had promptly cut her off and turned evasive until she had understood through oblique gestures that this avenue was closed.

That had been around the time his braces had come off and he was getting interested looks from the prettier girls in class, and Tristán, greedily delighting in the opportunities his eroding shyness afforded him, had decided Montserrat's earnest affection was not as enticing as miniskirts and plunging necklines.

She'd never made any overtures when they grew up, and they'd buried that episode, but then of course he hadn't forgotten it.

"Well, fuck! I didn't mean it like that. Sorry," he said, attempting an apology that would not earn him a tirade from her.

She seemed to take it well enough, shrugging.

"You saw him, then?" he asked, tentative, a little afraid of the answer.

"I didn't see anything. Not really. But I felt it. I think it's him."

The semaphore was red at the intersection they were approaching. Two teenagers wearing dirty Santa Claus hats were going from car to car, selling bubble gum. Tristán took out a couple of coins and handed them to the kids. Everything was turning American. The Three Kings were giving way to the fat guy in the red suit. Downtown, buildings were decorated with traditional piñatas but also glowing reindeer.

"Why is he following you?" he asked as the lights changed and the car began rolling down the street again.

"I don't know. Why did you see Karina? But it's happening, and I don't trust Marisa or her aunt. They're playing at something."

"Yeah, I know," Tristán said. "The problem is we're playing, too, but we don't know the rules of the game."

Montserrat did not reply. He sank back in his seat and glanced at the city streets. The posadas were starting the day after tomorrow. A time for joy and parties. Meanwhile, they were being chased by dead people.

Merry Christmas, 1993. It was going to be a hell of an end to the year.

20

Tristán was still trying to deal with the debacle at his photo shoot and spent a whole day on the phone, talking back and forth with Dorotea and other people. That meant they didn't head to Clarimonde Bauer's house until Thursday evening rather than tackling the issue immediately. This suited Montserrat fine because she wanted to see Araceli before her sister left for Morelia.

With a strange presence following her and the possible existence of cultists, Montserrat didn't have time to shop for a fancy gift and ended up hastily stuffing a couple of candy boxes in paper bags and pasting bows on them. She handed them to her sister—one for Araceli, one for their mother—and they had coffee at a joint that sold churros and hot chocolate.

"How's work? It seems you're busy every day I call."

"Shifts here and there," Montserrat said. She was not going to mention Ewers or his spells, so she jumped to the question she wanted to ask without preamble, figuring she might as well know. "What about you? Are you feeling okay?"

She was worried that whatever good luck might have been generated by the spell they'd cast when they dubbed the movie had vanished. Abel was dead, Tristán was probably out of an acting gig, and Montserrat couldn't even collect a check. This might mean a complete reversal of fortunes.

"I'm great. I went to the basilica on Sunday to thank the Virgin of Guadalupe for helping me out," her sister said.

"It must have been packed," Montserrat replied, remembering the processions, the people carrying their statues of the Virgin in their arms and their bouquets of flowers.

The Virgin's Day marked the beginning of the festivities that would bleed into the first week of January. Their mother had been devoted for a single day of the year and lit her candle and said a prayer every December 12. But others took it much further. Montserrat remembered the people, moving like ants downtown, heading to venerate her image.

It was a spectacle, as were the pastorelas where people dressed up as devils and angels and enacted the play of the Nativity. She wondered what Ewers would have made of those, interested as he was in performances. Religion and magic were not the same, but maybe Ewers had caught the scent of something when he walked downtown and saw such forms of entertainment.

Mexico was syncretism in motion, and Montserrat supposed in a weird way so was Ewers's magic system. Of course, he bent it the way he wanted, talked his talk of Aryan superiority and ancient lay lines, but he was not exactly original.

There she was again. She wished to chat with her sister and forget about Ewers, but she kept going back to him. Tristán wasn't wrong about her compulsions.

"Have you put up your Christmas tree?" Araceli asked.

"I forgot," Montserrat admitted.

"Wow, you must be busy. But you have figured out how you're spending New Year's, right? You're not going to be all alone?"

If Montserrat even hinted that she was planning on being alone, Araceli would never leave the city without her. She shook her head vehemently. "Of course not. I imagine Tristán and I will order takeout."

"You are an adventurous duo. Then he's not going anywhere, either."

"No. It's the two of us."

"You should make sure you have a smidgen of Christmas cheer. Put up the tree, go to a party."

When they were done with their hot chocolate, Montserrat drove her sister back home. Araceli surely noticed that she was distracted, but Montserrat hoped she chalked it up to the imaginary shifts she was working.

On the way home, she stopped at the same store where she'd bought books on Crowley and other occultists and bought more items. She didn't have money to burn on this stuff, but Tristán was right: they didn't understand the rules of the game they were playing. More reading material might be useless. Then again, her growing collection, spread across her desk, or resting atop a chair, comforted her. It wasn't exactly Christmas cheer, like Araceli suggested, but it was keeping her busy.

In the back of a closet Montserrat stored an old plastic tree. She pulled it out and dragged it to the living room, along with a box full of glass ornaments. She strung lights around it. The tree looked shabby, but she plugged the lights in and contemplated her handiwork.

Montserrat pulled the curtain aside, looking at the building on the other side of the street where someone was having a party. On the floor below her they were playing "Campana Sobre Campana." She went to her office, pulled out the headphones, and put on a tape with Huizar's "Pecado Capital" that she'd traded in exchange for a couple of bootleg Motörhead tapes two years before and listened to "Nota Roja."

She opened one of the books she'd bought and found a story about a group of amateur sorcerers in Washington who, in January of 1941, had tried to cast a spell against Hitler. The story had made it into an issue of *Life*. "The death that comes to you, let it come to him," they had said as they stuck pins into a doll made to look like Hitler.

Wilhelm Ewers had a section on sympathetic magic—though he didn't call it that—and another on reflecting hexes, and now she turned to that. She wondered what Ewers would have been up to if he hadn't died. Would he still be roaming around Mexico? Or would he have tried his luck somewhere else? He was an opportunist, after all. And what flavor of magic would he serve his acolytes nowadays? Clarimonde Bauer had reprinted his book with no changes to the text, but he would have altered it. Made it sound attractive for modern readers.

You are special and therefore you deserve this knowledge, he would have said. Or else, *You are not special, but I could make you so very special*. Either way worked; he had tried both approaches depending on whom he spoke to. Ewers contradicted himself when it suited his purposes; one section of his book negated a previous one. Yet his words had a rhythm to them, a musicality. It was a bizarre comparison, but it made sense to her. Ewers made you dance to his waltz. After the first few notes, you knew the steps and kept on going.

The practice of hitobashira in ancient Japan involved the self-sacrifice of a person to ensure the safety of a building. In China human victims were sacrificed to the spirits of ancestors; nowadays human figures drawn on painted paper are offered instead. Aun, King of Sweden, offered his nine sons in sacrifice to prolong his life. In Iceland we find the term blót, which means to sacrifice, though, after the introduction of Christianity, the meaning was changed to "curse."

Her finger carefully underlined the word "curse." She turned the page.

To reverse the flow of a curse, reflect it. Should the sorcerer cast a spell for illness, respond with a spell for health to neutralize it. Should the curse be of a more significant proportion, then a sacrifice may be required. The greater the magic, the greater the price.

Montserrat looked at the corkboard decorated with Ewers's photos and crossed her arms. She tried to picture him this time not as a grinning fellow at a Mexican high-society party, performing parlor tricks for Alma Montero and her friends, but younger. In the days when his parents organized boisterous reunions. Merely a kid with an imagination, and this made her remember Tristán and the times she wrapped him in old bedsheets and pretended he was a ghost rising from the grave.

But Wilhelm Ewers had been neglected after his brother's death. He'd grown up alone in a distant, large house, with no playmates to joke with him. *My parents heaped praise upon my older brother and left me to spend lonely afternoons in my room, anticipating my early demise,* he'd written.

An angry little kid who had been informed he was special and the rest of the world was beneath him. She slid her headphones off her ears, letting them rest on the back of her neck.

She picked up Tristán the following evening around seven. The palm trees lining the avenue that led them into Las Lomas were glowing bright with Christmas lights, but otherwise the festivities were subdued in this part of the city. Neatly trimmed hedges hid expensive houses, and sober driveways sneaked behind tall walls. People in Las Lomas had real gardens, with purple bougainvilleas and pale roses, unlike everyone in Montserrat's sphere, who made do with potted plants.

This area was "exclusive," which also meant people had good security.

Even if Clarimonde Bauer was still living at the address on the invitation, they could be chased away by bodyguards. They could also end up in jail, if the lady got nasty, and Montserrat did not want to have conversations with cops again. But there was nothing left to do but roll the dice.

They turned left, taking a side street. It was practically impossible to see the numbers on some of these houses or the names of the streets. Nobody cared to put up the proper signage, because if you lived there, you knew where you were headed.

"I think it's that one," Tristán said.

Montserrat stopped the car and stared at the house Tristán had pointed out. A white wall surrounded it, and there was a silver metal gate. Behind it you could glimpse a house with a coarse gray exterior. Las Lomas had no single overwhelming style. The rich constructed their homes in whatever fashion they fancied, with Spanish-inspired stucco houses sitting next to Porfirian style mansions. The Brutalist also had its place, as evidenced by Bauer's home.

Montserrat rang the bell. A servant came out and peered at them through the bars of the gate.

"We're here to see Clarimonde Bauer," she said.

"Do you have an appointment?"

"No. But please hand her this and tell her it's about Wilhelm Ewers," Montserrat said, pulling out one of the sheets of paper with Ewers's writing.

The servant did not look convinced, but he came back after a few minutes and opened the gate for them, and they walked the wide stone path leading toward the front door of the house.

The inside of Clarimonde's home was pure and simple: bright lights, polished cement floors, rough white walls. It had the feeling of a fortress, impenetrable, and the living room was all steel and glass furniture, except for the white couch where Clarimonde Bauer sat, dressed in matching white, as if color had been drained from this home.

Clarimonde Bauer's hair was a light blond, worn in a low chignon. Her blouse and trousers were made of linen, and she had silver bracelets around her arms and rings on almost every finger. A vase with a flower and a bowl with fruit had been set atop a coffee table. There were markers and pencils stacked on one end of the table.

She had a large sketchbook and a piece of charcoal and was busy sketching when they walked in. She was drawing a still life. The first page of Ewers's letter lay by her side.

"One must have hobbies," Clarimonde said, still focused on her drawing. "Or else the mind atrophies."

"When you were young your hobby was acting," Montserrat said.

"That was a long time ago. I know your voices, but not your names. You are Abel's little friends."

"How do you know our voices?" Tristán asked.

"From the dub you made."

"Then you have the film," Montserrat said.

Clarimonde's glasses were rimless and her eyes, when she glanced up at them, were green. "Of course."

They were standing in front of her now. Clarimonde gestured for them to sit and they did, trying to balance themselves on an uncomfortable white couch that matched the one Clarimonde sat on. The woman set her drawing pad down on the table.

"Did you take it from Abel's apartment?" Montserrat asked.

"You ask many questions but have not even introduced yourselves. It is a bit rude."

"We're Abel's little friends," Tristán said.

The woman smiled, although Montserrat wasn't sure she appreciated the jest. "You brought with you a letter."

"Yes, and we'll hand you the other half of it if you'll tell us the truth," Montserrat said.

"You *are* rude," she replied, but her smile only grew wider as if now she was becoming truly amused. "You already have the answers, but I'll play. What do you want to know?"

"Abel is dead," Montserrat said bluntly.

"A pity, that."

"You were not aware of it?"

"I suspected. It's why I have the film. He gave it to me."

"Why would he do that?"

"He sold it. For protection."

"From whom?"

"Can't you guess?"

"Alma."

Clarimonde Bauer looked directly at her. She did not nod, but Montserrat knew she'd gotten it right.

"How were you going to protect him?" Montserrat asked.

"Guess."

"Magic."

"See? You already have the answers."

"Not all of them. You are a sorceress and you've tried to maintain Ewers's cult. It didn't quite work like you planned it, right? That building downtown, it's abandoned."

For the first time Clarimonde Bauer raised her eyebrows at them, a trace of irritation coloring her eyes. She had been a pretty girl when she was young, but the years had corroded her easy beauty. What was left was a hard shell. It reminded Montserrat a little of Ewers's look. He'd had that trace of resentment in his mouth as if something had been denied to him. A hunger, in the pit of their bellies.

"The building is to be sold. It belonged to my husband. But tides do turn; 1987 was a bad year for us. The stock market tumbled. Our building sustained damage during the earthquake of '85 and needed repairs I could not fund. I've had to economize. Now, the letter, please."

Montserrat wondered what "economize" meant to this woman. She still had a grand home in Las Lomas and servants. Maybe it had not been the performance of the stock market that had pushed her to shutter her book business. Had she grown tired of idolizing a dead man?

Montserrat reached into her purse and took out the piece of rice paper. Inside the purse she carried her charm. She noticed that Tristán kept a hand in one pocket, no doubt clutching his own talisman.

Montserrat held the letter up. "We do have a few more questions."

"What more will you ask? You *know* what you did."

"No, no, we don't," Tristán said, shaking his head. "We're trying to understand."

"You and Abel cast a spell, and in doing so you've reset the clock, you put things in motion again. Now, hand me the letter and perhaps we can chat more."

Clarimonde's voice was smooth and rich. The voice of someone used to making demands and writing down orders. For a moment Montserrat thought to refuse her request, but she didn't think it mattered. The letter, by itself, held no special magic. Neither did Ewers's book. She knew this instinctively.

Montserrat slid the letter across the table. Clarimonde picked it up carefully, smoothing its creases with her ringed fingers. "Where did you find this?"

"He hid it in a book."

"Clever boy. He was ever so clever."

Tristán wet his lips and leaned forward. "Listen, you're telling us we put things in motion. How do we end that motion? How do we go back to the way it was? Because Abel is dead and things are getting weird around us."

"I would not have killed Abel. I made a deal with him. That is Alma's doing."

"Why would she kill the guy?"

"Wilhelm was murdered thirty-two years ago, but Alma still fears him. Now, as to the 'weirdness' you've experienced, I cannot say exactly what you've seen, but Wilhelm loved setting snares and curses. When he didn't get his way, things could become complicated."

"When his film wasn't finished everyone had a bout of bad luck," Montserrat said. "And now that we dubbed that reel he's not satisfied with that."

"Of course not. The spell needs to be finished. See? I told you that you had all the answers already."

"Except how we set things back the way they were," Tristán said. "How do we undo this snare?"

"There's only one solution: by finishing what Wilhelm started. Finishing the spell. You must have the silver nitrate print."

"Alma says we should burn anything that belonged to Wilhelm."

"Of course she would say that. The murderous bitch," Clarimonde said in a slow voice. Each word was the stab of a knife.

"You think Alma killed Abel," Montserrat said.

"It's nothing I could prove, and yet it is the obvious answer."

"You didn't think to kill her yourself in all these years?"

Clarimonde smirked. "Let's say she's been off limits."

"What happens if we finish what Ewers started, if we finish the spell?" Tristán asked.

But, oh, even before he asked the question Montserrat already knew. It was like Clarimonde had told them: she had the answers. It was in the pages of that book she read, in Ewers's letter, which now rested on Clarimonde's lap. She'd been circling around the inevitable answer.

"He comes back," Montserrat said, her words low.

Clarimonde looked pleased, like a teacher who is about to award a prized pupil a gold star. She grabbed her sketchbook and her charcoal, turned the page, and began delicately tracing the outline of an apple.

"Despite the problems in '87, I still have certain resources, even if that building is no longer in use. It's quite a lovely space; we used to meet there, once upon a time. The others remain around the city, at least a fair number of them, and there have been a few new converts. We still meet to share in Wilhelm's wisdom. The congregation is eager to greet him."

Montserrat saw the look Tristán shot her. He wanted to get up and run to the door. *Fear is not the answer, fear gives a sorcerer power over you.* She wanted to tell him that but since she couldn't, she pressed her palm firmly against his knee. Tristán froze in place.

"You do not need to be one of us. I wouldn't ask that," Clarimonde said.

Clarimonde's voice was soft, but her face was ice. Something about them offended her sensibilities. Their appearance or their dress or the combination of them. She supposed they looked like a couple of people who'd grown up playing near the train tracks in Pantaco. Kids from slightly squalid apartment buildings. Their hues, their mannerisms, were flawed. Wilhelm would have disapproved. Clarimonde Bauer, Abel Urueta, Alma Montero. He'd recruited his disciples from the upper echelons of Mexican society, which were also the whitest. The purest. The most suitable to his purposes.

"I know. It was an exclusive country club," Montserrat said.

Clarimonde seemed offended by the remark. "They don't let everyone go into the discotheques, do they? There's a velvet rope."

"You can keep the rope."

"Careful. You're being rude again."

Clarimonde looked fixedly at her, eyebrows arched. "I want the silver nitrate film, and I want your cooperation. There is a ritual that must
be completed. You'll be part of it. Afterward, you may go on with your
ridiculous lives, same as you did before you'd ever heard of us. It's not
much to ask, is it?"

"I guess it depends. Maybe we don't want dead sorcerers walking
around Mexico City, making snares and curses."

"What do you care? It won't affect you."

"We need to think about it," Montserrat said, standing up. Tristán
stood up, too.

"I've been very kind. Very understanding. But now I'm growing a little
impatient."

Clarimonde's irritation was poorly masked by an attempt at an air of
chilly indifference. Underneath it all, the woman burned with anger at
them. She must have expected them to agree to her request immediately.

"We've given you the letter. It was meant for you, anyway. But the
nitrate print, that's for us to think about," Montserrat said.

"Consider carefully what you're saying. You don't want to refuse me,"
Clarimonde told them as her hands fluttered back toward her sketchpad;
she gripped the piece of charcoal and slid it across the page with a hard
motion.

"We should get going," Tristán said weakly, grabbing Montserrat by
the elbow.

"Sit down, the both of you."

Clarimonde drew another line across the page.

"No," Montserrat said.

"You cannot refuse me," Clarimonde said, and her hand drew a third
stroke.

Montserrat could see, on the page, the crude shape of one of Ewers's
runes. Clarimonde Bauer was attempting to cast a spell on them; each
line she drew was a word in an incantation. To run out at that moment
might have been the most instinctive solution, but if Montserrat understood something it was that curses are not outrun. And although fear
or a strangled scream might have been an understandable reaction, she
gritted her teeth.

Montserrat extended a hand and grabbed one of the pieces of charcoal and began to draw her own symbol on the surface of the white table, each stroke hard, staring back at Clarimonde. The woman's anger was almost palpable, and Montserrat pushed back against that anger with a smooth determination and rage of her own. There was plenty of anger inside of her, after all. Plenty of kindling. Let it burn.

"I refuse you," Montserrat said and at the last word tossed the piece of charcoal away.

Smoke rose, and the paper Clarimonde had been drawing on turned black, the page curling and burning away into ashes within seconds.

Clarimonde's eyes were very wide. She stared at her in surprise. "A counter-spell. Who taught you that?"

"I read it somewhere," Montserrat muttered.

Clarimonde was shaken; her eyes looked a little wild. She raised a hand, as if to touch Montserrat, then seemed to think better of it. "You will not be safe, ever, unless you give me that film. Only I can protect you."

"Yeah, it didn't work for Abel, did it? Come on."

Montserrat grabbed Tristán by the hand and pulled him toward the entrance. They moved fast. She feared someone would bar the door, but they made it out and into their car without any issue.

She began driving toward her apartment. Her heart was pounding, and her fingers were wrapped tight around the steering wheel. In her ears there was a soft ringing. She reached for the dial and turned on the stereo, but Tristán immediately switched it off.

"How did you do that back there?" he asked. "Did you read it in that book?"

"It's . . . kind of. I mean . . . I don't know."

"You don't know?"

"She was trying to cast a hex, drawing runes. I stopped it. Reflected it. I don't know . . . I'll take you to your apartment." She winced and pressed one hand against her ear.

"I don't have any booze in my apartment, so let's go to yours. You look like you need a drink."

"Make it three."

She did have a bottle of tequila that she hadn't opened. As soon as they walked in Montserrat grabbed the first two cups she saw on the drying rack and filled them with booze. They were not proper tequila glasses, but she placed them on the table.

"That was messed up."

Tristán sipped his drink. Montserrat downed hers so quickly she thought it would burn a hole in her throat. She was a light drinker. One glass was enough for her. Tristán almost spat out the drink in his mouth when he saw her pouring herself a second one and downing it with equal haste.

"Holy shit, slow down," he said. "Are you okay, Momo?"

She pressed a hand against her forehead. It felt warm, like she might be starting to run a fever, but the ringing was growing muffled.

"I feel a little shitty," she said, setting her cup down.

"Well, of course you do, Charlie McGee."

"Don't fuck with me tonight, Tristán."

"I'm saying that you set a piece of paper on fire."

"Reflected a spell," she muttered.

"That too. And you're not sure exactly how you did it?"

Montserrat frowned. It was hard to put it into words. *There's a rhythm to his words*, she thought. *Three beats to the bar. It flows. Learn the pattern, you can dance it.*

"I was looking at Ewers's book. He discusses the rudimentary idea of it," she said at last. She poured herself more tequila, drank it quickly.

"You're still reading that thing," Tristán said, grimacing.

"Among other titles, it's over in my office," she said, pointing in its direction.

"What did you draw on her table? I didn't see."

"Just the word 'no.' The way we used to write it."

"Why would that work?"

Montserrat opened her mouth to explain Ewers's ideas about magical actions and reactions, his florid mixing of knowledge gleaned from here and there, plus her own scribblings, which had now multiplied and took up many pages in her notebook. It was like trying to explain poetry to someone who wants to read a recipe. Ewers's book had a system, but it was beautifully, sometimes surprisingly arranged, and depended not only on logic but emotion. Sound was much the same way. You can show someone how to splice tape, but getting the feel of it is a different tale.

Montserrat threw her head back. "I'm nursing a migraine, and I need to drive you home."

"You're not driving me home looking like you were just mashed by a steamroller and stinking of tequila. Come on, let's tuck you in bed."

Montserrat protested, but he hauled her up by the arm, and they headed to her bedroom. She lay down and watched wearily as Tristán took off her shoes. She'd done that for him on numerous occasions, and now the roles were reversed.

She didn't relish it.

Then he took off his own shoes and dumped his jacket in the corner.

"What?" he asked. "I'm not sleeping on that stupid couch of yours. It's lumpy."

"You could go back to your apartment."

"And be killed by an axe murderer? You don't split up in a movie."

"It's not a fucking movie," she said, rubbing her hands against her eyes, but Tristán was already taking the left side of the bed. She considered unbuttoning her jeans and slipping out of her t-shirt since Tristán had no problem stripping down to his underwear, then decided against it after throwing him a weary look.

He laughed. "Calm down, I'm not going to start rubbing myself against you."

"So you claim," she muttered.

"Fine. I'll make a wall of pillows."

She closed her eyes. "Sure."

Sleep came easily, which was an oddity for her. She was nocturnal and welcomed insomnia like an ardent lover. But she felt absolutely drained, and although the ringing had subsided, the migraine remained, making the blackness of sleep a welcome escape. It was three a.m. when she woke up. The numbers on the clock by her bedside glowed a bright red.

Montserrat felt Tristán's soft breath against the back of her neck. He was too close to her. Probably accustomed to sprawling across his king-size mattress, he was driving her toward the edge of the bed. She could feel the bulk of him curled against her.

She tried nudging him with her elbow. Instead of turning away, he moved closer to her, an arm settling against her midsection.

Montserrat sighed, and for a couple of minutes she thought to simply let him be, but she was in an uncomfortable position and wanted to turn around, and she couldn't when he was practically draped over her.

"You're crushing me, you idiot," she said and tried elbowing him again, which had no discernible effect.

He simply lay there, flush next to Montserrat, one hand now curling against her stomach, as if trying to hold her in place, his breath loud against the base of her neck. She was considering kicking him when he spoke in a whisper.

"Follow me into the night," he said.

And maybe if she hadn't heard Tristán's voice hundreds of times, dubbing him on more than a dozen occasions . . . Maybe if they had not grown up together and she hadn't watched him playing parts on TV from the moment he said his first lines . . . Maybe she would not have been alarmed by those words.

But that faint voice, with a hint of mockery, did not belong to Tristán.

She sat up and slammed her palm against a button, turning on the bedside lamp. On the other side of the bed, his body turned in the opposite direction, and with a decorous pillow placed between them as a demarcation line, Tristán was fast asleep.

21

S crambled, right?"

"You don't need to make breakfast."

Montserrat stood by the refrigerator, eyeing him with suspicion. She'd stepped out of the shower and was wearing a white bathrobe that reached her shins. Her hair was wrapped in a towel, and she wore blue plastic slippers, as if she were an old lady. The shoes made a loud *wap-wap* sound as she walked.

Check out the boner killer outfit, that's what he would have said any other morning. He would have said it loud and clear, but right now he was trying to be nice. Hence the eggs.

"Food is the only thing I'm good at. Maybe I should have been a cook. No, not that coffee. We can go home after I'm finished cooking and have a proper coffee there."

Montserrat held the jar with coffee and frowned. "What's wrong with it?"

"It's instant coffee. I've told you a hundred times, toss it in the garbage."

Montserrat leaned against the counter with a sigh. "I'll pour us orange juice, unless his majesty wants it fresh squeezed."

Tristán stirred the eggs with a spatula. He didn't look at Montserrat as he spoke, trying to sound casual.

"Are you going to tell me what Ewers said to you last night?"

"It's not important. I think he wanted me to be aware that he knows me, that he's following me."

"If he's following you around, he could be slipping into your bathroom while you are showering for all you know. A dead sexual deviant."

Montserrat walking around the bathroom in that outfit was not an enticing sight. But there were all types of perverts. And without the granny shoes and bath towel, who knew. He believed Montserrat at her plainest was the best Montserrat for him. He felt weird on the random days when she dolled herself up, smearing the mascara thick on her eyelashes and picking a dark lipstick.

There had been that guy, the one she'd dated before Regina, and she'd dressed up and curled her eyelashes more often because the dude was super social and took her to several parties and functions. Tristán had panicked for a bit, fearing Montserrat would marry that pompous ass. He never wanted to have to compete for Montserrat's attention. Fortunately, that guy was gone, and Regina had also fizzled out.

Boy, was he a bad friend for thinking that. Tristán knew it and shook his head, promising himself he'd be nicer, more generous, kinder in the new year. That would be his resolution.

"Ewers was playing. He wants to scare me," Montserrat said.

"He would have succeeded if it was me."

Montserrat did not reply. Tristán plated the eggs. He'd found corn tortillas in the refrigerator, but he clung to his northern customs and preferred flour ones, so he warmed one for Montserrat but none for himself. They took the plates and the glasses filled with orange juice to the table.

They ate quietly. The silence strained the ears. Although Tristán had been dancing around the words, he decided to finally say it. "We've got to pick a side, you know?"

"Excuse me?" Montserrat asked, glancing up at him.

"Alma Montero or Clarimonde Bauer. We have to give one of them the film."

"No," she said firmly.

"Why not?"

"Because they both want something."

"Everyone wants something."

"You know what I mean."

"You have a lot of notes about him."

"Excuse me?"

"I was in the office while you were showering. You have Ewers's book and a bunch of other books on magic, and all these little notes spread out over your desk."

Montserrat winced but did not reply. Her hermetic silence was starting

to get annoying. He would have understood if she had yelled and flailed at
the discovery that Ewers had been in her room, but all she had done was
wake him up with a tap on the shoulder and tell him what had happened.
Then she'd gone back to sleep while Tristán stared at the ceiling, afraid
if he set a foot on the floor a hand would reach out from under the bed
and clutch his ankle.

"What did he say?"

"For god's sake, it doesn't matter," she muttered, banging her fork
against the table.

"You don't always have to act tough, Momo."

"I also don't need to have a nervous breakdown. I'm not going to give
him what he wants. He wants me scared, all right? He can't have it."

Montserrat picked up her fork again and poked at her eggs. Whether
she liked it or not, Ewers and his spells loomed all around them, embit-
tering the morning. By the time Tristán placed the dishes in the sink it
was close to ten a.m. Tristán combed his hair with Montserrat's brush,
gargled a mouthful of Listerine, put on his sunglasses, and they went in
search of Montserrat's car.

Montserrat played her heavy metal music during the drive, therefore smartly avoiding any more conversation. Still, Tristán frowned and
chewed on his lower lip, wanting to prod.

She'd brought Ewers's book with her. It poked out of her purse, and
Tristán eyed it as if it were a venomous snake. Despite Montserrat's protestations he wanted to shred it page by page and toss the pieces in the
air as if they were confetti. Not only because witchcraft was creepy, but
because he was starting to feel jealous of Ewers.

Jealous! About a dead warlock. But Montserrat's office was filled with
things that yelled "Wilhelm Ewers." She'd taken photos from Abel's
album and pinned them to the corkboard where she normally pinned
tickets from old concerts or movies they'd watched together. Tristán did
a similar thing with Karina's photos, especially when the anniversary of
her death came around. He recognized this impulse. It wasn't healthy,
and it wasn't good to be leaving Post-its filled with scribbles or to mark
pages in Ewers's book, either. She was too interested in this magic stuff,
and not only interested.

She might be good at it.

It gave him the shivers, this whole business of runes, spells, and ghosts. Montserrat was drawing symbols on tables and making things catch on fire like a character out of a Corman flick.

He comforted himself with the thought of a good cup of coffee. Maybe Montserrat would relax after that. She might not be scared, but she was wound up tight, like a piano string that is in danger of snapping. So was he, for that matter. He had yet to have a smoke, and as soon as he was back in his apartment he'd open a window, lean out, and light a cigarette.

The sky above them was a muddled gray, courtesy of the winter season. In a few hours the city would be impassable, with vehicles clogging the streets, but at this time of the day and with folks starting to depart for the holidays, it was drivable. They left the car at the parking lot that was a couple blocks from his building.

Tristán went into his apartment thinking of warm coffee and a change of shirt, but froze as he walked into the living room. It was an absolute mess. His magazines were strewn over the floor, the couch had been sliced with a knife, and stuffing had been pulled out of the cushions. The telephone had been slammed against the floor with such force its plastic shell had cracked. His answering machine was smashed as if someone had taken a hammer to it.

"What the fuck?" he whispered.

"They must have come looking for the film," Montserrat said, rounding the couch and avoiding the shards of a broken cup.

"Who? Alma or Clarimonde?"

"Take your pick."

They walked slowly, moving toward the bedroom. There, drawers were open, his clothes littered the floor, and his bedsheets had been torn into ribbons. Above the bed someone had painted a familiar-looking symbol in bright red using rough, harsh strokes. The paint still looked fresh. If it was paint.

"Vegvísir," Montserrat said.

"Fuck," Tristán replied. He hurried out of the room and back to the living room. He felt as though his body was entirely fluid, devoid of bones, and had to plant a hand against the wall to keep upright.

They were not safe. They would never be safe. They ought to leave the city, now, this instant.

A loud buzz made him practically jump in the air. For a moment he didn't recognize it. Then he realized it was his intercom. It buzzed again. He gave Montserrat a wary look and slowly pressed his index finger against the button.

"Yes?"

"Listen to me, they are after you. You have maybe ten minutes before they get here, so you need to come down quick," said a rough male voice.

"Who is this?"

"It's José López."

"Who's after us?"

"Hurry down."

The intercom went quiet. Tristán turned to Montserrat. "What do we do? That could be a trap."

"Yeah, it could. But we've been looking for that man," she said.

"He could be an impostor."

"We're not safe here."

"I know that! We'll call the cops."

"With what phone?" she asked, glancing at the broken phone.

"The neighbors have phones," he said, realizing how foolish this sounded. What exactly would they tell the cops? That two different sorceresses were after them? That ghosts hunted them at night and someone had drawn magic runes above his bed, attempting to hex him?

Before Tristán could begin to craft a coherent story, Montserrat was already bolting out the door. Tristán muttered a curse and followed her. She didn't even wait for the elevator; instead she took the stairs. When they reached the lobby they saw the man waiting outside. He didn't look like a murderous sorcerer, but then again Tristán had not met a sorcerer before.

José López was leaning on a cane. His hair was peppered with gray, and his beard was almost entirely silver. He wore a navy-blue raincoat that was stained white with what might be bird droppings and frayed at the bottom. He'd slung a battered canvas messenger bag over his shoulder. He looked like the kind of guy who would carry a paper bag and a bottle in his pocket, half a vagrant and half a regular at a dirty, dark cantina.

"Montserrat and Tristán," López said.

"That's us," he said.

"My car is right there, across the street," the old man said, pointing to a sad-looking Taurus in need of a new paint job. "Let's go."

"Look, buddy, we don't know you; maybe we could go to the coffee shop—"

"Damn it. They're here. Whatever you do, stay behind me and do not flee. You'll die on your own."

Tristán looked in the direction López was staring and saw two men walking their dogs. They seemed ordinary, dressed in suits and ties. The dogs were Dobermans with spiky collars. The only thing that he thought was a bit funny was that they should look so well dressed for a dog walk, as if two bank executives had taken a break to pick up their pets.

Yet as he looked at the dogs they seemed to change, or perhaps it was that the longer he looked, the more he was able to see the seams of their construction. Those were not dogs. Their fur was a liquid black, as if they were etched with a brush. Their eyes, when they raised their heads and bared their razor-sharp teeth, were a murky yellow, the color of a wavering candle. A black liquid, tar-like, slipped down the corner of their panting mouths.

"I'll handle this," López said. "Stay close and do not interfere."

The men undid the leashes, and the dogs sprang forward, rushing toward the spot where they stood, their jaws snapping in the air. Tristán had a clear picture of his demise and raised his hands in a futile attempt to ward off an attack, but López stepped forward and swung his cane, hitting one dog and then the other. The handle of the cane was decorated with the silver head of a bird, and where it touched the dog's flesh, black ink oozed out and dripped on the ground, then bubbled up, sizzling and evaporating, leaving only a faint tendril of smoke.

The dogs came again, teeth bared, their ugly yellow eyes without any pupils staring at them, and tried to bite José, but he swung the cane a second and a third time. The dogs dripped ink upon the ground and retreated when the silver handle brushed against their skin.

The men in suits did not say a single word. They were watching them, their hands stiffly holding the leash of each dog in a complicated knot. Their lips were moving, but Tristán couldn't have heard the words even if he'd wanted to.

José took two steps back, motioning to Tristán and Montserrat to also step back. He was trying to shield them while they crossed the street. The dogs lowered their heads, sniffing the ground and growling, as they slowly made their way to the car. When they had almost reached the Taurus, the dogs edged closer to each other and suddenly seemed to merge. It was a violent, chaotic fusion of limbs, with sinews loudly snapping and bones popping as the two dogs became one larger creature with a single head and four eyes that narrowed into tiny pinpricks.

"Hold this," José said, grabbing the messenger bag and the cane and slamming them against Tristán's chest. He managed to clutch both items with clumsy hands while the old man took off his raincoat and tossed that to Montserrat.

Yellow claws clacked against the pavement as the dog-thing shifted and pulsed.

"We should run," Tristán whispered to Montserrat.

"He said to stay close to him."

"I know what he said. I also know what I'm seeing. That's a fucking Cerberus."

"Cerberus has three heads."

"Of course! That makes it much better!"

Under his raincoat José López wore a baggy beige sweatshirt and matching sweatpants. He pulled each sleeve up to the elbows, revealing a series of intricate black tattoos that looked like Ewers's runes. They covered his forearms completely.

"Bag," López said, and Tristán handed him the messenger bag. The old guy stared at the gigantic dog-thing while his hands searched for something inside until he took out a bottle and poured its contents on the ground. The greenish, viscous liquid resembled mucus and smelled foul. It made Tristán wince in disgust.

"Cane," López said, and Tristán handed him that, while pressing a hand against his mouth to keep himself from retching.

López grabbed the cane, dipped its silver-plated ferrule in the green liquid, and began drawing with it. Faint symbols that had been carved into the wood of the cane glowed a light green, and Tristán thought that for a second López's tattoos were also imbued with this green glow, the hue glittering beneath the ink. The sorcerer then folded both of his hands atop his cane.

But Tristán could not observe this strange process with more care because in the blink of an eye the dog was no longer a lump of ink shivering and twisting on the ground. The dog-thing rose, fully formed, huge and lean. Its long snout opened, making it look not much like a dog anymore, but a primeval wolf.

On the sidewalk the men in suits were whispering their incantations.

The creature shook its head and rushed forward, showing innumerable gleaming teeth and letting out a screech that made Tristán slam his back against the cold metal of the car.

From the angle where Tristán stood he did not have a view of López's face, nor could he hear what he was saying; the snatches of words that reached him were senseless blabbering that were muffled by the dog's screech as it lurched forward and then took one monstrous leap, landing on López and knocking him to the ground.

The dog-thing growled, fixing its eyes on Tristán, and Tristán felt Montserrat's fingers digging into his shoulder, holding him in place even though his first instinct was to run.

Then López kicked or elbowed the thing, and the creature snarled, opened its mouth with too many teeth, intent on tearing through the man's throat, but this must have been what López had expected, for he shoved the cane into the dog's open mouth.

There was a sudden, incredible splintering of flesh, as if the cane had been acid instead of wood, corroding the creature's body. The dog's head became a spray of black liquid that fell on the ground, on Tristán's shoes, and even on the car.

The rest of the dog dissolved, becoming rivulets of blackness that began to smoke and disperse.

López was trying to stand up, and Tristán helped him to his feet. The man leaned on him, gripping his cane with his left hand and holding it up, as if he were about to brandish a sword. The two men in suits stared at them but did not move from the spot on the sidewalk where they had stood, impassive, watching the dog-things. Their mouths were closed in two firm, angry lines.

"The keys to the car are in my raincoat," López said. "I would appreciate it if you'd drive."

Montserrat unlocked the car, and Tristán helped López into the back, sitting next to him. The men in suits started slowly walking toward the car. The leashes were wrapped around one hand, and their mouths opened, whispering a word.

López rolled down the window, reached into his messenger bag, and tossed out a handful of feathers and nails. The men in suits stumbled and glared at them. As Montserrat sped away, López sprinkled more nails out the window, then coughed and fell heavily back against the seat, his hand resting on the messenger bag.

"Where are we going?" Montserrat asked.

"Near the Pemex tower in the Anzures," López muttered. "My house has safeguards."

On a window there was a Garfield plush toy with sucker cups, and three air fresheners in the shape of pines dangled from the rearview mirror. Tristán stared at them with incongruous wonder, astounded by the sight of these ordinary trinkets. He was unable to suppress a laugh, which earned him a glare in the rearview mirror from Montserrat. He reached for the cigarettes in his jacket pocket and turned to López.

"Smoke?" he asked.

22

José López's home was indeed close to the Pemex tower, on a quiet side street lined with houses from the forties and fifties. It had a double metal door painted green that led to a tiny courtyard and then the door of the house proper, which was also made of metal. The elements had nibbled at this door and were eating the paint away. López muttered and took out his key ring, and they walked through a minuscule vestibule and into the living room, which had a fish tank. The curtains were drawn tight, and it wasn't until Montserrat was right next to the tank that she was able to see its contents: leeches.

"For spell casting," López said as he placed his cane in a ceramic umbrella stand and the canvas bag on a rattan couch, next to a sleeping white cat. This was no secretive antiquarian's lair, and López did not look the part of a wizened sorcerer. The living room reminded her of a tacky Polynesian restaurant Tristán had once taken her to.

"How do you use them?" Montserrat asked.

"You can get bones for spells easily at the Mercado de Sonora. But blood is a different matter and some spells require it. When I need it, I use my own blood and the leeches."

"You let the leeches bite you?" Tristán said, glancing at the tank in disgust.

"Self-sacrifice. It also hurts a lot less than cutting your palm or any of that nonsense."

Montserrat walked toward a bookshelf, pressing a hand against a spine embossed with gold letters while López went around the room and pulled the curtains with a banana leaf print aside. Then he took off his shoes, sat down, and rubbed his feet with a sigh.

"My blood pressure must be through the roof," the man said, reaching into a pocket and uncapping a bottle. "At least Clarimonde Bauer has style, I suppose. A neat trick, the dogs."

"That was Clarimonde, then?" Tristán said.

"Clarimonde's people, at any rate. Can you hand me that can of soda there?"

Tristán grabbed a can of Pepsi that had been left by the aquarium and gave it to the man, who promptly swallowed a pill and took a sip. "They were also inside my apartment. They painted one of Ewers's runes on the wall."

"It wouldn't have been Clarimonde in your apartment," López said, wiping his mouth with the back of his hand. "Now, I'm going to need food, and then I'll have a nap."

"What? Why?" Tristán asked.

"Because I'm seventy-three years old. And I'm not what I used to be," López said, shuffling in the direction of a hallway.

"No, I mean why are you sure it wasn't Clarimonde?"

"Because if it had been her, they would have ambushed us while we were inside," Montserrat said. "Therefore, the person who broke into your apartment must have been Alma."

"Good! She gets it. Basic deduction skills," López said and continued walking into a kitchen that had barely enough space for two people to stand in it. Instead of a door, there was a curtain with beads, which Montserrat supposed served to make moving around easier.

López opened the refrigerator, took out a milk bottle, and poured himself a glass. He also took out a bar of cheese and began slicing it.

"Oh, so both of them want a piece of us," Tristán said. "That's awesome."

"A piece of the film, too," López said. He pointed at Montserrat's purse and the book poking out of it. "I'm assuming that is Abel's copy of *The House of Infinite Wisdom*?"

"You assume correctly," she said, placing a hand on the strap of her purse. "How did you know we'd be at Tristán's apartment, and how did you know they were coming?"

"Alma called, wanting to know if you'd spoken to me. That's when I realized Abel was dead."

"You had no idea?"

"My house has multiple safeguards. I keep to myself and live a quiet life. I also prefer to know little of what my former friends are up to."

"But Abel wasn't your *former* friend. You sent him a box filled with feathers and nails."

"I did. Because he asked for a protective charm but did not specify why. Later, he phoned to say he had tried his hand at a spell, and not any spell, but he had used Ewers's old nitrate film and was having unexpected side effects. That is when I learned of your little experiment. I told him to come over and we'd try to straighten the matter out, but he never did."

"What do you mean by straighten the matter out?"

López grabbed two slices of bread and began spreading mayo on them. "We'd have to undo the spell, of course. There was no other way. Only he was afraid that would undo his good luck. He said he needed to consider things and left it at that."

"And you didn't get curious about the situation until Alma contacted you?"

"I was curious. I simply decided not to get involved until today."

"What made you change your mind?" Tristán asked. He was hovering by the doorway. Montserrat had wedged herself next to the refrigerator.

"I had a premonition."

"Then you're like Abel. You can see the future. Like in 'The Whispers of the Earth,'" she said, reaching for Ewers's book, wanting to clap it open and stilling her hand.

"I don't slavishly rely on Ewers's runic system and elemental divisions for my spells."

"The tattoos on your forearms—"

"Defensive symbols, but not duplicates of Ewers's runes," López said, pulling up a sleeve and showing them his arm. "They're altered; refined designs of my own making, if you will." Indeed, those were not clones of Ewers's runes. Montserrat recognized certain elements, but López had put his touch on them. She supposed it was like fingerprints: no two were identical. López pulled his sleeve down and continued building his sandwich.

"A premonition doesn't explain why you saved our lives."

"Those dogs outside your building: I had never seen that. Theoretically, Ewers talked about such spells. Practically? We didn't have that. Yet

in the past few days I have felt a thread of magic weaving around me unlike anything I've ever experienced. You've caused a nuclear explosion,"
López said as he took a big bite of his sandwich.

The white cat picked that moment to wander into the kitchen and rub
itself against Montserrat's leg.

"In 1961 Ewers died and his spell was ruined. Afterward, most people
associated with the film had bad luck, I understand that. But I don't see
how we ended up with a nuclear explosion," she said.

"I'm not entirely sure, either, because I didn't design the spell: Ewers
did. I wasn't aware of all its components; he kept certain details hidden.
But magic is energy. It has to go somewhere. You can picture what happened in 1961 as an accident at a power plant. An amount of radiation
leaked when Ewers died. It affected us. Then imagine if a damaged reac-
tor was powered up again. You'd end up with a big explosion, and anyone
in the control room drenched in radiation. Only instead of dying a horrible death you became Spider-Man."

It made Montserrat think of frequency-shifted keying, one of the easi-
est ways to synchronize electronic instruments. Easy, yes, but you could
also mess it up. If you recorded your FSK tone too loudly it would leak
onto adjacent tracks. That's what Ewers had done. His magic was leaking
onto others, distorting not sound, but lives.

López took a sip of milk. "What, you don't read comic books? Peter
Parker was bitten by a radioactive spider."

"Maybe it's more like *The Fly*," Tristán suggested.

"Pick your metaphor, kid. Anyway, it needs to be shut down for good,
before Clarimonde and her army of crazies try to bring Ewers back to life.
Or Alma keeps taking advantage of the situation."

"But she wants Ewers destroyed," Tristán said.

"Don't be silly, of course she doesn't. Alma is the only person who
has benefited from this whole thing. All these years she's been using the
magic Ewers originally invoked in those nitrate reels to keep herself
young."

Montserrat shook her head. "That didn't happen. The spell was supposed to give her back her youth, but Ewers was working behind her
back, and the spell was never intended for Alma."

The old man scoffed and looked at her as if he were talking to a student who had failed a quiz. "She didn't get her youth back: she has not aged since the day Ewers died."

Montserrat remembered the remarkable similarities between Marisa and her aunt. Her nose was different, yes, but that could be a simple prosthetic. Alma had worked in movies, after all. She might know all kinds of makeup tricks to change her appearance. With a different haircut, different clothes, she might not be immediately recognized as Alma.

"Then Marisa Montero is Alma," Montserrat said.

López had gone back to nibbling his sandwich and bobbed his head.

"Is that even possible? How would she have managed it?" Montserrat asked.

The cat was now rubbing itself against Tristán's legs, and he picked it up and began scratching its head.

"Ewers didn't give enough credit to some of the people around him," López said. "He didn't think Alma was capable or smart enough, but she's crafty. Of course, he didn't think I'd amount to much, either, and I was not stabbed in the back ten times."

"You were the one who told Alma he was cheating on her. Why?"

"Why not?"

"Wasn't Ewers your friend?"

López brushed crumbs off his shirt. "Ewers had no friends. Only followers."

A thought occurred to Montserrat, and her fingers danced upon the top of the book poking out from her purse. "Alma didn't kill him. You *both* did."

López tossed his dirty glass in the sink.

"I need to nap," he muttered as he elbowed Montserrat away and went back toward the living room, parting the bead curtains, making them rattle. She followed him, moving quickly; her leg ached again. Damn polluted, cold Decembers. They wreaked havoc on her body. The stress probably didn't help.

"Why did you do it?"

"I'm tired. At my age, spell casting is not easy."

"I asked why."

López spun around and stared at her. "I saved your life today."

"I'd like to know the reason."

López sat down on the rattan couch. The center table was also rattan, as were two matching chairs with a pattern of palm trees on the cushions. Montserrat leaned against the back of a chair but did not sit down, watching the old man.

"The reason won't make any difference."

"Indulge me," she said.

He sighed. "Alma was a great actress in her day, but by the time Ewers came along her career was finished. He appealed to her vanity, but what's the harm in that? We all want to be admired, once in a while.

"Ewers promised things. Wealth, fame, fortune. To Alma he promised her lost beauty and her youth. The spell he was designing was supposed to achieve that. He lied. The spell was for him. He'd weave it on film with his runes and his special alchemy of sound and movement. And then, when the film had been screened and hundreds of people had seen this glorious movie, he'd commit suicide in a special ritual and be reborn a healthy man. I told Alma his true plan, and she was the one who stabbed him."

"And then, she did what?"

"She must have used the film stock for her own rituals. I don't know and did not ask. Magic does not easily dissipate, it lingers in the air," López said, raising a hand, his fingers tracing a beam of light that illuminated a section of the floor. Tiny dust particles floated in the sunbeam.

"Like radiation," López continued. "Or a recurring infection, I suppose."

"Then Alma benefited from this but everyone else was cursed?" Tristán asked. He was also standing behind a wicker chair, in imitation of Montserrat. Perhaps he feared to sit down. In his arms he still carried the cat, which was beginning to wriggle, impatient.

"Not everyone. Just as radiation may give someone cancer, it could leave the person standing next to them in good enough shape."

"You haven't said why you wanted him dead," Montserrat said.

"Because I knew who he was."

The cat tried to bite Tristán. He put it down, and it ran off to a dark corner of the room. Montserrat sat down on the chair and placed her purse on her lap.

"When I met Wilhelm Ewers I was forty-one years old. Clarimonde and Abel were still practically kids, but I was on my way out. Abel was not even thirty yet. I'd been writing since I was sixteen with no luck. I worked on minor projects, polished a few lines here and there. I earned most of my money as a copy editor, which is what I still do to this day to pay the bills. José López the copy editor and Romeo Donderis the writer. I thought it sounded more distinguished."

"But then you did get the gig writing for *Beyond the Yellow Door*, and you worked on other films before and after that," Montserrat replied.

"Sure. I almost wrote a movie for Karloff when he was shooting flicks in Mexico. Low budgets and low salaries, that was my life. It was Alma who approached me for this gig. She was interested in astrology, as was I. Magic practices, the occult, the whole thing. I'd been fascinated by it for a few years. She called me over to her apartment, and Wilhelm was there. He shook my hand, we discussed his theories on runes and magic, and he decided I was the man he needed to co-write this script. I had talent, that's what he said."

"As a screenwriter or as a magician?" Montserrat asked.

"Both, according to him. It was fine in the beginning. The job paid well. No surprise, Alma was putting a nice amount of money into the production, and she signed checks without wincing. The team was pleasant, and I had worked with Abel before, so there were no issues with him. He was a bright, young director and Clarimonde, who was hanging around him all the time during the shoot, was a delightful girl. My conversations with Ewers were invigorating, his theories, although wild, were interesting, and our arguments were intelligent. There were two small matters that soured our relationship. I noticed one almost immediately; the other it took me a long time to accept.

"Ewers organized people into a pyramid. People like him, brilliant Aryan stock, were at the top. Then came all the mutts of the world. That's what he called them. The 'mutts.' The mixed people of Mexico. And then all the other races that made him shudder; each level of the pyramid was carefully color-graded."

"He thought he descended from Atlanteans," Montserrat said. "He said the Aztec and the Inca had been great but they had—"

"Degenerated," López said. "Yes, that was the line he took."

"It would seem to be a bad idea to call the people around him 'mutts,'"

Tristán said. "Pretty ballsy since they were working with him. Didn't anyone punch the guy?"

"Have you not met Clarimonde? Did you not realize what her last
name is? Her father moved from Munich in 1938. Carl Wilhelm Kahlo
changed his name to Guillermo to sound more like a local, but Clarimonde's dad never wanted such a thing. Abel Urueta would get a sunburn
if he stood at the beach for three minutes. Alma: same story. The elites in
Mexico are proud of their European roots. Do you know who came up
with the theory that Atlanteans founded Tiwanaku?"

"Edmund Kiss," Montserrat said. "He wrote adventure novels and was
an amateur archeologist. His name popped up when I was doing research."

"No, it was Belisario Díaz. A Bolivian man. Why? Because to imagine
Indigenous intelligence and power would have been unthinkable. We are
all taught to despise the whiff of darkness, of Indigenous blood and of
Blackness. We speak about 'bettering the race,' and by that we mean in-
jecting more European blood into our veins. What Wilhelm said wasn't
considered outrageous at the time. It's not even outrageous now, sadly."

"Okay, maybe he appealed to Clarimonde's 'pure' German genes and
such. But you do not look German," Montserrat said.

"No, I don't. Ewers told me perhaps I descended from Aztec royalty,
to please me and himself. An idiocy."

"And so? What happened?"

"What happened was that I was good at magic. I'd tried it before, it
was a hobby, and working with Ewers it became obvious I had talent. He
might have liked Abel and Clarimonde better than me, but I was twice as
good as them. So, for a while, I simply enjoyed my job, enjoyed the connections I was making, enjoyed Ewers's praise. I accepted that he had . . .
flaws, but that didn't bother me. Not anymore."

López's mouth turned down into an ugly grimace, and he shook his
head. "We were finishing the picture when I accepted the second truth
about Wilhelm Ewers: that he had no limits."

The cat had wandered back toward the rattan couch and now jumped
on it, giving Tristán an irritated look. López petted the animal absent-
mindedly.

"The spell for the movie had complicated components. There were six
runes that were to appear in the credits at the beginning of the film and

then at the end. There was the silver nitrate and the dubbing that would
have to happen in post-production. Ewers also mentioned blood, to cement the runes, as a sort of binding agent. We killed a chicken every two
weeks we were shooting, one for each rune. Then there was the last rune
that would flash on screen. I was the one who had obtained the chickens
for the other ceremonies we had, so I asked Ewers if I should go to the
market, get the chickens. He told me there was no need for it: for the final
rune we'd use the blood of a man."

"Like your leeches?" Tristán asked.

"No. He said there were many homeless people in the city and no one
would miss one from a corner. I thought he might be joking. Ewers exag-
gerated and lied to suit his purposes. But then he looked me straight in
the eye and said: 'You knew it would come to this.'" López took a deep
breath. "He was right, I did know."

Tristán, who had been standing up until this moment, sat down and
gripped the arms of his chair. "He was going to murder someone?"

"I believe he'd killed before and he'd kill again."

"He did, in Europe," Montserrat said, remembering Ewers's dead as-
sociate, from whom he'd purloined documents and a fresh identity. "It
was in his letter. He thought it gave him power."

Before that, there had been Ewers's father, who had been left behind to
perish. Ewers didn't write of other deaths in his letter, but it didn't mean
he hadn't killed more people. He thought himself better than everyone
else, an Übermensch surrounded by untermenschen. Across the ages she
had read something cold and calculating in his gaze: only *I* matter, that
was what Ewers's photos said.

"You didn't mention a murder," Tristán told her. "You carry his book
in your purse, you pin his photos to your wall—"

"I need to understand," Montserrat said angrily.

"What? That he was a murderous, mean little man who thought the
Holocaust was cool?"

No, the spell. She wanted to understand how the pieces of Ewers's
magic fit together, the same as she might want to know how you trans-
ferred data between sequencers or how you record a FSK sync tone.

There was an awkward silence. Tristán sat there, smoldering, while
López simply looked tired.

"How could you be sure Alma would kill him?" Montserrat asked instead of replying to Tristán.

"We planned it. The whole of it," López said. "He was sick and tired at that point, and he depended on me for several tasks. It wasn't that difficult. Alma was the one who did the actual stabbing. After it happened, she was supposed to destroy the film, but she did not. I did not know immediately what had taken place, but a few years later I heard her niece was handling her affairs. A niece I had never heard of before, and when I saw Marisa, I realized the truth."

"Did she pay you off so you'd stay quiet?"

"No. I think she fears me a little because I knew the full story of what happened to Ewers. Now Clarimonde, I'm sure she has guessed what happened, but I have my wards, and Alma must have even stronger ones. After all, she gained a great measure of Ewers's power. That is why she must be interested in you."

"God. You two are giving me a headache," Tristán protested. "We don't have anything to do with this. Can't you cut us loose?"

"But you do have something to do with it, Spider-Man. You caused a second bigger explosion, remember? It must be affecting her, too. Before it was only Alma siphoning off that radiation, now you opened a valve and we're all soaked in it. Clarimonde and Abel helped Ewers cast his spell on film, Alma and I killed the bastard, and you two allowed him to wake up and start bothering us again. You made yourself part of the story, buddy."

"Fuck me, just what I needed. Some good old thermonuclear black magic," Tristán muttered, then he turned his head slightly and looked down, as if he were interested in examining the arms of the chair.

It was like splicing a new piece of film onto a reel, then running it smoothly through a projector. In the beginning of this tale there had been Ewers and his associates, but now Tristán and she had made their way into the picture. Their voices had been used to dub the movie. That performance couldn't be erased. She wondered about the other players in the film, the ones who had come before them.

"You never told Abel the truth about Alma?" Montserrat asked. "That she'd used Ewers's film for her own purposes?"

López laughed and shook his head. "No. I made a mistake, telling him that Clarimonde was in love with Ewers and she was cheating on him. I implied I'd told Alma about it, too. He was furious. He said I'd ruined his picture. He said that was why Alma had shut us down. Can you believe it? We didn't talk for years. A while back we got in touch. He was a very lonely man."

Montserrat remembered Abel Urueta, inviting them into his apartment, showing them his trinkets, asking them to accompany him on errands. Yeah, she supposed he'd been lonely. Lonely and desperate enough to reach deep into the past and attempt one last spell, one last shot at greatness. The only problem was he had never informed them what he was getting them into.

"You haven't said why you saved us," Montserrat told López.

"This spell never ended. But I intend to put an end to it now," López said firmly.

"Well, no, it didn't end. Ewers's death did something to the film, didn't it?" Montserrat mused. "You thought by killing him you'd be rid of the man, but instead you made sure he stuck around. You said his magic was never this powerful when he was alive, but *now* . . . I mean, it's blood magic. That's what you did. He didn't kill himself, but you offered a sacrifice anyway."

"We didn't plan it that way," López said. "But yes, and now you've both made it even worse. We need to get rid of him permanently."

"Then you know what to do?" Tristán asked hopefully. "It's been awful. I've seen my dead girlfriend."

"Oh?" López replied. "Necromancy? I never cared for that trick. It makes people jumpy."

"Sure it does. Ewers haunts Montserrat, which I guess is worse."

López leaned forward, lacing his hands together, and looked her in the eye. "He loved grooming talent. Maybe he thinks he's found his next eager pupil."

"I was never much for formal schooling," she said, trying to sound nonchalant, even if López's words made her weary.

"How do we exorcise him?" Tristán asked with an anxious lift of his eyebrows.

"There's a way. At least I *think* there's a way." López stood up, wincing. "I need to take a nap. My doctor says it's good for my blood pressure."

"Yes, but—"

"You should also take a nap. You both look like you haven't slept."

Montserrat had not. She had rolled to one side of the bed and closed her eyes tight, but she had not slept. She had been acting, pretending she was fine. She didn't want Tristán to panic, but she also feared *someone* else might be watching her, *someone* might be hoping she would shiver in fear.

"Follow me," López muttered, as he began shuffling his feet out of the living room. They went behind him, up the stairs until he pointed at a door. "That's the guest room. There are wards in the house, so you're safe. Now let me sleep, and we can talk later."

Once inside the room Tristán fell upon the bed with its brown knit blanket, making the mattress's springs squeak. There was a desk with pictures of a man and a woman in sepia above it and a brass lamp with a green glass lampshade. Montserrat pulled up a chair and took the book out of her purse, setting it on the desk.

"What are you up to?" Tristán asked.

"The dogs he mentioned . . . Ewers doesn't talk about dogs specifically, but he has a section on manifesting animal—"

"You're going to keep reading his book?"

"What do you want me to do instead?"

"Not read it. Nap. He's right: we're tired."

"You're scared."

"But I'm also right."

Montserrat sighed and sat on the bed. Tristán made a motion until she scooted closer to him, and he wrapped an arm around her shoulders.

"This is an old lady's room," Tristán said. "It probably belonged to López's mother."

"Maybe. Or a sister or a wife."

"No, his mother. Everything is older here."

The wooden headboard against her neck was mahogany decorated with a profusion of flowers. The guest room looked removed from the rest of the house and had been furnished by a different hand. López's rattan furniture and his wallpaper with a pale green bamboo print in the living room had the whiff of the tiki craze of the early sixties. But Tristán was right: this room was from a previous era, and the doilies on the night table made her think of her grandmother.

"Maybe he was a surfer when he was young," Montserrat suggested.
"Or played the ukulele."

"He carved faces into pineapples."

Tristán snickered, then paused, thoughtful. "You think we can trust him?"

"He hasn't tried to kill us."

His mouth twisted into a grimace. "That's a low bar."

"We could leave while he's taking his nap if you don't think he's honest."

"Alma also said she wanted to destroy the film."

"But she pickled herself in magic, so she was lying."

"You're sure she was passing herself off as her niece? It might be a family resemblance."

"There was something wrong about her. Didn't you feel it?"

"When I met her the second time she looked older. I thought it was the light or the makeup she was wearing, but maybe she is finally aging. It could be the unintended consequences López talked about. Or maybe I'm going nuts."

"No, you might be right."

"I suppose," Tristán muttered. "I guess Alma's a dead end. And those dogs might be outside, anyway. I wouldn't want to see those creatures again."

Montserrat glanced at the window with lace curtains and wondered if that was indeed the case. Were López's wards as strong as he claimed? She was not entirely sure what he meant by that term. Protective charms somehow tied to a building? He'd tattooed symbols on his arms; maybe he'd also carved them beneath the wallpaper or under the floor. The thought of hidden magic made her frown.

"What?" Tristán said.

"Spookiness," she muttered, unwilling to elaborate.

The sleepless night and bizarre encounter with Bauer's minions had drained her, and the pillows were soft. She curled up without another word and closed her eyes. Tristán must have had enough, too, because he was snoring after a few minutes. Montserrat figured that if López decided to walk into the room and murder them, he'd have an easy time accomplishing the deed.

23

Karina used to say Tristán slept like a starfish, limbs extended, attempting to take over the entire bed. It was hard to sleep with him because he tossed and turned. But Tristán must not have been terribly restless because when he woke up, Montserrat was next to him, and she remained fast asleep.

It was getting dark and it was Friday. The posadas had started. They ought to have been out, eating tamales, venturing forth to a party. They should have been planning a New Year's celebration for the two of them, with champagne and streamers and a scary midnight movie. *Black Christmas*, perhaps, or *Gremlins* for something lighter. Instead, they were trapped in this odd house and a room that was filling with shadows.

He figured the best thing would be to nudge Montserrat and find their host, but he lay quietly for a while, slowly wrapping a strand of Montserrat's hair around his fingers.

Hair that couldn't belong to a human woman, it was more like a pelt than anything else. Never dyed, haphazardly cut, almost always tied back up in a practical ponytail and now undone. Quite wonderful in its own way, that hair. Quite wonderful Montserrat, too, with her t-shirt that had been washed too frequently, her eyebrows that were too thick, a nose that was too wide for any magazine to want to take a snapshot of her, the sullen, generous mouth that preferred to offer barbs rather than kisses. A mutable, witchy Circe rather than a demure, well-behaved Penelope.

You are pretty, sometimes, Momo, when it's you and me at dusk, he thought.

"What are you doing?" Montserrat asked, blinking and looking at him, with his hand in her hair.

"Analyzing your split ends," he replied, feeling embarrassed, his cheeks warming up as he conjured up a light laugh and tried to make fun of it. "You don't condition your hair."

"I don't shave my armpits, either. Are you going to tell *Cosmopolitan* to arrest me?" she replied, sitting up and shaking her head, as if getting rid of a kink in her neck.

"They'd execute you for crimes against fashion and personal grooming."

"I know."

A knock at the door made Tristán sit up.

"You two, I made supper," López said. "Come and eat."

The supper consisted of a watery chicken soup that had Tristán yearning for his mother's lentil soup with chard and the comforts of his apartment. He should cook more often, he thought. He'd stopped doing it because he felt it was useless to make a feast for one, and there were many days when he simply wanted to remain in his PJs and surf through the television channels for hours on end.

"What we need is to wrap Ewers's spell up, like tying a knot and cutting the thread," López said as he reached into a paper bag and took out a bolillo, then shoved the bag in their direction. "The way to do it, I think, is to replicate as much as we can Ewers's original magic. He used six runes that were going to be shown in the credits, so we write down those six runes in the order he intended, with the help of my leeches and a little blood."

"Whose blood?" Tristán asked.

"Yours, hers, mine. Whoever volunteers for it. Anyway, we draw the runes on the can of the silver nitrate print. You do still have that, correct?"

"It's in storage," Montserrat said.

"After we say the proper words and draw the runes, we can destroy the film."

"It's that easy, then?" Tristán said. "We draw runes and it's done?"

Tristán poured himself a glass of water from a plastic pitcher. At the center of the round table where they were sitting there was a figurine of a Hawaiian dancer, and when Tristán accidentally brushed his hand against it, the dancer moved her hips in a quick motion.

"It's a spell," López said, tearing off a piece of the bolillo and frowning. "It takes energy and effort. Spells feed off willpower, strength, life. Plus, you must remember what I'm saying is merely theoretical. I suspect that the only way to dispel Ewers's magic is to essentially screen the credits, as he would have done at the end of his film."

"But drawing runes is not the same as screening the credits."

"Magic is symbolic," López said. "We basically tell the film that we are screening the credits, that the movie is over."

"You *tell* the film?"

"Yes, we talk to the can of film. We say, 'You are Ewers, and your story has reached its conclusion.'"

"Sympathetic magic," Montserrat explained. "Spells like that appear many times in Ewers's book. You establish a link between two objects. When one object is affected, the other reacts. If Ewers's magic was preserved in the reels that he shot, then he was preserved, and he can be destroyed."

"We only have one reel," Tristán said. "Won't he still remain around if we don't destroy every remaining reel?"

"That is why we speak to the film, and we tell it that the story is concluding," López said. "If I'm right, then he will cease to be. It'll be like the lights turn on and you step out of a screening room. Any reels in Alma's possession will lose their charge."

There was a certain logic to what they were saying, but it still sounded odd. Tristán ate his bread instead of replying, mulling the idea.

"There are, of course, issues we have to deal with first," López said.

"Which ones?"

"I don't know what runes Ewers intended to use in the credits. He kept details from me. Abel would have had that information, but he's dead."

"Then what? Trial and error?"

"Impossible. We need to speak to Abel. Twice you've seen your dead girlfriend, correct?"

"Yeah," Tristán replied, frowning. "You're not saying—"

"You seem to have a certain affinity for necromancy. We're going to need that skill."

Tristán laughed. López was chewing loudly and staring at him. "No," Tristán said. "I don't know anything about necromancy. I'm trying to *avoid* ghosts."

"We'll hold the séance together. We'll be in the room with you."

"I'm not a sorcerer."

"It's not as if we have many candidates for the post."

"*You* do it. Or Montserrat," Tristán said. "She's seen Ewers, she's also seeing ghosts, she could to a better job at it than I ever could since she actually understands what is happening."

"Ewers is not a ghost. Ewers is neither dead nor alive."

He'd thought that López was talking in jest. At least, he had hoped he was. But now the man was staring at him and so was Montserrat. He felt as if they were backing him up against a wall.

"I don't care if he's a vampire, why the hell do I have to be the one who talks to a ghost? If we don't know the right runes, we'll guess. Trial and error, like I said."

"There are dozens of runes in Ewers's book. You must summon Abel," the old man replied, immutable, like he was asking him to go to the corner store and buy him a beer.

"I wouldn't even know how to do it. I have no idea how to summon ghosts."

"You have been summoning your girlfriend."

Tristán slammed his hands down on the table, making the Hawaiian dancer tremble. "I have not."

"You don't realize it, but you do it," López said. "Now you can be a stubborn coward and live the rest of your life inside my guest room, or maybe you can help me put an end to Ewers's spell."

López carefully wiped his mouth with a napkin and then fished out a piece of corn from his bowl and began gnawing at the kernels. Tristán pushed his chair back and stood up, glaring at the old man.

"I don't summon anything," Tristán said, wishing to choke the geezer if he as much as said another word about ghosts, but the crusty bastard seemed unfazed.

"You probably have something that belonged to her. That's useful when summoning ghosts. Anything personal or of significance to the deceased helps form a link. A picture also helps do the trick. Then you think about them, you call them forth, you ask them to speak to you."

Tristán remembered Karina's picture, tucked inside his wallet, almost forgotten and yet never out of mind. That little snapshot that was bent at the corner. He swallowed.

"Would he be in any danger?" Montserrat asked.

"Ghosts are not dangerous," López said. "They're shadows, immaterial."

"Ewers chased Montserrat through a building," Tristán said. "I'm sure she didn't feel safe."

"I said he's not a ghost. He's caught between life and death. Besides, we won't be asking him to join us."

"Why not? I'm a great necromancer. Let's call my girlfriend, Abel, Ewers, and hey, maybe Napoleon is available. We'll play poker together, okay?"

"Your sarcasm is not solving anything. Ewers cast one hardy spell, and when you dubbed his film, you released power unlike anything I've ever felt," López said. "For good or ill, you can see and speak to ghosts right now, and we need that skill."

"Or we could do nothing," Tristán said stubbornly.

"I told you this is power unlike anything I've ever seen."

"How much have you seen? Are there many sorcerers around the city? Do they all wear dirty raincoats? I don't think I should be following orders from a guy who can't figure out how to launder his clothes."

"That was my father's raincoat," López said. "I wear it because it protects me; it's bewitched, as are my tattoos. And yes, there are sorcerers in this city. Magic requires many elements to work, and most people don't have all of them at once. Ewers managed to essentially secure all the components to a bomb, and instead of defusing it, you made it tick again."

"Maybe he's too powerful to beat. Maybe he's superhuman. Have you thought about that?"

Montserrat scoffed. "Ewers was no Atlantean, he was a kid who became a good thief. If Ewers had a talent, it was that he was a magpie. In his letter he said he learned from every single person he met, even stealing when he needed to. He was clever and creative. He was also determined. It doesn't make him infallible."

"It also doesn't mean we should be getting more involved in this shit," Tristán said. "You're asking me to speak to the dead like I'm making a phone call and chatting with the operator."

"You are already speaking to the dead," López said. "You might want to hang up on your dead girlfriend instead of dialing her every day. All I'm asking is that you use whatever power you have to help me and your friend. A bomb, okay? You activated a bomb."

"Well, I didn't make that bomb, old man. Thirty-something years ago, you and your friends decided to manufacture a cursed film with an insane Nazi screenwriter, and now you want *me* to defuse your mistake. Guess what, I'm fed up. The answer is no."

Rather than reply López spat a kernel out into the palm of his hand and kept on gnawing at his corn. Tristán shook his head and stepped out of the dining room and headed upstairs, back into the bedroom. He paced around, waiting for Montserrat to find him. But she didn't come. On the night table there was a bowl with mints and candy that could only be found in an old lady's house. He tossed the candy away and lit a cigarette, collecting the ash in the bowl.

Montserrat finally stood at the doorway, watching him, arms crossed.

"He wants to help us," she said. "But we also have to help him."

"Yeah? What's he doing? What are you doing? I'm the one being asked to play around with ghosts, not you."

"He'll draw the runes with his blood. And I'll make the film burn. We need to work together."

"Don't ask this of me. What if I summon her instead of Abel? What then?" he asked, dropping the cigarette into the bowl and placing it back where he'd found it, on the night table with the doily.

Montserrat did not reply, but he could see by the slant of her mouth that she was growing restless and irritated. He considered pushing back, demanding other solutions, but then he reached into his pocket, took out his wallet, and carefully retrieved Karina's photo. He held it up, offering it to Montserrat.

She stepped into the room and took the snapshot from his hand. Then he lowered his head.

"You don't know the whole story. We had a fight the night of the party. It started as a small disagreement and spiraled out of control. She said I didn't love her, that I was with her for the publicity and because of her connections. She started drinking, and I ignored her. I flirted with other people, I laughed, I danced.

"When she said she was driving home, I knew she was sloshed, but I didn't try to take her keys. I simply got in the car and shrugged. I wanted to teach her a lesson. I thought maybe she'd bump into another car when she tried to park, or she'd vomit over the expensive upholstery. And I was tipsy myself, and irritated.

"My eyes were closed as she drove. I could hear her crying, but I was tired and I was angry, so I kept them shut and pretended I was trying to sleep."

Montserrat's face was expressionless. He would have preferred it if she'd made a motion, replied with a nod, something. He'd always told Montserrat that he'd been blind drunk that night and sitting in the passenger's seat. He had not described the party, nor hinted at a fight. The papers had whispered about trouble between the lovers, but he had not admitted it. Oblique references through the years had never crystallized into a full story.

"I didn't see what she crashed into. I heard the screech of the tires and then there was glass everywhere and I was being hit so hard I lost my breath. It was all pain after that. I opened my eyes and I saw blood. It was everywhere, over her face, over mine . . . I passed out."

Something flashed in Montserrat's eyes then. Neither disapproval nor understanding. It was only that she'd heard this part before, or at least knew enough of it to recognize that section of the narrative: the awful taste of the blood in his mouth, his injured eye, the chaos of an ambulance and nurses. But he steered in another direction; instead of speaking of the surgery or the recovery, he paused.

"The funny thing is that I wanted her to break up with me. At the party, she said I didn't love her, that I was stringing her along. She was right. I liked her, but I didn't love her, and by then I didn't even like her that much. I wanted her to go off and find someone else so I wouldn't have to be the one doing the breaking up. I hate that. It's always messy, and I knew it would get even messier with Karina; she was dramatic, which I enjoyed and hated. I figured we'd have a shitty night and she would dump me."

He stood up and glanced at the photo in Montserrat's hand.

"Look at that picture, look at that girl. She's twenty-four there. She's a kid stumbling around, making dumb choices, but still a kid. She deserved to grow old, to grow up. To have a whole life."

"You didn't kill her."

"No," Tristán said, scoffing. "I didn't start the ignition, I didn't turn that wheel and crash that car, but I knew her. I knew she was fragile; I knew she needed me to calm her down or to at least ask someone to watch over her for a bit. I knew she was hurt."

He touched his eyebrow, slid his fingertips against the corner of his eye and smirked, feeling the scar there and beneath it the titanium mesh holding his eye in place.

"When I woke up, you know what the first thing I asked was? Not if Karina was fine, not if anyone else had been harmed . . . I asked if my face looked okay.

"I've never visited her grave," Tristán continued. "I always thought it was silly to bury people. She should have been cremated. She wanted her ashes spread near the ocean. But her father wouldn't hear of it. Just like he wouldn't hear that she wanted to kill herself that night."

"Her and you."

"Yeah. I hated her for it, right after the accident, when they said . . . the eye, you know. The other injuries, the surgeries . . . I thought she should have had the decency to swallow pills or slash her wrists in the bathroom, like a normal person. You're not supposed to enact the libretto of *Madame Butterfly* in a moving vehicle."

He let out a low, brittle half-laugh as he took the photograph from Montserrat's open palm. "You're correct, Momo. I'm a selfish bastard. I've let everyone I've ever known down. And I'm always running away."

"López says the living hold on to ghosts. You made a haunted house out of your own flesh and bones."

"How poetic," he muttered, sitting down again.

"It's true. There's no exorcism that has ever worked for you. But right now, you could do something for all of us."

"I don't want to talk to Abel any more than I want to talk to Karina."

"You have to," she said, moving closer to him, until she was right in front of him. "López says it needs to be you. He has a picture of Abel somewhere that can be used for the summoning. He'd tell you what to say and do. But the most important part is that you need to be willing to do it. You can't be forced into it."

She sat down on the bed. He turned to look at her. Montserrat raised a hand, her fingertips tracing the scar he'd been touching before. Then her hand went down, toward his chest, to the spot where the other scars lay hidden under his shirt. She'd looked at him at the hospital many times, she'd helped him clean himself and bathe in the awful months of his recovery. She remembered all the marks, like a map.

But he still inhaled in surprise.

"I guessed the whole story, Tristán, because I know you."

"You realized I'm an idiot, then."

"I knew that the first time you agreed to jump into the grain containers. Who does that because their friend suggests it?"

Tristán smiled, thinking about the feel of the grain against his body, almost tickling him, and Montserrat's delighted laughter as they tried to climb their way out.

"I don't think you'd abandon me, would you?" she asked, with a solemnity that made him wince.

"That's cheating, Momo," he said. "It's a cheap and dirty trick."

He lowered his gaze, looked at Montserrat's hand still pressed over his chest. She moved away from him slowly, as if fearing he'd bolt away.

"If López is right . . . if it's me calling her . . . if I tell Karina I'm sorry, do you think I would stop seeing her?"

"Maybe. López says you want her with you."

"I've spent ten years thinking about her. It's a habit. God, Momo, it's like sinking in quicksand. I don't want to hear any more talk of sorcerers and spells and runes."

"Then let's get this over with! We made a mistake when we dubbed that film; we helped wake Ewers and we can't pretend we didn't. We have to finish this," she said with a certainty that he expected but equally dreaded.

"But what if we don't?" Tristán insisted. "What if we let things be?"

"You heard López: we caused a nuclear explosion. We need to clean it up."

"What's the worst thing the guy is going to do? Maybe, I dunno, he'll wake up and simply want to watch a movie and see the elephants at Chapultepec. He won't bother anyone."

"He'll want to do more than see the elephants."

"You don't know that."

"I think I do. He'll be angry, he'll be hungry, and he'll want to fuck up the world."

"How can you be sure?"

Because she knows the guy, he thought, and she was glad she didn't actually say this, instead making a vague gesture, but it was the truth. She'd spent enough time reading his book that she had a pretty good idea of who he was. Tristán didn't like that; it made him nervous.

"All right, yeah, I don't think he and his cult want peace and world harmony. And I know I can't carry Karina with me anymore, I know now is the time to let her go, but it's hard."

Tristán pressed both hands against his face. He felt Montserrat's hand on his shoulder. He brushed her aside, as gently as he could, then walked out of the room and into a small bathroom. He'd been near water the previous times he'd seen Karina. He didn't know if water was necessary, but he thought it might help. He also wanted to be alone. He couldn't attempt this with Montserrat by his side.

He held up Karina's photograph with two fingers, carefully looking at every feature and detail of the snapshot.

"I should have taken flowers to your grave. You loved pink roses," he said. "I'm sorry."

He tried to think of Karina as she'd been in the photo, energetic, full of possibilities, instead of the way he'd seen her in the bathroom the last time: bloodied, with cuts on her face and body. He hadn't loved Karina the way she needed to be loved, but he did miss her, and he felt true sorrow at the memory of her loss.

The bathroom remained cool and quiet. He didn't notice a change. He wasn't sure how you were supposed to formulate spells with nothing but need and loneliness. He drew a "K" on the mirror in front of him and squeezed his eyes shut and whispered her name. He remained like that for a long time, until his head was throbbing and he heard the faint whisper of footsteps on the tiled floor.

He turned his head and she was there, standing next to him. Karina, with her mournful eyes. She did not cough blood, and glass did not spill from the folds of her clothing. She simply stood by his side, and he raised a hand in a mute goodbye.

He took out his lighter and pressed the flame against a corner of the photo. Tristán let the photograph fall into the sink, where it curled up and smoldered, a bitter trail of smoke rising in the air. He stared at the tiny bits of black left behind, opened the faucet until the ashes swirled down the drain. When he lifted his head again, she was gone.

24

They decided they would conjure Abel's ghost the next night and then head to Antares the morning after that to pick up the film. Montserrat said there wouldn't be anyone working on a Sunday, especially the weekend before Christmas. Although Montserrat had keys to the building, she didn't have keys to the vault where the film was stored, and she was going to have to tinker with the lock. They'd break in, essentially. Fortunately, from what Montserrat told them, the security system at Antares was useless due to recent budget cuts. They wouldn't be tripping any alarms.

López warned them the conjuring would tire them, so he didn't want to attempt both things in a single day. Tristán thought it was better this way because that meant whatever spell they worked on would take place during the daytime on Sunday, after their prompt return from Antares. Daytime seemed like a much safer time for magic than midnight. The séance, however, would unfold Saturday evening.

"I am not a wind-up toy," López said. "I'm not going to have a séance before a proper breakfast and careful preparation. Well? Pull up a chair for yourself."

A "proper" breakfast consisted of eggs without bacon or even a glass of orange juice. López had a few bags of cheap green tea in his kitchen, but nothing else that could function as a suitable drink.

"No coffee?" Tristán asked.

"I was going to go to the grocery store, but then I got stuck with you two," López told them. "You can go outside and order yourself a latte at a fucking Sanborns, but if you get killed on the way there don't blame me."

"Forget I asked," Tristán muttered.

There was no way he was going to walk to a Sanborns for a lousy cup of coffee that might get him murdered. Instead, Tristán threw himself on

López's couch, sipped a terrible cup of tea, and tried watching the rickety TV set. López had apparently never heard of cable, so he was stuck with a movie featuring Tongolele while Montserrat inspected the books on the shelves and talked to López about spooks, spells, and charms.

In the afternoon, the scent of beer wafted down the streets from the Modelo brewery a few blocks away. If he took a taxi, he would be back in his apartment in less than twenty minutes, even accounting for traffic. But Tristán merely peered out a window into the front courtyard with its metal gates.

"Is there a reason for the tropical décor?" Tristán asked when López told him he needed help with a couple of boxes and they ventured into a room wallpapered with a banana leaf print.

"Ever heard of the Winchester house in California?"

"It was in an episode of *Ripley's Believe It or Not.*"

"The legend says Sarah Winchester constructed stairs that go to no-where and designed meandering hallways to confuse spirits."

"Is that what you're doing?"

"No. I like tropical things. But it sounds better if I tell you it has a higher purpose," the old man said dryly.

Tristán laughed. He took the boxes to the dining room and placed them on the round table. López opened one and began taking out red candlesticks that were wrapped in newspaper. "I don't have much use for fine dining. But we'll need candlelight."

"Why? I saw Karina last night and didn't have a candle with me."

"You bid her goodbye?"

"Yeah," Tristán said, bunching up the newspaper between his hands.

"It sounds like it was about time," López said and shook his head. "You had a long-standing connection with your girlfriend. It will be harder to reach Abel, and you'll need any help you can get. Darkness will be benefi-cial, and these are no ordinary candles. They've been blessed. Instead of chasing away ghosts, like white candles do, these candles will draw them in and protect you. Sometimes you can use other things to catch the at-tention of the dead. Spoiled meat or bones can do the trick, but I think red candles should be enough for you."

"Good. I didn't want to have to find a spoiled hamburger patty in the garbage."

"We'll need a picture of Abel." López took off the lid of a file box and began thumbing through folders inside. "I kept a bunch of things from my film career. I didn't think they were valuable until a few years back when I began talking to Abel again and he said memorabilia can sell for big bucks. Now, here we go," López said as he took out a photo and placed it on the table.

It was a snapshot of Abel Urueta, as he had looked during the production of *Beyond the Yellow Door*. The photo reminded Tristán of the reality of Abel's death, and the fact that he would have to attempt to speak to his ghost.

"You think this will work?" Tristán asked.

"Yes, if you make an effort. It won't be like those chance glimpses of your girlfriend. It's one thing to see a ghost and another to hear their words."

"Maybe Abel won't want to talk to me."

"Draw him forth. I'll explain how, but the most important part is you need to *want* to do this."

In the afternoon, there was a supper that consisted of sandwiches with a single slice of mortadella, and afterward López had them sit down in the dining room so he could paint symbols on their hands using a dark ink that had Tristán questioning its provenance.

"What is that?" he asked, disturbed by the smell. The ink had an acrid, unpleasant scent, and he wondered if López hadn't macerated a couple of leeches from the tank, then ground them in a molcajete. He wouldn't put it past the guy.

"Several things mixed together," López said, carefully sliding the tip of a thin brush against Montserrat's wrist. "The symbols should protect you, just in case."

"Just in case what? I thought you said ghosts were not dangerous."

"It's an extra precaution."

"And that?" Tristán asked, pointing at the large box of table salt sitting on the table.

" 'First burn ye therein sulphur pure, and then sprinkle about it with a wool-wound branch innocent water mingled, as the custom is, with salt,' " López said. "Theocritus."

"What?"

"Salt. Sprinkle it around and it can repel many noxious beings."

"What does pepper do? Allow you to summon demons?"

"You must take this seriously."

"Sure. I will. What time are we doing this, anyway? It's getting late."

"After dark," López said.

Tristán looked at his wristwatch. "I might as well take a nap before we start with all the witching."

López gave Tristán an exasperated look and shook his head, his fingers wielding the brush delicately. Tristán promptly walked back into their room and plopped himself on the bed. Later, Montserrat wandered in, her hands inked with runes.

"You need to have your hands painted," she said.

"Yeah, yeah, I'll do it in a bit."

"Why are you being annoying?"

Tristán was sitting on the bed with one hand behind his head. He leaned on his elbows and sat up, watching Montserrat as she crossed her arms and stared at him.

"I'm not going to chicken out, Momo. You'll have your séance. But it doesn't mean I want to spend my day listening to the old man whisper about magic."

"You're not taking this seriously."

"And you take it too seriously."

"What is that supposed to mean?"

"You're enjoying this. Spells and wizards and Wilhelm Ewers. The way you act about all his stuff," he said, pointing at the book she'd left open on the desk. "Or the things he wrote and thought . . . What did he say to you? That night, when he woke you up, what did he say?"

Montserrat sat on the bed, by his feet, and shook her head. "You're a stubborn fucker. Fine. He told me to follow him into the night."

"What does that mean?"

She frowned. "It's a phrase in his book. He's trying to scare me, that's all. I said so already."

"No, it's bigger than that," Tristán insisted. "The more you become immersed in his books, in his magic, the more you become immersed in him. You don't realize it, but sometimes you sound like you *admire* the guy. He was clever, creative, and determined, right?"

"That's not what I—" Montserrat began to say, her frown deepening, but he cut her off.

"You told me I was summoning my dead girlfriend, but have you thought that maybe the reason why you've seen Ewers is because you're calling out to him?"

"He could write a decent turn of phrase, okay? And he could figure out the components of a spell, and neither of those things means—"

"Do you want to be a sorceress, like old Willie? Cast hexes instead of mixing audio? Fess up."

She stood up. "Get the runes on your hands."

Tristán felt tempted to be contrarian, but in the end he submitted to the process and listened patiently to López as he explained what he had to do in order to summon a ghost.

By ten p.m. López had placed a white tablecloth atop the table and re-moved the Hawaiian dancer from its center, relegating it to the sideboard. The box with the salt took the doll's place. López placed two candlesticks on the table and struck a match. Between the candlesticks there was a glass of water.

"Water is a good conduit, and the candles, like the box of salt, should protect you while also providing a welcoming space for the ghost. Now you understand the instructions," López said as he handed Tristán a large notepad and a pen. "Do you need to go over the words again?"

"I'm an actor. I can memorize lines," Tristán replied. He wanted to get this done with before he thought it over and backed out.

"You simply ask him to join us and then you write down whatever he says."

"In the movies people hold hands, you know."

"And they probably have a Ouija board manufactured by Juguetes Mi Alegría. Will you simply sit down?"

Tristán muttered a curse word but obeyed. López turned off the light and sat to his right. Montserrat had already taken his left.

The room was rather dark with only the two candles. He wrapped his hands around the glass of water and asked the water to bless him and protect him before he embarked on this journey. He placed the notepad and the pen on the table, resting his hands lightly next to them. Then he

recited the words López had told him to memorize, which were easy
enough.

López handed him Abel's photograph, and Tristán held it up. In the
dim light it was hard to make out the features, but he tried his best to
keep his eyes on the photo and listen to his own breathing. The minutes
stretched by. His hand was beginning to ache from holding the photograph up.

"Concentrate," López said.

"I am concentrating," Tristán said, switching hands.

"Repeat the incantation again, from the beginning."

Tristán said the words. Nothing happened. After many more minutes
López pushed his chair back. "Perhaps we might try something else. I
have incense in the sideboard," he said, as he moved toward a lumpy shape
that must be said sideboard, hidden as it was in the dark.

Tristán set the photograph down next to the notepad with a sigh. It
was cold that night. Tristán hadn't noticed before, but suddenly the chill
of the evening overtook him, making him shiver. His hands brushed
against the pen, restless, as López grumbled and opened a drawer, rum-
maging among what sounded like cutlery.

"Where is it? Why, you stupid . . ."

López kept muttering, and Tristán shivered again, his fingers wrapping
around the pen. He felt nauseated and pressed one hand against his belly.
He closed his eyes.

"Tristán?" Montserrat said.

He blinked a couple of times. The nausea was dying down, but there
was a sharp pain in the back of his skull, as if someone was inserting a
needle there. His hand twitched. He wrote down a word and glanced
down at the letters. He clutched the edge of the table with his free hand.

"Momo," he said, quickly looking up and staring at her. She stared
back at him in confusion.

"What?"

"That's not my handwriting."

Montserrat looked at the pad where he had written "Abel" with clean,
neat strokes, the letters in cursive in a style that was very much unlike his
own. López looked down at the paper and sat down, nodding.

"Keep at it," López said.

"How? You said he'd speak to me, but this isn't speaking. I'm not hearing anything."

"It's fine. Give it a try."

"Okay, sure . . . ah . . . Abel, is that you?"

He wrote down the word "yes." López nodded and motioned for him to continue. López had been right: this was different from the times he had seen Karina. The sharp stabbing pain in his skull was new. Tristán wetted his lips.

"I'm sorry for what happened to you. We are trying to end Ewers's spell, but we need your help. There were runes he wanted to project during the credits, do you remember that?"

Yes.

"I need the runes and the sequence in which they were going to be projected. Can you help me?"

I'll try.

"Go ahead," Tristán said, not knowing what else to say.

His hand moved across the page as if of its own volition. He traced a triangle and two lines, adding smaller strokes to the sides.

"The first one. This is the first one," Tristán said.

"Air," Montserrat said.

Earth and *water* came next. Then there was a rune López identified as *life*. "The opener" was the fifth. Neither Montserrat nor López had to identify the last rune for him: he recognized it as the vegvísir. Funnily enough the symbol for fire had not been called. He'd expected it to be part of the sequence, seeing as they'd started with an element. He felt something was subtly wrong but could not pinpoint what, exactly. His fingers trembled.

"Is there something else?"

Yes.

His fingers trembled even more. Even if Abel couldn't speak to him Tristán felt something had gone askew. A cloud of anxiety wrapped around his brain.

Yes.

"What is it?" he asked, the sensation that Abel was trying to warn him was thick and almost tangible.

His hand twitched against the page again.

You are afraid, Tristán.

The words bloomed before his eyes; the pen was harsh against the page. Those letters . . . that handwriting . . . it was different than what he'd been writing moments before. This was very compact, the letters pressed against each other, tiny.

Every day of your life you are afraid, Tristán.

"It's Ewers's handwriting," Montserrat said.

Tristán watched as his hand descended upon the page, almost slashing it apart with one violent stroke. He swallowed.

"Yes, it's Ewers," López said. "Crafty bastard, what do you want?"

Fear me.

The candles wavered, and Tristán felt a wave of terrible cold. It was as if the cold pressed against him, and he tried to slam the notebook shut, he tried to lift his hand away, but instead his fingers closed around the pen with an iron grip as his stomach churned.

Follow me into the night, Mont—

Tristán knocked the notebook off the table with his free hand, but the pen dug into the white tablecloth, staining it, drawing the rest of the letters.

—serrat.

"Make it stop," Tristán told López.

"You miserable bastard," López said, reaching for the box with salt and tossing liberal amounts of it across the table. "Leave. You are not welcome. My wards repel you."

Tristán bent over the table. Something had shoved him down, something of great strength, and for a moment he feared it would crush his spine. The candles sputtered, and they were plunged into shadows. He felt Montserrat's hand, clutching his wrist, as his chair squeaked and seemed to shiver. His mouth was coated in bile, and he clenched his teeth.

"My wards repel you," López said again. Tristán could hear and feel the salt being scattered around the room, blindly tossed in all directions.

He dropped the pen and shoved a hand into his jacket pocket, his fingers sliding against his lighter, producing a dim flame.

"Light those candles again," López ordered. He had thrust one hand inside the box with the salt.

Tristán obeyed, attempting to press the flame against the wick, but the tablecloth slid forward, slick as a snake, toppling with its motion both candlesticks and the glass. It launched itself against López with such force that the man was flung back. The box he was holding fell to the ground.

Tristán stood up and helplessly watched as López was wrapped in the tablecloth and pulled or shoved back fast, colliding against the sideboard with a resounding crash.

"José!" he yelled.

The man groaned in response, and Tristán stepped forward, but Montserrat yanked him back.

"Look," she said.

The cold had intensified. Tristán's breath rose like a plume of smoke, and his teeth were near chattering. The furniture creaked all around them, vibrating, as if the chairs and the table were about to splinter, and then the noises ceased. The room was quiet. For a moment he thought it was all over and the entity had departed, but Montserrat did not move a muscle.

With only the lighter to illuminate the room it was hard to see anything, but slowly she raised an arm and pointed to a shadow that stood close to López. The shadow had the dim shape of a man, taller than López, taller than Tristán, too. The shape had no features, it was a void, it drew the eye even though there was *nothing* there.

"Get the salt," Montserrat whispered to him, and to the shadow she spoke in a louder voice. "Our wards repel you."

Tristán bent down and grabbed the box. The lighter in his hand trembled with the motion of his body, and the shadow seemed to shift, to almost blink in and out of existence. The tablecloth fluttered a little, moved by an invisible wind. His ears ached, as if he was sitting on a plane during a landing. Montserrat's voice had grown muffled, and the shadow stood still but it was *breathing*. He could hear it, faint as the whisper of an insect's wing.

"Our wards repel you," Montserrat said, stepping forward. "Tristán, say it."

"I . . . our wards repel you."

"Our wards repel you," she said as she took another step and held up an open palm.

The sound of breathing quickened. Tristán wasn't even sure he could hear it anymore, but the shadow rippled, as if it were gasping for breath, its chest rising and falling. Silver, then dark, a sharp, quick blinking, a flash frame.

"Our wards repel you," he mumbled. The words were so muffled he doubted anyone would have understood what he said.

"At the same time as me," she said.

"It's not working!"

Montserrat pressed her hands against her ears and closed her eyes, grimacing, and Tristán felt the darkness crash like a wave against them, tinged with aggressiveness, with a need and a quickness that made him stumble back. The thing in the room had almost thrown him to the ground, as it had thrown López back, but he regained his footing.

"Tristán," Montserrat said. Her hand grasped his arm, holding him as the darkness pushed against them. A chair slid and lurched up, shoving Tristán, attempting to knock him down a second time, and Tristán might have screamed, but he was too surprised. A candlestick flew through the air, then another, smashing against a wall. Dishes rattled inside the sideboard, cups and glasses crushing and splintering against one another. He shrank away, intending to reach the door to the dining room, but Montserrat's hand was still on his arm, gripping him tight.

"Don't stop!"

The table slid fast across the floor, and Montserrat pulled Tristán back, moving him out of its path, while he held on to his lighter. He dropped the box of salt, and it spilled in front of their feet. The grains of salt crunched underneath the soles of their shoes as they jerked away and stumbled against a wall.

Tristán groaned, and Montserrat's hand was on his shoulder. "Say it with me."

Darkness boiled up, making the tiny flame Tristán still clutched in his trembling hand blink into nothingness. Blinded, lost in the darkness, he panicked as he tried to flick the lighter back to life. But Montserrat's hand slid down his arm, lacing her fingers with his.

"Tristán, don't stop. On the count of three, all right?"

"Yeah . . . yes," he said.

"One, two, three."

"Our wards repel you!" they yelled.

Something hurtled against the wall. Perhaps it was a chair, or even the table. The noise was like a cannon being fired, and it made the walls shiver. He clutched Montserrat against him, hugging her tight.

The room grew still and quiet. The tidal wave of darkness, having crested, withdrew.

"He's gone," she whispered. "For now."

25

Together they lifted López and hauled him to his room, with the man moaning and complaining every step of the way. He was not badly hurt, although there were bruises around his neck, as if the tablecloth he'd been wrapped in had been pressed tautly against his flesh. López's skin was clammy, and Montserrat took out blankets and piled them atop him until the man spoke with a raspy voice.

"He shouldn't have been able to sneak into my house. He's more powerful than I thought."

"Calm down, old man, you're going to give yourself a heart attack," Tristán said. He reached for a pitcher and a glass that were placed atop a table next to several images and statues of saints. "Here, have a drink."

López nodded and took a long sip before he handed the glass back to Tristán.

"That monstrous, greedy bastard," López said as he tried to sit up and Montserrat placed another pillow behind him. "You must fetch the film. Tonight. We cannot wait any longer."

"You said it would be too difficult to attempt two spells in a single night," Tristán protested.

"Yes, it would be too much for me. But I'm an old man and you're not."

"Now we're going to exorcise Ewers by ourselves?"

"You know the general plan, and I'll be here to guide you through it. We cannot wait. Ewers is becoming stronger. I think he's feeding off you."

"Ewers is dead," Tristán said. "He's a ghost. How can he be feeding off anything?"

"He's not a ghost! He's caught between life and death, manifesting in our physical reality."

"Okay, you're still not explaining how he can be feeding off anything and why that matters."

"Because he's becoming more powerful," Montserrat said, looking thoughtful. "The first time I saw him, he was a vague reflection, and now he can throw things around a room. When he was murdered, Ewers empowered the film; it was a blood sacrifice. It gave it great might. And then all that bad luck tied to everyone who worked on the project, all those deaths and bad things that happened. They accumulated over time. And now, it's no longer just a print in a freezer, it's somethings that *lives*. The more we use magic and the more he interacts with us, the stronger he becomes. Yes, he's feeding off us, but we're feeding off him, too. That's why suddenly there're magic dogs and furniture flying around. It's like Abel said: pressure building up inside a pot. It's decades of deaths and malice and spells."

"How much more powerful can Ewers get?" Tristán asked worriedly.

Powerful enough that he might actually be able to return to life, Montserrat thought. Oh, she hadn't been sure his ritual would have worked in the first place back in 1961, but she thought it might work *now*. Alma Montero had drawn on Ewers's spell, his old magic, for her own purposes, but she had not drained it completely, and Ewers's magic had also remained latent in that nitrate film. It persisted, Montserrat and Tristán's tinkering with this magic made it worse, and at this point Montserrat was certain that if Clarimonde Bauer and her associates got hold of the nitrate print they would somehow be able to restore Ewers to pristine health.

They were two steps from encountering Ewers in the flesh. This would surely be disastrous for Montero and López. Montserrat wasn't sure it would be better for her and Tristán. They were not members of his cult, and Ewers was no friend of theirs. Who knew, maybe the first thing Ewers would do after returning to life might be to kill both of them.

"He's concerned, otherwise he wouldn't have come here," López said. "He wanted to stop us. He knows he's in danger. We will use the sequence of runes as dictated by Abel—"

"There was something wrong with Abel," Tristán said, cutting him short. "There, toward the end, before Ewers interrupted him. He was trying to tell me something and couldn't."

"You need to get that film," López said and pointed to an armoire across the room. "There are blessed nails in there. Take my car, sprinkle the nails behind you as you get into the vehicle . . . the wards I drew, they haven't washed off . . . that should suffice. I will not survive a second attack. You need to go, now."

Montserrat opened the armoire's door and began pulling out drawers. She found a plastic bag filled with copper nails and turned to Tristán, who took her aside.

"If we go out there we are completely exposed," he said, his voice low. "And should we be leaving the man alone like this? What if Ewers comes back?"

"He's coming back one way or another," Montserrat said.

"You don't know that."

"He is not going to give up. But neither are we."

Montserrat hurried back to the room where they'd slept and put on her jacket, slinging her purse over her shoulder. The keys to the car were on a shelf by the front door, under a postcard from Hawaii that had been taped to the wall.

Tristán pressed a hand against the door, blocking her way. "Have you paused to think Ewers might want us to leave this house?"

"What do you mean?"

"It could be a trap. Abel was trying to warn me about something."

"What?"

"I don't know."

Montserrat rubbed a hand against her head. She felt tired, and her body ached. López could say everything he wanted about them being younger and stronger, but this spell casting hit you like a punch to the gut. She'd felt it when she'd reflected Clarimonde's spell, and it was thrice as bad now. Yet there was no avoiding it, and she knew it even if Tristán wanted to deny it: they had to hurry.

Montserrat grabbed the key ring and stared at Tristán resolutely. "We need to vanish him."

She opened the door and walked toward the front gate. Despite his protestations Tristán followed her. She tossed nails as they walked toward the car and flung some more out the window at stoplights. No vehicle seemed to be following them, and the street in front of Antares was deserted when they parked.

She threw more nails and quickly dug her hand into her purse, finding her keys and opening the door. The lobby was a mess, filled with streamers, plastic plates, and cups. She saw pizza boxes piled in a corner. The office Christmas party must have taken place on Friday, and nobody would clean up until Monday. She had completely forgotten about the celebration.

"Come on," she told Tristán and guided him down the long hallway flanked with tall mirrors and doors leading to the offices and editing bays. They turned left. The storage rooms were closed at night, and as Montserrat jimmied the lock she thanked God that it was the holidays. There was no chance they'd be interrupted.

She flicked on the lights and they were in a vast room with shelves filled with blank cassettes for the duplicates they made. Past a tall pile of boxes there was a door with a sticker that said "Vault One" on it.

"We keep the masters there," she told Tristán.

There too they stored some of the older equipment that nobody had the heart to throw out, including a Moviola that had supposedly been used by Carlos Savage. On the other end of the room there was a door with a sticker that said "Vault Two." It was a glorified closet rather than a room. Inside it was the steel fireproof cabinet where she'd stashed Ewers's reel. Montserrat forced the lock to the small vault, opened the cabinet, and quickly stuffed the film can into her purse. She was still carrying Ewers's book with her, which she supposed was oddly fitting.

She closed the cabinet, and they headed back the way they'd come. When they reached the long hallway that would take them to the lobby, they paused.

An old woman stood at the other end of the hallway, wrapped in a dark navy coat, her white hair pulled back from her face and pinned perfectly in place. Montserrat did not recognize her at first but then something in the way she held herself up allowed Montserrat to connect the dots.

"Alma," Montserrat said. She had aged a decade in the span of a few days.

"I want that film," the woman said. Her voice was hoarse, but her eyes remained sharp and knowing.

"We're going to destroy it. Like you should have done."

"That film is power. Ewers's magic has kept my old age at bay for over thirty years."

"It doesn't seem to be working anymore."

"No," Alma conceded, slowly walking toward them. "You and Abel did something. You threw everything off balance. It's cost me a lot to find you and come here. All my reserves of power, every inch of my magic . . . but it'll be worth it."

Before Montserrat could reply there was a great popping sound and the lightbulbs above their heads began to waver and fizzle out, plunging the hallway into darkness. Then there came a hissing, almost a hum, and Tristán let out a loud grunt, pushing against Montserrat.

"Fuck, it stings," he said. She turned around and saw what he meant.

A faint rope of light had woven itself from one side of the hallway to the other. It sparked, a live wire, except there was no wire. It was as if the electricity was being siphoned from the outlets on the walls and dragged as a rope across the hallway. Tristán had come in touch with it and been electrocuted, although it must have been a mild pain, perhaps not unlike a child toying with a wall socket and a fork.

"We can probably jump over it," Montserrat suggested, but other ropes of light had started weaving themselves. It was a spider web, quickly knotting itself together and glowing brighter.

They began to walk away from it, toward the spot where Alma must be standing in the darkness, awaiting them. But they didn't have much choice as to their path. The doors on each side of the hallway led to production rooms, editing bays, or offices: dead ends. There was no alternate escape route they could follow. As they walked, the tendrils of light extended along the wall and ceiling, humming with power. It was like listening to a loud generator.

Tristán clutched Montserrat's hand, and they moved slowly, avoiding stray whips of light that appeared before them, illuminating the floor for a moment and then disappearing. The tendrils on the wall continued expanding, as if they were a monstrous, glowing mesh of ivy. They snaked around the tall, decorative glass panels and the doors but otherwise seemed to be able to crawl upon any surface.

"I didn't want to kill you," Alma said, from the darkness. "I won't, even now, if you give me the film."

Montserrat clutched her purse and shook her head. "You'll use it to cast a new spell and he'll keep existing. He won't cease to be."

"He's been asleep for a very long time, and he can sleep again."

"What if someone awakens him once more?"

"I'll deal with it, like I'm dealing with you. I won't hurt you, I promise. But you must give me the film."

The lie was easy to read. "You killed Abel," Montserrat shot back.

"Because he wouldn't do as I said. You're better off taking your chances with me than with Clarimonde, and I doubt José is any use to you. If I was able to track you, it means his power is waning."

"So is yours."

Those words must have angered Alma because a rope of lightning stretched suddenly taut in front of them with such strength and speed that Montserrat felt the sting of it. It was like pressing your tongue against a nine-volt battery and tasting its charge. It didn't hurt Montserrat, but then again it hadn't really touched her. The rope of light hung inches before her, yet she could still perceive its power. Should she come in contact with it, it would seriously harm her.

More ropes of light spread in front of them, creating another spidery web. Tristán pulled Montserrat back. They began retreating. Montserrat rested a hand against the jamb of a door but immediately let it go with a loud yelp as the metal seemed to sear her flesh: it was electrified.

She fell to her knees, and Tristán bent down to help her. "Momo," he said, urging her up.

The hallway, which had been plunged into darkness moments before, now was blazing with light. Ahead of them, standing close to the web of electricity, she could see Alma staring at them. She began walking. The web seemed to move with Alma, sliding forward. Behind them were more tendrils of lightning. They would soon be sandwiched between these webs of electricity, burned to a crisp.

The strain of this magic seemed to be taking a toll on Alma: her hands were shaking and her eyes were wild. But she still had reserves of power and strength that neither Montserrat nor Tristán could counter.

"The film," Alma demanded.

Montserrat swallowed. From the corner of her eye Montserrat noticed a flutter of movement, a burst of light. She turned her head a fraction and saw the wall-to-ceiling mirror decorating the hallway had a small crack, and when she looked more carefully, she saw a shape—rough, more a blur than anything else—and for one second a slender finger traced that tiny fracture.

She stopped and looked again, staring at the mirror, seeing herself and Tristán and the blinding arcs of light above their heads. Nothing else. Except, for one flickering moment—there, like the flash frame in a film— Wilhelm Ewers in his beige trench coat, his hands pressed against the glass, staring back at her with an expression that almost seemed amused.

Push, he said. Wordless, though. She simply knew what he meant, his eyes narrowing and glancing in Alma's direction.

The carpet down the hallway was becoming singed from the electricity licking its edges, its threads blackening and unleashing a disgusting smell. If they didn't die from being electrocuted perhaps they would perish from inhaling noxious fumes.

"Here!" Montserrat yelled and held up the can of film. "You can have it!"

Alma began walking forward, stepping through the taut web of electricity blocking the path ahead of them, sliding through it like a knife, arms extended, making the filaments sing.

"Tristán, help me push," Montserrat whispered.

"Push what?" he replied. He looked up worriedly at the ceiling lights, which were flickering on and off and giving off sparks.

"The glass."

"How?"

On the mirror there were now multiple cracks, and Montserrat wasn't exactly sure what they were supposed to do, so she couldn't even attempt to explain it to Tristán. Except that her instinct told her that both of them against Alma were no match for the woman, and Ewers wasn't up to the task, either. But three . . . *a triangle*, as Ewers had said. He'd wanted three sorcerers.

It was probably a bad idea to join forces with Ewers for anything, but they were out of options, and she knew Ewers hated Alma. It had been right there, in his narrowed eyes, a searing, long-festering rage. Alma had feasted on Ewers's magic for many years, and now he intended to pay her back for her impudence.

"Will it to break," she ordered Tristán.

"Will it how?" Tristán asked in return. His voice was almost a hiss, and they had stepped back as far as they could; they were unable to retreat any farther. Alma had slipped through the mesh of light and now stood mere steps from them, her hair fluttering around her head.

"Tell it to break," Montserrat said.

"Mother fucker . . . okay, break. Break, damn it," he said and clutched Montserrat's hand while she muttered under her breath.

Alma had extended an imperious hand, and Montserrat felt the sting of a cord of light against the back of her legs, as if it were a whip, making her stumble forward. She gripped the can of film tight.

"*Break*," she said.

The crack that had been growing across the mirror gave way, and there was a harsh, sharp sound that made Alma turn her head. She saw the mirror and held her hands up, as if meaning to ward off the spell. But it was too late. In a flash the mirror had shattered, and its shards, rather than rolling to the floor, seemed to explode; they were hurtled away, in Alma's direction, and embedded themselves in her flesh with a terrible fury.

The woman screamed. Both Tristán and Montserrat fell to the ground, as if pushed back by a powerful gust of wind, away from the flying fragments of glass. The tendrils of electricity all around them glowed a searing white, giving off sparks, before they dissipated into nothingness.

The hallway smelled of burned plastic and wood, the walls were crisscrossed with dark marks, and patches of carpet had been completely singed off. Several light bulbs had simply burned out, leaving the hallway a patch of shadows.

Montserrat coughed. Tristán leaned against a wall with a groan and, clenching his teeth, helped Montserrat to her feet. They shuffled next to the spot where Alma lay on the floor. A fragment of glass had sliced her throat with clinical expertise, and blood welled profusely from the cut. Blood also poured from her mouth, and her eyes stared up at them as she stretched out a hand, as if still trying to reach for the film can Montserrat was carrying. Then her arm fell down limply.

She was dead.

A transformation overtook the body, the skin atop it dissolving as if it were painted on, and then the muscles turned to gelatin, bones poked out from this mess of melting flesh so that the natural process of decomposition seemed to take place in the blink of an eye. A second more and Alma was nothing but a mound of dust, and even this seemed to then break and decay even more, becoming nothing but the faint outline of a body upon a dirty carpet.

Montserrat was breathing fast, and there was a thundering pain in her head. Tristán looked worse than her. She thought he would vomit, but he shivered and grabbed her hand, and they stumbled through the messy lobby and then outside.

The night air was good against her face, and Montserrat thought in a few minutes more she'd be able to get into the car and attempt the drive back. But then the men came out from the shadows, with their dogs at their sides, and although Montserrat held up a feeble hand with a smudged rune, she knew they could do nothing except stand still as the dogs circled them, black bile dripping down their open mouths.

26

On one occasion, when she'd ventured to a nightclub with Tristán, Montserrat had been served an adulterated drink. This was not uncommon. Many bars cheated their customers, selling shoddy products to increase their profits. It was the only time this had happened to her, thankfully, because it had been one of the most horrible experiences of her life. Until now.

As the men with dogs shoved them into the back of the car, Montserrat felt as if she was going to pass out. Her head throbbed. When they arrived at the building downtown that used to house the offices of Clarimonde's publishing house, as she was forced out of the car and stumbled through the sturdy front doors, she felt something different. It was a jolt, as if a liquid river of gold had suddenly been injected into her veins.

As she walked into the old ballroom, she tasted not the fog of intoxication, but a clarity of thought that seemed to render everything brighter.

The room, which during her first visit had lain empty and in shadows, was now lit by massive chandeliers, the glass in them glittering. More than three dozen people clustered at one end of the ballroom. Their clothes seemed formal but not extravagant, with suits and ties and nice dresses; the kind of attire suitable for a cocktail party. A mixture of ages were represented among the crowd. Some older guests, their hair white and gray, whispered next to yuppies who looked fresh-faced. Montserrat wondered about the provenance of these younger recruits. Were they the children of the older ones? Had they heard about Ewers and his marvels at bedtime? Or perhaps Clarimonde's copies *of The House of Infinite Wisdom* had found success among a new niche group of people.

The room remained mostly barren, though toward the middle of the vast space they had set up two portable projectors and a portable screen against a wall. They probably intended to run the nitrate print she carried in her purse, even though no one should do this without a fireproof, well-ventilated booth. Then again, Montserrat did not suppose it was the time to do a quick safety demonstration and ask if there was a working sprinkler system.

Next to each of the projectors someone had set a large porcelain bowl. One was filled with water, the other was empty. In addition, to the left of the bowl with the water there was a low table, covered with a yellow cloth.

She counted two doors, one on each end of the ballroom, and neither one reachable with the men and the dogs at their side. Montserrat and Tristán were ushered into the back of the room, any escape route further barred by the multitude of guests. After a few minutes, Clarimonde Bauer walked in with two women behind her. Clarimonde's attire was more flamboyant than that of her associates. She had traded her linen blouse and skirt for a flowing dress that was a dark, mustardy yellow. Around her neck she wore a silver pendant in the shape of Ewers's vegvísir and silver bracelets around her wrists. She stood in front of the projectors and held up her arms in a dramatic pose. People clapped. When the applause died, Clarimonde spoke.

"My brothers and sisters, we gather tonight to welcome back our great father into our fold. Our lord has been absent for too many years, but his power is with us, bathing us in his glory."

"We follow him into the night," the cultists said.

Ewers had written this script a long time ago: the setup, the attendants, the instruments, they resembled the ones that showed up in the scene they dubbed. *Movie magic*, Montserrat thought. Ewers had loved movies and wanted everything to play like one; he wanted the thrill of the spectacle. He was going to give them a show, all right. Behind her she could hear soft whispers, the excitement of the crowd, an invisible wave, lapping at their feet. It would rise and crest higher. This was but the beginning. She understood as much.

Two men made their entrance. They dragged someone with them. The man's arms were bound behind his back and his face was covered with a cloth so she could not make out his features, but she could see the slow rise and fall of his chest.

She thought perhaps the man was unconscious, but no. Although he had been effortlessly brought into the room, now he attempted to struggle, his entire body shivering. It was no use. He was brutally shoved down. They held him in place, making him kneel next to the porcelain bowl, and he bowed his head, whimpering.

"What are they doing?" Tristán asked softly.

She knew, of course. She remembered what José had said about the runes, the chickens sacrificed, the natural next step after that: the blood of a man.

"Don't look now," she said, like she did when they went to the movies and she warned Tristán about certain scenes. *Don't look now*, like when they had been small and Tristán grabbed her hand, except it was not the movies and she could not look away after all.

Slowly, almost gently, Clarimonde took out a dagger from between the folds of her clothes and sliced the man's neck with an expert hand. The sight of the spray of blood sent Montserrat reeling against Tristán's chest, clutching his shirt.

Her fingers felt unnaturally warm, blistering almost, and in her mouth there was a sour taste.

The blood dripped into the bowl, turning it crimson. Clarimonde Bauer motioned to her assistants, signaling for them to come closer. Tristán and Montserrat were pushed forward. She moved mechanically, one foot in front of the other, heart thumping, until Clarimonde stepped behind the projectors and greeted them with a half smile.

The woman extended her hands, and one of the men gave her the can of film and the book Montserrat had been carrying in her purse. Clarimonde looked at the objects reverently.

"I'm so pleased you could come," Clarimonde said, carefully handing back the film and the book to one of her men. "Wilhelm has given me exact instructions as to how we should proceed."

Now that they had approached the projectors, Montserrat could smell the blood that was dripping into the bowl, as well as another sickly, pungent, almost sickeningly sweet scent. The aroma of rotting meat.

"The three of you must be present to cast the spell," Clarimonde said. "All six runes must be drawn using fresh blood, while the nitrate print plays. The dubbed copy you made will play at the same time, mixing sound and image. There are a few words to be said: we shall speak them. Then we will coax Wilhelm back from the dead."

Clarimonde motioned to one of the women who had walked with her into the room, and who now drifted toward the low table with the yellow cloth. The woman slipped the cloth aside, revealing the corpse of Abel Urueta. This was the source of the stench in the room.

"That . . . my god, you are all insane," Tristán said, shaking his head. He turned, looking at Ewers's congregation. "All of you! Bunch of crazies!"

As Tristán spoke, Montserrat tilted her head and looked at one of the mirrors decorating the ballroom. She'd caught sight of a blurred reflection there, a swift, subtle movement that made her swallow. Ewers. Behind the glass. Watching and listening. Her hands were trembling, but she clasped them together.

"I said all three," Clarimonde replied, her half smile now a wide grin. "A corpse is better than an item from the deceased. You should have no trouble conjuring Abel."

"What?" Tristán asked. "I'm not doing a single thing."

"Yes, you will. You both have your parts to play. In return, Wilhelm has promised to be generous," she said, looking at Tristán, then turning to Montserrat.

Clarimonde expected them to nod quickly and agree. Or else, perhaps to cower in terror. Montserrat released her hands and stared at the mirror.

"And all we have to do is summon a ghost, draw a few runes, and chant a sentence," Montserrat said. "Well, guess what, we aren't idiots. We bring your friend back to life, you'll cut our throats like you did to that man. Maybe we should sit here and keep our mouths shut and our hands in our pockets."

"What are you trying to do?" Clarimonde asked. Her voice was an icy warning.

"Nothing. That's what we are doing. Nothing unless we hammer out the terms of this contract. You heard that, dead boy?" she asked mockingly.

Behind them, the dogs growled, and Montserrat was certain Clarimonde wanted to slap her, perhaps even stab her with that knife of hers, still stained with fresh blood, but the woman stared at Montserrat. As she'd expected, her hand was stayed.

"He wishes to speak to you. Personally," Clarimonde said. Her eyes were hard. She yanked Montserrat forward, thrusting her in front of the beam of light traced by one of the projectors. It was so bright, she had to raise her hand up to shield her eyes. It was one blazing flash of white, engulfing her.

The ground beneath her feet was smooth black onyx. The light that had blinded her was gone, replaced by a dim glow and stark shadows. Fog enveloped her; it seemed to shiver and shimmer, flashes of silver punctuating the darkness. Wilhelm Ewers stepped out of that darkness laced with silver, hands in the pockets of his beige trench coat, head held up high. He looked not like the elusive image she'd spotted in mirrors and reflective surfaces, but a solid, tangible presence. His flaxen hair was side-parted, sleek, and his smile even sleeker, looking very much like he did in the photo album. Only the eyes were wrong. Wilhelm Ewers's eyes had been a light blue, but now they were rendered a strange silver-gray, as if they were tinted with the same mist that surrounded him.

"I'm glad to meet you, Montserrat," he said. Previously he'd been a paper-thin whisper, but no more. His voice was self-assured and strong.

"I thought we'd already met. You were in Abel's apartment and then you chased me down the stairs," she replied.

"I was curious. I wanted to take a good look at you."

"You tried to kill us during the séance."

"Not *you*, my dear. I tried to kill José. Were you frightened?"

"No. Even though you've been attempting to frighten me for a while now."

"Has it worked?"

"Fear gives others power over you," she said.

"I know. You're a stubborn little thing, aren't you? I like it, although you're being too stubborn just this instant. Won't you take my offer? It is most generous; I can assure you that."

"Where are we?" she asked, unwilling to reply to him, hoping to buy herself time, if she could. She'd told him she wasn't afraid, but she also was no fool and knew herself to be in danger. There had to be a way for

Tristán and her to escape this situation unscathed, and for now, at least, Ewers was not trying to hurt them. The answer was to maintain her composure, to affect a calm and cool demeanor. She suspected he would use any wavering wisp of emotion against her.

"Technically you're still standing in the same room, although some fraction of you is now with me, in this liminal space between spaces," Ewers said as he began walking around her.

"Is this where you live, then, when you're not trying to toss me down the stairs?"

"Or saving you from being electrocuted to a crisp."

"You did that for revenge."

He raised his shoulders in a minuscule shrug. "For my amusement, too. You awoke me and here I am, growing stronger by the minute after decades in a slumber. You can't blame me for having a little fun. Thank you, by the way, for playing with me. I enjoy the taste of your strength, even the nervous anxiety of your Tristán, although it doesn't taste the same as you. Too . . . scrawny," he declared. "Did you enjoy your first murder, by the way?"

"I didn't murder anyone."

"You did. I wouldn't have managed on my own. Feel it, there?" he asked, casually brushing a hand across her shoulder and sliding a finger onto the hollow of her throat. "That's death."

She thought she could feel it, for one second, as the tip of his finger pressed against her skin. A sharp pull, the source of the dizziness that had made her almost trip at the building's entrance and then the warm wave upon her fingers when the blood splashed against the bowl. In his letter Ewers had said he'd felt power in the wake of his father's death; his magic had come into full bloom after that. Were Tristán and Montserrat stronger now? She'd felt faint in the car. Almost drunk. Drunk on Alma's death, perhaps.

"Montserrat, let's talk about us. I am willing to alleviate your financial woes and provide you with the other trinkets you desire, including Tristán. The love of your life, am I correct?"

"I can get a raise and go on dates on my own, asshole," she said, unable to maintain a composed tone against the mockery of his voice.

His amused laughter reverberated around them. "You're trying to use anger as your shield. If you won't be afraid, then you'll be furious and insolent. It's a cheap trick."

"It's from your book," she replied.

"I know. That is why I'm partial to it."

There was glee in his eyes, smugness. *You know me, you saw me*, the eyes said.

"Let's try another route. How about power, Montserrat? The power you've craved since you were a little girl, when they mocked you and shoved you and called you dirty names. The power you lack when those men sneer at you and ignore your contributions, your brilliance. The power to make the whole world see you."

"You're talking about what *you* want, not me," she said, although her mind immediately jumped back to the old taunts, the nicknames she knew well. *Peg-leg, where's your pirate ship?* the kids at school had asked, and her cheeks burned with mortification at this memory.

He noticed the blush, seemed amused. "I think we're very much alike. You'd like to know all the secrets that hide between the pages of musty books, all the ways spells can be woven with runes, and the meaning of words you've never heard before. You want to know, you've always wanted to. I've seen into your heart as you've slept and discerned your dreams."

She wondered if he could spy into people's minds while they slept, or if his knowledge was gained from lurking in shadows and hearing her speak to Tristán. He wasn't wrong, though, and if she denied it, he'd discern the lie.

"You're not to be trusted," she told him instead.

"And you have potential," he replied.

She stared at him mutely, wondering exactly how much knowledge he'd wolfed down through the years, and the how of it, and many other things.

The potential for what? she wondered, and she didn't like that she tilted her head at him, unable to contain her instinctive curiosity. She didn't like that she had to strain to swallow her words, but to ask questions would be a mistake, a detour onto a dangerous path.

He gave her an indulgent look, as if it didn't matter she wasn't talking, as if he'd guessed what she was thinking: the tilt of the head gave it all away. And she was thinking how lovely it might be to learn how to etch a red rune on the back of a spider and crush your enemies as you crushed the insect's body.

"You're special," he said, and Montserrat almost sighed in relief because the words were utterly wrong; they reminded her of the conversation she'd had with José.

"I see. Perhaps I'm an Aztec princess," she replied tartly. Her hands twitched, but he'd said it himself: anger was a shield. She clung to it. "You tell people what they want to hear. You're trying to sell me the same bullshit you sold José and Alma. How did they trick an all-powerful sorcerer such as yourself, who knows the secrets of the universe?"

He didn't care for that. His smile, cold and perfect, wavered in irritation. He was tiring of her. Or maybe tiring, period. How long could he stay here in this netherworld? Not too long, she thought. He'd toss her from this place soon, although that wouldn't be great, either. She'd be back in that room with Clarimonde and her cultists.

"Maybe that's why I am being generous. I learn from my mistakes," Ewers said.

"You want to bribe me a little better than you bribed them so I won't turn against you."

"José had talent but he is old, Alma and Abel are dead, and that leaves only Clarimonde. Let there be three."

"The son to rule the West, the mother Lady of the South, and the Eastern King, the Mighty father united by the might of man," she recited, remembering what was written in the book. "But then, I thought you'd reserved the spot of the mother for Clarimonde. The love of your life, am I correct?" she asked mockingly.

"Magic is about symbols," Ewers said. "Things spoken that have a second meaning. Magic is ritual. You and Tristán fit perfectly within this play, like slipping on a mask. Follow me into the night."

Poetry, rhythm, musicality. He spoke well, had a knack for it, and she had a good ear.

"You've said that phrase before. What does it mean?" she asked, tasting something in his words. Dynamism and symmetry, the heady perfume of magic upon each syllable.

"You know what it means. Words are also ritual, gestures are spells. Promise to obey me, be a servant to a great lord, and I'll grant you immense power."

He had ceased in his walking and stood very still. Watching her carefully. Sizing her up. "Here, take my hand," he said and almost casually lifted said hand. Not for her to shake, no. Perhaps for her to bow her head and kiss the fingertips. It was lofty, an almost laughable and theatrical gesture, but he had a grandiose swagger. *Hollywood*, she thought again, *spectacle*. But a spectacle with purpose. It's what he had written in his book, in his letter.

She had the disturbing realization that the fog was closing in on them, the endless expanse they walked in was growing smaller. When she jumped into the grain containers she'd had a similar sensation, one panicked moment when she felt the grain would close above her head and she'd never be able to push her way out.

"You can't be trusted," she said rather than responding to his languid gesture. "You lie and cheat. If we let you, you will consume us."

"It's natural for the strong to feast on the weak. I am meant to rule over you. The Opener of the Way—"

"Is a concept you invented," she said, cutting him off. "Or a story you heard about and perverted. There's nothing natural about it."

Montserrat shuffled one, two steps away from him; watched as the corners of his lips lifted into a caustic smile.

"Maybe I'll fix that lame leg of yours. You move like a wounded bird, how awkward," he said, glancing down at her feet.

She had a sudden wish to hit him. He reminded her of the neighborhood bullies, of the boys who mocked her cane. Rather than folding she wished to hold her ground, and rather than bowing she wished to snarl.

"You must have been a very unhappy boy, Wilhelm Ewers," she said. "Scrawny, sickly, no match for your big brother. Your parents preferred him. Your mother took her own life when her favorite kid died. Maybe she thought you should have been the boy who perished. And your father had always been distant. You could not impress him with anything you did, not even when you tried, reading all those books, amassing all that knowledge."

"You have a vivid imagination," Ewers said dismissively, and his hand now curled into a fist, falling by his side, "and a talent for fabrications."

"I read your letter. And you said we're very much alike."

She thought she was correct. Somewhere, in between the lines in his book and his letter, in the leaden gaze imprinted on the photographs, Montserrat had recognized a familiar tale. It had beckoned her. She didn't even have to look into anybody's dreams to figure as much.

"You are brave because I'm being exceedingly kind. Do not doubt that I can still harm you. In this and any other place. You and your little friend. You'll never be free of me; you'll never be safe."

"You need us, that's what this is all about," she countered.

"No, this is about you trying to find a solution to your predicament, trying to find a chink in my armor, a weakness to exploit. You think I can't tell? Your little mind is spinning, but while it's been amusing, you must know that you can't possibly best me."

Then, for a second, she felt unmoored, as if the ground beneath her was shifting. Perhaps it was. The fog was a rolling carpet of black, the light dimmer, and his eyes flashed bright, with the glow of silver.

There was so much power in this place, in him, and as Ewers had said, he was only growing stronger. She understood why he wanted so badly for her to agree to obey him. It was as José had told them: he fed off them. He was fueled by whatever unnatural reaction they had started, his power, meshed in silver nitrate, boiling up on its own but also augmented by the loving adoration of his acolytes, of Clarimonde and the others. Unwittingly, too, amplified by Tristán and Montserrat, like at the studio when they had cracked the glass. Together, they could do more. And this, now . . . Ewers was not even *alive*. What could he accomplish if he was resurrected, what spells might he conjure, what horrors? She did not doubt his threats.

It was stupid to attempt to defy him. All she was doing was stoking his anger. It was a pointless strategy. How had José attacked him? How did Alma kill him?

"If you continue like this, I'll ask Clarimonde to cut each finger on your Tristán's hand and feed it to you. Tell me, afterward, how much I need you," he said.

The world around them had become a slab of blackness, compressed, so that they rested in a small halo of light. An iris shot signaling the end of a scene.

"One way or another, Montserrat," he said, "you will bow your head to me."

How? How to get rid of him? She recalled: José and Alma had worked together. Her eyes widened. He looked at her, curious, a question on his tongue.

Montserrat stumbled forward and extended a hand, gripping Ewers's arm before he could ask it.

"I'll follow you into the night," she said.

He looked pleased with this answer. "I knew you would."

27

B efore Tristán could object, Clarimonde had shoved Montserrat forward, pulling her in front of a projector. Tristán attempted to follow them, but the moment he took two paces a man stepped in front of him, blocking his path, with his ugly-looking dog showing its teeth at him in warning. Tristán desisted. He stared at Montserrat. She was not moving. She stood there, looking down at her feet, bathed in the light of the projector. Her expression was dazed, her eyes half-lidded.

"She's not in danger," Clarimonde told him. "Everything will be fine as long as you do his bidding."

"You should let us go. You can talk to Abel without me, you can bring Ewers back without our help. We're not going to tell anyone about you. We pose no danger. Please!"

"Wilhelm needs you," Clarimonde said simply.

The minutes ticked by. At last Montserrat stepped back and shook her head, fixing her eyes on Tristán. She stumbled, dazed, as if she were about to fall.

"Momo," he said. This time, even with the dog growling at him, he sprang forward and reached her, putting his arms around her. "Momo, are you okay?"

"I'm fine." Her lips sought his ear. "Tristán, you need to summon Abel."

"We're going to go through with this?"

"Summon him and tell him to help us. It's going to take all three of us to stop Ewers. I'll begin drawing the runes, but I'll pause and cause a distraction. You and Abel finish drawing them and order the spell to cease. The three of us awoke Ewers, the three of us can get rid of him."

"I don't know how to do that. I'm not a sorcerer."

"Abel knows."

"Did you speak to Wilhelm?" Clarimonde asked as she reached their side. Behind her Tristán saw people busy with the projector, prepping it for the grand screening.

"We agreed on our terms," Montserrat said. "Tristán will summon Abel, and I'll draw your runes."

"Good. Then we should begin."

The chandeliers above their heads grew dim, plunging them into darkness. The only sources of light now were the projectors in the middle of the room.

Tristán looked at Montserrat helplessly and nodded. He walked toward the bowl with water and the low table with Abel's corpse. Yeah, fine, he could do this. He'd done it before. Not with a dead man next to him, but he supposed it couldn't make much difference. Maybe it would even be easier.

Tristán dipped his hand in the water. He wasn't sure that was strictly necessary, but when he'd called Karina he'd run his hands under the tap. He pulled his hand out of the water and licked his lips, trying to remember the words López had told him to use, trying to reproduce the elements of the séance while the projectors hummed. He wondered how much it had cost Clarimonde to organize this gathering, with projectionists and complicated equipment including speakers so the audio could be blasted around the room.

Then he glanced at Abel's corpse and felt like gagging. He'd been a bit sick every time he had conjured a ghost, but this time his queasiness was augmented by the presence of a dead body. He tried not to look at Abel and wrapped a hand around the man's wrist, closing his eyes and whispering the words he'd learned from José López. There came that sharp pain, like a needle sliding into his head, and Tristán shivered.

The light from one of the projectors seemed to grow stronger; it even changed hue. For a moment it was yellow, the shade of wilted marigolds.

"Have you come to us, old friend?" Clarimonde asked Tristán. "Is that you, Abel?"

He let go of Abel's hand, his fingers twitching nervously. "I have," he said. The words seemed to emerge from someone else. The voice was different, even though it was him speaking. A murmur went through the crowd.

"Thread the projector," Clarimonde said excitedly. "He has come."

Tristán couldn't tell if that was the case or not. Nothing else had changed inside the ballroom, except that he now had a blazing headache. He heard people whispering. Montserrat was handed a long stick with a silver tip. For the runes, he supposed.

Frame lines jumped on screen, and before Tristán could ask for any further clarification, before he could beg for a moment to sit down and close his eyes, twin images popped up on screen, side by side, partially overlapping.

It was Ewers's reel on the right, the glorious nitrate print popping and shimmering even against a crude portable screen, and Montserrat's duplicate on the left. Not half as beautiful, it had not quite captured the shape of shadows and the starkness of the light, but that print had sound. That print spoke.

On the screen, a young Clarimonde and Abel opened their mouths, but it was the voices of the older Abel and of Montserrat who read the script. The dubbing, making it all come to life.

"I greet you upon this most sacred of hours."

"I greet you as the moon bares her face to the sky."

The crowd repeated the lines. He could almost feel the tumultuous adoration of his followers, their admiration was a kiss, brushing the screen. Their voices bounced off the tall ceilings, created echoes, while the people on film shimmered with the stark beauty of the monochrome palette. Black and white, white and black. The images dizzied him.

He turned and looked at Montserrat, who was dipping the stick with the silver tip into the bowl with blood. He turned to look again at the screen in time to see a hooded figure step forward from behind a curtain. When Ewers removed his cape and showed his face, his voice was provided by Tristán in the duplicate print. He watched himself granting life to Ewers, making those lips emit sounds, every word fanning an unseen power that was nevertheless palpable.

Film, motion, chanting.

Light, movement, sound.

He felt a bit tipsy, as if he'd done a line of tequila shots.

The image flickered. One quick second, the blinking of an eye, and a pillar of smoke began to emerge in front of the screen.

It coalesced with astonishing quickness, and although the smoke was black, Tristán saw flashes of silver among its threads. He didn't know how smoke could have threads, of all things, but this apparition seemed to be soot, mist, and sinews. It gave the impression of both muscularity and vapor; it recalled the contours of a human body.

On the screen Ewers's silver pendant glittered.

"Give me your hands, dearest brother and sister, for now we call upon the Lords of Air, the Princes in Yellow, to witness our rites."

Behind Tristán the cultists parroted the lines. Clarimonde seemed to practically scream hers, gazing at the screen in adoration. Montserrat had dipped her stick in the blood again. She raised her head, pausing. Her eyes sought him.

Tristán nodded.

Montserrat made a quick motion with the stick, tracing a rune. A second later, a solitary spark lit the corner of the room before flames jumped up and began gnawing at the screen.

Three things happened at once. The crowd, which had been happily babbling and holding their hands up in the air, began to protest, pointing and yelling at the spreading flames. The pillar of smoke that had been coalescing in front of the screen grew faint. Clarimonde yelled, motioning to the men with the dogs. They rushed toward Montserrat, their hands wrapped around the dogs' leashes, and she stepped back quickly, the stick in her hands. José López had faced off against the dogs like that, but she wasn't López. Tristán thought of following her, even of grabbing one of those creatures with his bare hands and punching it, but the pain in his head increased. He fell to his knees and clutched the back of his skull, digging his fingers against his skin.

He heard a sound, a high-pitched wailing, or static, a noise that was not words although he could hear a faint murmur. He squeezed his eyes shut.

Runes.

"Abel," he whispered. "Is that you?"

Yes.

Tristán stood up, shaking, one hand still pressed against the back of his head. He moved toward the spot where Montserrat had been standing. There were six runes on the floor, the same as Tristán had drawn during the séance, except the last one was the fire rune instead of Ewers's vegví-sir. That was missing and must be traced for the sequence to be correct. He bent down, wiped the fire rune with his foot, and stared at the floor.

"I can't remember how to draw it," he told Abel. "And I have nothing to draw it with. Hey, are you there?"

Abel did not reply. Fuck. He'd worry about the silence later. Tristán turned around looking for a tool, something he could use, while on the screen Wilhelm Ewers smiled.

Montserrat's heart was beating fast. With one hand she carefully traced a rune, while she pressed a hand against her throat with the other, her fingers settling on the spot where Ewers had touched her. He'd been right, she could feel it, there—power, coiled tight, tainted with death. Or perhaps enhanced by it. Power in the blood she smeared on the floor. It seemed to go from the silver point of the stick up the wooden handle and tickled her hands.

She'd felt sick in the car, almost faint, but now she was wildly alert. The encounter with Ewers had sharpened her senses. *This is how he felt*, she thought, *when he cast his spells and wove his complex conjurations.*

Air, earth, water, life, the opener. Her movements were elegant. Both prints were playing in smooth synchronized motion; the dialogue echoed around the room. She paid little heed to it, or to the cultists who chanted in unison. The runes held her attention.

Then she paused, breathing in slowly. Tristán's voice had started play-ing. He was reciting Ewers's lines. She saw Ewers on the screen, with his gleaming, treacherous eyes, and turned her head, seeking Tristán.

He was staring at her, and she breathed a sigh of relief as she looked at his familiar face, those mismatched eyes, one narrower, placed a fraction higher than the other, and the scar from the accident she couldn't see in the dark but that she knew was there.

The sight of his face, the sound of his voice, jolted her back to the real-ity of the ballroom, of the night thick with the scent of magic. She drew the sixth rune, but conjured fire instead, wishing for it, willing it forward. Ordering flames and heat to manifest.

They did. Fire tore through the screen, like a mirror that cracked, tracing a spidery line of golds and reds. There was power in death, in blood, as Ewers had said. Power that lingered and could be re-formed, directed, and she took that feeling of might and hurled it at the screen.

She clamped her hands tight around the stick, expecting a reprisal, and within seconds the attack came. Two men stepped forward, their hands wrapped around leashes, charging forward with their dogs.

When a dog lunged at her, she hit it hard. The tip of the stick sunk into the dog's skin as if it were made of tar, and the animal turned its head, viciously snapping at the wood. The other dog went for Montserrat's leg, fangs sinking into her thin, atrophied ankle.

The pain was tremendous; the fangs were sharp even if the dog was not a real animal, but a dreadful mix of magic and illusions. Her eyes watered, and she opened her mouth, but she recalled Clarimonde's living room. *Reflect*, she thought. *Not outrun.*

At Clarimonde's house she'd had charcoal to draw with, and here she had nothing.

No, not quite.

One dog savaged the wooden stick, chomping at it, and she kicked the other dog away, though the motion ruined her balance. When she fell back on the floor she still had a free hand, and her fingers glided quickly in the air, tracing a rune.

Fire, she thought again, as she'd thought about it only seconds before, setting the screen ablaze.

Almost immediately the two dog handlers burst into flames, crowned in fire, and whirled around in shock. The dogs evaporated while the men rolled and screamed on the floor. Montserrat groaned. She sat up only to find Clarimonde moving in her direction, clutching her knife.

Montserrat managed to trace another fire rune, but Clarimonde grinned fiercely and returned the rune with another motion of her own. Montserrat's fingers burned, as if she'd touched a candle's flame, instead of affecting Clarimonde.

"Fuck," she said. Montserrat managed to stand up, using the stick to help her steady her limbs. Magic was a quick-burning fuel, one second whipping through your body, then draining you. She could feel the power that she'd wielded only seconds before already receding. The boost blood and death had given her were evaporating. Beneath that there remained a charge she could access, the force that both she and Tristán had been using all this while: the infectious energy of Ewers's spell. Of Ewers himself, although this too seemed to almost be wavering, as if Ewers were angrily clawing at it. Perhaps because he needed this reserve of energy in order to manifest in the room, or maybe because he wished to stop them from ruining his plans.

Montserrat, weakening, could only grasp the stick like a baseball bat and swing it at Clarimonde as she approached. Swing left, and right, in an attempt to force her to stay back. Clarimonde laughed and held an elegant hand forward, pressing it against her chin, and opened her mouth, as if blowing cigarette smoke in her direction. A strong gust of wind shoved Montserrat. It made the chandelier above their heads tinkle and blew out the simmering flames that were chomping at the screen as easily as if they were birthday candles.

Montserrat slammed the stick down firmly to keep from losing her footing again, but the wind was growing stronger, whipping her hair around her face. She held up a hand trying to negate the spell with a haphazardly chosen rune.

"Cease," she muttered.

The wind kept blowing, and the chandelier above shivered and groaned. Suddenly, Clarimonde was standing in front of Montserrat, her silver knife glinting dangerously, almost glowing. She recoiled, expecting a blow, but before metal bit flesh Clarimonde was shoved out of the way. Tristán pushed her back, and the woman landed on her knees, the knife tumbling from her hands, sliding by Tristán's feet. He picked it up and held it up, a poor safeguard against the woman's magic.

"Momo!" he yelled, the wind still whipping at them.

"The runes!" she yelled back.

The tails of the films made a flapping sound, the screen suddenly flooding with white light. Clarimonde pulled herself to her feet. She threw them a venomous look and closed one of her hands into a fist. The chandelier shook, its chain snapping and plummeting toward Montserrat and Tristán.

"Cease!" Montserrat ordered, and without a rune, with nothing but instinct and fury, she pushed back.

The chandelier exploded. Metal and glass bounced against the ceiling and the walls, rained down all around them. The cultists began yelling and rushing for the doors, frightened by the spectacle.

The blast had knocked Clarimonde off her feet. She lay on the floor, facedown, one of the sections of the chandelier pinning her in place, like a butterfly. Montserrat had a hand closed into a fist and trembled, holding the chandelier in place as Clarimonde grunted and scrabbled at the floor, attempting to push it off her, while Montserrat kept pushing down.

Tristán stared at Montserrat, surprised. "The runes," she said, breathless, and pressed the stick against his chest. He grabbed it clumsily with one hand while he still clutched Clarimonde's knife in the other. "Worry about the runes."

"Right," he replied.

Montserrat took another deep breath and pressed a hand against her throat. She bent her head down, trying to clear her mind, which was nothing but a tangle of black threads. Clarimonde was yelling, she was even scratching the floor, and although injured she was stronger than Montserrat.

"Stay," Montserrat said, pushing down.

The light of the projectors kept hitting the wall, an eye that remained eternally open and blind, but now a shadow passed before it, as if the lens was fogged, and in the bits of crystal on the ground Montserrat recognized a familiar reflection.

A hand closed around her neck.

The bowl with the blood had been overturned in the commotion, and the runes had been painted over red. Tristán let out a loud groan. He needed to draw all six again.

"Fuck me," he whispered. "Abel, we're doing this together, buddy," he said, clutching the stick. The piercing needle in the back of his skull seemed to radiate down his column, as if a muscle had been pinched.

Your blood, came the muffled reply.

"What?" Tristán asked, outraged.

Your blood. Sacrifice.

He remembered José López with his leeches. "Mother fucker," he said.

Sure. Okay. He'd use his own blood. Six runes. It couldn't take that much blood, would it? He dropped the stick and held up his hand, slicing across his palm with the knife. The sting of the cut made him squeeze his eyes shut, but then he knelt and began scribbling with the knife on the floor.

"Abel," he said. "First one."

There came no reply. That static inside his skull had returned. He felt tired, weaker, and his stomach was in knots.

"Abel, you have to guide my hand, please."

God, he was scared. He was scared and nervous and could hardly think, never mind speak to ghosts. He wasn't sure how to go about this, and any second now he would piss his pants.

There was no sound, not a whisper from Abel. Nothing. He raised his head and saw that Clarimonde remained on the ground, but Montserrat kept walking back, as if retreating from something. He thought he saw a figure, dim, more a faint vapor than the pillar of smoke that had manifested before, but coalescing again, in front of her. It was becoming solid.

Ewers was in the room.

"I command you to show me the runes," Tristán said, resolutely, despite his nerves, despite the fear, because there was no time to waste and Montserrat needed him.

He slammed the knife down and his hand scribbled quickly, possessed, moved not by him but by Abel. Air, earth, water, life, the opener. He said each rune out loud, rubbed his hand against the blade, smearing it with more blood, and kept going. One by one. Vegvísir. The final one. He drew it and felt like heaving.

Tristán raised his head, looked at Montserrat again. The vague outline of smoke that had stood before her now was a real and solid shape. At least it was, for a moment, as it seemed to flicker, like an image that was out of focus. That gray shape had shoved Montserrat against a wall.

"Ah . . . it's the end of the film," Tristán said, looking down at the runes. "It's the end of the film, go away, Ewers. Cease to be."

Nothing. The shape was still before Montserrat. The room sizzled with a dark and terrible force.

"Fuck! It's not working, Abel!"

Your rune.

"I drew the runes! I drew the runes!" Tristán yelled, pointing at the floor.

Abel did not say anything else. There was a garbled sound, then silence, and Tristán was definitely going to vomit. More than that, he was going to pass out. Three more seconds and he'd be out cold. He felt utterly drained.

Helpless, he raised his head and stared in Montserrat's direction.

"Momo!" he screamed, and it wasn't fair because he didn't know what to do, he didn't understand anything about runes. She was the one who knew. Willpower and you make them your own and he couldn't do a thing without Montserrat.

"Draw our runes!" she yelled.

He stared at her in confusion, and then he knew. He remembered. Determined, focused, he began tracing a line.

Power. That was what Montserrat felt as icy, strong fingers wrapped around her neck. She didn't see Ewers at first, then he was smoke, then he was ash, his hand still tight around her neck as he kept pressing her back, making her retreat, one step at a time. His hold was not so tight that she could not breathe, but it still hurt, and she could feel the terrible strength in him.

"I warned you. One way or another," he said. He was silver and black-blue smoke, he was ash that was reshaped into sinews.

He was real. But he shouldn't be. He shouldn't. They had not finished the spell. Yet he flickered into existence before her wide eyes. She stepped backward.

"How?" she asked.

"You gave me a voice. You drew my runes. You even joined the audience in watching me," he said, his mouth curling in glee, ash and smoke somehow able to smile. "You made me real."

She shook her head.

"Say it now, say I'm alive, and you'll follow me into the night."

"You can't—"

"No, *you* can't. Those are my runes, this is my magic, this is my power. Give in. Say it."

"You're choking—"

She tried to shove him away, but his grip on her throat grew more vicious. She squeezed her eyes shut. He released his hold on her, instead sliding his hands down her shoulders and holding her in place like that.

"Better?" he asked, almost innocently. She coughed and opened her eyes, shocked to see he was indeed alive.

No, not quite. For a moment he looked to be flesh and blood, nostrils flaring, and then he flickered. The edges of him were smudged one second, crisp the next. He was still a half-thing, existing between spaces. Oh, but he was more real than she'd ever seen him before.

She could almost taste the power of the sorcerer, trace the edges of the magic holding him in place. She was afraid she'd inhaled some of this power, of Ewers, that it would settle in her lungs like the smoke of tobacco.

"I'm already there," he said and pressed a finger against the hollow of her throat. "Make me live."

She was tired and he was right. It was as José López had explained. All she and Tristán had done was essentially cause an explosion and they'd been exposed to a radioactive element, to poison, because of it. This magic she commanded wasn't hers. It was *his*. Bits of Ewers, his runes and his spells, channeled and making their way around them. It was heady, this well of strength, it made her head spin.

"Will me to life. Say it. Say I live."

"Words are ritual, gestures are spells," she muttered, dazed.

"Yes."

Her pulse drummed madly. They'd done exactly what he wanted anyway. Drawn his runes, played his game. She had not given in to fear but still she'd bent to his will. One way or another, as he'd promised. Dancing to his tune, following the steps he traced . . .

"Momo!"

"Complete my ritual."

A thought cleaved her mind. *His* runes, *his* ritual. He'd stolen bits of knowledge, remade it, remixed it, took from here and there. He'd painted a canvas, but he had not invented colors. Even now, even this spell they were completing was not how the original ritual would have gone. It was not the way he'd planned it.

No, this magic, this moment, it belonged as much to them as it did to him. They'd shaped it. He wished to crush the world in his fist and name it his, yet this could not be.

The room was very dark. Even the projectors seemed to be malfunctioning, the light streaming from them no longer blazing white but gone dim. Yet even though he was half-shrouded in shadow, she looked beyond Ewers's shoulder at Tristán.

"Draw our runes!" she told Tristán.

"Complete me, for without me there is nothing," Ewers said. He looked almost amused as he gazed down at her, and she stared back at him knowing what he meant. Force, authority, magic, all of it, there for the taking, if she should want it. No more eating crumbs from the ground, no more groveling and wishing for greatness.

She was tempted to parrot the words he asked of her, to turn the key and unleash him. She gaped at him, afraid for the first time not of him but of herself and the selfish, covetous corner of her heart that wished to simply submit and reap the prizes he'd promised.

Poetry, symmetry in a world that was chaos and grime.

"I drew the runes!" Tristán yelled. "Be gone!"

"How he squawks. He's a weakling," Ewers said. "You don't want to be weak, do you?"

She looked at him, thinking back, to the train tracks and the grain and the streets of her childhood and the day she'd met Tristán, leaning on her cane and peering at a little boy with dark, large eyes.

"I've never been weak," she whispered. "And neither has Tristán."

Ewers began to turn his head, lazily, in Tristán's direction, but she extended a hand and held his chin in place, forcing him to look into her eyes. "But *you* are weak. Yes. You are dead, Wilhelm Ewers. Dead and buried and nothing but ash," she said, abruptly, fiercely; each word was thought made will and emotion.

She remembered exactly who she was talking to. A thief who snatched secrets from other warlocks across the continent, a liar who told others what they wanted to hear, a swindler who conned his lovers, and a murderer. A voracious predator. But as she gritted her teeth, she was not afraid of him, and as she looked at him, she didn't covet any of his secrets. She wished him gone.

"It's the end of the show," she said. "Your movie is over. And so are you. We will it and therefore it is."

The projectors burst into flames, popping and sizzling. This fire would not be quenched the second time around. Ewers's eyes, which were luminous silver, reflected only scorn. But then his skin began flaking off, turning gray, and Ewers looked at her in bewilderment.

He opened his mouth to yell, perhaps to attempt an incantation, some countermove, but his face was dissolving, as if someone had pressed the tip of a cigarette against a bit of film, blackening it. His jaw fell and broke, then sizzled on the ground, a cinder that was being quickly consumed. She pushed him away, and the entirety of his body was twisted, stretched, it seemed to shift colors, turning violet and yellow and blue; red hot blisters ravaged his chest, his hands. He bent and his skin bubbled, his body shrank and it was no longer a body, but a smudge on the floor.

Clarimonde screamed, pinned beneath the chandelier, stretching out a hand in Ewers's direction while the acrid scent of nitrate filled the room and fire began blooming on the walls and creeping up the ceiling. The cultists who had not yet fled yelled and ran, bumping against one another and rushing to the exits, attempting to escape the cauldron that the room had become.

She ran to Tristán, who was kneeling, head bowed, one arm wrapped around his belly. On the floor she saw the two symbols Tristán had traced next to Ewers's runes, negating his spell, reversing it, making it theirs: their childhood signatures, the two small figures that represented Montserrat and Tristán in the secret messages they'd passed around.

"You okay?" she asked, pulling him up. Her leg hurt horribly, and she grimaced when Tristán leaned on her.

"No. I'm going to vomit for three days straight," he promised.

"Let's get out of here."

Tristán nodded and shook his head. He grabbed her by the hand and they hurried behind the throng of panicked cultists. The fire was moving abnormally fast; the ballroom was now enveloped in black smoke, and even when they reached the hallway there was smoke there, too. Someone shoved her aside, and Montserrat tripped, lost hold of Tristán and was suddenly alone, lost, in the shadows of the building.

Startled, confused, her heart pounding in her chest, she could not see anything. The world had gone dark. It was as if someone had slid a shutter, blocking out all the light. Whatever this was, it was not natural. These were the dregs of Ewers's magic, trying to hold her tight, or perhaps Clarimonde's spells, slicing the world away, plunging her into an endless jet-black night.

The smoke scratched his throat, but Tristán glimpsed the dim outline of a door ahead and dashed forth, stumbling into the street. He took a deep breath and looked around with watery eyes.

Momo. She wasn't behind him. She'd been there a second ago and had vanished.

Panicked, he stared at the door of the building, picturing her trapped inside, trying to make her way in the dark. He ought to go back for her, but he had no flashlight to light the way, and dark smoke was streaming from the building.

He could run down the street, raise the alarm, find a pay phone and summon the cops. It would take too long, though, and Momo was inside, alone.

He stood still, one hand resting against the doorway, and peered back into the darkness, trying to glimpse the vaguest of shapes.

"Momo!" he yelled. "Momo!"

No answer. The darkness was warm and thick as tar. He felt sick again, like he might really throw up this time, and he'd never been brave anyway. It was Momo who covered his eyes during the gory scenes in movies, Momo who gripped his hand tight when they jumped together into the grain. It was Momo who forgot to fear, and he who feared everything.

Every atom in his body demanded that he flee. For a second, he considered it. Considered a world without Montserrat, sterile and icy.

Magic is willpower, that's what Momo said. He didn't know what that meant, but he knew he needed Momo as much as the flames inside that building needed oxygen to burn.

He took a desperate breath.

He pressed into the darkness of the building, into the clouds of smoke, and held out his hand. "Momo, I'm here!" he yelled.

Even if the darkness never ended and swallowed him whole, he'd still run to her.

The building was boiling Montserrat alive. Sweat drenched her forehead, and she stood in darkness. No answer came to her, no magic; whatever power she'd held now trickling out of her body.

Montserrat was alone. Tristán had gone. She knew it. Her hand rested on a wall, and smoke swirled around her ankles, and the world was darkness. This was how Ewers must have felt when he died and was confined to oblivion; a part of himself trapped in the frames of a film and sealed in a can. This nothingness prickled her skin, suffocated her more than the smoke.

Her bones were leaden, and tears trickled down her cheeks. She bumped into a door, ran her hands down the crumbling plaster of a wall.

She felt a desperate, clawing force.

Stay! it said, wordless, invisible, this something that clung to her, squeezing her tight, making her stumble. Their gaze, their voices, their will, had once revived Ewers, and he desperately yearned for that spark of life they'd granted him. With his gasping, last breaths he pulled at her, begging her to save him, follow him, grant him life . . . once again . . . this one time.

Montserrat was tired, and in the darkness of the building, with nothing to anchor her, she thought perhaps she might heed that mournful call.

Everything was dark, motionless.

Then, she heard a couple of stumbling, heavy footsteps and squinted.

"Momo, where are you?!"

"Tristán!" she yelled back. "I don't know where to go!"

"Find me!"

But where was he? His voice came from nowhere and everywhere at once. She coughed, pressed an arm against her mouth, and without thinking she moved toward him, even though he could be anywhere.

"Tristán!"

She felt his fingers on her arm, the pull of him.

"I'm with you!"

She wasn't sure he knew where they were headed. In the past it had been Montserrat who guided him, who made him jump into the grain containers. But now it was her turn to follow him, to let herself be dragged, fast.

Their fingers were laced tightly together, and they rushed forward.

She followed *him* into the night, not Ewers, but Tristán. She shook off the sick pull of rotting magic and pressed onward.

The darkness ruptured like a membrane. Breathless, they emerged into the startling prickle of cool air and an ordinary street, with its dim lampposts and businesses that were shuttered at that late hour. They could hear a siren in the distance and the barking of dogs. Montserrat winced as she walked, and Tristán thrust his arm around her, holding her steady. They headed nowhere, directionless, yet confident in their steps.

FADE

TO

BLACK

28

Don't treat me like an invalid. I can get a refill when I want to," José said, slapping Tristán's hand away and sipping his soda with suspicious eyes. Then the old man leaned back against the couch and kept on petting the cat sleeping next to him.

"Are you sure you feel okay, José?" Montserrat asked.

"I'm fine. You both look worse than me."

Montserrat supposed he was right, although it wasn't too bad. Montserrat's ankle was sore and bandaged, Tristán's hand was wrapped in gauze, and they both sported multiple cuts and bruises. It seemed a small price to pay considering everything that had happened. Forty-eight hours. Ewers had been gone for forty-eight hours.

"Now, hand me that."

"Oh, yes, here you go," Tristán said and he passed the photo album to José.

The nitrate print was gone, burned away to a crisp, and so was Ewers's book. Montserrat had burned all photos of Ewers when she got home, not because any power remained in them but simply because she didn't wish to remember him. But there were other photos in the album, pictures of Abel that José might want to keep.

José flipped the pages, his hands touching the edge of a photo, and he smiled.

"Thank you for this," he said, closing the album. "Now, I don't want to be rude, but I'm feeling tired, and it is the longest night of the year, a dangerous evening. It's best we head to bed early."

"But Ewers and his cultists are gone," Tristán said, frowning. "Right? You said so yourself, his magic has vanished, and they can't harm us."

"Of course. You have nothing to fear from them. You feel it, don't you? The absence of his magic?"

Montserrat wasn't sure about Tristán, but she did. It was like having a tooth removed, almost painful. She had grown used to Ewers's power, the spells and runes. She hadn't realized how enmeshed she was in his web until he had disappeared. The loss of magic, of power, hurt worse than the scrapes on their bodies.

"Okay, then what's the problem?" Tristán asked.

"Problem? Nothing, maybe. But sometimes, when you've been around magic, you tend to attract the attention of other things that lurk in shadows. Monsters, ghosts, and the evil eye. I've tattooed myself for a reason," José said, showing them his wrist, with its circle of ink.

"We should tattoo ourselves against monsters and ghosts?" Tristán asked, raising an eyebrow at him.

"Sure. Top to bottom." When Tristán stared at him in anguish José laughed and slapped his leg. "Look at you! God, I think you turned purple right there."

They rose and shook hands. José shuffled after them, walking them to the door. He paused, giving Montserrat a curious look as she took her coat from a hook.

"I have to admit, I wasn't sure you'd actually destroy him," he said.

"That was the plan, wasn't it?" Montserrat said, toying with the collar of her coat.

"Yes. But Alma didn't do it. She stole a piece of his magic and kept it hidden, used it for herself."

"Then thirty-two years later he returned. It would have been foolish to attempt to subdue him and play with his toys," Montserrat said, and then, noticing José's expression, she cocked her head. "Did you think you might do that?"

"The thought crossed my mind. I was tempted. I thought you might be, too."

"Ewers offered nothing that was true."

The cat had not moved from the couch, simply regarding them with one open eye before going back to sleep. By the time they stepped out it was dark. Montserrat buried her hands in her coat pockets. They had come to return José's car to him, to give him the album, and to make sure he was fine, and now that their tasks had been accomplished, they walked down the street in amicable silence.

She thought of magic, the spells she'd cast and that had now vanished. She told herself it was fine, that she didn't miss them and wouldn't seek such power again. The streets around them, with their cars and houses and tiny corner stores, offered a sea of mundanity to her where once before there had stood wonders. The coat she was wearing reached her ankles, and she wrapped it tight around herself.

"You were tempted, weren't you?" Tristán said as they rounded a corner and walked by a liquor store that had decorated its windows with strings of lights.

"For one millisecond," she admitted.

"You would have made a powerful sorceress," he mused. "You're very brave."

"You were brave, too. You came back for me."

"I was self-serving. Can't live without you," he said.

Montserrat looked up at him, the weightiness in the tone of his voice surprising her and making her go quiet. She stuffed her hands deeper into her pockets and wiggled her fingers.

"What did you think about what José said? About things that lurk in shadows?" he asked.

"You want to get a tattoo?"

"I'm unsure about that. But, you know, it being the longest night of the year and all, maybe we should be careful."

"Sure."

"We should go home."

"Okay."

"Back to your apartment. It would be wiser if I stuck around tonight," Tristán said.

After they'd rushed out of the burning building they'd headed to her place and slept late. Many hours later, Tristán had gone back home, but he had returned alleging that even though he'd washed off a gigantic rune from his bedroom, and even though he'd tidied up, he didn't like his apartment anymore and felt uncomfortable there. He associated it with too many bad things. They ordered Chinese, and over chop suey Tristán talked about finding a new place. Something bigger, perhaps. She let him take over the couch and figured he'd change his mind come morning.

"You stuck around yesterday, too."

"Sure. On account of the fact that we were almost murdered Sunday night and I took three aspirins for my head. I needed to crash."

"Fine. We'll go to my apartment and order the first thing we can think of," Montserrat said. "I didn't want to head out for dinner, anyway."

"Maybe I should stick around your apartment until Christmas. It makes no sense to be shuffling back and forth when we are going to have dinner together anyway."

"Okay."

"In fact, we should make it until New Year's." He shook his head. "Nope, nope: Epiphany."

"Why don't you forget about finding a new apartment and stay on my couch," Montserrat replied mordantly.

"Why don't I?"

She stopped walking and looked up at him. Tristán gave her a shrug and a big grin. He wasn't wearing his stupid sunglasses that night, so she had a perfect view of his dark, mismatched eyes.

"You're crazy," she said, and began walking quickly, except with her bad leg and the fact that right that second the limb was still sore, she managed an extremely awkward shuffle rather than the dignified getaway she had hoped for. She remembered how Ewers had said he'd mend her leg and bristled at the memory of his taunt. But he was gone now, Ewers, with his mesmerizing tricks and spells, with his power that had once invaded her veins. Maybe they'd been idiots to turn their backs on that. If there were indeed dangers lurking in the shadows, as José López pointed out, it might have been better to keep a measure of magic, like Alma had done all those years before. But that would have been repeating the same story. She wanted a different ending.

"Momo, where are you going? Momo!"

"Away!" she yelled back.

"Let's discuss this," Tristán said, catching up with her in a few quick strides.

"It's not the right time to talk about that." Her voice sounded uncharacteristically sharp.

"When would it be a good time? Should we wait until another sorcerer tries to come back from the dead? Maybe a French one this time?"

"You're an idiot," she answered archly.

Tristán's grin had been wiped off his face. They gazed at each other gravely. "Why?" she asked.

"You'd save on the rent. We probably shouldn't inflict ourselves on other people." When she didn't laugh, he sighed. "Well, I don't know . . . or . . ."

He'd jotted down a dozen good reasons why that morning when he gazed at her across the dining room table while they had breakfast, but he'd only written them in his mind and now they escaped him. He was as nervous as a kid who got his first callback after an audition and didn't want to ruin his delivery, but he could not remember a single line in the script he'd written for himself.

"You had a near-death experience and your brain is fried," Montserrat replied simply.

"Momo, it's not that!"

"Oh, I hate you," she whispered, walking again, her long coat whipping past him, her heavy boots crushing a stray can of soda, and then she turned around, furious. "You couldn't have asked this twenty, even five years ago? When we were young?"

"What's the big deal with being older? Getting close to forty is not a death sentence," he said.

"It's old enough to be set in your ways and to know better. When we were kids, maybe I would have, maybe I did—"

"Jump into the grain, play on the tracks? Make stupid choices involving me?" he asked.

It might have been fun to take a chance on each other back then, when they were kids. It would certainly have saved them from a few doses of heartache. But he figured a performer only gets better after doing several shows, and maybe it was the same with affection. It's honed, not found. She spoke before he could explain himself.

"Bones heal a lot better when you're eighteen. You get to be our age, then you must be careful," she said, her voice strained, thinking of how they both had a lousy record when it came to human hearts. "We're not children to be playing house."

He huffed, bruised by her refusal. He hadn't expected her to swoon, but this felt like a military siege; he'd have to fight tooth and nail for her. But it only emboldened him, made him realize he'd have to dig deep, and he wouldn't be able to do things in halves.

"Call me immature then, because it sounds reasonable to me," he said, spreading his arms. "It's twenty years of foreplay, Momo. Do you want to wait a few more decades until I can't masticate my own food? 'Cause I'll love you until then and feed you pureed prunes, but it would be a shame to start living together at eighty-nine and die of a heart attack the first time we have sex."

"That is the most disgusting declaration I've ever heard," she said flatly, and then she couldn't help it, she laughed. Tristán laughed, too, and now he felt stupid, but he supposed that was fine. It was okay to be stupid when it came to Montserrat.

"It is, isn't it?" he said.

They hugged. She clung tightly to him, tighter than she'd ever held him. His arms wrapped around her, chasing shadows away.

"What do you want me to say? I recite dialogue, I can't write it," he whispered, his voice soft against her ear.

"You're a silly tomato," she blurted, not even knowing what she said. She was forgetting the meaning of words and how to speak them.

"A silly tomato!"

She could feel his smile, but her face was buried against his chest, and he was running a hand through her hair. She couldn't bear to look at him.

"You can't drive my car, I won't let you. I won't do your laundry, I won't sew your buttons, and if you don't pick up after yourself, I'll toss you out," she said, whip-quick.

"I'll cook. Believe me, we'll live longer," he said, his fingers sliding down her cheek, tipping up her chin.

"You're an asshole," she said.

"You going to kiss me or what?" he asked, voice husky, and was rewarded with the tremor of her lashes. "At least I'm not the only nervous one," he said, savoring the startled look on her face as she stared up at him.

She wanted to punch him. "You probably kiss like in the movies and I'll die of embarrassment."

"Well, fuck me, I kiss well, yes. That's a plus. Now who's the silly tomato?" he asked, stepping back and arching an eyebrow at her. "Wanna make out in your car tonight?"

She did punch him on the arm then, not hard, but to make sure he didn't get too cocky.

Across the avenue, a vendor of tamales was pushing a cart, his strident whistle calling forth customers. A boy carrying a big boom box was walking on the other side of the street, spewing loud notes through the night air. "Don't Fear the Reaper," or at least a cover of it, was playing on the radio.

"Come on, dinner is on me," Tristán said, pointing at the vendor and slipping his hand in his jacket, looking for his wallet.

This was life, they figured. Not a fabulous medley of spells, hexes, and intoxicating power, but the simple, ordinary assembly of sights and sounds that were nevertheless a wonder, for they were viewing and listening to them together. She laced her hand with his and they crossed the street in a hurry, laughing and telling the man to wait one second for them.

Author's Note

In 2010 I published a story called "Flash Frame" in a very small press anthology titled *Cthulhurotica*. That story was reprinted in *The Book of Cthulhu* in 2011 and gave me a certain amount of caché among the Lovecraftian circle. It was the tale of a pornographic film screened at an old movie theater that seems to attract a disturbing crowd and has eerie side effects on the narrator, a journalist looking for a scoop. This was the seed from which *Silver Nitrate* was born. Cultists, old movies, and a fire appear in the short story, and re-emerge in the novel, albeit in radically different ways.

The color yellow showed up in "Flash Frame" and became something of a leitmotif in my fiction. It appeared in the short stories "The Yellow Door" and "Sleep Walker." It again popped up in the mushrooms of *Mexican Gothic* and the novella *The Return of the Sorceress*. Over and over again, this color yellow. Why? There is of course *The King in Yellow*, that well-loved example of Weird fiction by Robert W. Chambers. Yellow is associated with romantic decadence thanks to *The Yellow Book*, a British quarterly literary periodical that was published in the nineteenth century. "The Yellow Wallpaper" details the descent of one woman into madness. Gautier spoke of language "veined with the greenness of decomposition," but my color is yellow.

The Nazis did have a bizarre medley of occult interests. From lay lines to astrology, hollow earth theories to Tibetan expeditions, they built a mythology that supported their racist concepts. Goebbels believed that cinema was one of the most effective propaganda instruments and sought to consolidate and control this industry.

There is a common phrase I grew up with in Mexico: "mejorar la raza." It translates to "better the race" and means you should marry whiter, more European-looking people, so, although there was no Wilhelm Friedrich Ewers in the 1950s in Mexico City, he might not have been unwelcome.

Ewers is a composite of many occultists, although the spark of inspiration for him was Arnold Krumm-Heller, who indeed made his way to Mexico. Ewers derives his surname from Hanns Heinz Ewers, a novelist, early scriptwriter, correspondent of occultist Aleister Crowley, and Nazi supporter. He might have also been a secret agent, who traveled to Mexico to persuade revolutionary Pancho Villa to attack the United States. Ewers fell out of favor among Nazi officials due to his homosexuality. His assets were seized, and his books were banned in 1934. He died in 1943. His most famous story, "The Spider," is the tale of a man who falls in love with a mysterious woman named Clarimonde who lives across the street from him.

Much of the information on films is true even if Abel Urueta is made up. He is named after Mexican film director Chano Urueta, who was responsible for dozens and dozens of films, including many horror flicks (*El Monstruo Resucitado*, *La Bruja*). His first name comes courtesy of actor Abel Salazar, who played Alberto de Morcef in an adaptation of *The Count of Monte Cristo*.

Nitrate film is highly flammable, and it's also true that although in the United States there was a switch toward a safer alternative in the 1950s, other countries continued to use nitrate stock because it could be purchased cheaply. Francoist Spain bought large amounts of nitrate film at a discount.

In the United States foley art, the reproduction of sound effects, owed its name to Jack Foley, but in Mexico it was a different story. The efectos de sala were nicknamed after a different man: sound technician Gonzalo Gavira. Hence the terms "hacer un Gavira" or "montar un gavirazo."

There are several lost films I thought about when writing this novel. One is *London After Midnight*: the last existing print of this movie was destroyed in a fire in an MGM vault in 1967. Another is Carlos Enrique Taboada's *Jirón de Niebla*, which was supposedly stolen as part of a complex case of political intrigue. In life, like they say, truth is stranger than fiction.

Acknowledgments

Thanks to Barton Hewett, Jeremy Lutter, Carlos Morales, and Gabriela Rodriguez for their information and assistance in matters of film and audio editing. Thanks also to my editor, Tricia Narwani, and my agent, Eddie Schneider.

If this book had a soundtrack, it would probably consist of John Carpenter's film scores, the Italians Do It Better collective, the Canadian band July Talk, the obscure Mexican post-punk band La Sangre de Alicia, Kate Bush's *Hounds of Love* album, Death Cab for Cutie's "I Will Possess Your Heart," and the soundtrack from *Phantom of the Paradise*, all of which I listened to on rotation while writing *Silver Nitrate*.

About the Author

SILVIA MORENO-GARCIA is the *New York Times* bestselling author of the critically acclaimed speculative novels *The Daughter of Doctor Moreau, Mexican Gothic, Gods of Jade and Shadow, Signal to Noise, Certain Dark Things,* and *The Beautiful Ones;* and the crime novels *Untamed Shore* and *Velvet Was the Night.* She has edited several anthologies, including the World Fantasy Award–winning *She Walks in Shadows* (aka *Cthulhu's Daughters*). She lives in Vancouver, British Columbia.

silviamoreno-garcia.com
Facebook.com/smorenogarcia
Instagram: @silviamg.author

About the Type

This book was set in Dante, a typeface designed by Giovanni Mardersteig (1892–1977). Conceived as a private type for the Officina Bodoni in Verona, Italy, Dante was originally cut only for hand composition by Charles Malin, the famous Parisian punch cutter, between 1946 and 1952. Its first use was in an edition of Boccaccio's *Trattatello in laude di Dante* that appeared in 1954. The Monotype Corporation's version of Dante followed in 1957. Though modeled on the Aldine type used for Pietro Cardinal Bembo's treatise *De Aetna* in 1495, Dante is a thoroughly modern interpretation of that venerable face.